THE MURDER GAME

An avid reader since childhood, Beverly Barton wrote her first book at the age of nine. Since then, she has gone on to write well over sixty novels and is a *New York Times* bestselling author. Beverly lives in Alabama.

For further information about Beverly Barton go to her website at www.beverlybarton.com and www.AuthorTracker.co.uk for exclusive updates.

By the same author:

Close Enough to Kill
Amnesia
The Dying Game

BEVERLY BARTON

The Murder Game

AVON

This novel is entirely a work of fiction.
The names, characters and incidents portrayed in it are
the work of the author's imagination. Any resemblance to
actual persons, living or dead, events or localities is
entirely coincidental.

AVON

A division of HarperCollins*Publishers*
77–85 Fulham Palace Road,
London W6 8JB

www.harpercollins.co.uk

A Paperback Original 2008

First published in the U.S.A by Kensington Publishing Corp.
New York, NY, 2008

Copyright © Beverly Barton 2008

Beverly Barton asserts the moral right to
be identified as the author of this work

A catalogue record for this book is
available from the British Library

ISBN-13: 978-1-84756-059-9

Set in Times New Roman

Printed and bound in Great Britain by
Clays Ltd, St Ives plc

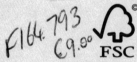

Mixed Sources
Product group from well-managed
forests and other controlled sources
www.fsc.org   Cert no. SW-COC-1806
© 1996 Forest Stewardship Council

FSC is a non-profit international organisation established to promote the
responsible management of the world's forests. Products carrying the FSC
label are independently certified to assure consumers that they come
from forests that are managed to meet the social, economic and
ecological needs of present and future generations.

Find out more about HarperCollins and the environment at
www.harpercollins.co.uk/green

In loving memory of my mother, Doris Marie.

Many thanks to my friend Marilyn Puett for putting me in touch with a retired FBI agent who generously agreed to help me with research.

Thank you, Former Special Agent William C. Rasmussen. Your assistance proved invaluable during the course of writing this book. Any mistakes are mine, probably because I assumed I knew something or I either misunderstood the answer to a question or simply asked the wrong question.

Prologue

I am not going to die! Damn it, I refuse to give up, to let him win this evil competition.

Kendall Moore pulled herself up off the ground where she had fallen, face-down, as she ran from her tormentor. Breathless and exhausted, she managed to bring herself to her knees. Every muscle ached. Her head throbbed. Fresh blood trickled from the cuts on her legs and the gashes in the bottoms of her callused feet.

The blistering August sun beat down on her like hot, heavy tendrils reaching out from a relentless monster in the sky. The sun was her enemy, blistering her skin, parching her lips, dehydrating her tired, weak body.

Garnering what little strength she had left, Kendall forced herself to stand. She had to find cover, a place where she had an advantage over her pursuer. If he caught up with her while she was out in the open, he would kill her. The game would be over. He would win.

He's not going to win! Her mind screamed orders—run, hide, live to fight another day. But her legs managed only a few trembling steps before she faltered and fell again. She needed food and water. She hadn't eaten in three days and hadn't had any water since day before yesterday. He had been pursuing her from sunup to sunset for the past few days, apparently moving in for the kill. After weeks of tormenting her.

The roar of his dirt bike alerted her to the fact that he was nearby, on the narrow, rutted path to the west of her present location. Soon, he would come deeper into the woods on foot, tracking her as he would track an animal.

At first she had been puzzled by the fact that he had kidnapped her but then set her free. But it hadn't taken her long—only a matter of hours—before she realized that she was in the middle of nowhere and that she wasn't free, no more than a captive animal in a game reserve was actually free.

Day after day, he stalked her, hunted her down, and taught her how to play the game by his rules. He'd had more than one opportunity to kill her, but he had allowed her to live, and he'd even given her an occasional day of rest. But she never knew which day it would be, so she was forced to stay alert at all times, to be prepared for yet another long, tiring match in what seemed like a never-ending game.

Pudge parked his dirt bike, straightened the cord holding the small binoculars around his neck and the leather strap that held the rifle cover across his back. Kendall didn't know it, but today was the day she would die. He had brought her here to this isolated area three weeks ago today. She would be his fifth kill in this brand-new game that he had devised after several months of meticulous planning. Only recently had he decided that he would hunt his prey for three weeks, then go in for the actual kill on the twenty-first day.

After his cousin Ruddy's death on April first of last year, he had discovered that he missed his one-time opponent and lifelong best friend more than he'd thought he would. But

Ruddy's death had been inevitable. After all, he been the loser in their "Dying Game" and the consequences of losing was forfeiting one's life.

You'd love this new game, dear cousin. I am choosing only the finest female specimens, women with physical prowess and mental cunning. Only worthy adversaries.

Kendall Moore holds an Olympic silver medal in long-distance running. Her slender, five ten frame is all lean muscle. In a fair fight, she might actually win the game we're playing, but whenever did I fight fair?

Pudge chuckled to himself as he dismounted from the dirt bike.

I'm coming for you. Run. Hide. I'll find you. And then I'll kill you.

As he stomped through the woods, Pudge felt a surge of adrenaline rush through his body, heightening his senses. He had missed the thrill of taking a human life, of watching with delight the look of horror in a woman's eyes when she knew she was going to die.

Soon, he told himself. The next victim in The Murder Game is only a few yards away. Waiting for you. Waiting for death.

Kendall knew that if her captor chose to kill her, her chances of escape were nil. He had proven to her several times that she was powerless to stop him from tracking her and finding her. He had pointed his rifle at her, dead center at her heart, more than once, then grinned with evil glee, turned, and walked away. But the time would come when he would not walk away. Was today that day?

She heard his footsteps as he crunched through the underbrush, drawing closer and closer. He wasn't trying to sneak up on her. In fact, he seemed to want her to know that he was approaching.

You have to keep moving, she told herself. *Even if you can't get away, you have to try. Don't give up. Not now.*

Kendall ran for what seemed like hours but probably wasn't more than ten minutes. Her muscles ached, her heart raced. Out of breath and drained of what little energy she had left, she paused behind a huge, towering tree—and waited.

Keep moving!

I can't. I'm so tired.

He's going to find you. And when he does . . .

God, help me. Please, help me.

Suddenly, as if from out of nowhere, her captor called out her name. Just as she turned toward the sound of his voice, he stepped through the thick summertime foliage surrounding them. The trickle of sunlight fingering down through the ceiling of sky-high treetops hit the muzzle of his rifle, which he had aimed directly at her.

"Game's end," he said.

He's never said that before, Kendall thought.

Breathing hard, she lifted her head and stared right at him. "If you're going to kill me, you son of a bitch, then do it."

"What's wrong, Kendall, are you tired of playing our little game?"

"Game? That's all this is to you, isn't it? Some sick, perverted game. Damn it, this is my life."

"Yes, it is. And I hold the power of life and death—your life and death—in my hands."

His cold, self-satisfied smile sent shivers through her.

"Why me?"

"Because you're so very perfect."

"I don't understand."

"You don't need to understand. All you need to do is die."

She swallowed hard. *He's actually going to kill me this time.* Icy fear froze her to the spot. "Do it, damn you, do it!"

The first shot hit her in her right leg. Pain. Excruciating

pain. She grasped her bloody thigh as she fell to her knees. The second bullet hit her in the shoulder.

She stared at him through a haze of agonized tears and waited for the third shot.

Nothing.

"End it," she screamed. "Please, please . . ."

The third shot entered her chest, but missed her heart.

The pain enveloped her, taking her over completely, becoming who she was. No longer Kendall. Only the torment she endured.

As she lay on the ground, bleeding to death, her captor approached. When she felt the tip of the rifle muzzle pressing against the back of her head, she closed her eyes and prayed for death.

The fourth and final bullet answered her prayer.

Chapter 1

He had killed before and he would kill again. Nothing could compare to the godlike feeling of such power.

For five years he had played the dying game with his cousin and their rivalry had been part of the excitement, part of the thrill. But Ruddy was dead, their wonderful game over.

His new game was only a few months old, yet he already realized that without an opponent, without the psychological stimulation of competition, it just wasn't the same. The hunt was exhilarating, the kill a sublime climax, but the titillating pleasure of the preparation and planning as well as the triumph afterward were missing from his murder game. He now had no one with whom to share either.

He trusted no one the way he had trusted Ruddy, both of them knowing from their teens that they were different from others. Special. Superior. He could hardly run an ad in the paper for another partner, could he? Wanted: Cunning sadist to compete in a highly skilled game of hunt and kill. Winner takes all. Loser dies.

As Pudge crossed over the Arkansas border into Louisiana,

heading toward Bastrop, he chuckled at the thought of advertising for an adversary.

It wouldn't take long to reach Monroe, then he'd go on to Alexandria, where he'd hit Interstate 49, which would take him home. He might even stop for dinner somewhere along the way.

He had put a bullet into Kendall Moore's head only three days ago and had returned her body to a secluded area just outside her hometown of Ballinger. As he had done with the others, he had taken a trophy. A little souvenir. Something to add to his growing collection.

Removing his gaze from the road momentarily, he glanced down at the small, round box nestled securely on the passenger side floorboard. Kendall had possessed a mane of short brown hair. Thick and curly. Like heavy satin to the touch.

Sighing deeply, he thought about touching her hair again, about caressing it tenderly as he recalled, over and over again, those final moments of her life.

Griffin Powell envied his old friend. Judd Walker had been to hell and back. Now, thanks to the love of a good woman, he had survived and had a wonderful life. A life that he appreciated in a way only a man who had come close to self-destructing could. Seeing the happiness in Judd's eyes every time he looked at his wife and infant daughter, Griff knew how much Judd valued the priceless second chance he had been given.

If anyone knew about second chances, Griff did.

Judd slapped Griff on the back. "Come on outside and help me put these steaks on the grill." He held up the tray of marinated meat in his other hand. "Cam's got it all fired up and ready to go."

"Just how many chefs do you need manning the grill?" Griff asked before upending his beer bottle to finish off the last drops.

Judd shrugged. "Suit yourself, but I thought you might want to get away from the ladies for a few minutes. That is, unless you're dying to listen once again to all the details of how we decorated the nursery, went through childbirth classes together, and how I nearly fainted during Emily's delivery."

Griff smiled as he glanced across the room to where the visiting ladies—Rachel Carter, Cam's latest girlfriend, and Griff's date, Lisa Kay Smithe—sat at the kitchen table chatting with Lindsay Walker. Little Miss Emily Chisholm Walker slept soundly in her mother's arms. Lindsay McAllister, now Lindsay Walker, had traded her Private Investigator license and 9mm for a bucolic life out in the country with her husband and baby.

Griff had never seen her happier.

Lindsay deserved to be happy. She'd earned it.

He loved her like a little sister and wanted only the best for her.

"I think I'll leave all the baby talk to the ladies," Griff said as he followed Judd outside and onto the patio. Judd had added the patio to the old Walker family hunting lodge that he and Lindsay had renovated shortly after their marriage last year.

Griff wasn't much for family get-togethers and backyard barbecues. Not that he wasn't enjoying himself today. Not that there was anywhere else he'd rather be. He could count true friends on his fingers, a short list, with Judd and Lindsay among the chosen few. Griff and Judd went back quite a few years, pre-Lindsay years. They'd been playboy pals even before Judd's first marriage. And Judd had been buddies with Camden Hendrix since the two attended law school together. Like Griff, Cam had come from nothing and was a self-made man, while Judd came from generations of old Tennessee money. And Griff and Cam were both confirmed bachelors fast approaching their fortieth birthdays.

"How do you like your steak, Griff?" Cam asked as he took the tray from Judd and placed it on the side table by the state-of-the-art built-in grill.

Realizing that through all the years they'd known each other, this barbecue was a first for them, Griff eyed Cam with a raised eyebrow. The All-American blue-eyed, sandy-haired trial lawyer was casually dressed, wearing a white apron over his University of Tennessee T-shirt and cutoff jeans. "Medium," Griff replied to the question.

Cam grinned. "Really? I'd have pegged you for a rare kind of guy."

"Nope."

"Don't like it raw, huh?" Cam chuckled as he nodded toward the back door. "Wonder if Ms. Smithe would prefer a guy who does take it raw?"

Griff's good-natured smile never wavered. "You're more than welcome to ask her. But what about the lady you brought to the dance? Won't she expect you to dance that last dance with her?"

"We could swap partners," Cam suggested.

"Will you two stop that?" Judd glanced at the screened door that led from the patio to the screened porch. "I'm an old married man and if my wife heard such talk out of you two, she might forbid me to ever invite y'all back."

Cam and Griff laughed out loud.

"How the mighty have fallen," Griff said.

"He's pussy-whipped," Cam joked.

"Sure am," Judd told them. "And damn proud of it."

Griff knew that if any man on earth was devoted to his wife, Judd was. And he didn't blame him. If a woman ever loved him the way Lindsay loved Judd . . .

There had been a time when they had exchanged girl-friends, had passed them around, and none of the women had objected in the least. As a matter of fact, Judd, Cam, and he had speculated that the ladies they dated were probably keeping score, comparing each man to the other two and sharing their preferences with one another. When Jennifer

Mobley entered their lives, they had vied for her affection, each of them dating her in turn. Judd had won that particular prize. He'd fallen head over heels for Jenny. They were still newlyweds when Jenny had become one of the Beauty Queen Killer's victims. That had been more than five years ago.

And lucky son of a bitch that he was, Judd had found the right woman for a second time.

Griff figured that sooner or later, Cam would succumb to love. When he least expected it, the right woman would come along and knock his socks off.

But Griff didn't expect to ever marry or father a child. He had far too much baggage to bring into any relationship. A past that no woman would understand. Demons plagued him. Soul-deep demons, from which he could never escape.

Nicole Baxter sprawled leisurely on the rustic wooden chaise lounge with thickly padded cushions in a hideous floral print. The day was hot, the breeze slightly humid, the air heavy. She lifted the large glass from the deck floor up to her lips and sipped the sweet tea. As she glanced high overhead and saw an eagle in flight, she rubbed the cool glass across one cheek and then the other. Nearby the soft trickle of a small stream drummed melodically in her ears and the rustle of the moist air through the towering treetops reminded her that the weather forecasters had mentioned an afternoon rainstorm.

If it rained, she'd go inside the rental cabin, choose one of the half dozen paperbacks she had brought, then curl up on the sofa and read. If it didn't rain, she'd probably change clothes and go hiking.

Glancing down at her seen-better-days shorts, oversize cotton T-shirt, and bare feet, she sighed. Maybe she wouldn't go anywhere. Maybe she'd sit right here for the next four or five hours, drinking tea, napping, trying her best to get the rest and relaxation her boss had told her she needed.

Maybe Doug was right. Maybe she'd become so consumed with her two-killer theory that she wasn't thinking straight. And an agent who couldn't think straight couldn't do her job.

Besides that, she hadn't taken a vacation in years, not since Greg died and she'd thrown herself into her work. Work had saved her sanity when she lost her husband. Work had become her passion, her only passion.

Hell, who was she kidding? From the day she'd been recruited by the FBI, a green kid fresh out of college, she'd been consumed with proving herself, showing everyone that a woman could be the best. The very best.

And, yeah, maybe her attitude had a great deal to do with her male chauvinist father.

Damn it, Nic, let it go. You came to terms with your father's overbearing influence a long time ago. Don't rehash the past. It serves no purpose.

Six months of grief counseling had done more than help her deal with Greg's death—it had made her open up to a therapist about her life in general, especially the formative years that had created Nicole Baxter, the real woman, the woman few people ever truly knew. To be honest, there were times when she wasn't sure even she knew who she was.

"Take two weeks off." Doug Trotter, one of the Special Agent's in Charge at the D.C. field office where she worked, hadn't given her much choice.

"I'll go nuts," she'd replied.

"Give it a try. Go somewhere fun. Go to the beach. Put on a bikini. Flirt with beach boys. Get drunk and get laid."

If she and her boss hadn't been good friends as well as colleagues, he never would have added that final comment.

"I'll take two weeks off," she'd told him. "But I'm not

into boys. If I'm going to get laid, I want a man doing the job."

Doug had laughed.

So, here she was in a rental cabin in Gatlinburg, Tennessee, in the heart of the Great Smoky Mountains. She had arrived last night. Slept like the dead. Ate a big breakfast she'd cooked herself. Soaked in the hot tub for twenty minutes, then showered and thrown on some old, comfy clothes.

Day One in her first week of R&R and she was bored out of her mind.

Pudge exited off Interstate 49, took a right turn at the end of the ramp, and went in search of Catfish Haven, which was advertised on the FOOD AND LODGING sign. There it was, up ahead on the left. The restaurant was housed in a new building, constructed of old lumber to give it that aged quality, and possessed a rustic metal roof, a sprawling front porch, and a large parking lot half-filled with vehicles.

Pudge eased his rental car into a slot near the entrance. Good parking karma. He smiled. The gods were looking down on him today.

Before he went inside and dined on the local cuisine, he had two phone calls to make. Thinking about a solution to his problem as he'd been driving, he had come up with a brilliant idea. Just the thought of it excited him.

He didn't need a *partner in crime* in order to have a competitor. All he needed was an adversary. Someone with whom he could share certain aspects of his planning, execution, and subsequent triumph. Someone intelligent. Someone who would have no choice but to play the game with him. What fun it would be to outsmart that person, to stay one step ahead of him or her.

Leaving the motor running so that the air conditioner would keep him cool—Pudge hated to be uncomfortable—

he opened the glove compartment and removed one of the four prepaid phones he had placed there before leaving for Arkansas three days ago.

He had both cell numbers memorized, of course.

Which to call first? Hmm . . .

Save the best for last.

As he tapped the first number into the cell phone, he imagined the look on the man's face the moment he realized there was a new game under way.

Griff had forgotten to put his phone on vibrate, so when it rang during dinner, he apologized to the others and excused himself. While everyone continued their meal that was spread out on the two tables near the pool in Lindsay and Judd's backyard, Griff walked around the side of the house and found some shade under a couple of massive old oak trees.

Even though he didn't recognize the caller's number, he answered on the fifth ring. Only a handful of people had his private number.

"Powell here."

"Hello, Griffin Powell. How are you today?"

Griff didn't recognize the voice. Clearly not disguised. Southern accent. A tenor voice, bordering on alto, soft and slightly high-pitched for a man. But it was definitely male.

"Who is this and how did you get my number?"

Laughter. "There's a new game afoot."

"What did you say?"

"Does Mrs. Powell's little boy want to come out and play?"

Griff's muscles tightened as he gripped the phone. A rush of pure adrenaline raced through his system.

"That depends on the game," Griff said.

"Tell me what you and I know about the Beauty Queen Killer that others don't know and I'll tell you a little something about my new game."

Griff's heartbeat accelerated. Goddamn! Was this guy for real?

"Cary Maygarden had a partner," Griff replied.

More laughter. "Very good, Griffin. Very good indeed."

Griff's instincts told him that this caller was the second Beauty Queen Killer, the one who had gotten away because no one knew he existed. Only Griff and Special Agent Nic Baxter believed Maygarden had had a partner. And try as she might, Nic had been unable to convince her superiors to reopen the Beauty Queen Killer case because she had no substantial evidence, no way to prove there had been a second killer.

"When do you intend to start your new game?" Griff asked.

"I've already begun the new game."

A sick feeling hit Griff square in the gut. This lunatic had already killed again?

"When?" Griff asked.

"I'll give you a clue—Stillwater, Texas. Four weeks ago."

Before Griff could respond, he heard dead silence at the other end of the line. His caller had hung up, effectively ending their conversation.

As lightning streaked the sky and rumbles of thunder echoed through the mountains, Nic sat curled in the chair-and-a-half in the corner of the cabin's wood-paneled living room. The paperback she'd been reading lay open in her lap as she struggled to stay awake. If not for the occasional booms of thunder, she'd probably be snoring right now.

Suddenly a vicious crackle of lightning hit somewhere nearby and startled Nic from her semiasleep state. Mercy! That was close. She shifted in the chair, accidentally dumping the book and the lightweight cotton throw she'd wrapped around her bare legs onto the floor. A gentle surge of cold air coming from the nearby floor vent wafted across Nic and created tiny goose bumps on her bare legs and arms.

Just as she reached down to pick up the book and the throw, she heard her cell phone ring. Why hadn't she just turned off the damn thing? Since she was officially on vacation, the call wouldn't be work-related. That meant it was personal. So it was probably her mother, her brother, or her cousin Claire.

If it was her mother, she'd call back. She always did. She would call and call and call until Nic responded.

If it was her brother, he'd leave a message and she would return his call. She and Charles David had been close all their lives and despite the fact that they lived three thousand miles apart—he in San Francisco and she in Woodbridge, Virginia—they spoke often and visited at least once a year.

Kicking aside the cotton throw at her feet, Nic got up and walked across the room to where she'd deposited her purse, key chain, and cell phone last night.

She picked up the phone, checked the caller ID, and realized she didn't recognize the number. Not that many people had her cell number, so unless it was a wrong number . . .

She flipped opened the phone. "Hello, you've reached Nicole Baxter's—"

"Hello, Nicole Baxter. How very nice to hear your lovely voice."

"Who is this?"

"A man who admires you for your beauty and your brains."

"How did you get my cell number?"

"I have my ways."

"I'm going to hang up. Don't ever call me again."

"Don't hang up. Not yet. Not before I tell you the good news." He paused for effect. "There's a new game afoot."

Nic's heartbeat went wild. "What did you say?"

Laughter. Sinister and chilling.

A shiver of foreboding tiptoed rapidly up Nic's spine.

"Now, aren't you glad you didn't hang up?"

"What kind of game?" Nic asked, all the while knowing the answer. Fearing the answer.

"What do only you and I and Griffin Powell know about the Beauty Queen Killer?"

Nic barely managed to stifle her gasp. "Cary Maygarden did not act alone. There were actually two killers."

"Very astute of you, my dear Nicole. Now, I'm going to allow you and Griffin to play my new game with me. And here's your first clue—Ballinger, Arkansas. Yesterday."

"What kind of clue is that?"

Silence.

The son of a bitch had hung up on her.

Nic flipped her phone closed, curled her fingers around it, and clutched it tightly.

My new game.

Damn it. Did this mean he planned to start a new killing spree? After five years and more than thirty murders, Cary Maygarden had been shot in the head and stopped forever. After his death last year, Nic had tried her best to convince the powers-that-be at the bureau to investigate further, but without any real proof that there had been two Beauty Queen Killers instead of just one, the case had been closed and her concerns had been put on the back burner.

During the past year, she had moved on to other cases. Unfortunately, a nagging certainty lingered in the back of her mind, a certainty she shared with only one other person. They both believed that Cary Maygarden had worked with a partner in a series of murders in which each death represented a certain number of points and at the end of the game, the loser lost not only the game but also his life.

Nic paced the floor. The last person on earth she wanted to see ever again was Griffin Powell. The billionaire playboy owner of Powell Private Security and Investigation Agency was a swaggering, macho asshole. And because Griff was the only other person who believed as she did, Nic now realized that fate had a really warped sense of humor.

She would rather eat glass than contact Griff, but her gut instincts told her that this guy—whoever the hell he was—knew that she and Griff believed in his existence. So, the odds were he either had or would call Griff.

Suck it up and do what you have to do.

Damn it, had she kept Griffin Powell's cell number on her list or had she, after the Beauty Queen Killer case had been closed, deleted it?

She flipped open her phone and scanned her personal phone book. His number was still there. Why she didn't know. She should have deleted it last year.

Hesitating for a moment, she glanced outside as the summertime storm washed across the mountainside. High winds and a torrential downpour. But no more thunder and lightning.

Stop procrastinating. Call him. Do it now.

Nic hit CALL and waited as the phone rang.

"Well, well, if it isn't my favorite FBI agent calling." Griffin Powell's voice was a deep, gravelly baritone and sandpaper rough.

"Did he call you?"

"Did who call me?"

"Stop jerking me around and just tell me. Did he or did he not call you?"

"He did. Not five minutes ago. When did he call you?" Griff asked.

Nic swallowed hard. "Just now."

"We were right."

"Yeah, I know, but I wish we'd been wrong."

"Did he tell you that he's already begun playing his new game?"

Nic groaned. "Yes, so that means he's already killed again."

"Did he give you a clue?"

"Yes. Did he give you one?"

"Stillwater, Texas."

Nic shook her head. "The clue he gave me was Ballinger, Arkansas."

"Son of a bitch. He's already killed twice. One woman in Texas and another in Arkansas."

"We need to find out for sure," Nic said.

"Any chance the bureau will—"

"Not without some sort of evidence."

"Then I'll handle things."

"Not without me, you won't."

Griff grunted. "Are you suggesting we work together?"

It pained Nic greatly to reply, "Yes, that's exactly what I'm suggesting."

Chapter 2

"Do you want me to come to you or do you want to—?"

"I'm not at home," Nic told Griff. "I'm in a cabin in Gatlinburg."

"Alone?"

"That is none of your business."

Griff smiled to himself. He pictured the look of indignation on Nicole Baxter's pretty face. Such a shame that a woman so attractive tried so hard to prove to the world that she was the equal of any man. Not that he didn't think of women in general as equals, but he was old-fashioned enough to like women who enjoyed being utterly feminine. If that made him a male chauvinist, so be it.

"Since you're not far from Knoxville, why don't we make plans for you to come to my house?" Griff suggested. "I'm not at home either, but I can head out soon and be there in about three hours."

"Won't *she* object to your leaving?" Nic asked sarcastically.

Griff chuckled. "I'll drop Lisa Kay off on the way home.

We're outside Whitwell, near Chattanooga, at Lindsay and Judd's."

Silence.

"You still there?" he asked.

"I hadn't thought about how this would affect them," Nic said. "If they find out that there were two Beauty Queen Killers—"

"There's no need for them to know, now or ever."

"This guy has started a new game and has probably killed two women already."

"Unless his MO is the same and he's picking up where he and Cary Maygarden left off last year, then there's no way to connect him to the BQ killings."

"So you're saying that we start this case off as if it's not connected to—?"

"The Beauty Queen Killer case is officially closed. I can see no reason to reopen it, can you? How will that help us find this guy and stop him before he escalates his new game?"

"You're probably right. But if he's killing beauty queens again—"

"Let's find out," Griff said. "I'll put in some calls and see if there have been any recent murder cases in Ballinger, Arkansas, and Stillwater, Texas. If there are two with similarities, then we can bet it's our guy."

"The bureau probably won't become officially involved right now, but that doesn't mean I can't use my credentials to get information from local law enforcement. You should let me handle things. I can make those calls on the drive to your place."

"If we make this a competition, it's going to be difficult working together."

Nic groaned. "Oh, all right. You contact Stillwater and I'll contact Ballinger. See, I'm perfectly capable of cooperating."

"Do you need directions to my place?"

"I think I can find it."

"I'll leave word that you're to be admitted as soon as you arrive."

"What does it feel like, Mr. Powell, living on a compound with around-the-clock guards?" She wished back her damn sarcastic question the second it came out of her mouth.

"It feels secure, Ms. Baxter. Safe and secure."

Pudge arrived home well before dark, after turning in his rental car in Opelousas and picking up his own car. As a boy he had intensely disliked his family's hundred-and-sixty-year-old estate, the house an antebellum structure built before the War Between the States. But as a man, he had grown fond of the home place. He had a love/hate relationship with his heritage. He had adored his mother, hated his father, and tolerated his two sisters, Mary Ann and Marsha. Thank God he saw them only at holidays and on very special occasions. He could trace his ancestry back to Europe on both the paternal and maternal sides of the family. His father had been Ruddy's mother's third cousin, but in certain families even distant relatives were considered part of the clan. The two of them had met at a family reunion held here at Belle Fleur when they were boys and they had become friends for life.

He never would have guessed that he'd miss Ruddy so much, that his cousin's death would leave such a strange void in his life.

Pudge parked the BMW in the carriage house garage on the estate, retrieved his suitcase from the trunk, and made his way along the stepping-stone path to the back entrance. He no longer kept live-in servants. Decent help was almost impossible to find and he'd rather do without than deal with incompetence. He made do with a weekly cleaning service and a cook—old Allegra Dutetre—who, when he was in residence, came in at nine in the morning and left in the afternoon. He had known Allegra all his life. She'd been the family's cook as long as he could remember. She was probably nearly seventy, but was still quiet spry even if she wasn't all that bright. Not mentally retarded, just a little slow. He was good to Allegra because she was one of the few people who had always treated him with the respect he deserved.

And she never pried into his business.

Thank God the sun had set and a humid breeze was blowing in off the river. He'd walked from the garage and already his skin was damp with perspiration. Going into the house through the back porch and kitchen, he tapped off the alarm code on the keypad as he entered, then dropped his suitcase and round trophy box on the floor. There was very little in the suitcase except his disguises. Wigs, makeup, fake mustaches, and beards. Even several sets of colored contacts. He had disposed of all the clothes he'd worn on his trip to and from Ballinger, placing them in various Dumpsters along the return route.

After removing his jacket and hanging it over the back of a kitchen chair, he unbuttoned his shirt to midchest, then sat down and removed his shoes and socks. He eyed the trophy box and smiled. He supposed he could wait until tomorrow to add the new acquisition to his small but exclusive collection. But why wait? After all, his special room in the basement of the mansion had been empty for over a year, until a couple of months ago. When, in April last year, he had won his five-year game with his cousin and had taken Ruddy's life as the ultimate prize, he had removed all the mementos from his numerous Beauty Queen kills. That game was part of the past, as was Ruddy. Now he was playing a new game, with new adversaries and new rules.

Pudge stood, picked up the box, and headed for the door that opened to a set of wooden steps leading into the basement. He flipped on the light switch just inside the door and made his way carefully down the stairs. The first room in the

musty cellar was used for storage and was piled high with
discarded items from generations past. To his left was the
pantry, empty now and never used. To the right was the wine
cellar, to which only he had a key. Straight ahead at the far
back side of the basement, past the row of rusting chains
hanging from the ancient brick walls, lay a very private
room, one he had personally converted into a trophy room.
And like the wine cellar, only he possessed the key.

With trophy box in hand, Pudge approached the locked
door. The dim lighting along the narrow passageway cast shadows across the slimy walls and the remnants of the heavy,
rusted chains that had once bound unruly household slaves.

His sisters had been afraid of the basement and to his
knowledge had never set foot down here. But he had been
fascinated by the subterranean area, especially the chains.
Even as a boy he had fantasized about what it would be like
to bind a person to the wall and whip them into submission.
Unfortunately, the years had taken a toll on the chains, leaving them all but useless.

When he reached the door, he paused, stuck his hand in
his pocket and removed his key ring. After unlocking the
door, he shoved it open. He felt along the inside wall for the
light switch, flipped it on, and then walked into the 14' x 14'
room. The wall to the right was lined with shelves and sitting
on the shelves were glass cases, all of them empty except for
four. Soon the fifth case would contain his latest prize.

He set the box on the round table in the center of the
room, removed the lid, and reached down inside. The moment his hand touched the silky softness, he closed his eyes
and sighed.

Kendall Moore had been the strongest, the bravest, and
the fiercest prey he'd ever hunted. He hoped that his next
quarry would provide him with as much pleasure during the
hunt.

* * *

Nic could not believe she was doing this. Never in her wildest nightmares would she have thought the day would come when she would join forces with Griffin Powell. The man was charming and could play the part of a gentleman quite well. But underneath all that *GQ* cover-model façade beat the heart of an uncivilized warrior.

You're not joining forces with him. You're simply working with him on a temporary basis and only because he is, as far as you know, the only other person the second BQ Killer contacted with the news that he has started a new game of murder.

When she drove her rental car up to the front gates of Griffin's Rest—how like the egotistical man to name his estate after himself—she realized she'd have to contact the house to be allowed entry. Two massive stone arches, with huge bronze griffins embedded in the stonework on both, flanked the locked gates. The moment she pushed the CALL button, a man's voice responded. She gave him her name and nothing more, and it wasn't until the gates opened that she realized there had to be a hidden camera that had conveyed her image to the house and she had been instantly recognized.

The road to the house wound around through a heavily wooded area before opening up onto a lakefront view. Although the mansion was an impressive two-story structure with a columned front portico that faced away from the lake, Griffin's home was not as large as she had expected. Probably somewhere between eight thousand and ten thousand square feet. Rather modest for a man reported to be worth billions. Although twilight was descending over the lake, with the dying embers of sunlight reflecting off the surface of the water, the outdoor security lights along the road and surrounding the house kept the property well lit.

Slinging her leather bag over her shoulder, she emerged from the car, stretched to her full five ten height, and marched confidently across the drive and up the front steps. She crossed the veranda and rang the doorbell. In less than a minute, the front doors opened to reveal Sanders, Griffin Powell's right-hand man.

Nic had to admit that she was as curious as everyone else was about those ten missing years of Griffin's life, when he had disappeared off the face of the earth at twenty-two and reappeared again a decade later. He had returned from only God knew where, filthy rich and accompanied by a mysterious man named Damar Sanders.

"Please come in, Special Agent Baxter." Sanders stepped back to allow her space to enter.

She hesitated for half a second, something elemental within her warning her of danger. Entering Griffin Powell's home was the equivalent to a princess entering the dragon's lair.

When she stepped over the threshold, Sanders gestured with a sweep of his arm. "If you'll follow me, I'll show you the way to Griffin's study."

"Is Mr. Powell here?"

"He just arrived." Sanders looked directly at her, the expression in his dark eyes emotionally neutral, neither friendly nor unfriendly. "He asked that you wait for him in the study."

She nodded, then followed the stocky, middle-aged man with the leather-brown skin and shaved head. His ethnic heritage was as much a mystery as the man himself, but his voice possessed a hint of an English accent, although she doubted that English was his native language. He left her at the open door to the study, excusing himself with a curt head bow. After taking a deep breath, she entered the two-story room.

Wow! A massive rock fireplace, so large that several

people could easily stand upright inside it, dominated the impressive den. This was an extremely masculine room with paneled walls and hardwood floors. A seven-foot green leather couch resided parallel to the fireplace and sat far enough away from the opposite wall to allow for the placement of a sofa table behind it. Two brown leather armchairs flanked the fireplace and a sturdy antique desk claimed the corner by the windows overlooking the lake.

Griff had put his stamp on this room. Knowing him as she did, she recognized the den for what it was. His sanctuary. This was where the great man came to escape from the world.

Nic felt his presence before he entered, before he spoke her name. Every nerve came to full alert. Every muscle tensed. She took a deep, closed-mouth breath and turned to face him.

"Hello, Nic."

She liked her nickname, but on his lips it sounded like an insult.

With her gaze meeting his head-on, she replied, "Hello, Grr . . . iff." She made his nickname sound like a two-syllable word by stretching it out.

"Would you care for a drink?" he asked, his gaze traveling to the decorative liquor cabinet in the opposite corner from the desk.

"No, thank you, but feel free to—"

"Sit."

Command or request? With Griffin, she figured they were the same thing.

She chose the right side of the large sofa.

He sat on the sofa, taking the left side.

"What did you find out about the Texas victim?" she asked.

"Not much. There have been two murders in the Stillwater, Texas, area in the past couple of months. One man was stabbed to death by his business partner. The other victim was a young woman whose body was found by some kids in a city park.

She was hanging from a large tree limb, upside down, her feet bound together."

Nic closed her eyes for a split second before looking at Griff. "Had she been shot in the head?"

Griff nodded. "Yeah."

"Had she been scalped?"

Clenching his jaw, Griff grunted. "Damn! You found out about an identical murder in Ballinger, didn't you?"

"It wasn't enough that he killed them, execution style. He had to scalp them, too."

"Trophies," Griff said.

Nic shot up off the sofa. "I want this guy. I want to stop him before the body count rises. But my boss will tell me that two similar murders in two different states do not mean there's a serial killer on the loose."

"Not even when you add to the scenario the information that this guy made phone calls to you and me?"

"All those calls prove is that there's a nut job out there who has our private cell numbers."

"Then we need to find enough evidence to prove our theory. I'll go to Ballinger and Stillwater and see what I can find out beyond the basic police reports."

"I'm going with you." As Nic hovered over him, their gazes locked.

The corners of Griff's mouth curved upward with a hint of a smile. "You know how some local police chiefs and sheriffs are about the FBI sticking their nose into local business. You're liable to make 'em nervous, honey, a big, important special agent showing up and asking questions."

She cringed at the generic endearment, one he'd no doubt used with hundreds of women. No, make that thousands of women. But she knew he had called her honey for one reason only—to piss her off.

"Well, honey," she replied, "I tell you what—I'm on vacation so I could go with you in an unofficial capacity and not flash my credentials around unless it becomes absolutely necessary."

"Do you suppose you could try to be charming instead of commanding?" Griff asked, a devilish twinkle in his cold blue eyes. "We might get more information that way."

"I think you have enough charm for both of us."

"Why, thank you, ma'am. I take that as a compliment."

Nic groaned quietly. "You can take it any way you want to."

Griff stood. "Do you think there's any way we can put aside our personal feelings and actually work together? We could call a temporary truce."

Nic squared her shoulders and faced him. "I'm willing to try."

"Good enough."

"The murder in Ballinger was recent," she said, considering their truce to be in effect now. God help them both. "The body was found only yesterday. What about the woman in Stillwater?"

"Her body was found the first of the month, nearly four weeks ago."

"Then we should go to Ballinger first, gather what info we can, and go from there to Stillwater."

"Agreed. I'll have the Powell jet ready to take off first thing in the morning."

"All right. I'll meet you back here at—what time in the morning?"

"Where are you going tonight?" he asked.

"I saw several halfway-decent-looking motels on the drive here."

"You'll stay here. I have plenty of room."

"I wouldn't feel comfortable staying here."

"Why not? Because you don't like me? Or because you're afraid you won't be able to resist me if I come on to you? Believe me, you're safe with me." He put up his hands in an I-wouldn't-touch-you-with-a-ten-foot-pole gesture.

"I don't like you," she freely admitted. "And we both know that I do not find you irresistible, so thank you for the invitation to spend the night. I'll get my bag out of the car and—damn, I'm in a rental car."

"Give me the keys and I'll have Sanders get your bag and tomorrow he'll take care of returning the car."

She smiled at Griff. "My goodness, it must be nice to issue orders and have everyone around you snap to it."

Griff clicked his tongue. "Now, now, Nicki, what happened to our truce?"

Forcing herself not to react to his taunt, she unzipped her shoulder bag, delved inside, and brought out the car keys. "Here you go." She dropped the keys into his open palm, careful not to touch him. "Thank you. And please thank Sanders for me."

Griff closed his fingers around the keys, all the while not taking his eyes off Nic. "Why do you think he called us? Why alert us to the fact that he's killing again? He could have killed a dozen or more women before anyone connected the dots and realized there was a bizarre connection between the murders."

Nic sighed deeply. "I have no idea, but my gut tells me that sooner or later, he'll tell us his reason. And I don't think we'll like it."

Pudge removed the mannequin's head, placed it on a stand, and set it on the round table where Kendall Moore's scalp lay. With the utmost care, he gently placed the bloody scalp on the bald plastic head, working with it patiently to position it just right. When he was satisfied with his handiwork, he opened one of the glass cases on the shelf, the fifth one in the top row, then lifted the head and eased it into the case. Next he opened the small file cabinet under the metal desk in the corner and removed the label he had made weeks ago. The label was typed in neat, black Times Roman print, and read:

Kendall Moore, #5.

He closed the glass case, walked back across the room, and sat in the desk chair. As he gazed lovingly across the room at his five beautiful trophies, Pudge smiled.

Wonder how long it will take Griff and Nic to discover that there are five victims and not just two?

Despite their mutual animosity, Griffin Powell and Special Agent Baxter would join forces against him. Of course, that was exactly what he wanted them to do. They didn't know it yet, but they were going to be major players in his new game.

He suspected they would head for either Ballinger or Stillwater tomorrow, if they weren't already on their way tonight. By now, they should have found out that a victim's body was found in Ballinger yesterday and another in Stillwater nearly a month ago. Both women had died in the same manner and both had been displayed in an identical way— hung by their bound feet from a tree branch. And both women had been scalped.

§Pudge whirled the swivel chair around and stared at the blank computer screen sitting atop the desk. If he kept to his self-imposed schedule, he had no time to lose. He had to choose his next quarry immediately. Tonight. Tomorrow at the latest. He had already narrowed down his choices. He chose only specimens in their prime, physically and mentally superior women who would make the hunt a challenge for him.

He turned on the computer and opened the file he had been compiling for quite some time. One name stood out from all the rest. She would be his ultimate kill. The prize of a lifetime.

Nicole Baxter.

Chapter 3

All things considered, Nic had slept amazingly well. Griff had shown her to a guestroom. Large, elegant, and quite feminine. She'd wondered just how many other ladies had used this room over the years.

When Sanders had brought her suitcase, he'd said, "If there's anything you need, please don't hesitate to ask."

"Thank you, I'll be fine."

"Do you prefer to set your alarm clock for in the morning or would you like for me to wake you?" he'd asked.

"Uh, I'll set the alarm, but I forgot to ask Mr. Powell what time I should be ready."

"Breakfast will be served in the kitchen at seven in the morning," Sanders had told her.

Nic checked her wristwatch. It was now six forty-three AM. Last evening, she had set the alarm on the beside table for six. The clothes she had on today were not part of the daily "uniform" she wore for work. She was stuck with the clothes she had packed for a semisecluded vacation in the mountains. Her choice in apparel had been shorts, jeans, or the one skirt she had brought with her. She chose the jeans and topped them with a white short-sleeved pullover.

Squaring her shoulders and tilting her chin, she resisted the urge to glance at herself in the cheval mirror she passed on her way to the door. She knew she was clean and presentable. That was enough.

Once downstairs, she simply followed her nose. The aroma of coffee and cinnamon led her straight to the large, modern kitchen. After entering, she paused when she saw Sanders at the stove and Barbara Jean Hughes, in her wheelchair, buzzing around setting the table. Barbara Jean's younger sister had been one of the BQ Killers' victims, and Barbara Jean had been one of the few people who had gotten a glimpse of the killer as he left the scene. She should have been under FBI protection while they'd hunted down the Beauty Queen Killer, but instead, she had succumbed to Griff's persuasive charm and accepted his offer of protection. Apparently, even after Cary Maygarden had been killed and she was no longer thought to be in danger, Barbara Jean had chosen to stay on and was now in Griffin's employ.

The moment Barbara Jean saw Nic, she paused and smiled. "Good morning, Special Agent Baxter. It's so nice to see you again, but I wish it were under more pleasant circumstances."

"Yes, me, too. And please, call me Nic."

"You're a bit early. Breakfast isn't quite ready." Barbara Jean eyed the table, neatly set with placemats, silverware, and china. "Griffin and Maleah should be down shortly." She glanced sweetly at Sanders. "Damar has prepared his special breakfast casserole and homemade cinnamon and raisin scones."

"It smells delicious." Nic tried her best to curb her curiosity about Maleah. Was she one of Griff's women? Probably.

"Would you care for coffee?" Sanders asked.

"Yes, I'd love coffee, but I can get it myself."

"Yes, ma'am."

By the time she'd poured the black brew into a china cup and was about to take the first sip, a woman entered the kitchen. Pretty and blonde and stacked.

Nic could certainly see why any man would be attracted to her.

"Morning all," the woman said as she visually scanned the room. Her gaze settled on Nic. "Hi. You must be the infamous Nic Baxter." She smiled and held out her hand as she approached. "I'm Maleah Perdue, the Powell agent assigned to Griffin's Rest this week."

Nic returned her smile, feeling oddly relieved that she wasn't being subjected to breakfast with Griff's latest girl-friend. "So, I'm infamous around here, am I?"

"Most definitely," Maleah said. "During the BQK case, your name was synonymous with The Devil."

"I wouldn't have it any other way, not with Griffin Powell. Believe me, his name is synonymous with arrogant SOB in my office every day."

Nic and Maleah were laughing when Griff entered the kitchen. He glanced from one woman to the other, nodding at each in turn. "Something tells me that all this early-morning good humor is at my expense."

"Could be," Maleah admitted.

Sanders brought Griff a cup of coffee immediately and said, "Breakfast will be served momentarily."

Griff motioned to the table. "Ladies."

He waited until each of them had taken a seat and Bar-bara Jean had positioned her wheelchair in front of a place setting before he sat down at the table.

He turned to Maleah, on his left. "Have you received any information this morning?"

Sanders placed a canned cola and a straw in front of Maleah, who popped the lid and inserted the straw before re-plying. "Actually, some info came in overnight. I haven't printed it out yet, but I can give you a rundown from memory."

"What sort of information?" Nic asked. "About the two victims?"

Maleah nodded. "With only their names and the basic info on both women, I was able to get quite a bit of personal information. The Web has made everyone's personal life an open book."

"Other than similarities in the way they were murdered, did the two women have anything else in common?" Griff asked.

"Hmm . . . I suppose the answer is yes and no. There's nothing in their backgrounds to connect them. They were born in different states, lived in different states, and were, we assume, abducted in different states. Different religions—one Catholic, one Methodist. Kendall Moore was a pure WASP—white, from an upper-middle-class family. Gala Ramirez's parents migrated from Mexico before she was born and were dirt poor."

Sanders placed the casserole dish on the table so unobtrusively that Nic and the others barely noticed.

Griff glanced on the other side of Maleah where Barbara Jean sat. "Are you sure you want to sit in on this discussion?"

She nodded. "Yes, I'm sure. If Cary Maygarden had a partner, I want to know everything about the man. After all, we can't be a hundred percent sure which one of them killed my sister, can we?"

"Cary Maygarden fit your description of the man you saw," Griff reminded her.

"I know. It's just . . . just . . ." Her voice quivered and then trailed off into silence.

Sanders set the tray of scones on the table, walked over to stand behind Barbara Jean, and curled his fingers gently over her shoulder. Nic spied his actions in her peripheral vision, but neither she nor anyone else looked directly in Sanders's direction.

"Okay, so you've told us how Gala Ramirez and Kendall Moore were different," Griff said. "Tell us what they had in common."

All eyes turned to Maleah. "Well, to start with, they were both brunettes. Both of them were born and raised in Southern states, assuming we, as many people do, consider Texas a Southern state."

"Is that it?" Nic asked.

"There is one other thing—both women were athletes. Gala Ramirez was a tennis pro and at only twenty, her career was just beginning. She had a good chance of becoming a national champion," Maleah said. "And Kendall Moore, who was twenty-nine, held an Olympic silver medal as a long-distance runner."

Silence.

No one spoke. A ticking clock and the distinct sound of breathing prevented the room from being absolutely quiet.

"Athletes, huh?" Griff reached out and spooned a large helping of the casserole onto his plate. "This could mean that he switched from beauty queens to athletes for his victims in the new game."

"Possibly," Nic said.

"Was either woman married? Have children?" Griff asked.

"Both were single," Maleah said. "No children."

Nic stated the list of similarities. "Brunette, unmarried, no children, Southern, and more specifically an athlete. Do y'all know how many women that description fits?"

"Thousands." Maleah flipped back the cloth covering the scones and retrieved the one on top. The scent of cinnamon and sugar permeated the air. "Maybe tens or hundreds of thousands of women, depending on your definition of an athlete. That could be anyone from an Olympic gold medal winner to a woman who plays softball for her church team."

As Nic and Barbara Jean served themselves and Sanders took a seat at the opposite end of the table from Griff, the discussion turned from the two murdered women to the trip to Ballinger, Arkansas. And by the end of the meal, Nic had gained a new insight into Griffin Powell. As much as she disliked him and as badly as she hated to admit it, everyone else at the table seemed to like and respect Griff. He treated the others with an easy warmth and cordiality usually reserved for friends, which led her to believe that he considered them more than employees and that they felt the same.

Twenty minutes later, Griff slid back his chair, dropped his linen napkin on the table, and stood. "If you're packed and ready, we can leave by eight," he told Nic.

"I'm ready to go whenever you are."

"Good." He eyed the cup she held. "Finish your coffee. I have a couple of phone calls to make. I'll meet you in the foyer in ten minutes." Not waiting for a reply, he walked out of the room.

Nic drank the remainder of her coffee hurriedly, then excused herself and went upstairs to brush her teeth, finish packing, and make one phone call of her own.

Josh Friedman answered his cell phone on the third ring. "Hey, good looking, what are you doing up so early while you're on vacation?"

Josh had been a member of the BQK task force she'd been on for several years. They were presently in the same squad working out of D.C. and under SAC Douglas Trotter's command, who took orders from the ADIC, the Assistant Director in Charge.

"Officially, I'm still on vacation," Nic said. "For now, I

don't want Doug to know anything about what I'm doing unofficially."

Josh let out a long, low whistle. "I don't like the sound of that. What are you up to and is it going to get you into trouble?"

"Yes, it could get me in trouble." She hesitated telling Josh everything. God, was he going to get a laugh at her expense. If anyone on earth knew how much she detested Griffin Powell, it was Josh. He'd had to listen to her curse the man's very existence on a fairly regular basis while they were on the BQK task force.

"I'm listening," Josh told her.

"If you laugh, so help me—"

"Now, why would I laugh at you? Unless you've gone off and married Griff Powell—my God, Nic, you haven't—!"

"Of course not!" Nic sucked in a deep, courage-building breath. "But I am with Griff."

"You're shitting me, right?"

"Swear to me that you'll keep this under wraps until I find out more."

"More about what?"

"You know my theory about there being two BQ killers? That supposedly unprovable theory that I've shared only with you and Doug, the theory that Griffin Powell and I both believe to be true?" She added hastily, "And it's the only thing that man and I share. Get that straight here and now."

"Good God, don't tell me that you and Powell are off on some wild-goose chase to prove your theory."

"He called us," Nic said.

"Who called you? And is that the royal *us* or are you referring to you and Powell?"

"The second BQ Killer called me on my cell phone yesterday and he called Griff, too. He phoned us only minutes apart. He all but admitted to both of us that he'd been the second BQ Killer. He told us he has begun a new game. And he gave us both a clue."

"Crap! Are you kidding me?"

"We know he's already killed two women and both women were athletes, but we need to find a way to prove that the two crimes are connected. I'm flying to Ballinger, Arkansas, with Griff this morning. That's where one of the victims was found." Nic hurriedly filled Josh in on what information she had, then ended the conversation by saying, "If I call you for unofficial help—?"

"Look, I think you should tell Doug right away and bring him up to speed on this."

"No. Not until I'm certain that I can prove to him this guy has started a new killing game and the bureau needs to be involved."

"Doug is not going to like your teaming up with Griffin Powell," Josh reminded her.

"I don't like teaming up with him, but right now I'm not calling the shots and neither is Griff."

"Then who is?"

"Our killer is."

*　*　*

Amber Kirby had the oddest feeling that someone was watching her, and the sensation gave her the creeps. But she didn't slow down, didn't alter her pace one iota. After all, it wasn't as if she were out here on this walking/jogging trail alone. She had overslept and was running late this morning; otherwise she'd be finished with her three-mile run and be showered and dressed for the day. But Sundays were her day of rest, the only day her hectic schedule allowed her time off, and that would change during basketball season. She didn't really mind all the hard work—both on the court and off—because her basketball scholarship to University of Tennessee was the only way she could afford college. That or join the army. And since she'd been the star of her high school team, with a natural athletic ability, she preferred playing basketball to running the risk of getting killed or having her limbs blown off in Iraq.

The farther along the trail she ran, the more relaxed she became, and the more certain she was that she had imagined someone peering at her through the bushes. No one in their right mind would try to attack someone on such a wide-open and often-congested trail. She'd seldom run this course without seeing at least half a dozen people. And no one was likely to be staring at her because they were fascinated by her beauty. At six one, big-boned, and with a flat chest, she wasn't exactly the type who attracted attention from the opposite sex. How often had she wished she'd inherited her body build from her mother instead of her father and his two big, gangling sisters.

Despite being taller than the average man, Aunt Virginia and Aunt Carole had found husbands. And neither aunt was a great beauty. So, there was hope for her. Sooner or later, some six foot six guy would come along and decide he liked his women tall, raw-boned, and plain. But until then, she'd just keep on doing what she did best—playing basketball. And loving every minute of it.

* * *

Pudge sat on the front porch in his favorite chair, an old wicker rocker that had belonged to Grandmother Suzette. He had no memory of her because she had died when he was only two. She had drowned in one of the numerous ponds on the thousand-acre estate, her death ruled an accident. But he had once overheard his mother and aunt talking about Suzette, about her being as crazy as a Betsy Bug and how the nutty old woman had killed herself.

Balancing the saucer in his palm, he lifted the cup to his lips and sipped the strong espresso as his gaze traveled over the lush, moist land spread out before him, land that had been in his family for nearly two hundred years. If all was as it should be in the world, he would be the king of a vast empire, with underlings kissing his feet and begging for his favors. But instead, he ruled over land that hadn't produced a crop in his lifetime and a decaying antebellum mansion that reeked of mildew and pulsated with the ghosts of countless ancestors whose spirits haunted the rooms. He'd never seen a ghost, mind you, but he had felt their presence. Even as a child, he'd known evil spirits resided here at Belle Fleur.

But in the light of day, the sunlight invading every nook and cranny, banishing the shadows, Pudge preferred to dwell on more pleasant thoughts. He would be traveling to Tennessee soon, tomorrow at the latest, to pick up his next quarry. Once he brought her home with him, the fun would begin. She would spend her first night in the basement, just as the others had done. Then the next morning, before Allegra arrived to prepare his breakfast, he would take his prey and release her into the wild.

Just the thought of beginning the game again, of spending three weeks stalking Amber Kirby, then capturing and killing her, excited him. A sensation of pure glee tingled through his whole body.

* * *

Ballinger, Arkansas, located south of Little Rock, appeared no different from most small towns comprised of less than ten thousand people. Griff drove up Main Street, which apparently had undergone a recent restoration, in search of the B&B Sanders had booked for Nic and him. He figured they would learn what they could about Kendall Moore today and tomorrow, then head for Stillwater, Texas, late in the day.

"Is that it?" Nic asked, pointing to what appeared to be an old, remodeled hotel right in the middle of town.

"Hmm . . . Yeah, I believe it is. The Ballinger Hotel." Griff chuckled. "I suppose, for a little town like this, it was something in its heyday, which was probably 1925." The two-story building possessed a dark red brick façade, clean lines, and Craftsman-era styling.

"There's a sign with an arrow," Nic told him. "PARKING IN THE REAR."

Griff turned right at the sign and eased their rental Ford Taurus between the two structures until he reached an alley-way that led to the parking lot behind the B&B and a law-yer's office.

"We'll check in and leave our luggage, then take a walk over to the police station we saw on our way into town."

When they got out, Griff removed their suitcases from the trunk, intending to carry them both. But Nic didn't budge. She held out her hand.

"I'll take it," she told him.

"Why?" he asked.

"Why what?"

"Why not let me carry your bag for you?"

"Because you have your own to carry and I'm perfectly capable of carrying my suitcase."

"Hmm . . ." What was she trying to prove? That she didn't want or need a man's help? Sometime in her past, some guy had done a real number on Nicole Baxter and Griff would lay odds that it hadn't been her husband.

She twitched her fingers at him. "My suitcase, please."

"Sure thing." He handed the case to her.

Side by side, they walked through the alley, around to the sidewalk on Main Street, and up to the hotel's front entrance.

Griff held the door open for her. Let her chew him out for being a gentleman. But his mama had taught him good manners and he wasn't about to let a lady open her own door.

Surprisingly, Nic said nothing. But she did give him a disapproving sidelong glance. The foyer of the old hotel was small but clean and rather appealing with brown marble floors and oak paneling. A plump, silver-haired woman who was running a feather duster over the framed photographs of the town, circa early twentieth century, that hung on the wall, paused in her chore when she realized she was no longer alone.

"May I help you?"

"I'm Griffin Powell and this is Ms. Baxter," Griff said. "We booked rooms for tonight."

"Oh, yes, of course. Check-in isn't until two, but since y'all are our only guests, it won't be a problem." She glanced from Griff to Nic. "I'm Cleo Willoughby. I'm the owner."

"Now, tell me, dear, do you want rooms with a connecting door or not?"

"Not," Nic said lightning fast.

Cleo's brows rose with a hint of speculation and curiosity.

"Ms. Baxter and I are business associates," Griff said.

"Indeed. And what kind of business are you in, Mr. Powell?"

"I'm a private detective," he told her, without hesitation. In a town this size, news would travel fast, so there was no point in trying to keep his identity secret.

Cleo smiled broadly. "How very interesting. Can you tell me what brings you to Ballinger?"

"We're hoping to speak with the police chief about a recent murder," Griff said.

"Is that right? And is Benny expecting y'all?"

"Benny?" Nic asked.

"Yes, Benny's the police chief. He's my nephew. If you'd

like, I'll give him a call and tell him you folks want to talk to him about a murder. I assume it's Kendall Moore's murder, isn't it?"

"Yes, ma'am, it is," Griff replied. So the police chief was her nephew? Ah, the interwoven relationships of small-town families.

"Well, you two come along and get signed in and I'll show you upstairs." Cleo motioned for them to follow her into the room on the left, apparently her office. "While you're settling in, I'll call Benny. It's nearly eleven, so he'll probably be heading over to Mot's for Sunday dinner as soon as he leaves church." She lifted her head from where she'd been fiddling with the credit card machine and looked right at Nic. "I went to nine o'clock services this morning. Don't want y'all thinking that I'm not a good Christian woman."

"The thought wouldn't have entered our minds, Ms. Willoughby," Griff said.

"Call me Cleo. Everybody does."

"Yes, ma'am," Nic and Griff said simultaneously.

"If you'd wanted connecting rooms, I could have given you the Fred Astaire and Ginger Rogers rooms, but the Jean Harlow room is bigger and has a view of Main Street. And the Cary Grant room is very nice, too." She patted Griff on the arm. "The last gentleman who stayed in it said he couldn't remember when he'd slept better."

"That's good to know." Griff wished Cleo would hurry things along, but he suspected there was no point in trying to rush her.

She ran Griff's credit card, handed him the slip to sign, and swapped him his card for the bill.

"Do you get many visitors?" Nic asked.

"Not many, but enough to keep the doors open. The gentleman I mentioned who last stayed in the Cary Grant room spent only one night. Said he was just passing through. I wonder if those boys finding Kendall Moore's body in the park had anything to do with him leaving so fast."

"When did this man arrive and when did he leave?" Griff asked, an odd notion hitting him at the mention of the man being here so recently.

"He came in on Friday evening, rather late, and paid in cash." Cleo said. "And he left Saturday morning, right after we heard about them finding that poor gal strung up by her heels and her head scalped. Have you ever heard of such a gruesome thing?"

Nic and Griff exchanged glances and in that moment, he knew that she was thinking the same thing he was: the recent occupant of the Cary Grant room might well have been Kendall Moore's murderer.

Chapter 4

A six foot, auburn-haired, good old boy with an easygoing manner and an infectious laugh, Benny Willoughby seemed like a nice guy. Nic guessed that he was in his early fifties, and the gold band on the third finger of his left hand indicated he was married. When they arrived at Mot's, which was apparently the town's most popular restaurant, at least for the Sunday lunch crowd, he greeted them cordially and suggested they order the chicken and dressing.

Nic wondered where Benny's wife was.

After they placed their order and sat down at the table with the police chief, at least six different men stopped by to speak to Willoughby. Finally, just as the waitress brought their drink order, he turned and glanced from Griff to Nic.

"Aunt Cleo tells me you folks are private detectives interested in Kendall Moore's murder."

"That's right," Griff replied, giving Nic a don't-contradict-me glance.

"Did the Moore family hire y'all or—?"

"No," Griff said. "We're not working for anyone on this case."

"Then I don't understand." Benny frowned.

Griff leaned in closer to the chief and lowered his voice. "I'm not at liberty to reveal my sources—not yet—but we have reason to believe that Ms. Moore was murdered by a serial killer and if that's true, her murder could be connected to a case we worked on in the past."

Benny's eyes widened in surprise. "If what you say is true, then I sure do need to know the source of your information, Mr. Powell."

"I'll make you a deal, Chief Willoughby." Griff glanced from right to left, then focused his full attention on Benny. "If you're willing to give us what information you can about Ms. Moore—nothing that would get you in any trouble, of course—I'd be willing to tell you who our source is."

"Humph." Benny looked down, his gaze not quite centered on anything in particular as he shook his head while he considered the proposition. "How about you divulge your source and then I'll see what I can do about answering any questions you've got."

Griff looked at Nic, as if wanting her agreement. She smiled and nodded, knowing damn well he couldn't care less what she thought.

"Fair enough." Griff grasped the back of Benny's chair and moved in, right up against his shoulder, then whispered, "Kendall Moore's killer called us and told us. There was another murder identical to Ms. Moore's out in Stillwater, Texas, about a month ago."

"Well, I'll be." Benny shook his head again. "If that don't beat all. A serial killer, huh? Somebody that didn't even know Kendall. That girl was Ballinger's pride and joy, you know. She went to the Olympics nearly ten years ago and won a silver medal. She was on the track team in high school, just a few years ahead of my oldest, Benny Jr. Came from a good family. She'd been living in California until about six months ago." Benny grunted several times. "I sure couldn't figure out who'd want to do such a terrible thing to Kendall. It was a real puzzle to me and everybody else."

"How long was Kendall missing before her body was found?" Griff asked.

"Her folks contacted me when she didn't come home from an aerobics class one night over three weeks ago," Benny said.

"Could you tell us if she was sexually assaulted?" Nic asked, knowing he'd be more likely to respond to that type of question if a woman asked it.

"We haven't gotten back the autopsy report yet, but our coroner said it didn't look like it to him. Of course, you know she was shot in the head and had been scalped. And our coroner, Larry Kimball, said he was pretty sure she hadn't been dead more than ten or twelve hours. Three teenagers, the Oliver brothers and Mike Letson, found her body hanging from a tree in the park. By the time we got to the scene, there was already a crowd there and in no time, reporters were swarming like maggots. Information that shouldn't have been released to the press got out before we could do anything about it."

"Those things happen," Griff said.

"If you're right about the serial killer, then I sure am relieved. I hated to think anybody around these parts was capable of doing something like that."

"Is there anything in particular you can share with us?" Nic asked. "Anything at all, even something you might consider insignificant."

Grunting, Benny shook his head. "Can't think of anything. Of course, y'all know that she wasn't killed in the park. She was killed somewhere else. We're waiting for the state boys to get back to us. If I let 'em know we think it could be the work of a serial killer, that might get us an autopsy report a little faster." His gaze connected with Griff's. "You were involved in the Beauty Queen Killer cases, weren't you? I

saw your name and picture in the paper on and off for years."
He glanced at Nic. "And you look familiar, too." He snapped
his fingers. "Damn it all, you're the FBI agent who headed
up the task force, aren't you?"

Nic nodded, but before she could respond, Griff took
over. "This isn't an official FBI case. Not yet. Special Agent
Baxter is here in an unofficial capacity. We're putting together
a few pieces of a puzzle, that's all. If enough pieces fit together and we can prove there's a killer who is crossing state
lines, then the bureau will step in."

"As you know, any case with an interstate aspect to it
comes under the FBI's jurisdiction," Nic added.

"Well, I tell you what—when I get more information,
probably within the next few days, I'll share it with you and
whatever you find out about that murder in Texas, you share
with me." Benny picked up his fork and dove into his chicken
and dressing. After a couple of bites, he continued the conversation. "You're welcome to go out to the park and take a
look at where we found her. And you can talk to the first officer on the scene, but I'd rather you not talk to the boys who
found the body. They were pretty shook up about it and their
folks don't want them having to retell it again and again."

"Mr. Powell and I appreciate your cooperation," Nic said.

"We sure do," Griff said. "Nic and I will take you up on
your offer. We'll stay overnight and then head for Stillwater
in the morning."

Apparently, Benny had talked all the business he intended to for the day. He concentrated fully on his meal.
Griff ate heartily, seeming to enjoy the down-home country
cooking. Nic ate two-thirds of the delicious food on her
plate, then stopped. She had learned long ago that if she ate
all she wanted, she gained weight easily. At five ten she
could carry some extra weight, but God knew she wasn't
model thin. She worked out regularly and watched her diet
in order to keep her body fit.

* * *

Thirty minutes later, after she'd drunk another glass of iced tea while Griff and Benny had finished off huge slices of German Chocolate Cake, they headed for Ballinger Park. Located in the center of four downtown streets and comprising an entire block, the park boasted a central fountain, a gazebo, brick walkways, towering trees, neatly manicured flowerbeds, and a variety of wrought iron and stone benches.

"You folks take your time," Benny said as he led them directly to the corded-off crime scene. "The Crime Scene Investigation folks are finished, so you can't bother nothing. If you need anything, you've got my number, so just give me a call. I'm fixing to head to Pine Bluff. I've been seeing a lady over there for the past six months and if things keep going along the way I hope, we'll probably get married before Christmas."

"Congratulations," Nic said, even more curious about the wedding band he wore.

"Thank you, ma'am. I've been a widower nearly three years and my kids are all grown and gone. A man gets mighty lonely." He looked at Griff. "You're not married, are you, Mr. Powell? Don't put it off too long. A man your age ought to be thinking about settling down with a good woman and having a couple of kids."

Nic almost laughed out loud. If only Griff could see the expression on his face. But she managed not to laugh or make a snide comment until after Benny disappeared up the brick walkway. Then she laughed.

Griff gave her a hard stare.

"Sorry," she told him. "But the way you looked, you'd have thought Chief Willoughby had suggested you should get yourself castrated."

"Marriage isn't for everyone, is it, Nic? You tried it once, didn't you?"

That certainly achieved the desired effect. Wiped the smile right off her face. She wondered just how much Griff knew about her marriage. The fact that he obviously knew she was a widow was more than she'd like for him to know. What had he done—investigated her past? Probably. Okay, so he'd found out she had been married and that her husband was dead. That didn't necessarily mean he knew how Gregory had died.

"No, marriage isn't for everyone," she replied.

He didn't respond. Instead, he stepped over the yellow crime scene tape and walked around the massive oak tree. He stopped and studied the low-hanging branch from which Kendall Moore had been hung.

"A guy would need a ladder and some sturdy rope," Griffin said. "And he'd have to be fairly strong to lift a dead body."

Following Griff, she stepped over the yellow tape. "He probably laid her on the ground, tied her feet, then climbed up and tied the robe around the limb and hoisted her up."

"This guy is smart," Griff said. "And careful. During the five years of the BQK murders, he didn't leave any clues that would lead us to him. Hell, nobody even realized there were two killers."

"Not until the end. Not until one partner killed the other."

Griff jerked around and stared at her. "He didn't have to kill him that day. My sharpshooter's bullet would have taken him out. He killed Maygarden because it was part of their game. That tells us that he plays by the rules, even if they are his own rules. He's organized, methodical, and—"

"Evil," Nic said. "He's capable of just about anything."

"He abducted Kendall and kept her somewhere for three weeks, then brought her here to the park. Where did he take her? Why keep her alive for three weeks before killing her?"

"We need to find out if she was tortured."

"Do you think that's why he kept her alive, to torture her?"

"Probably."

"The BQ Killer's MO didn't involve prolonged torture. He moved in for the kill pretty damn quick and got it over with, then left the body there. This is a completely different scenario."

"A new game," Nic said.

"A solo game, one without a competitor."

"No scorecard this time. No one to compete with—" Nic gasped. "That's the reason he called us."

"To tell us this game is different, that there are new rules, a completely different—"

"Yes, all that, but more. He wants us to play the game with him. Isn't that what he said? He even gave us the first two clues. He's daring us to play the game, to see if we can outsmart him, maybe even catch him."

"We're his competitors." Griff snorted. "That son of a bitch!"

"We don't have to play his game."

"Yeah, we do. And he knows it."

"Why us? How could he know that you and I were the only two people who believed he existed, that believed Cary Maygarden had a partner?"

"It was either a lucky guess or a logical conclusion. Whichever it was doesn't matter, does it? We were the two investigators who followed the BQK cases for years. We were the two people who knew all there was to know about the murders and the murderer. And he had to know the ballistics reports would show that Maygarden was hit with two different bullets that day and that somebody would get suspicious."

"He probably felt pretty sure that the bureau wouldn't try to track down a possible second killer when we had no solid proof of his existence and there were no other BQK murders after Cary Maygarden was killed."

Griff walked all the way around the tree and Nic followed him. When he stopped abruptly, she almost collided with his big, broad back. She caught herself just in time. Another two inches and she'd have slammed up against him.

"This is useless. We made a mistake coming to Ballinger first," Griff said as he turned around to face Nic. "We should have started with the first murder, the one that's nearly a month old. The sheriff in Stillwater will have more info."

"What makes you think the woman in Stillwater was his first victim?"

Griff narrowed his gaze until his eyes were hooded slits. "Good question. I'm hoping she was, but it's possible there have been others."

"We need to know for sure, don't we?"

"Do you suppose you could find out for us?"

"Are you asking me to use my position as a federal agent to acquire the information?"

"Would you?"

Nic knotted her left hand into a fist and squeezed it a couple of times, damning herself for being in this situation. "I knew hooking up with you would come to this, but I didn't think it would happen so quickly. Just because you cut corners and push the boundaries as far as possible and steamroll right over the law when doing things the legal way doesn't suit your purposes does not mean that I will, now that we've formed this unholy alliance."

Griff chuckled. "Unholy alliance, huh? Does that make me the Devil? Probably does. And you'd be—?" When she opened her mouth to protest his taunting, he held up his hand in a STOP signal. "No, don't tell. I figured it out. I'm the Devil and you're a fallen angel."

"You have no idea how much I'd like to slap that stupid smirk off your face."

"But you won't slap me, will you? That would require your actually touching me and you don't want to do that, do you?"

"No. I'm going to resist temptation and avoid possible

contamination," Nic told him. "But I am going to call Doug Trotter first thing in the morning."

"I take it that Doug's the supervisory special agent over your squad in D.C. So, why do you think he'll bend the rules for us?"

"Doug's one of the SACs. And he will not bend any rules for us. If I can persuade Chief Willoughby to play along with us, all he'll have to do is tell Doug that he suspects the same person who killed Gala Ramirez in Texas also killed Kendall Moore in Arkansas."

"You know what will happen if we find out that there were other murders before Kendall and Gala," Griff said.

"There is a distinct possibility that once all the law enforcement agencies in the states where the bodies were found are informed, then the FBI will become directly involved and a task force will be formed."

"When that happens, you'll want to cut me out of the action."

"You're smiling." Nic really hated that smug look on his face. "As much as I do not want you involved, you will be. Not just because you make a habit of sticking your nose in where it doesn't belong, but because the man who called you and me isn't going to allow me to cut you out of the action."

"Already figured that out, have you? Yeah, for some reason he wants us to be a team on this one."

"Maybe he has a giant ego and outsmarting just one of us isn't enough of a challenge."

"Maybe."

"After we finish up here and talk to the first officer on the scene, I want to call Chief Willoughby in the morning and see if he'll contact Doug."

"Make it early, okay? I want us on the plane and heading for Stillwater by nine."

* * *

Griff sure as hell hoped that Nic didn't think he had requested this special romantic dinner. Miss Cleo had pulled out all the stops in arranging an evening under the stars for them.

Griff looked directly at Nic, who sat across from him at the small table decked out with a linen tablecloth. "I hope you know that I didn't—"

Nic burst into laughter.

Griff grinned. "It seems Miss Cleo is a romantic."

"Undoubtedly. And delusional as well. How anyone could think that you and I . . ." Nic laughed again. "We are the last two people on earth who'd ever be a couple."

"Yeah, I agree. But neither of us ever thought we'd become crime-solving partners, either."

"I don't like to think of us as partners," Nic said. "There's just something unnatural about it."

"Yeah, I know. It's an unholy alliance."

Nic smiled; and when she did, Griff realized that in all the years he'd known her, he had seldom seen her smile. She was downright pretty when she wasn't frowning.

"We aren't friends," she reminded him, her smile vanishing. "We don't even like each other, so there's no point in pretending otherwise. But I can and will act in a professional manner, if you will. And I'll try my best to be civil, even cordial, if at all possible."

"Tell me why you dislike me so much?" *Good God, why had he asked her that?*

"Do you really want to know?"

He nodded.

"You're an arrogant, egotistical, womanizing bastard who thinks because you're rich, you can do whatever you want, that the rules others have to live by don't apply to you. I've got news for you, Mr. Powell, you're not all that special. You're no different than any other man."

Griff glared right into her eyes. She shivered.

"That's where you're wrong. I am different. And not because of my sizable bank account." She had no idea just how different he was. Neither she nor the rest of the world would ever know. And he would give all he owned if he could forget.

"There's that gigantic Powell ego speaking. Mr. Big-Bad PI with the mystery past and women swooning at his feet. You love it, don't you? You love being Mr. Macho."

Griff lifted the crystal flute and sipped the wine. Not great, but he'd tasted worse. He studied Nic, noting her flushed cheeks and rapid breathing. She was angry, and all that emotion was directed at him. But was he really the one she was upset with, the one who had prompted her anger?

"Go ahead," she told him.

"Pardon? Go ahead and do what?"

"Tell me why you don't like me."

"If you really want to know."

"Turnabout is only fair," she said.

"I don't like women who need to prove they can do anything a man can do and do it better. Men and women are inherently different. I like being a man and I prefer women who enjoy being female."

"Fluttery and feminine and helpless and silly," Nic said, her eyes flashing with anger. "Can't get along without some big, strong man taking care of her. Good for fucking and having babies and not much else."

Griff took another sip of wine, set his glass on the table, and asked, "Who put that enormous, ugly chip on your shoulder, Nicki?"

Gritting her teeth, Nic groaned; then she shoved back her chair and stood. "I've lost my appetite."

When she turned to leave, Griff pushed back his chair, got up, and went after her. When he caught up with her, he grasped her arm, intending to apologize. But before he could say a word, she whirled around and gave him a killer glare.

"Let go of me."

He looked at his hand holding her arm, then looked directly at her before releasing her.

"Don't ever touch me again," she told him.

When she turned and walked away, he didn't try to stop her.

Chapter 5

Stillwater wasn't much more than a wide place in the road. The only street in town was Main Street. A single row of ramshackle old buildings, all but two empty, looked like they were about to fall in. The two occupied structures had been remodeled. One housed a beauty shop and the other, a two-story building, boasted a big green sign that read FEED AND SEED.

As they drove through town, Nic kept her gaze focused either to the right or straight ahead, pretending to be interested in the local scenery. Neither she nor Griff had mentioned anything about how their evening had ended yesterday. Actually, when she'd met him in the dining room of the Ballinger B&B for breakfast this morning, he'd acted as if nothing had happened. While Cleo Willoughby had served them a big country breakfast, complete with grits and hash browns, Griff had informed her that the Powell jet was ready to leave, that he'd already spoken to the sheriff of Stillwater, and had taken a call from Ballinger's chief of police.

"What did Chief Willoughby have to say?" Nic had asked.

"He promised that he'd do as you asked and get in touch

with Doug Trotter today to request that the bureau compare the murder here in Ballinger with the murder in Stillwater."

During the plane ride from Arkansas to Texas, Nic and Griff hadn't talked much. For a good part of the trip, she had pretended to be asleep. She'd been sure Griff would hassle her about the way she had overreacted to him grasping her arm last night. She had kept waiting for him to say something, to ask her why the hell she'd run from him as if she were afraid of him. But to her surprise—and relief—he hadn't said a word.

If he had, how would she have responded? She could have admitted that she overreacted because she'd been tired and edgy. She could have told him that she hated being forced to work with him. That would have been the truth. Just not the complete truth.

"Look for a sign that reads Old Stillwater Road," Griff told her as he maneuvered the rented SUV through town.

"Sure." Nic looked right and left, but avoided direct eye contact with Griff. "What time is Sheriff Touchstone meeting us?"

"He said he'd be there by twelve thirty and it's"—Griff glanced at the Rolex on his wrist—"twelve twenty now."

"I was a little surprised that he agreed to meet us at the scene," Nic said. "Apparently, he intends to be as cooperative as Benny Willoughby was."

She felt Griff glance her way, so she kept her gaze riveted to the windshield.

"Does it surprise you that local law enforcement is willing to cooperate with a private detective?" he asked.

"If that private detective was just any old PI, yes, I'd be surprised. But let's face it—there aren't many people who haven't heard of *the* Griffin Powell."

"My name does open a few doors for me, but as a general rule, most local lawmen don't cross the line and give me privileged information. Once in a blue moon, somebody will offer a little more info than they should, but for the most part, I have to resort to other methods to acquire my information."

"Illegal methods," Nic snapped.

Griff grunted. "Rarely illegal, but I admit we bend the rules near the breaking point when necessary. And often our methods could be perceived as unethical."

"*Perceived* as unethical?" Nic harrumphed.

"Look, years ago, you and I established the fact that you do not approve of me, my agency, or our investigation tactics. And I don't fault you for trying to be a by-the-book federal agent. I respect you, Nic, I just don't like you personally."

Slap! Why should she care that the high and mighty Griffin Powell didn't like her? Heck, she should be grateful that he didn't. What was the old saying about there being people you wouldn't want to like you?

"We're actually in agreement on something," she told him. "You don't like me and I don't like you."

"So it would seem. Now, the question that remains is, can we set aside our personal differences and actually work together to put a killer out of commission before he kills again? I'm man enough to do it, are you?"

Slap! Nic knew that Griff saw her as a man-eating feminist who had something to prove to every man she met. Maybe he was partially right. If there was one thing she hated, it was being told she couldn't or shouldn't do something because she was a woman.

"Sure," Nic said. "I've got the balls, if you do."

Griff chuckled under his breath.

Nic smiled to herself, an internal don't-screw-with-me smile; but outwardly her facial expression remained unchanged.

"There it is—" Nic pointed to the left. "Old Stillwater Road."

Griff slowed the SUV, and then turned left onto the two-lane country road. After going over two miles, they had seen little except open fields, probably once planted annually in cotton, but now planted in corn. The pavement, filled with potholes and covered with cracked and crumbling asphalt, needed repairs.

Nic saw two vehicles parked alongside the roadway about a quarter of a mile ahead of them. As they got closer to the truck and the Jeep, she noticed two men standing in the shade of a large maple tree near a narrow bridge. Griff pulled the SUV in behind the other two vehicles and killed the engine.

"Be nice," Griff said. "Act like a lady and not a hard-ass FBI agent."

Glaring at him, she made a hissing sound.

Laughing, he opened his door and got out. Before he had a chance to round the hood and open her door, she jumped out and met him at the right front bumper. He nodded in the direction of the big tree.

"Ladies first," he said.

She walked ahead of him, up the side of the road and into the area near the bridge. The two men standing there watched as she and Griff approached. The younger man, wearing a tan Stetson and brown leather boots stepped forward.

"Mr. Powell?" he asked as he held out his hand. "I'm Sheriff Touchstone."

Griff shook hands with Dean Touchstone, who appeared to be in his early thirties. He was hazel-eyed, brown-haired, Texas-lean, and sported a thick, old-cowpoke mustache.

He turned to Nic, removed his hat, and nodded, "Ma'am."

"This is Nicole Baxter," Griff said. "She's working with me on this case."

Nic had to bite her tongue to keep from correcting him and saying that he was working with her and not the other way around. But she forced a smile and shook hands with the sheriff.

"This is Vance Coker." The older man nodded to Griff

and gave Nic an appreciative appraisal, the kind men give most women at first glance. "Vance is the one who found Gala Ramirez's body hanging from that tree right there."

Vance was probably sixty, short, wiry, and gray-haired. At least what hair he had left was gray. He had the kind of weathered skin that a person has after years of sun exposure.

"Vance owns this land," the sheriff said.

"Been in my family over a hundred years," Vance added.

"He found Gala's body hanging from that maple tree there by the bridge, the first of August. Me and Ellis, one of my deputies, came out just as soon as Vance called us." Dean Touchstone turned his head and stared at the tree. "It's been over ten years since we had a murder in Durant County."

"Sure was a troubling sight," Vance said. "That poor little gal was strung up like a piece of beef, her ankles bound together and her head scalped. You can't imagine what that looks like if you ain't never seen it. Real troubling." Vance shook his head back and forth.

"Was she naked?" Nic asked. "Was there any evidence she'd been sexually assaulted?"

"She wasn't naked," Vance said. "She was wearing shorts and a blouse, both of 'em bloody. Real bloody."

"She wasn't sexually assaulted," Sheriff Touchstone said. "The coroner's report ruled out rape."

"What did the coroner's report tell you other than she hadn't been raped?" Griff asked.

Ignoring Griff's question, Touchstone looked at Vance. "Thanks for meeting us here. I appreciate it." He turned to Griff. "You folks have anything else you want to ask Vance before he leaves?"

Beating Nic to the punch, Griff asked the farmer half a dozen questions. His answers were succinct, but not very informative.

"If that'll be all, Mary Lou's holding lunch for me." Vance looked to the sheriff for permission to leave.

Touchstone nodded. "Thanks again, Vance."

As soon as the farmer got in his truck and drove off, the sheriff faced Griff and Nic. "I'll give you folks the basic facts of the case, but that's all. I'm not opening my files to you and I'm not sharing privileged information. Understood?"

Nic smiled. "Yes, Sheriff, we understand. You can't divulge privileged information to just anybody, not even private detectives."

"Yes, ma'am." Touchstone smiled at her, a flirting twinkle in his eye.

Griff cleared his throat. "As I mentioned when we spoke on the phone, what we need is to confirm that the similarities between Kendall Moore's murder and Gala Ramirez's murder are enough to indicate a link between the two and possibly point to a serial killer."

"I understand," Touchstone said. "But I don't want y'all bandying around the words 'serial killer' in Stillwater. Folks are upset enough by the Ramirez girl's murder without hearing that there's a serial killer on the loose."

"We don't intend to speak to anyone else in Stillwater," Griff said. "You've already told us that Gala was hung upside down from that tree." Griff nodded to the grand old maple. "Her feet had been bound and she'd been scalped, but she hadn't been raped and she wasn't naked. Could you confirm her cause of death?"

"She'd been shot in the head."

"The scenario you described fits Kendall Moore's murder," Nic said. "What we need is for you to contact SAC Doug Trotter at the FBI field office in D.C. and tell him you suspect that the same person who killed Kendall Moore in Ballinger, Arkansas, might have killed Gala Ramirez."

Squinting against the noonday sun, Touchstone replaced his Stetson and focused on Nic. "I tell you what I'll do—I'll call the police chief in Ballinger and if he backs up everything y'all have told me, I'll contact the FBI."

"Thank you." Nic rewarded him with a wide smile.

"You folks staying on overnight? If you are—"

"We're not," Griff said. "My plane is waiting for us in Lufkin and we'll be taking off from there and heading back to Tennessee. But if you need to get in touch with me, with us, you have my cell number."

"Sure do," Touchstone said. "But I don't have yours, ma'am."

"If you need to reach Ms. Baxter, just call me," Griff told him.

Pudge booked a first-class ticket from Baton Rouge to Nashville. Once there, he would use a fake ID to rent a car and then drive on to Knoxville. He would check into a cheap motel as close to Amber Kirby's apartment as possible and the following day he would begin observing her. Within a couple of days, he should know enough about her daily routine to choose the best time to abduct her. He couldn't be certain, of course, but because she was an athlete and had to stay in superb physical condition, he assumed she ran at least once every day. If he was lucky, her routine would include either an early-morning or a late-night run.

Before he packed, he needed to choose a disguise. Nothing elaborate, just enough to change his appearance so that if anyone remembered seeing him, they wouldn't describe him as he actually looked. After unlocking the wooden chest at the foot of his bed, he sat on the floor and casually went through the contents. He laid out a brown mustache that matched the color of his hair; then he found a pair of black-framed glasses. He added an Atlanta Braves baseball cap to the subtle masquerade items he would use. While in Nashville, he'd find a Wal-Mart and buy some inexpensive clothes. Nondescript. A cotton shirt and trousers. A pair of athletic shoes.

A couple of loud taps on his locked bedroom door reminded him that he was not alone in the house. Allegra was here. But he never worried about the old woman. She was a trustworthy old soul and even if she saw or overheard anything unusual, she didn't have enough sense to figure out what was going on.

"Lunch is ready," she called through the closed door. "I fried up some of them fresh catfish that Pappy Rousey brought by this morning."

"Thank you, Allegra. I'll be right there."

"Don't you dawdle too long and let my fried conrbread balls get cold."

Pudge heard her shuffling away, going back down the hall. He wasn't sure how much longer she'd be able to make the trip out here to Belle Fleur every day. Her daughter, Fantine, dropped her off and picked her up on her way to and from her job as one of the maids for the Landau family who lived about ten miles down the road. He supposed when Allegra either died or retired, he'd have no choice but to find a new cook. When that day came, he would have to be more careful about playing his games.

Surely there's a halfwit out there somewhere who knows how to cook.

Pudge picked up his disguise, got up out of the floor, and carried the items over to the bed where his open suitcase lay. He removed a small plastic case, laid the items inside, and put the case back into the suitcase.

As he left his room, he whistled to himself, some nonsensical tune from his childhood. He didn't think he'd ever heard the words to the song, didn't even know the name of the song, but he found himself humming it whenever he was plotting a new adventure. It was a happy song. His mother had hummed it to him to comfort him after she rescued him from his father's wicked temper tantrums. Why his father had lashed out at him and never at Mary Ann and Marsha, he didn't know. But whenever Daddy got in one of his moods, he had always called for Pudge to be sent to his study.

Don't think about how mean Daddy was to you. Think about how kind Mommy was to you afterward.

Nic hadn't chewed Griff out the way she had wanted to and it had taken every ounce of her willpower. She had wanted to scream at him, to tell him that he had no right to speak for her, that maybe she had wanted to give the handsome sheriff her cell number. And if she had, it wouldn't have been any of Griff's business.

On the drive from Stillwater to Lufkin, he'd glanced at her every once in a while, as if trying to gauge her mood, but she'd remained calm and silent, speaking to him only when he asked her a direct question.

Finally aboard the Powell jet and waiting for a powerful summer thunderstorm to pass before taking off, she and Griff sat in the luxurious cabin, sipping on early-evening drinks. Crown Royal and Coke for Griff. Plain Coke for Nic.

"He'll contact us again," Griff said, the statement coming after endless minutes of complete silence.

"Who?" Nic asked.

"The killer." Griff pivoted on the leather sofa and faced Nic, who sat across from him. "Who did you think I meant—Sheriff Touchstone? Hell, what kind of name is that, anyway—Touchstone? A pretty name for a pretty boy."

"He was rather handsome, wasn't he?"

"He took an instant shine to you."

"Do you find that so hard to believe, that a good-looking man would find me attractive?"

Griff downed the last drops of his drink, set the glass on the side table at the end of the sofa, and replied, "No, of course not. You're attractive. I never said you weren't. It's not your physical appearance that I object to, it's your personality."

"What's wrong with my personality?" *That's it, Nic, ask him and he'll no doubt tell you.*

"You're abrasive, aggressive, bossy, and—"

"Traits that you would admire in a man."

"Why do you want to act like a man?"

Answer that one, she told herself. *Damn him!*

Nic finished off her Coke but didn't put down her glass. Instead she shook the tumbler, making the ice chips click together as she absently stared into the glass.

The distinctive ring told Nic that it was her cell phone and not Griff's. She removed the phone from her pocket, checked the caller ID, and flipped it open. This just might be the call she'd been hoping for.

"Hello, Doug."

Griff's eyes widened. She didn't pay any attention to him. Let him wait.

"I received two rather interesting phone calls today," Doug Trotter said. "First this morning, Chief Benny Willoughby from Ballinger, Arkansas, called me and then this afternoon, Sheriff Dean Touchstone from Stillwater, Texas, called. Seems they've each got an unsolved murder and they think the same killer committed both crimes. You wouldn't happen to know anything about either of those, would you, Nic?"

"I might."

"Might, my ass. Just where the hell are you? And don't give me any bullshit about your being in a cabin in the Smoky Mountains."

Nic sensed Griff's impatience. He was dying to know what her boss had to say. Tough shit. The longer she could make him wait, the better.

"I'm on a private jet that will soon be taking off from Lufkin, Texas," Nic said.

"How'd you get yourself involved in this?" Doug asked.

"Does it matter?"

"It does if you've gone over to the dark side."

Nic laughed softly. "I take it that you've heard I'm in league with Lucifer."

"Lucifer?" Griff asked, faking an indignant expression as he pointed to himself.

"What are you doing with Griffin Powell?" She heard the obvious disapproval in Doug's voice.

"Remember my theory that there were two BQ Killers?"

"Yeah."

"Well, Griff and I both received calls a couple of days ago from a man who implied that he was that second killer. And he told us that he has begun a new game. He gave us both clues, each the name of a town and state and a time frame."

"Go on."

Nic wondered why Doug didn't seem surprised. "There had been murders in each of the towns he named, and the time frame he gave us fit the time frame for each murder. Four days ago and four weeks ago."

"So, instead of contacting me, you went with Griffin Powell to Ballinger and on to Stillwater. Want to tell me why?"

"Because Griff and I knew we needed some sort of proof that the murders were connected and that the local law had to get on board before—"

"You're calling him Griff now, traveling on his private jet with him, partnering with him. I don't like it, Special Agent Baxter."

"Yes, sir. I'm not thrilled with the arrangement myself."

"I want you to part company with Powell as soon as possible," Doug told her. "Then I want you to hop a commercial jet to Atlanta. I want you to speak to a couple of detectives there. After I heard from Benny Willoughby this morning, I set some wheels into motion and discovered a really ugly trail of scalped female bodies hanging from tree limbs."

A ripple of fear zipped through Nic's nervous system as a sick feeling hit her in the pit of her stomach.

"What is it?" Griff asked, a concerned look on his face. "What's going on?"

Nic shook her head and motioned for Griff to be quiet, then she asked Doug, "Are you saying there were others besides Gala Ramirez and Kendall Moore?"

"Yeah. So far, we've discovered three other similar murders in three states—Georgia, Oklahoma, and Virginia. All three women were young—under thirty."

"Virginia?"

"Yeah. I've got Josh on it until you get back here."

"Were all three women brunettes?" Nic asked as she absorbed the facts.

"There were three other murders?" Griff asked.

Nic laid her phone on her chest, glowered at Griff and told him, "Yes, there were three more. Now, will you please shut up until I finish talking to my boss!"

"Nic?" Doug called her name.

She lifted the phone to her ear. "I'm here. I had to swat a pesky mosquito."

"To answer your question, no, they were not all brunettes. The first one, killed back in April, was blonde. The second one, killed in May, was a redhead, but the third one was a brunette. She was killed in late June."

"Then her hair color may not have anything to do with his choice. It may not play a part in his new game the way it did in the BQK murders."

"There is a connection between the women, other than the fact that they're all young," Doug said.

"And that would be?"

"Five of the four women were athletes."

"Interesting. We already know that Gala was a tennis pro and Kendall was a former Olympic silver medalist in the long-distance running competition."

"Dana Patterson was a gymnast and Candice Bates was a rodeo athlete."

"And what was the fifth one?"

"Angela Byers was an Atlanta police officer."

The wheels in Nic's mind turned at lightning speed. "My guess is that Angela Byers was in tiptop physical condition. We can check it out, but I'd bet my pension on it." Nic took a deep breath. "What all five women definitely have in common is the fact that they were physically fit. For whatever reason, our killer either wants or needs only women in their physical prime."

Chapter 6

Anxious to know every detail of the information Doug Trotter relayed to her, Griff waited impatiently for Nic to finish her conversation. From listening to her side of the exchange, he surmised that Gala Ramirez had not been the first kill and that three other women's murders fit the same MO.

Nic looked at Griff and wiggled her fingers. "I need a pen and paper," she said as she held the phone sideways to prevent her boss from overhearing her request.

Griff hurried to a built-in desk, opened a drawer, and grabbed a notepad and paper, then slid the pad into Nic's lap and handed her the ink pen. She nodded her thanks, then began writing rapidly as she straightened the phone and said, "I'll get to Atlanta as soon as possible. Want to give me the names of the officers I should contact and where I can locate them?"

Griff watched while she continued writing furiously, nodding her head occasionally and giving simple, one-word replies. Finally, just as his patience wore thin, Nic said goodbye, closed her phone, and slipped it into her pocket.

"Well?" Griff asked.

"Doug unearthed some information that led him to believe there have been five connected murders, not two."

"And?"

"The bureau is looking into each. He's contacted the various law enforcement agencies in the affected states—Georgia, Virginia, and Oklahoma. He's also contacted the field offices in those areas. He wants me to go to Atlanta before I return to D.C."

"No problem," Griff told her. "I'll just have Jonathan file a new flight plan and we'll head for Atlanta instead of Knoxville."

"I don't remember inviting you." Clipping the ink pen to the top of the thin notepad, she looked directly at Griff. "Doug told me to go to Atlanta. He didn't say anything about bringing you along with me." She pressed the pad to her chest. "As a matter of fact, he disapproves of your involvement up to this point."

"Tough." Griff had no intention of letting Doug Trotter shut him out. He didn't take orders from the bureau and although he tried to cooperate with all law enforcement agencies, he always did what he believed was in the best interest of everyone involved. He felt a special need to assist the victims' families and to see that justice was served. Of course, it wasn't always the type of justice he would prefer. His type of justice would be swift and deadly. No mercy whatsoever for vicious murderers like Cary Maygarden and his unknown partner, who had already begun a new killing spree.

"Look, Griff, it's not going to work, our partnering up. Not now. It's only a matter of time before this case is official FBI business. And when that happens—"

"You know that I'll either be one step ahead of you or one step behind you. It doesn't make sense for us not to cooperate."

"I'd ask you to stay out of this and allow the proper authorities to handle the matter, but I know you won't listen to anything I say." Nic clutched the notepad to her chest with both hands, as if she were determined that he not catch even a glimpse of the info she'd jotted down during her conversation with Trotter. "You're going to do whatever you want to do and damn the consequences. You want to solve this case and be the big dog in the news. You want everyone saying what an amazing PI Griffin Powell is, how he's doing law enforcement's job for them."

"Do you honestly believe that I get involved in these cases because I like the publicity?" Good God, she really didn't know him at all, did she? But then, he probably didn't know her any better and might be judging her as unfairly as she was him.

"Are you saying you don't love the publicity?" She snickered mockingly. "Odd, huh, that you wind up with your picture in the paper on a regular basis. If it's not a story about Griffin Powell on the trail of a killer, then there's one about your appearance at the latest highbrow social event with some gorgeous heiress on your arm." She huffed. "Admit it—you love being in the public eye."

Griff glanced at the notepad she held so protectively. She tightened her grip on the edges of the pad, eased it away from her chest, turned it over, and laid it in her lap. She pressed her folded hands down on top of it.

"I like solving crimes," he said. "I like helping put criminals behind bars. I like doing what I can to stop evil people from harming others."

"Then become a police officer, join the FBI, or get a law degree and—"

"There are enough police officers and lawyers"—he looked her square in the eyes—"and enough FBI agents. And you're all required to work within the system, to follow the rules and walk the straight-and-narrow. Sometimes that works. Sometimes it doesn't. I have the freedom to cut a few corners, to sidestep a few rules. Sometimes my way works better. Sometimes it doesn't."

"What is it with you?" she asked. "Why do you care? If it's not for the thrills and the publicity, then why do it? You've got more money than God, so why not enjoy your playboy lifestyle and not get your hands dirty with murder and mayhem? I've never understood why you opened a PI firm in the first place."

"Why I care is a personal matter," he told her. "And because I do have more money than I could spend in several lifetimes, I have the means to help other people. Powell's takes all kinds of cases, from people like Judd, who can pay dearly for our services, as well as from people who can't pay us a dime. It doesn't matter to us—to me—as long as we do our job."

"So, you want me to believe that the Powell Agency is some philanthropic organization and you're the benevolent benefactor?"

"Believe whatever you want."

Nic looked down at the notepad in her lap. "This is information you'll find out sooner or later." She flipped the pad over. "I'll share this with you, and then I need to get off your plane and book a reservation on the next commercial flight out of here for Atlanta."

"As soon as we can get airborne, I'll have Jonathan fly us to Atlanta." Before she could protest—and she was on the verge of doing just that—he held up a restraining hand, asking her to wait. "Once we're in Atlanta, we'll go our separate ways. You'll investigate for the bureau and I'll find a way to look into things on my own."

She hesitated, apparently considering his offer.

"Fly with me and you'll not only be more comfortable, but you'll arrive in Atlanta much sooner," Griff told her.

She released a heaving sigh. "Oh, all right." When he smiled, she added, "But once we get to Atlanta—"

"You can take a taxi and go to headquarters alone, talk to the police and the SAC at the Atlanta office, while I check into a hotel and get a good night's sleep."

She eyed him skeptically.

Using his index finger, he drew an invisible *X* on his chest. "Cross my heart."

She nodded agreement.

Suddenly Griff's cell phone rang at the same moment his pilot, Jonathan Mills, emerged from the cockpit.

"We've been given clearance to take off," Jonathan said.

"Hold off on that," Griff told him as he glanced at the caller ID on his cell phone. "There's been a change in plans. We're going to Atlanta, not Knoxville."

"Yes, sir."

Griff answered on the fifth ring, his gut warning him who the caller was. "Powell here."

"Hello, Griff."

Apparently sensing the tension in Griff, Nic reached over and tapped his arm, then mouthed, "Is it him?"

Griff nodded to Nic, then spoke to the caller. "What can I do for you?"

A soft chuckle. "It's not what you can do for me, but what I can do for you."

"And just what would that be?"

"I can give you a new clue."

"On one of the five past murders or one of the future murders?"

"Ah, you and Nic have been busy, haven't you? I'm impressed that you've already discovered information about all five of them."

Then there really had been only five. But that was five too many. Five innocent young women who had died at the hands of a monster. "Yeah, we know that there were five."

"I'm going to capture Number Six day after tomorrow, so you see, I'm giving you thirty-six hours' notice."

Griff held his breath. Damn this arrogant, crazy son of a bitch.

"Did you hear me?" the caller asked.

"Yeah, I heard you."

"That was the first part of your clue. Want the second part?"

"You're going to give me the second part whether I want it or not, so why ask me?"

"Frustrated already?" Another nasty chuckle.

Griff didn't respond.

"Debbie Glover," the caller said, then hung up.

Griff lifted his phone away from his ear and clutched it in his hand as he repeated the name over and over in his mind. *Who the hell was Debbie Glover? The intended victim? No, that would make it too easy.*

"What did he say?" Nic asked.

"He's abducting another victim day after tomorrow, in thirty-six hours, which means sometime early Wednesday."

"Was that all he said?"

Before Griff could answer Nic, her cell phone rang. Their gazes met and locked.

"He's calling me this time," Nic said as she removed her phone from her pocket.

"He's enjoying himself," Griff told her.

Nic flipped open her phone. "Hello."

"My darling Nicole, how lovely to hear your voice."

"I can't say the same. I hate hearing your voice."

Laughter.

"I have two clues for you," the caller told her. "Two for Griff and two for you."

Nic waited.

"She's a blonde," he said. "I have a personal preference for brunettes, but I don't want to discriminate against blondes and redheads, now do I?"

Nic swallowed hard.

"If you don't say something and let me hear your sweet voice again, I won't give you the other clue," he told her.

"Give me a really good clue—tell me where you are," Nic said.

"Ah, that's my girl. Feisty as ever."

Griff was right. This sick bastard was enjoying himself. He loved drawing Griff and her into his game, into the planning and preparation stage. He needed them, needed their participation in order to achieve the optimum pleasure. But unfortunately, they couldn't simply refuse to play along, not if even one thing he said to them could help them figure out who he was or who his next victim might be.

"I'm at home," he told her. "I'll be leaving in the morning, on my way to stalk my prey before I capture her and . . . But you don't want to hear about all that, do you? You want your other clue."

Nic held her breath.

"Rubies and lemon drops."

He hung up.

Nic frowned, totally puzzled by his statement.

"Well?" Griff asked.

"He's crazy."

"We already knew that."

"Blonde," Nic said. "He told me that his next victim is blonde."

"And he's going to capture her Wednesday."

"What was your other clue?"

"It didn't make any sense."

"Neither did mine," Nic said. "But what was it?"

"A woman's name—Debbie Glover."

"Does the name mean anything to you? Do you know a Debbie Glover?"

"The name is meaningless. I have no idea who she is," Griff said.

"Maybe there's a connection between her and rubies and lemon drops."

"What?"

"His second clue for me was rubies and lemon drops."

"Contact Trotter," Griff said. "And I'll get in touch with Sanders. We'll run a trace on the name and put a few more heads together to work on figuring out the clues. Agreed?"

"Agreed." She lifted the notepad from her lap and handed it to Griff. "In the meantime, I need to get to Atlanta tonight."

"Your wish is my command."

Their gazes met and held for a split second, a silent understanding passing between them. They were still unwilling partners, at least for the time being.

Griff had dropped Nic off at police headquarters over two hours ago, where she was meeting with the local police and an agent from the Atlanta FBI field office. Griff had driven to the downtown Sheraton and checked in. Before they'd left Lufkin, he had contacted Sanders, who had made arrangements for a one-bedroom suite and a separate single room at the four-star hotel.

"When you finish up with what you need to do, catch a cab and come on over to the Sheraton, downtown, on Courtland Street," Griff had told her. "If you'll call me on the way, I'll order supper and when you get there we can see if we can make sense of our four clues."

Kicking back, with his jacket and tie off, Griff relaxed in the suite's lounge. He'd ordered coffee when he first arrived and was now on his third cup. He wasn't concerned about caffeine consumption. He figured he wouldn't sleep much tonight anyway.

As he was studying the notepad filled with Nic's scrawling handwriting, going over the information once again, his cell phone rang. Checking the caller ID, he answered on the second ring.

"You have something for me?" Griff asked.

"Yes and no," Sanders replied. Damar Sanders was more than Griff's right-hand man. He was his best friend, his confidante, his father confessor, and sometimes his conscience. Their relationship went back eighteen years and nothing short of death would ever sever their unique bond.

"Give me the yes first," Griff said.

"Very well. I compiled a list of all the Debbie Glovers I could find in the U.S. and then I narrowed them down to those in the South, including Texas, Oklahoma, Kentucky, and Maryland."

"And?"

"And there were far too many to be able to find out even the most basic facts on all of them before Wednesday morning."

"Narrow the search to only those between twenty and thirty."

"I did."

"And?"

"And I am now running a search on those women, but it will take time to discover their professions."

"Anyone whose profession implies she would be in really good physical condition is to go on the list," Griff said. "As soon as we've narrowed it down to a reasonable number, we'll start narrowing them down to the ones who are blondes."

"Do you think he has actually given you the next victim's name?" Sanders asked.

"I have no idea," Griff admitted, "but unless we can figure out what else the name Debbie Glover could mean, how it could connect to his next victim, then I'm stumped. At least for now."

"I have called in several agents who are not presently on assignments to assist me," Sanders said. "We are working on the clues, seeing if anyone can come up with any ideas as to what they might mean."

"At least everything made some sort of sense—day after

tomorrow, Debbie Glover, and blonde—until the last clue. What the hell kind of clue is rubies and lemon drops?"

"A cryptic one, wouldn't you say?"

"I hate like hell that he's having so much fun doing this. He's stringing us along, keeping us guessing, knowing damn well that we won't refuse to play his game on the off chance we might be able to outsmart him."

"He needs the challenge."

"We know what kind of game he's playing with Nic and me," Griffin said. "What I need to know is what kind of murder game he's playing with his victims. We found out that, at least with Gala Ramirez and Kendall Moore, he kept them alive for approximately three weeks before he killed them."

"Can Special Agent Baxter find out more detailed information about each victim?"

"I'm sure she can, but whether she'll share that info with me is iffy."

"I'll make some phone calls," Sanders said. "If I find out anything, I'll contact you immediately."

No sooner had Griff ended his conversation with Sanders than someone knocked on the outer door. He got up, but before he reached the door, a feminine voice called, "It's me, Nic."

Although he'd told her he would book her a room for tonight, he hadn't been sure she'd actually show up.

When he opened the door, he found her standing there, shoulders drooped, makeup faded, eyes bleary, and an expression of pure disgust on her face.

"I'd better have my own room," she told him as she shoved past him and walked into the suite.

"Naturally. I am a gentleman."

"That's debatable." She eyed the coffeepot on the table. "Tell me that's not decaf."

"Good God, no."

She tossed her shoulder bag onto the nearest chair and

headed straight for the coffee. After pouring herself a cup, she kicked off her shoes and sat down on the sofa.

"You look beat," Griff said. "Are you hungry?"

"Starving."

"Since you didn't call, I haven't ordered dinner. What would you like?"

"Red meat."

Griff chuckled. "I'll make it two steaks. How do you take yours?"

"Medium-well," she replied. "And I want a loaded potato."

While Nic sipped on the coffee, Griff placed their dinner order, then came over and sat down beside her. She gave him a sidelong glance.

"I called Doug on the taxi ride over," she said. "Earlier, I had asked him to find out what he could about the two other murders, the one in Oklahoma and the one in Virginia, and let me know if he unearthed anything."

"And?"

When she didn't immediately reply, he wondered if she had no intention of sharing what she'd learned with him.

"So far, not much," Nic said. "But putting together the info on what I found out about the murder here in Atlanta with the info on the four other murders, there is one more thing that definitely links all five, other than their all being shot in the head and scalped." She heaved a deep sigh. "From the time each woman was discovered missing until her body was found hanging from a tree was between twenty-two and twenty-three days."

When Nic's hand trembled just enough to shake the cup she held, Griff reached out to take the cup from her, but stopped short of touching her. Realizing his intention, she handed him the almost-empty cup.

"All five, huh? So, why keep them for three weeks?" Griff set the cup aside, then leaned back into the sofa and faced

Nic. "We need to know. Is he torturing them? Keeping them drugged? What? We know he didn't rape Kendall and Gala, so he probably didn't rape the others."

"Why does he scalp them?" Nic asked. "What does that convey about him, about the game? He shoots them in the head, apparently execution style, then he scalps them after they're dead."

"The scalp is a trophy, as well as a memento."

"That means he's keeping the scalps so he can look at them and relive each kill. Looking at the scalp triggers the memories and he can get high on recalling whatever led up to the final moments before he put a bullet in the woman's head."

"Why would he need only women in superb physical condition?" Griff turned partially around, lifted one leg over the other, positioning his right ankle over his left knee.

Nic rested her head against the back of the sofa and closed her eyes. "Does he *need* them in great shape or does he *want* them in great shape?"

"Take your pick. Either or."

"They're all young, physically fit, and some are athletes. Their hair color varies, as does their physical description. Gala Ramirez was of Mexican descent, so she was different in that aspect." Nic yawned. "Sorry. I'm tired."

"It's been a long day. Why don't you just relax until dinner arrives, then take a shower and go to bed. We can start fresh in the morning."

Nic shook her head and looked right at Griff. "I'm heading back to D.C. in the morning."

He had figured as much. "You'll be in charge of the bureau's investigation, right?"

"Probably. Doug knows it's what I want."

"And if he thinks you're in cahoots with me, he won't give you the assignment."

She lifted her head from the sofa and leaned toward him ever so slightly. "If the killer continues giving each of us clues, we'll have no choice but to cooperate with each other, but for that reason only. You understand?"

"Oh, yeah, I understand."

"So, while we're together this evening, let's not waste our time. Let's discuss the clues. I assume your team has been searching for women named Debbie Glover, right? And maybe combining brain power to figure out what on earth rubies and lemon drops could mean."

"There are countless Debbie Glovers, but Sanders is narrowing the search. Whether or not we can narrow it down enough to do any good before Wednesday morning is doubtful."

"I've been going over various thoughts about rubies and lemon drops," Nic said. "One is a precious gem and the other a candy. One is expensive, the other is cheap. You wear one and eat the other."

"Our guy knows we'll drive ourselves crazy trying to figure out the clues and in the meantime, he's making plans to abduct his sixth victim."

Griff's cell phone rang.

Both of them froze instantly.

Griff retrieved his phone and checked the caller ID. "It's not him." He answered the call. "Yeah, what is it?"

"We've just come across some rather interesting information," Sanders said. "Actually Maleah came up with the idea of cross-referencing all the Debbie Glovers on the original list with a list of female athletes from all sports, professional and college, in the past thirty years."

"And?"

"And there was a Debbie Glover who played basketball for Boston College fifteen years ago. And another Debbie Glover who was a golf pro back in the eighties."

"Are they the only two who are athletes?"

"As far as we know."

"Both would be too old to be our victim, if our guy stays true to form," Griff said. "But Debbie Glover's sport—whichever Debbie Glover it is—could be the clue. The next victim might be a basketball player or a pro golfer."

Chapter 7

Nic and Greg had bought a home in Woodbridge, Virginia, shortly after they married. It had made sense for them to live within easy driving distance of their jobs. She had worked in D.C. and he'd worked in Alexandria. When Greg died, she had taken a month off, then went to her boss and asked for a transfer to another field office. Anywhere in the U.S., just as long as it was away from D.C., away from all the memories, both good and bad. She'd worked in two states during that time and wound up heading a task force on the Beauty Queen Killer case when the Special Agent in Charge, Curtis Jackson, had retired. But when that case, for all intents and purposes, had been solved, she'd decided it was time to go home. Back to the D.C. field office, with a territory that covered not only D.C. but also cities surrounding the capital. Arlington. Alexandria. Quantico.

Although she'd thought about selling the house in Woodbridge, she had, after letting it remain empty for over a year, put her furniture in storage and turned it over to a realtor to lease.

If she'd thought time and distance would erase the memories, would heal her broken heart, and appease her guilty conscience, she'd been wrong. Moving back into the home she and Greg had purchased, decorated together, and lived in for the three years of their marriage hadn't been easy. But she liked her house, liked the neighborhood, and felt comfortable here. So what if from time to time, she felt Greg's presence? If his spirit lingered here, perhaps simply in her memories, then it was a kind, gentle spirit.

Gregory Baxter had been a kind, gentle man.

Nic turned over in bed—a king-size bed that she had bought new when she moved back into the Woodbridge house last summer—and glanced at the alarm clock. Five ten. The alarm was set for five thirty. She tossed back the light covers, slid to the edge of the bed, and sat up. After shutting off the alarm, she stood, stretched, and headed for the closet. When she was at home, she walked every morning in her neighborhood and the one adjoining it. Two miles. And she worked out at the gym three days a week.

Once dressed and fully awake, she headed out the back door. It was barely daylight and already humid. She could feel the heavy moisture in the air. Early morning was the best time to walk, run, or jog in the summertime. In her twenties, she had jogged, but a knee injury had forced her to take her doctor's advice and change to brisk walking. Better on the knee joints.

As she set her pace and headed up the street, her body went on automatic pilot. Her route never varied. Although she might speak to a fellow walker or jogger, she never lingered to talk to anyone and really didn't know her neighbors beyond her own block.

For the past thirty-six hours, her thoughts had centered on one thing: somewhere out there a woman was going to be abducted this morning and there was nothing she could do to stop it from happening. It didn't help that she and Griff had figured out three of the four clues. They knew that a blonde would be kidnapped this morning and in all likelihood she was either a basketball player or a golfer. How many women fit that description? Too many.

Nic rounded the corner of the second block, picking up speed, pushing herself, as her mind replayed the final clue. Rubies and lemon drops. She had driven herself crazy trying to figure out what the hell that meant. Griff had half his staff at Powell's trying to come up with something.

Griff. She'd spoken to him once since they'd parted company early yesterday morning. He had called her shortly after eight last night. He was back at Griffin's Rest and doing what she was doing—waiting for the inevitable. And hoping beyond hope that they could figure out who the next victim might be.

Before it was too late.

There would be no way to get Griff out of her life now. If the killer continued to phone them both with clues, they would have to compare notes on a regular basis. And, as Griff had told her, he would stay either one step ahead of or one step behind the authorities on every case.

She had talked to Doug again. "I think the killer wants me heading up this case. Why else would he choose a victim from Alexandria, in my territory? I think he picked me just like he picked his victims."

"Isn't that reason enough not to play along?" Doug had asked her.

"I have to do this. He knows that. Talk to Ace Warren. Persuade him to use his influence to see that I'm put in charge. Make us the office of origin on this case and the others the Auxiliary offices. After all, our killer is talking personally to me and not to any other agent."

"He's also talking to Griffin Powell," Doug had reminded her. "Want me to put him in charge, too?"

"Very funny."

"I'll talk to Ace."

"Thanks."

Nic had spent more than four years of her career tracking down the BQ Killer and when Cary Maygarden had been unveiled as the murderer, that should have put an end to it. Unfortunately, one small but significant clue had kept her from writing "The End" to the story that everyone else had said was concluded. Two bullets had been found in Maygarden's body. One bullet had come from Powell's sharpshooter Holt Keinan's rifle and the other from an unknown source. Although the bureau and the local authorities in Knoxville had looked into the matter, nothing had ever come of it. Dead end. Only she and Griff had been convinced that there had been a second BQ Killer, one who had ended the deadly game—the dying game—by shooting his partner.

The second killer had laid low for a whole year, killing again almost a year from the day that Cary Maygarden had died. Coincidence? No way.

As Nic power-walked block after block, her mind moving as quickly as her feet, her brain jumped from thought to thought. But she finally realized that it all came back down to that final, perplexing clue—rubies and lemon drops.

By the time she had come full circle and returned to her block, dawn light was spreading across the eastern horizon in vibrant splashes of color. A pink glow so dark it was almost red, fringed in pale gold. Something she'd heard her grandmother say when she was a child came to mind. "Red sky in the morning is a sailor's warning." A red morning sky forecast rain.

Nic slowed when she reached her driveway, tossed her head back, and sucked in huge gulps of fresh air. Her gaze lingered on the sky, alight with color, red and gold, pink and yellow.

Red and yellow.

Rubies and lemon drops.

Damn! Could it be that simple?

Had the final clue been the colors red and yellow? If so, what could it possibly mean? The color of her hair? Blonde. The color of her car? Red? That couldn't be it.

Colors. Think colors. Paints, crayons, eye color, hair color, skin color.

Wiping the perspiration from her cheeks with the back of her hand, Nic paused at her kitchen door. She removed the mint green plastic spiral wristband with her key attached and unlocked the door.

Think sports. Colors. School colors?

Was there any college with red and yellow as school colors?

Nic closed the door behind her, walked into her kitchen, and saw that the coffeemaker she had set the night before had brewed eight cups of heavenly smelling black coffee.

Shower first. Coffee later.

School colors. Red and yellow.

If you mix red with yellow you get—orange.

Orange was the dominant color for how many colleges?

Nic yanked her cell phone from the clip on her walking shorts, hit the programmed number, and held her breath until she heard his voice.

"Rubies and lemon drops," she said. "Red and yellow. Mix those colors and you get orange."

"So you do." Griffin Powell sounded wide-awake and not the least surprised to hear from her.

"Think school colors—what comes to mind when you say orange?"

"My first thought is UT, of course." He cursed softly under his breath. "That's too simple, but—"

"What if the woman he intends to abduct this morning is a basketball player from UT? I know it's a long shot, but—"

"It's better than nothing."

"I can contact the campus police," Nic said. "They may think I'm crazy and I can't say I'd blame them, but—"

"Let me handle this," Griff told her. "I've got an *in* at UT. I know the head of campus security and if I ask him to check on all the blonde players on the UT women's basketball team, he'll do it."

"Thanks, Griff." She hesitated, hating that, in this case, he could do more than she could and do it quicker. "Call me as soon as you find out anything."

"You realize this could turn out to be nothing. Yes, red and yellow make orange and orange is a UT color. But you've already admitted that it really is a long shot. We've probably got it all wrong."

"You mean I've got it all wrong."

"If we're partners, then we're both wrong or we're both right."

"We are not partners."

"Whatever you say, Nicki."

Before she could come up with an adequate snappy come-back, he hung up. *Smart-ass.*

Nic eyed the coffee. She could almost taste it. Resisting temptation, she hurried to the bathroom, placed her cell phone on the vanity, and stripped. Once under the shower-head, she closed her eyes and let the warm water pepper down over her head and body.

The odds were her guess about the color orange was wrong, which would make their second guess that the potential victim was a UT basketball player also wrong.

Oh, God, please, please let me be right. And if I am, don't let it be too late to save her.

Amber Kirby went for her morning run. During the week, she got up earlier than on weekends and usually had the trail to herself for at least part of her run. When the fall semester started and there were more students on campus, the trail wouldn't be as solitary as it was today. She didn't mind the solitude because she often used earphones to listen to her favorite tunes on her iPod.

Just as she made it to the halfway point and was heading back, she met a man walking the trail instead of running or jogging as most people did. Because he was only the second person she'd seen in her three-mile jog this morning, she glanced at him, her gaze connecting with his for half a second. He looked like someone who needed exercise. Although he wasn't fat, his body looked soft and pudgy and his face was round and full.

He smiled as she whizzed past him. She returned his smile.

An odd shiver rippled along her nerve endings.

Okay, so there had been something strange about the guy. That didn't mean she should be afraid. After all, it was obvious that she could easily outrun him. And even though he was a man, she'd bet she was as strong as he was. Maybe stronger.

Ignore your gut feeling that something's wrong. Just keep running.

Amber glanced over her shoulder.

Walking in the opposite direction at a plodding speed, the man was almost out of sight. He hadn't stopped. He hadn't turned and followed her.

How silly of me to think that that pudgy-looking guy was dangerous.

Although Nic was still officially on vacation, she'd driven into D.C. to Justice Square and met Doug just as he arrived at the office. If she had stayed at home, the waiting would have driven her stark, raving mad. It had been over three and a half hours since she'd spoken to Griff and he hadn't called back. She figured he didn't have anything to report, that she hadn't solved the rubies and lemon drops word puzzle. After all, what were the odds that they'd actually been able to put all the pieces together using those last two asinine clues?

Nic had wanted to see ADIC Ace Warren, but Doug hadn't been able to arrange a meeting.

"Ace can't fit you in," Doug had told her. "I'll see if I can get you a few minutes of his time tomorrow. In the meantime, go home, take it easy. You're supposed to be on vacation, you know. A much-needed vacation."

There was no point in her hanging around here, accomplishing nothing except irritating Doug. She knew the wheels were turning, if somewhat slower than she would like. But the field offices in each state where a woman had been murdered—shot in the head, scalped, and hung by her feet—had been notified, and agents were checking into the matter and comparing notes. If she made a pest of herself, she wasn't likely to endear herself to either Doug or Ace Warren. And the last thing she wanted was to piss off either of them. What she wanted was for Ace to put her in charge of the bureau's investigation into this serial killer case when the bureau actually became officially involved.

Just as Nic slid behind the wheel of her Chevy Trail-Blazer, her cell phone rang. With shaky hands, she jerked the phone from her pocket, noted the caller ID, and flipped open the phone.

"Yeah, what?" she asked.

"You were right," Griff said, but he didn't sound pleased.

"Right about?"

"She's a basketball player for UT. Her name is Amber Kirby. She's twenty, blonde, and runs early every morning as part of her daily fitness routine."

Nic swallowed hard, her gut warning her that something was wrong. Bad wrong. "Just tell me."

"Amber Kirby went for her morning run three hours ago and hasn't been seen since."

"Son of a bitch!" Emotion tightened Nic's throat. "He's got her."

"Yeah, more than likely."

"If only we'd figured out that final clue sooner."

"Don't go there," Griff told her. "This is not our fault."

"If we just had some idea where he's taken her and what he's going to do to her. Assuming he stays true to form, we have twenty-one days to find her before he kills her."

"Twenty-one days or twenty-one years, it doesn't matter. We don't have the slightest idea where he's taken her."

"He'll call us," Nic said. "He'll give us more clues."

"Maybe."

"I'm right. You wait and see. He enjoys tormenting us far too much not to continue forcing us to play his game. He may not call today or tomorrow, but he'll call."

"Nic?"

"Huh?"

"Are you going to be all right?"

"Yeah, sure. Why wouldn't I be?"

"Right." He paused for a couple of seconds, then asked, "Are you still on vacation or have you—?"

"Officially, I haven't gone back to work yet. I was supposed to take two weeks, but I can't. Not now. I'll save a week for later on."

"I have a suggestion."

"What?"

"You could come here to Griffin's Rest for a few days."

"Why would I do that?"

"You could meet some of my team, work with us, and we'd be together when the Scalper calls again," Griff said.

"The Scalper, huh?"

"You and I both know that it'll take some time for the bureau to coordinate things with local and state authorities. It could be another week or two before they form a task force, if then. Work with me and we could be ahead of the game."

He made it sound so tempting. "Thanks for the offer, but no thanks."

"Okay. Have it your way."

"Griff?"

"Yeah?"

"If he calls you—"

"I'll let you know immediately."

"Same here."

"Take it easy, honey. And stop beating yourself up for not being Wonder Woman."

Griff had taken his small, single-engine fishing boat out onto the lake earlier today and had spent a couple of hours in the fresh air and sunshine. He owned several seacraft, everything from the fishing boat to a yacht he kept docked in Charleston, where he owned a beach house. As much as he enjoyed deep sea fishing, there was something to be said for hours of lazy, relaxed fishing on a tranquil lake. As a boy he'd gone fishing in any branch or stream he could find, and his mama had always fried up his catch for supper. Those had been lean days when a fat catfish on their dinner table had meant the difference between eating and going hungry.

A part of him missed that time in his life. Not the being poor or going hungry, but his mother's smile and her tender touch. Griff had been on the verge of being able to afford to give her a better life, a life of ease and luxury. Getting drafted by the NFL would have been only the beginning.

He couldn't go back, couldn't change anything that had happened. If he could, he would. He'd be twenty-two again, fresh out of college, with the world at his feet. His mama would still be alive and he'd take good care of her.

She had lived a hard life and had died far too young.

"There's a phone call for you," Sanders said, bringing Griff back to the present moment.

Griff lifted his gaze and looked up at Sanders. After lunch, he had gone into his study, chosen the latest presidential biography he'd purchased recently and sat down to read.

"Who is it?" Griff knew it wouldn't be the Scalper. He would call Griff's cell number.

"It's Ms. Smithe, sir."

"Lisa Kay? Tell her that I'm—no, wait. I'll take the call." There was no point in his sitting around here waiting and worrying. A pretty woman to distract him was just what he needed.

Griff got up, walked over to the extension on his desk, and picked up the receiver. "Hello, honey, how are you?"

"I'm missing you, sugar. You haven't called since I last saw you on Saturday."

"I'm sorry. I've been busy. I do work, you know."

She giggled. "How about working on me? You could come to Knoxville and spend the night or I could drive out there."

"Make reservations someplace nice," he told her. "I'll drive into Knoxville and pick you up around six thirty."

"Bring your toothbrush."

"I'll pack an overnight bag."

"Drive the Porsche, will you? I just love the way people turn green with envy when I step out of that thing."

Griff chuckled. "Sure thing. I'll drive the Porsche."

He had been dating Lisa Kay Smithe on and off for a couple of months. They'd met at a party in the home of a mutual acquaintance.

He'd turn forty in a few months, but he didn't feel forty and sure as hell didn't think of himself as approaching middle age. He kept his body in good shape and he wasn't a bad-looking guy, but he didn't kid himself about why women of all ages swooned at his feet. They were all impressed with his big bank account. Most men his age were either married or seriously considering finding a suitable mate.

But he wasn't most men.

If he wanted a wife, he could easily buy one. And he could have his pick. The only problem was, he didn't want a woman who could be bought.

Amber awoke slowly, her mind groggy, her eyes gritty, and her body sore. What was wrong with her? Why couldn't she hold her eyes open for more than a couple of seconds? Why did her head ache as if she'd been hit with a two-by-four?

Think, Amber. Focus.

What was the last thing she remembered? Her alarm had gone off at five twenty. She'd dressed quickly in her shorts and tank top, slipped into her running shoes, and . . . Had she fainted? Had a heat stroke? Been mugged?

She had gone for her usual three-mile jog.

Forcing her eyes to stay open, she tried to focus, but her vision remained blurred. Something was wrong with her. Was she sick?

She opened her dry mouth and licked her lips. God, she was thirsty.

"Hello," she called, her voice little more than a croaky whisper.

She leaned forward and realized she was sitting, her back braced against a cool, damp wall. *Get up. Move around. Figure out where you are and what happened to you.*

When she rose to her feet, her vision slowly cleared, then she realized her ankles were bound together and so were her wrists. She looked around, left, right, up, down. The area was dark, the only illumination coming from a bare bulb hanging from a socket in the ceiling. The ceiling? Old wooden beams covered with cobwebs. The floor was brick, and dirty and damp, as were the walls.

She was in a basement. Maybe the cellar of an old building.

How had she gotten here?

She tried the shackles that bound her and managed to walk two feet before the length of chain on her ankles and wrists stopped her. Glancing over her shoulder, she looked back and saw that the restraints had been attached to the wall. They were new, shiny chains, unlike the row of old, rusty, and broken manacles that lined the wall on either side of her.

Oh, God! Oh, God! Where was she? What had happened to her?

Amber opened her mouth and screamed.

Upstairs in the kitchen, Pudge sat at the table enjoying a slice of Key Lime Pie. A late-night snack before he went to bed.

When he heard the screams, he smiled.

Ah, she's awake at last.

Poor darling.

She would probably scream until she was hoarse and then cry herself to sleep. In the morning, he would go down into the basement, introduce himself, and explain the rules of the game they would be playing together for the next few weeks.

Chapter 8

Nic woke before the alarm chimed, but when she heard the rain, she turned off the alarm and rolled over, lifting one of the pillows over her head. She had spent another night tossing and turning, waking frequently with thoughts of Amber Kirby flashing through her mind. She wasn't sure if anything the Scalper would do to Amber could be worse than the horrendous things Nic had been imagining.

The Scalper.

Griff had come up with that malevolent title. Unfortunately, it seemed to fit the killer and his crime.

Four days ago, Amber Kirby had disappeared while out for her morning run. There had been no signs of a struggle anywhere along the trail she normally used, but the police had found evidence that someone had been dragged at least ten feet off the path and into the wooded area. Signs had led them to believe the killer had then hoisted her over his shoulder and carried her to his vehicle. Bloodhounds had led them from the woods to a secluded dirt road where the killer could have parked. From that point, the trail had gone cold.

"We figure he either came up behind her and knocked her over the head or he somehow drugged her," the Knoxville detective had told Nic when she'd spoken to him late Wednesday.

"Until she comes up dead, with a bullet in her head and scalped, we have no proof that Amber Kirby's disappearance is connected to the other five murders," Wayne Hester, the Knoxville field office SAC, had explained. "As for your mystery caller who's been giving you clues—he could be some nut job who has nothing to do with any of the murders."

"What about the fact that the clues led us to these women?"

"Look, Baxter, I don't doubt that you and Griffin Powell believe that you deciphered this guy's clues and it led to a specific conclusion, but the fact is the whole thing could be nothing more than coincidence. I'm not getting involved in something until I have some concrete proof."

How many women had to die before she could persuade her colleagues that they had a nomadic serial killer on the loose? At Doug's suggestion, she hadn't mentioned her theory that the Scalper was also the second BQ Killer, the one who had shot Cary Maygarden as a final triumphant act in their vicious game. Besides, Griff and she had agreed that there was no point in reopening old wounds for Lindsay and Judd Walker. Or for the families of any of the other BQK victims. Until this killer is apprehended and punished for his crimes, why put them through more misery? They had already suffered far too much.

Realizing that she wasn't likely to go back to sleep, Nic yanked the pillow off her head, tossed it away from her, flung back the covers, and got up. Her bedroom was chilly. She liked sleeping in a cold room, so during the summer, she turned the central air down to sixty-five at night.

She grabbed her robe off her maternal grandmother's cedar chest that she kept at the foot of the spindle bed, which had belonged to her paternal grandmother. It wasn't so much that Nic liked antiques as it was that she liked the idea of passing things down in families, one generation after another. She supposed her most prized possession was her great-grandmother's rocking chair, which was in the guest bedroom. When she and Greg first married, she had daydreamed about someday sitting in that rocking chair, holding their baby in her arms. That dream, along with so many others, had died the day Greg died.

Nic slipped on her robe over her comfy cotton pajamas, then headed for the bathroom. After hurrying through a quick wake-up routine—using the toilet, washing her hands and face, and running a comb through her tousled hair—she barely made it to the kitchen before a loud boom of thunder rocked the house. The rattling windows and flickering lights startled her.

Damn!

She offered up a prayer to the Almighty. *Please, don't let the electricity go off until I've had my first cup of morning coffee.*

For the past four days, she had resisted the urge to go to Knoxville and speak to Wayne Hester in person, as well as to the local police officers first called to the scene. But what good would it actually do? She'd been given all the facts. And as Griff had pointed out, they had no way of knowing where *he* had taken Amber.

If only he would call with another clue.

But he hadn't called either her or Griff.

Why not? What was he waiting for?

"He's letting us stew," Griff had told her when she'd spoken to him on Friday. "This is his game, his rules, and he wants to make certain that we know it."

She had wanted to ask Griff if he and his team of detectives had come up with anything that the local law hadn't. But she figured he would've told her if he had.

If she'd accepted his offer, she could be doing something constructive now, instead of waiting for her superiors to take action. When he'd asked her to come to Griffin's Rest for the few days she'd had left on her vacation, why had she turned him down instantly? Why hadn't she at least given it some thought?

"You could meet some of my team, work with us, and we'd be together when the Scalper calls again," Griff had said.

Gut instinct told her to join forces with Griffin Powell. Common sense told her otherwise. A battle between emotions and logic warred within her. As much as she disapproved of him and to some extent distrusted him, she could see why most women found him appealing. Not that she did!

Yes, he was good-looking, in a big, rugged, blond, Nordic sort of way. In a long-ago era, Griff would have been a marauding Viking, plundering and pillaging, taking what he wanted.

Her father had been one of those big, rough-and-rugged kind of guys. He had steamrolled right over her sweet, flighty mother and her equally sweet and gentle brother, Charles David. And he had tried to dominate her, treating her like he did her mother, as if she were some china doll with straw for brains. If only he had looked closer, he would have seen not a carbon copy of her mother but a strong resemblance to himself.

How different their lives might have been if their father could have allowed Charles David to be the sensitive, emotional child and she the strong, independent one. But no, his son had to be a man. A real man. No tears. No whining. And his daughter had to be fluttery and feminine and silly. In Charles Bellamy's world there had been no room for uniqueness, no quarter given to a son who constantly disappointed him and a daughter who would not bend to his will.

Nic eyed the coffeemaker. Thank goodness she had set it

last night and already the pot was half-full of the dark, gourmet brew. She poured herself a cup and took a sip.

Ah . . .

A good cup of coffee was one of Nic's few pleasures.

How many Sunday mornings had she and Greg sat in this kitchen, drinking coffee, reading the newspaper, discussing everything under the sun? Greg had been a wonderful conversationalist. Unlike so many men, Greg hadn't had a problem communicating. At least that's what she'd thought, up to the very end. She supposed that was one of the many reasons his death had come as such a shock to her. Why hadn't she realized that something was wrong? Why hadn't she sensed that something was troubling her husband?

If only she could go back in time.

Oh, Greg . . . I'm so sorry. If only I had known. If only you had told me.

Even now, after seven years, it hurt to think about her husband's death, to remember the way he had died. But she didn't cry anymore. She had shed all her tears of mourning long ago. All the tears in the world wouldn't bring Greg back, wouldn't change the way he died, wouldn't absolve her of her guilt.

Griff woke at ten thirty. He slept late only when he'd had a late night. He had stayed with Lisa Kay until two this morning, then had driven home. She had wanted him to stay over and share Sunday as a couple's day. He liked Lisa Kay, found her amusing both in and out of bed, but he had spent two nights at her place recently and didn't want her to get any wrong ideas. If he was looking for a permanent relationship, which he wasn't, his standards would be pretty damn high. Probably too high. Beauty mattered, but he had learned over the years that beauty truly was in the eye of the beholder. He'd had his share of gorgeous women, had been with younger women, older women, smart women, and dumb women. He adored women in general, appreciated each for what made her unique, but he'd never found a woman that tempted him to end his bachelor days.

Rolling over and out of bed, Griff stood and stretched. He slept nude. He liked the feel of his body against the satiny cotton sheets beneath and over him. Shards of morning sunlight crept through the dark wooden shades covering a wall of windows and French doors that overlooked the lake. When he had commissioned the architect to build his home, he had specified several must-have items. First and foremost had been that his second-story bedroom would face the lake and would have doors that opened up onto a balcony.

After a quick trip to the bathroom, Griff put on his silk robe, opened the French doors, and walked out onto the balcony. August had faded hurriedly into September, the end of summer as hot and humid as the beginning. The shimmering sunlight poured over him as it dappled through the nearby trees. The moist wind hinted of rain.

This was Labor Day weekend and all of his employees who were not on specific assignments had the three days off. Lindsay had called and invited him to spend the long weekend with her and Judd and little Emily, but he had declined. He appreciated that they considered him family, that they had honored him with godfather status for their daughter, but right now, he needed to keep his distance from them. Knowing what he knew—that the second BQ Killer could just as easily have been Jennifer Walker's murderer as Cary Maygarden could have been, and that this man had now begun a second killing spree—put Griff in an awkward position with his friends. They had been to hell and back in order to reach the point where they were now. He couldn't bear the thought that anything might disrupt their hard-won happiness.

There had been a time when Griff had thought Judd

would never find happiness again, that he was doomed to loneliness and misery. For years, Griff had watched Lindsay stand by Judd, take whatever abuse he dished out, and never stop loving him. When she had come to work for Griff at the Powell Agency, her single reason for existing had been to find the man who had killed Judd's wife. That type of single-minded devotion was rare. Few men were lucky enough to have a woman love them the way Lindsay loved Judd.

Is that what you want? Griff asked himself.

Did he want to be loved?

Yeah, sure. What human being didn't want to be loved?

Griff laughed at his sentimental thoughts.

He had a life most people would envy. A life he enjoyed. Not only did his great wealth afford him every luxury he could ever want, but it allowed him to make a difference in the world, to help people who might otherwise get lost in the system. His charity extended worldwide, but his own personal involvement centered on the Powell Private Security and Investigation Agency. Sanders had been the one who had come up with the idea when Griff had been searching for something to fill his days. He didn't have to work. He could easily live the life of a worthless playboy cavorting from one social hot spot to another, but that sort of life would have made him miserable.

"Think of all the people who never receive any type of justice for themselves or their families," Sanders had said. "Think of all the criminals who are never caught, who literally get away with murder."

The idea of bringing criminals to justice, criminals the law couldn't find or couldn't touch, appealed to Griff in a personal way that little else did. Sanders had realized that fact because he knew Griff as no other man knew him. They were brothers of the soul as only those who had stood together against great evil and triumphed over it could ever be.

Griff's gaze scanned the yard, all the way to the lake, and

his mind wandered back to another lake, a lagoon really, on a South Seas island. On the surface, it had been a Pacific paradise, but in reality it had been an inescapable prison.

Damn! Don't go there. Do not think about that place or what happened to you there. You put it all behind you years ago.

Griff went back inside his bedroom, slipped into a pair of leather house shoes, and went downstairs. He needed coffee and a decent breakfast before shutting himself off in his den to go over all the information he had on the Scalper's victims. Not that there was anything new, but every time he read over the reports, he gained a little more knowledge. He doubted that he'd find anything in those reports that would save Amber Kirby's life, but he had do something that made him feel as if he were at least trying.

There has to be a way out!

Not once in the three days he had let her run free had she seen any sign of a fence. But that didn't mean if she ever made it to the outside world, there wouldn't be some type of barrier to prevent her escape.

That first morning, at the crack of dawn, he had taken her from the damp, dank basement, marched her into an upstairs bathroom, and shoved her, fully clothed, under a warm shower. Leaving her in her wet, soiled clothes, he had then taken her to the kitchen and fed her a meal as if she were a helpless infant. She had spit the food in his face. He had merely cleaned his face, frowned at her, and called her a naughty girl.

"When you get hungry enough, you'll eat," he had told her.

He'd been right. This morning, when he'd set a plate of scrambled eggs and toast in front of her, she had eaten every bite.

Like a general issuing orders to his soldiers, her captor had recited the rules of his game. And that's what he'd called it—a game!

"I am the Hunter," he had told her. "And you are the Prey."

If his words had not convinced her he was mad, his actions would have.

What frightened her more than anything else was the way he looked at her, an insatiable hunger in his eyes that was both sexual and predatory. And yet, he hadn't raped her or removed her clothes or even touched her intimately.

How long will he leave me outside today?

That first day, he had taken her, hands and feet manacled, deep into the woods; and then he had removed the cuffs from her ankles and left her. It had taken her at least thirty minutes to realize she was alone, free to run away. And she had run as fast and as far as she could, falling a couple of times and quickly learning how to hoist herself back up, even with cuffs on her wrists.

Then suddenly, just as she was beginning to hope that she could get away, she had heard the roar of a dirt bike's motor. He had reappeared, chased her down, and aimed a rifle directly at her. He had forced her to walk back to the creepy antebellum house where he lived.

On each of the three days since she'd been here, he had taken her out into the woods and left her for an hour or two. She had tried to find a means of escape but had finally realized that there was no escape. Apparently, he had installed a tracking device in her handcuffs, which he never removed. Every moment she was out of his sight, he knew precisely where she was.

Amber heard his footsteps on the wooden stairs as he came down into the basement. Mixed emotions raced through her. Fear. Uncertainty. Excitement. Anticipation. She had no idea what he would do to her, but if he released her into the woods again today, that meant he was giving her another chance to get away.

Nic had spent most of her day scouring over copies of the reports she had accumulated this past week, hoping beyond hope that something—anything—would trigger a spark of brilliance. They had seventeen days to find Amber Kirby. But they had absolutely no idea where the UT basketball player was. He could have her hidden away in Knoxville somewhere. Or he could have taken her to a neighboring state or halfway across the country. If he was as wealthy as Cary Maygarden had been, he might own his own plane or at least could afford to hire a private plane to take him anywhere in the world.

Half-reclining on the sofa, a couple of decorative pillows at her back and her bare feet crossed at the ankles, Nic reached out and picked up a glass of iced tea from the coaster on the coffee table. Scattered file folders and sheets of paper littered the entire table as well as the floor area around it.

She had turned down invitations from her mother and her brother, who had each asked her to spend the holiday weekend at their homes. She loved her mother dearly, but she wasn't overly fond of her mother's husband, an air force colonel who reminded her of her father. When her dad had died, Nic had thought her mother would enjoy her independence from a domineering man who had ruled her completely. But what had her mom done? Within two years, she had remarried, choosing a man who was as much of a control freak as her father had been.

Nic adored her brother, Charles David, and had since the moment her parents had brought him home from the hospital when she was four. As a toddler, he'd been far too pretty to be a boy. With his large, luminous brown eyes and mop of curly dark hair, everyone had mistaken him for a girl, which had outraged their father. But Charles Bellamy had done what had to be done—he'd taken his tearful two-year-old to the barber shop and, to his weeping wife's dismay, had his son's pretty curls buzzed off.

Whenever she and her brother got away together, she loved every minute with him. And although she didn't fit in with his artistic friends—who wrote plays and poetry and music, who painted and sculpted, and lived in a world of transcendental, mystic ideas—she found that, from time to time, soaking in all that artistic genius was refreshing. Her life, her world, consisted of harsh reality, often the ugly side of reality. If not for the occasional trip to the West Coast to visit her brother, she might easily forget that there was still beauty and hope and peace out there in the world.

Nic had read and reread the reports on the five murder victims—Angela Byers, Dana Patterson, Candice Bates, Gala Ramirez, and Kendall Moore—until her vision was blurred and she had a slight headache.

She downed the last drops of iced tea, then set the glass on the coaster and lifted her arms over her head to stretch. The morning rain had continued all day, turning into a real soaker. She'd missed her morning walk and had been tempted to don her hooded raincoat and venture outdoors this afternoon. But she had become so absorbed in the various reports that she'd lost track of time and now it was nearly seven. Her rumbling stomach reminded her that she hadn't eaten since one, and then only a sandwich and chips.

Just as she tossed the files in her lap onto the sofa and stood up, her cell phone rang. *Maybe Griff's calling.* Now why had his been the first name that came to mind? Several times today, she'd thought about him, wondered if he might call her, had even hoped he would call and share some new insight he had gained about the case. She reached down and picked up her phone off the coffee table, noted the caller ID, and held her breath when she answered.

"Hello."

"If you'll promise to do something for me, I'll give you another clue."

Nic released her breath. Her heartbeat accelerated. "What do you want me to do?"

"I want you to call a press conference—you and Griffin Powell—and tell everyone that the Hunter is giving you clues to solve the mystery of his brilliant Murder Game."

Nic swallowed. The arrogant, egotistical son of a bitch! He wanted publicity. He wanted the whole country to become fascinated with his diabolical game.

"I can't do that," Nic said.

"Don't you want another clue?"

"Your clues aren't worth much," she told him.

"It's not my fault if you and Griffin and your teams aren't smart enough to figure out the clues in time for them to be useful."

"Give me a really good clue and maybe I'll think about calling a press conference."

Laughter.

God, how she hated that sound. How dare he take such sick pleasure from playing his evil game.

"I'll tell you what—I'll give you and Griff a really big clue, just to show my faith in you both. Then when you two hold a press conference, I'll call you back next week with another clue."

"I'm listening."

"You have sixteen days to find her before the day of the final hunt," he said, his voice filled with excitement. "But you won't find her."

The Hunter is giving you clues. The day of the final hunt. Hunter. Hunt.

Did he realize that those two words were clues?

Of course he did.

"I'm waiting for the clue. That's why you called, isn't it? To hear me plead with you for a clue, for any tidbit of hope."

"There's nothing I like more than hearing a woman beg."

"If you don't give me another clue, I'll hang up and I won't take any more of your calls."

"Threats, Nicole? You shouldn't make threats you don't intend to follow through with. We both know you'll take my calls. You want to save Amber Kirby, don't you?"

"You know I do."

"I've already given you two clues—I am the Hunter and Amber is the Prey."

She didn't reply. But she didn't hang up, either.

Waiting for him to speak again, she heard a muffled sound, then a cry and whispered words. "Tell her where you are, Amber. Talk to Special Agent Baxter."

"Hello? Hello?" Nic's pulse pounded, her heartbeat going wild. Was he actually going to put Amber on the phone?

"Help me," a female voice cried out in panic. "There are woods everywhere. And water. Streams of water . . ." A loud gasp and then a thud, followed by faint whimpers.

"Amber? Is that you? Are you Amber Kirby?" Nic asked.

Then she heard him whispering. "That's enough. Don't want to tell her too much and end all our fun too quickly." Then he spoke directly to Nic. "How was that for a clue?"

Before she could reply, he hung up.

Goddamn it!

Nic stood there trembling from head to toe, the sound of Amber Kirby's terrified voice replaying over and over again inside her head. Nausea threatened as images of the young woman filled her mind. Tall, slender, blonde. And young. So young. Only twenty. Little more than a child, really.

His game of killing—his heinous murder game—involved some type of role-playing where he was a hunter and his victims were prey. Was he actually hunting down these women as if they were wild animals?

Oh, God, that's why he scalps them.

Griff had been right—their scalps were trophies. In the same way a hunter had the heads of the animals he slaughtered preserved and hung on the wall, this sick son of a bitch was taking scalps and probably displaying them somewhere in his home.

Nic wanted to call Griff immediately, but she needed to wait and give the Hunter time to contact Griff with another clue.

Griff will call me. All I have to do is wait.

Twenty minutes, two shots of Johnnie Walker, and five miles of pacing later, Nic's cell phone rang again. She didn't bother checking the caller ID before answering.

"Just tell me what he said."

"You're letting him get to you," Griff told her. "Pull yourself together, honey. I can hear the panic in your voice."

"Screw what you think you hear. Did he or did he not give you a clue?"

"He wants us to call a press conference and make an announcement about his game. He's calling himself 'the Hunter' and his victims are his prey."

"Tell me something I don't know, something he didn't share with me."

"He put Amber on the phone and—"

"Yeah, he did that with me, too."

"All she got out before he ended it was a plea for help and to tell me that there were trees and water. Not much to go on."

"Was that it? He didn't give you a different clue, something to add to what he told me?"

"Not really," Griff said.

"You're not telling me everything."

"He ended the conversation with a cocky announcement."

"Which was?"

"He said that we'd find Amber, in two and a half weeks. All we had to do was find the one tree in Knoxville where he planned to hang her body."

Chapter 9

Maddie Landers screamed. And screamed. She wanted to move, but she couldn't. It was as if her feet were glued to the ground. She stood there staring at the body hanging upside down from a tree in her grandparents' apple orchard. She and her cousin Sean, who at seven years old was six months older than she, had been playing hide-and-seek after school. She'd known that the first place he'd hide was out here somewhere in the orchard.

It seemed like the longest time before Grams called her name. Maddie tried to answer her, but she couldn't. When she opened her mouth, nothing came out but a weak little squeak.

"Maddie, child, where are you?"

"Maybe she got snake bit," Sean said.

"Hush up and help me find your cousin," Grams told him.

"There she is, just standing there staring at the trees," Sean said. "What's that hanging in the tree? It looks like somebody hung up a dead animal."

"Mercy Lord, boy, that ain't no animal carcass. That's human."

Maddie felt Grams' soft, fat arms wrap around her and lift her off her feet. Finally, as if she'd been frozen in stone by an evil spell and was now set free, she gasped and flung her arms tightly around Grams' neck.

"Run to the house, Sean, and tell Pops to call the sheriff."

"Is that a real human body?" Sean asked. "Sure don't look human to me. It hasn't got any hair. And it's all bloody and—"

"Hush up and do what I told you to do. We need the sheriff out here right now."

Even with her eyes closed, Maddie could still see the body. It sure was an odd sight. Turned upside down, the feet tied together and all the hair on its head missing. She buried her face in Grams' shoulder and cried.

"Shh . . . Hush up now. It'll be all right. Your Grams has got you. You're safe. Ain't nobody gonna hurt my gal."

Maddie opened her eyes and saw that Grams had carried her away from the tree where the body was hanging. They were halfway out of the orchard and she could hear Pops hollering, telling anybody within hearing that he had a shotgun and damn well knew how to use it. She supposed Grams wouldn't fuss at him for cussing, not this time, anyhow.

He drove to Chattanooga and went straight to the downtown Marriott. He checked in with a fake ID, paid cash, and as soon as he locked the door to his fourth-floor room, Pudge removed the mustache and stored it in his suitcase, along with the clothes he would later dispose of before he returned home. After taking a shower and putting on a silk shirt and tailored trousers, he picked up his suitcase and headed for the elevators. Completely unnoticed, he walked outside, caught the downtown shuttle, and rode to the other end of town, where he promptly checked into the Chattanoogan Hotel, using a different fake ID.

God, he loved these little games of cloak-and-dagger. He really felt that under the right circumstances, he would make a brilliant spy.

After settling into his room at the Chattanoogan, he ordered dinner, and while waiting for his meal he removed his lightweight laptop from his suitcase and set it on the desk. He opened the file on the woman he had chosen as the object of his seventh hunt. She was older than any of the others, but not too old. Only thirty. And from looking at her toned body, the muscles in her arms and legs well defined, he knew she was in excellent physical condition. And why shouldn't she be? After all, she made her living teaching other people how to exercise.

Amber had disappointed him. She'd been too whiny and instead of fighting him, she had begged and pleaded for him to let her go. She'd been nothing like Kendall Moore. Kendall had made every hunt an adventure. Up to the last breath she took, Kendall had fought him, as had Angela Byers and Candice Bates. Dana Patterson had been as big a dud as Amber so that when he'd killed her, he had felt more relieved than triumphant. Gala Ramirez had been somewhere in between. At first she had posed a real challenge, resisting him, trying to outsmart him, doing her best to escape. But after two weeks, she had lost hope and stopped resisting.

He ran his fingertips over the pretty redhead's photo, one he had taken from her website. *I'm coming for you very soon. By the end of the week, you'll be mine.*

He hoped she proved to be as feisty as she looked.

Sheriff Gene Hood had known in his gut the minute he saw the scalped woman hanging from the apple tree in the Landers's orchard that she was that missing UT basketball player, Amber Kirby. She fit the general description and everything about the situation told him that the same man who'd killed those other women, in five other states, had committed this crime, too. Of course, the only reason he knew the basic details about those other murders was because his cousin Shaughnessey worked for the Powell Agency. Only last weekend when he and Shaughnessey had gone fishing, his cousin had told him all about how Griffin Powell was taking a personal interest in what was sure to become an FBI matter.

After contacting the state boys, Gene had debated whether to call Wayne Hester at the FBI field office first or to call Shaughnessey. In the end, he had done his duty. He'd called SAC Hester, but he had told one of his deputies to call Shaughnessey. So, it hadn't surprised him one bit when Special Agent in Charge Hester and Griffin Powell had shown up within ten minutes of each other. Gene and his deputies mostly manned the situation, keeping onlookers, who had swarmed in like a bunch of bees following their queen, away from the scene while the CSI team did their thing.

He had met SAC Hester a couple of years ago and felt he was an okay kind of guy. He'd never met Mr. Powell, but Shaughnessey had spoken highly of the man. As soon as the FBI agent saw Griffin Powell, he bristled, but he didn't say anything to Gene, even though he had to know Gene had contacted Mr. Powell or someone in his organization.

Wayne Hester actually shook hands with Mr. Powell.

"Looks like you and Nic Baxter were right," SAC Hester said. "It appears Amber Kirby was abducted by the same man who killed those other five women."

"Have you positively identified the body?"

"No, but I took a damn good look at her, as did Sheriff Hood"—SAC Hester hitched his thumb in Gene's direction—"and we agree that the woman is Amber Kirby."

"Have her parents been notified?" Powell asked.

"Yes, sir, they have," Gene replied. "But all they were told was that a body had been found that could be their daughter."

"I understand that a little six-year-old girl found the body," Powell said. "Is she all right? Something like that could traumatize a child."

"That poor little thing hasn't said a word since her grandma found her. But her cousin, a seven-year-old boy, said he didn't see nobody around, just the body hanging from the tree and his cousin screaming."

"More than likely the killer was long gone," SAC Hester said.

Powell nodded.

They all stepped aside and watched in sad reverence as the medical examiner and his crew carried away the body.

"She was shot in the back of the head and also scalped, right?" Powell asked.

"Yes, sir, she was." Gene shook his head. "I've never seen anybody scalped and I'm here to tell you that it's not a pretty sight."

Griff followed the path out of the orchard and back to where he'd parked his Porsche in the Landers's family's driveway. He opened the door, slid inside, started the engine in order for the air-conditioning to work, and then placed a call on his cell phone.

Nic answered on the second ring. Apparently, she'd been expecting to hear from him.

"It's bad news, isn't it?"

"I'm a few miles outside Knoxville, in Wayside, at an apple orchard," Griff said. "A six-year-old girl found a woman hanging upside down from a tree. She'd been shot in the head and scalped."

"It's Amber."

"Yeah, I'm afraid it is."

"Maybe we should have called that damn press conference," Nic said. "If we had—"

"Nothing would have changed, not for Amber. He would have killed her no matter what we did or didn't do."

"But if we'd done what he wanted us to do, maybe he'd have called back with more clues."

"You're doing just what I was afraid you'd do," Griff said. "You're beating yourself up again when what happened wasn't your fault and there was nothing you could have done to have prevented it."

"So, this happened outside the Knoxville city limits, huh? Does this mean you're dealing with a county sheriff?"

"Sheriff Gene Hood, a man with twenty years of experience. He's no dummy. He called one of your boys, SAC Wayne Hester, who is, as we speak, on the scene."

"And?"

"And he's saying that Amber Kirby was killed by the same man who murdered the five other women."

"Thank God, he's finally seen the light. I need to call him, but not tonight. He needs time to process everything. I'll call him in the morning, but I won't say I told you so. I want him backing me, not taking charge himself."

"You now have six different states involved, six different local law enforcement agencies and six different FBI field offices, each with equal input into the investigation in their territories. Take my advice and don't try to steamroll over these guys. You'll catch more flies with honey than you will with vinegar."

"Is that your not-so-subtle way of advising me to use my feminine charm to get what I want? Damn it, Griff, you know I don't work that way. I'm a first-class agent, not some eyelash-fluttering femme fatale."

"All I was suggesting was that you play nice."

"Humph."

"I'll call you again later," he told her. "I'm going to head back out to the orchard and talk some more to Sheriff Hood."

"I wonder where the killer is and what he's doing. I keep picturing someone who looks like Cary Maygarden, all soft and round and pink, and he's smiling. He's cocky and confident. He believes we can never catch him. And I hate him for being so smug. I want him to know he isn't invincible, that it's only a matter of time before we bring him down."

"Nic, honey, are you getting any sleep?"

"What?"

"You sound tired."

"I'm fine. You don't need to concern yourself with my health."

"Look, you need to take a step back and put things into perspective before he starts his game all over again," Griff said. "He's going to call us before he goes after his next victim. He'll want to give us our clues and draw us into the game with him."

Nic groaned. "If only I could get my hands on that sick, sorry-ass—"

"Are you eating?"

"What?"

"Are you sleeping? Are you eating? Are you reading or watching TV or going out on dates?"

"What sort of stupid questions are those?"

"Answer me."

"Those are personal questions," Nic told him. "The answers are none of your business."

"Don't let capturing the Scalper become the sole focus of your life. It's unhealthy for an agent to become obsessed with something like this."

"Go to hell, Griffin Powell. Go straight to hell."

* * *

Nic hated admitting that Griff had been right, that he had sized her up accurately. For the past few weeks, she hadn't slept all night through, not even one night. If she wasn't having nightmares about the Scalper, she was obsessing about various details in the reports she had scoured over dozens of times. And she'd lost her appetite. She hadn't weighed herself, but her clothes were fitting looser, so she figured she'd dropped four or five pounds. Usually she had a healthy appetite, sometimes too healthy.

She wasn't watching TV, but then it was only mid-September and the fall shows hadn't started yet. She had been reading, just not for pleasure. Her only reading material was the thick file of reports on the dead women.

Had she been dating?

No, not recently. As a matter of fact, her last date had been . . . Jeez! Back in April sometime, right after Easter. He'd been a friend of a friend. A really nice guy named Eric. Or had it been Derrick? Maybe just Rick? Anyway, she had liked him just fine and actually had been glad when he'd called her for a second date. Unfortunately, the second date had ended badly. Apparently, Eric—or whatever his name was—had thought a second date meant he got to spend the night. When he'd found out that she was one of those women who did not have sex on a second date, he never called her for a third.

Determined to prove to herself that she had not become as obsessed with the Scalper as Griff implied she had, Nic went into the kitchen, opened the freezer, and removed a pint of Toffee Crunch ice cream. After finding one of her long beverage spoons, she carried the ice cream and spoon into the living room and turned on the television to the History Channel.

See, I am eating and I'm watching TV.

The ice cream was rich and creamy. Totally decadent and

delicious. And the television program about the underground world in Paris was actually rather interesting. Every time a thought about the Scalper or about poor Amber Kirby crossed Nic's mind, she forced it away. When she finished off the whole pint of ice cream, she lay down on the sofa and concentrated fully on the next program, this one a documentary about Winston Churchill.

Nic yawned as her eyelids drooped. Maybe she'd take a short nap.

How long she had slept, she didn't know. Apparently, more than an hour because it was already getting dark outside. She roused from the sofa, intending to close the blinds, but paused when she heard the doorbell ring.

Who on earth?

She went to the front door, peered through the peephole, and groaned. What was he doing here? She did not want to see him, didn't want to talk to him face-to-face. Over the phone, she could handle him, but not up close and personal.

He rang the bell again.

You know he won't go away, so you might as well let him in.

She opened the door, planted her hands on her hips, and glared at Griffin Powell.

Chapter 10

"What are you doing here?" Nic asked.

"I don't suppose you'd believe me if I said I was in the neighborhood."

She glowered at him, but had to admit—reluctantly—that she was actually glad to see him. For the first time in the five years she had known him, she didn't think of him as the competition, as an enemy combatant she had to defeat. But he was not her friend. She needed to remember that fact. And she couldn't let down her guard, not even for a minute. If she did, she might fall under his spell, that hypnotic blend of macho good looks and Southern charm.

"Well, where are my manners," she said, faking a smile. "Please, come in. How nice to see you. So glad you could drop by."

He grinned. "Why don't you change clothes and run a comb through your hair, then we'll go out for a late supper."

"What's wrong with the way I look?" She stepped back, spread out her arms and posed for him. She probably looked like warmed-over mush in her loose-fitting cotton pants and baggy T-shirt. Add to that no makeup and her hair in a pony-tail.

Griff surveyed her from head to toe. "If you don't want to go out, we could order in."

"I'm not hungry," she told him. She nodded to the empty carton sitting on the coffee table. "I just finished off a pint of Häagen Dazs."

Griff stepped over the threshold and closed the door behind him. Suddenly he was much too close, his six four, muscular body less than a foot away, so near she could smell the barely discernable scent of his aftershave. Whatever the cologne was, it probably cost more per ounce than she made in a week.

"When's the last time you had a decent meal?" Griff asked.

"Ice cream is dairy, which is one of the major food groups."

Griff looked around in Nic's living room, noting the place was clean but untidy. File folders and loose papers were scattered on the sofa, the coffee table, and the floor. An empty glass rested on a coaster on the coffee table alongside the empty ice-cream carton sitting on a folded paper towel. The furniture was a mixture of old and new and the one common denominator in the room was the color scheme. Neutrals. Earth tones. The only real splash of color was the vibrant oil painting over the sofa. Griff made his way closer to the painting, wanting to inspect it up close.

Ah, just as he suspected—it was an original. The artist's signature in the corner was a sprawl of letters, his or her handwriting as free and fluid as the painting. C. D. Bellamy. Hmm . . . Nic's younger brother.

Over a year ago, Griff had asked Sanders to run a check on Nicole Baxter and find out what he could about her personal life. He had accidentally found out she had been married once, something he hadn't known about her. During that investigation, Sanders had put together basic facts that included: 1) Nic's father was dead, her mother alive and remarried; 2) She had a younger brother who was an artist and lived in California; and 3) Nic had been married for three years to DEA agent Gregory Baxter. Seven years ago, her husband had put a 9mm in his mouth and pulled the trigger.

If there was one thing Griff knew about human nature, it was that we all tend to blame ourselves for our loved one's shortcomings and failures. No doubt Nic blamed herself for her husband's suicide, whether or not she had any reason to feel guilty.

There hadn't been a damn thing he could have done to have prevented his mother's death, and yet, he felt guilty. If things had been different . . . If he had been smarter, less cocky, less trusting . . . If he had returned to the U.S. a few years sooner . . .

Griff studied the broad, enthusiastic strokes of the artist's brush that had created such boldness. Perhaps the trait was hereditary. It was plain to see that Charles David Bellamy expressed his strength, stubbornness, and tenaciousness in his paintings the way Nic did with her job at the bureau.

Had she always been so dedicated, so thoroughly focused on her career to the exclusion of everything else? Apparently there had been a time when she had wanted more, needed more, than to work 24/7. Had her husband's suicide taken away her hopes and dreams? Or was he assuming incorrectly simply because Nic was female? No, that wasn't it. Most people, male and female, wanted more out of life than to simply succeed at their chosen profession. They needed family.

Griff thought of Sanders as his brother and their dear friend Yvette Meng as a sister. But deep inside him, Griff had come to the point in his life where he wanted more. More than he had a right to want or ever expect.

Did Nic feel the same way? Was she as much a prisoner of her past as he was?

Dru Tanner lathered her body with sun lotion, SPF 15, just enough to give her a minimum of protection. She was lucky that along with her auburn hair and brown eyes, she had inherited her olive complexion from her mother. In the summer months, she kept her tan alive by sunbathing by the pool and in winter months, she made use of the tanning beds at the physical fitness center she managed. Her mother, who owned Great Bods, was semiretired even though she was only fifty-five. Dru was lucky, too, that after giving birth to her daughter, now three, she'd been able to get her body back in shape quickly and the pregnancy had barely changed her figure.

Dru knew she wasn't pretty, that her eyes and nose were too big and her mouth too small, so she prized her greatest asset, her body. Big boobs, long legs, slim hips. Of course, Brian was always telling her she was beautiful. God love him. Her husband adored her. Her brainy, bookish, nerdy husband. In their case, it was true—opposites do attract. The smartest thing she'd ever done was marry Brian and the best thing she'd ever done was have his baby. She'd worried that she was too self-centered to be a good mother and maybe she'd never be the typical mom, but she would die for Brianna. Nothing was more important to her than her child.

"Watch me, Mommy," Brianna called to her from the pool where Brian stayed at her side while she swam from side to side in the shallow end.

Dru clapped wildly. "Great job, sweet pea. Yea, Brianna!"

Brian lifted their daughter from the pool and set her on the patio. She rushed to Dru, who held open an enormous beach towel. She wrapped Brianna in the towel, then lifted her off her feet and onto the chaise lounge where she sat. Brianna giggled happily while Dru dried her off, from her curly auburn hair to her tiny pink toes.

Brian came up from the water and stepped out of the pool. He was short, slender, and tan. He came to the fitness center

three times a week, but only to please her. She knew he preferred reading and working crossword puzzles and playing
games on his computer to working out.

"I hate to see the summer end," Dru said. "I wish our pool
was heated so we could use it year-round."

Brian leaned over, kissed her on the tip of her nose, and
then sat down in the chaise beside hers. "Maybe you can talk
your mother into adding an indoor pool to the fitness center."

Brianna crawled out of Dru's lap and into Brian's. She
cuddled against his hairless chest, resting her cheek directly
in the center.

"I mentioned it to her back in March and she said she'd
think about it. But you know my mom. She hates change
worse than anything."

"Maybe you should get Jerry to talk to her. He seems to
have more influence with her these days than you or Ali or
Deb."

Brian was right. Her mother's new boyfriend could talk
her into anything. She liked Jerry well enough, even if he
was ten years younger than her mom, which made him only
ten years older than her sister Deb. People had been gossip-
ing about how Deb had dated Jerry first and that's how he'd
met their mom. She supposed folks had a right to question
his sincerity, and Lord knew Deb and Ali despised him. But
Jerry made her mom happy, happier than she'd been since
their dad had died, five years ago. As long as her mom was
happy, Dru figured that was really all that mattered.

"He asked her to marry him," Dru said.

"What!"

"She called me this morning while we were getting ready
for church. Last night, he proposed to her. He gave her a diamond, got down on one knee, even sang to her."

Brian chuckled. "You got to give the guy credit—he
knows how to romance a lady. He sure waltzed into your
mom's life and swept her off her feet."

"Do you think he loves her? I mean really loves her?"

Brian shrugged. "Who knows? He acts like he's crazy about her."

"Do you think it's just an act?"

"I didn't say that."

"They're both signing prenups."

Brian's gray eyes widened in surprise. "Are they really?"

"They're talking about an October wedding," Dru said. "Maybe going over to Gatlinburg and getting married in one of those little wedding chapels. She asked if we'd go with them, me be her matron of honor and you Jerry's best man." Dru reached over and caressed a sleeping Brianna's soft, pink cheek. "She wants sweet pea to be the flower girl."

"What about your sisters and their families?"

"Mom hasn't told Ali and Deb. She said she knows they'll both throw a fit and refuse to even come to the wedding."

Brian reached out and grasped Dru's hand. "I'll do whatever you want me to do. If you want me to be Jerry's best man, I will be."

She squeezed Brian's hand. "How did I ever get so lucky to find a man like you?"

Brian beamed with pride. "I'm the lucky one."

The meal had been delicious. Nothing fancy. Just the absolutely best lasagna and Italian salad she'd ever eaten. Nic had pigged out on the crusty toasted bread slices that had tasted twice as yummy dipped in the cheesy pesto sauce. The wine, which no doubt had cost a small fortune, had also been superb. And as much as she hated to admit it, Griff had impressed her with the impromptu supper.

"Are you sure you don't want some of this Italian Cream Cake?" Griff asked, then slid a huge bite into his mouth.

Groaning, Nic rubbed her stomach. "I'm so full, I'm about to pop. I probably gained five pounds tonight."

"Good. I hope you did."

Nic laughed. "Are you saying you'd like to see me fat as a butterball?"

"Nope. I'm saying you didn't need to lose weight, that you were a perfect size."

Nic froze, her body and her mind momentarily numb. But her emotions rioted. Had he really said that she was a perfect size? Not too tall, too Amazonian, too hippy, too busty, but perfect?

"Oh, Mr. Powell, you are good. No wonder you have women swooning at your feet. You certainly know all the right lies to tell a woman."

Griff chuckled. "Why can't you just take the compliment for what it was—an honest statement."

Now he was making her feel uncomfortable and she was sure that had not been his intention. All through dinner, he had been a charming companion. They had talked about everything from the weather to politics, from good movies to good wine. She had discovered that she and Griff agreed on more things than they disagreed on. Strange. She would have thought they had nothing in common.

Griff downed a couple more bites of the rich Italian Cream Cake, then shoved his plate aside and stood. "I'll clean this up later. Why don't we take our wine into the living room and relax?"

"It's getting late," Nic said. "I'll bet it's nearly eleven, isn't it?"

He glanced at his wristwatch. "Ten forty-eight."

"Maybe you should go. I assume you're staying over tonight and flying home tomorrow."

"My plans aren't definite."

"If you're staying in the area because you think you're

going to play my knight in shining armor, then don't." Nic picked up her wine, took a final sip, and set the glass back on the table; then she slid back her chair and stood. "I don't need you or any other man to come to my rescue. I can take care of myself. I always have and I always will."

Griff fell into step alongside her as they walked out of the kitchen. "I learned a valuable lesson a long time ago. There are times when we all need somebody. Sharing the load with someone else isn't a sign of weakness."

Nic paused in the doorway between the kitchen and living room. Looking directly at Griff she asked, "Did you learn that lesson during those ten years after you mysteriously vanished?"

Not missing a beat, not blinking an eye, he replied, "Yes, as a matter of fact, I did."

"You don't talk about those years, do you, not with anyone?"

"Those years are a part of my past and there is nothing any of us can do to change the past."

"You're right about that." She couldn't change the fact that Greg had killed himself.

Griff walked on into the living room. Nic followed.

"Mind if I stay long enough to finish my glass of wine?" he asked.

"Sit. Drink. Stay." She sat on the sofa and indicated for him to take one of the two chairs.

He eased down into the hefty brown leather lounger and took a sip of wine. He glanced at Nic, then looked past her to the painting hanging behind the sofa. "That's a striking painting," he said. "The artist has real talent."

She inclined her head to glance back and up at the riot of brilliant color, the painting Charles David had given her for her thirtieth birthday present, two years ago this past May.

"My brother is the artist. And you're right, he is very talented."

"I'd like to see more of his work. If the rest is as good as this one, I would like to buy something similar for my home."

"I must admit that I don't know much about art, modern or otherwise," Nic said. "But I do know that every time I look at that painting, it makes me feel good."

"If his purpose was to create a sense of excitement and happiness, then he achieved his goal with that painting."

"I never thought about it, but I suppose I should have realized that a man as wealthy as you are would be an art connoisseur."

Griff smiled. "I'm not a connoisseur. I just know what I like."

Oh, my, my. This isn't good. I'm feeling relaxed and comfortable around Griff and I'm actually enjoying his company. I'm seeing him in a different light, a flattering light.

Nic faked a yawn. "Excuse me. I can't believe I'm actually sleepy. Not after that nap I took. It must be the wine. I shouldn't have had that third glass."

Before Griff could take the hint and leave, his cell phone rang. He set his glass on the coffee table and eased the phone into his hand. She watched him frown when he glanced at the caller ID.

"Powell here."

He didn't say anything else, just listened.

Nic slid to the edge of the sofa and mouthed, "It's him, isn't it?"

Griff nodded.

Finally he said, "Yeah, I heard you. What do you want me to do, thank you for the clue?"

The entire conversation lasted maybe a minute.

Griff turned to Nic. "He's chosen his next victim and wanted to call and give me a clue as to who she is."

Nic swallowed. "And the clue was?"

"Fit as a fiddle."

"Oh, great. That makes as much sense as rubies and lemon drops."

"Not necessarily. We know all the women are in good physical condition, so they're all—"

"Fit as a fiddle," Nic finished the sentence for him.

"But this clue is supposed to be more specific to this one woman."

"I know something should come to mind immediately," Nic said. "But I'm tired, I've had three glasses of wine, and I've spent too many hours lately trying to put together pieces of his damn puzzle."

Suddenly Nic's cell phone rang. She could hear it ringing, but she couldn't remember where she'd put the darn thing. It must be here in the living room; otherwise, she wouldn't be able to hear it so clearly.

Griff leaned forward, raked a couple of file folders aside and picked up Nic's phone from where it had been hidden underneath. He offered her the phone. She grabbed it, flipped it open, and held her breath.

"Hello, Nicole."

She didn't respond.

"Griffin will be calling you shortly to share his clue with you, so I know you'd like to have one to share with him."

She remained silent.

"If you don't let me hear that sweet voice of yours, I'm not going to give you a clue," he said.

Damn him! He had the advantage in this game and he knew it. "Please, give me the clue."

"That's a good girl. I really shouldn't give you and Griff any more clues, since you still haven't held a press conference and told everyone about me. I want the world to know me as 'the Hunter.' "

"Are you going to give me the clue or not?"

"So eager." He laughed. "Very well. Listen carefully. Your clue is"—he paused for dramatic effect—"Hush . . . hush, Thomas Wolsey." He ended the call.

What? Another name? But this one sounded familiar for some reason. Something historical maybe.

As soon as she laid aside her phone, she looked at Griff. "My clue is another name. And it's one I should know."

"What is it?"

"He said, 'Hush, hush, Thomas Wolsey.'"

"Thomas Wolsey?"

"Yeah. Why should I know that name?"

"*The* Thomas Wolsey was a powerful English statesman during the time of Henry VIII," Griffin said. "He was also a cardinal in the Roman Catholic Church."

"Oh, well, knowing that should make it easy for us to put our clues together and figure out who his next victim will be and where she lives." Nic groaned, knowing that once again the killer's clues would have to be deciphered.

"He's playing with us, giving us clues that even if we figure them out will only indirectly lead us to the victim. And he knows that by the time we make a really good guess and act on it, even if we turn out to be right, the way we were with Amber Kirby, it'll be too late to save her."

"But we can't not try," Nic told him. "We have to give it our best shot."

"Yeah, and he knows that."

Chapter 11

While Griff had phoned Sanders to give him the latest clues from the Scalper so that their team could get to work on deciphering them, Nic had called Doug Trotter to fill him in.

"Looks like I just might get my wish," she'd said after hanging up. "As early as midweek, I may be heading up an official investigation into the murders."

Griff knew that was what she had desperately wanted, and he had no doubt that she could handle the job. She was a smart woman. And as determined as a dog with a bone. But he was concerned about her. She was already borderline obsessed with finding the killer. He'd never thought he would ever care one way or the other about Special Agent Nicole Baxter.

The woman had been a pain in his backside for years, all through the BQK investigation. From the moment they met, she had disliked him and done everything possible, short of spitting in his eye, to make sure he knew it. It hadn't taken him long to figure out that the lady had a massive chip on her shoulder about men in general and him in particular. While her former boss, Curtis Jackson, had been in charge, she'd been forced to downplay her animosity. Griff had liked Curtis, an old-fashioned man's man. But once he retired and Nic was put in charge of the BQK cases, things had gone downhill in no time. The cordial relationship Griff had cultivated with Curtis hadn't extended to Nic, who had let him know immediately that his involvement in the BQK investigation was unwanted and bordered on illegal.

"You're awfully quiet," Nic said.

"Hmm . . . Just thinking," Griff replied as he lifted his arms and stretched.

"Come up with anything?"

"No." He checked his wristwatch. "It's after one. We've been batting ideas around for the past few hours. Maybe we should call it a night and start fresh in the morning."

"Sure, if that's what you want. You can head out for your hotel anytime you'd like." Nic got up off the sofa, rubbed the back of her neck with both hands and moaned. "I think I'll put on a pot of coffee and—"

Griff reached out, grasped her arms, and lowered them. She shivered at his unexpected touch. He took her hands in his. She glared at him.

Always on the defensive, even when she didn't need to be.

"What?" she demanded, then jerked her hands free.

"You're dead on your feet and should get some sleep. The last thing you need is coffee. Why don't you sit down, relax, and we'll go over everything again?"

"I thought you were leaving."

"I'll leave when you go to bed."

"Then you may be here until breakfast." She sat back down, crossed her arms over her chest, and gave him a so-there look.

Griff picked up the notepad where he'd been doodling while they had discussed the case after her call to Doug Trotter. "Okay, let's go over what we think we know. We've decided that 'fit as a fiddle' might mean the victim is into physical fitness professionally. She could be a gym teacher, an aerobics instructor, a physical fitness instructor, someone who makes her living helping others get in shape."

"And that would be how many hundreds of thousands of women nationwide? Even if we could narrow it down to a state, even a city, what are the odds we can get to her before he does?"

Nic lifted her bare feet off the floor, turned sideways, and bent her knees to create a slanted table with her thighs. She picked up her laptop. "I'm going to try the words again."

"You've done that three times already," he told her. "You've got all the info we need. It's just a matter of figuring out what makes sense and what doesn't."

"Four words," she said. "Well, actually only three, with the first two repeated. 'Hush, hush, Thomas Wolsey.' "

"We've agreed that the most logical assumption is that Thomas Wolsey was a cardinal."

"Yeah. Ball teams came to mind first. St. Louis, Arizona, Louisville."

"Was he telling us that his next victim will be from one of those areas? If so, we've agreed that since all the other victims have been taken from Southern states, Louisville would be our top pick from those three."

"But what if it's not a ball team?" Nic pecked on the keyboard but glanced at Griff. "There's cardinal rule, cardinal number and, of course, there's the cardinal bird."

"Let's not forget the small towns throughout the country that are called Cardinal."

Nic groaned. "Damn! Why didn't I think of this before?"

"What?" Griff sat down on the sofa beside her and turned her laptop sideways so he could see what she'd brought up on the screen.

"I should have typed in the words 'hush, hush' earlier. Do you see what I see?"

"I see that there are restaurants and clubs and—"

"There. That one." Nic pointed directly to the title of a DVD.

"The movie title? *Hush...Hush, Sweet Charlotte,* the old Bette Davis film?"

"What if the 'hush, hush' part of the clue is Charlotte?" She typed furiously. "Of course, the first city that comes to mind is Charlotte, North Carolina, but that might be too easy."

"At this point, I'm ready for easy," Griff told her.

"Hmm . . . There's a Charlottesville, Virginia, a Charlotte County, Florida, a Charlotte, Tennessee, and—"

"What's the state bird of North Carolina?" Griff asked.

"Huh?"

"What's the state bird? Want to bet me that it's the cardinal?"

Nic kept typing and the info on the screen kept changing. "Holy shit! You're right, the state bird of North Carolina is the cardinal."

" 'Hush, hush, Thomas Wolsey' translates to Charlotte, North Carolina."

"His next victim is a professional in the fitness business and she lives in Charlotte, North Carolina." Nic shoved the laptop off her thighs and onto the coffee table, then she grabbed her cell phone. "I'm calling Doug. He needs to contact every law enforcement agency in Charlotte, including our field office there."

"Every woman the Scalper has abducted came up missing between six and ten in the morning, five of them while they were on morning runs or walks. If he goes after her in the morning—"

"Do you think he'll go after her so soon? Hasn't he been putting some downtime between killing one woman and kidnapping another?"

"Check the data," Griff said. "Unless I'm mistaken, the

time between one body being discovered and another woman being abducted has varied between two and four days. He's not consistent about that. Probably because the distance between his home base and the victim's location varies, as does his means of transporting them."

"Are you trying to tell me that even knowing the city and the woman's profession, more or less, there's no way to get to her before he does?"

"He's not giving us enough info to narrow it down to one woman. If he did, he'd be a fool and the Scalper is no fool. A psychopathic killer—yes. But a fool—no. He's smart, but probably not as smart as he thinks he is."

"If we could get out some kind of announcement to the women in the Charlotte area, those who are physically fit . . . God, would you listen to me? That was a brilliant idea, wasn't it? Can you say panic in the streets?" Nic twisted her neck in a clockwise motion.

"Call Doug Trotter," Griff told her. "I'll wait until morning to contact Sanders. There's not much the Powell Agency can do at this point."

Nic nodded, hit the programmed number and waited. He could tell by her end of the conversation that she had awakened her boss from a sound sleep and he was none too happy about it. But once she had soothed his ill temper, she relayed the information calmly and precisely.

She flipped her phone closed, laid it on the coffee table, and rubbed her neck. "He's making the necessary calls and he'll get back to me later. He needs to check with the SAC in Charlotte before he okays my going there in any official capacity."

"Sit back down." Griff patted the sofa cushion beside him.

She eyed the cushion, then frowned; but she sat down.

Griff clutched her shoulders, turned her around so that her back was to him, and then he massaged her neck, using his thumbs to administer deep pressure. Nic yelped, then moaned.

"Sorry, I didn't mean to hurt you, but you're so tight that the knots in your muscles have knots." He continued massaging, alternating between soothing and pain-inducing pressure.

"Ooh . . . That feels so good."

Suddenly, as if just realizing that she was intimately close to a man she didn't like and didn't trust, Nic pulled away and turned around so that her back was against the sofa.

"Thanks," she told him. "You're pretty good at that."

Smiling, Griff wiggled his fingers. "I've been told I have the magic touch."

Nic snorted. "I'll bet."

"Practice makes perfect. Just think, if I hadn't tried my skills on a host of other ladies and learned what I was doing, I wouldn't have been able to make you feel so good."

"I don't know if you're joking or if you're serious."

"A little of both."

"You know that I've spent quite a few years adamantly detesting you, don't you?"

He nodded.

"I disapprove of you on so many levels. As a private detective, you've stuck your nose into criminal cases without any legal right to do it. And you've delighted in showing me—the bureau—up whenever possible. And don't even get me started on what I find reprehensible about your private life."

"Hey, I draw the line there." *Here we go again,* Griff thought. *She's off on another tangent, citing all the reasons she shouldn't like me.* "You have every right to complain about our business differences, but you don't know the first thing about my personal life, except what you read in the newspapers."

"Believe me, that's enough. Actually, it's more than I really want to know."

"How would you like it if people judged your personal life without any firsthand knowledge of the subject?" Griff asked. "What if I judged you on hearsay, on rumors, on—?"

"Are you saying that you're not a filthy rich, bed-hopping playboy who thinks of himself as a cross between James Bond and—?"

"I've been rich and I've been poor and I must admit that I prefer being rich. Who wouldn't? Agreed?"

"I suppose so."

"As for the bed-hopping." He shook his head. "I'm a single man with a normal libido. I enjoy sex and I like to indulge frequently. But I don't go through women as if they were throwaway tissues and I don't make promises that I don't keep."

"So, you don't break any hearts along the way?"

"Not intentionally."

"You want me to think that I've been misjudging you all these years, don't you?"

Did he? Was what Nic thought of him really important? Apparently it was or he wouldn't be defending himself. As a general rule, he didn't explain himself to anyone. One of the perks of being Griffin Powell.

"Just to show you what a good guy I really am, what do you say I call Jonathan and have him get the jet ready to fly to Charlotte as soon as you can pack a bag?"

He could tell by the light in her eyes that she loved the idea, but she said, "I'm not authorized to go to Charlotte. I need to wait until I hear from Doug and—"

"Did I say anything about your going to Charlotte in any official capacity? We can fly down, get there in time for breakfast, and by then my guess is Doug will have okayed it with the SAC in Charlotte for you to take part in the investigation."

"Oh, Mr. Powell, you do know how to tempt a girl, don't you?"

He grinned. "So, what do you say?"

She jumped up. "I say give me fifteen minutes."

"Take your time, honey."

As she hurried out of the living room, she paused, looked back over her shoulder, and said, "You realize, don't you, that I'm actually doing you a favor by allowing you to accompany me to Charlotte?"

She winked at him, then rushed off down the hall.

Griff chuckled. There was much more to Nic Baxter than met the eye; and he was beginning to realize just how much he would like to peel back the outer layers, one by one, and get to know the real lady buried deep inside.

Dru started to hit the snooze button on her alarm one more time, but when she glanced at the lighted digital clock, she gasped. It was five forty. That gave her twenty minutes to get up, shower, dress, grab a protein bar in the kitchen, and make the fifteen-minute drive to Great Bods. There was no way she could accomplish the impossible and arrive on time.

She opened Great Bods every weekday morning at six o'clock and her mom was responsible for the weekend mornings. Mondays were always the most difficult for Dru because she stayed up too late on Sunday nights and felt horribly sleep-deprived the next day. She had found that going in early on Mondays so that she could work out before any of the customers starting showing up helped energize her. That certainly wasn't an option today.

Careful not to disturb Brian, she eased back the covers and slipped out of bed, then tiptoed to the bathroom. Good thing she was a creature of habit. Last night, as she did every night before a workday, she had laid out her shorts, tank top, clean bra, and bikini panties, as well as her socks and athletic shoes. With no time for a shower, she took a quick sponge bath and put on her working clothes, then ran a comb through her hair, pulled it into a ponytail and rinsed her mouth out with mint-flavored mouthwash.

Usually she took time to peek in on Brianna before going downstairs, but she had to forgo that pleasure this morning. If she drove like a bat out of hell, she should just make it there in time to unlock the doors by six. Most people didn't start showing up until between six fifteen and six forty-five, but occasionally someone would show up early.

Please don't let this be one of those mornings.

She didn't bother grabbing a protein bar. She kept a few in her desk at work, so after she opened Great Bods, put on a pot of coffee in the lounge, and ran a couple of miles on one of the treadmills, she'd grab a quick bite. She wasn't one of those crazy women who skipped meals or used laxatives or made herself throw up to stay slim. She ate three healthy meals a day, stayed away from processed foods like white sugar and white flour and limited her red meat intake. Managing a fitness center was a real plus, as was having inherited her mother's sleek figure and great metabolism. Of course, she did have one sinful weakness. Coffee. She could do without candy and cookies, without potato chips and nachos, but she'd rather die than live without coffee.

Dru went through the kitchen and out into the garage. Her black Mustang had been a present from Brian this year on her thirtieth birthday. She slid behind the wheel, started the engine, and backed out into the driveway.

Mondays seemed like the longest day of the week. Maybe that was because she put in twelve hours on Mondays, from six to six. Although Great Bods stayed open until nine, she had arranged for her assistant manager, Kim Worsham, to come in at one and stay until closing. Nothing was more important to Dru than being home to have dinner with Brian and Brianna every evening. She and Brian took turns giving their daughter her nightly bath and reading her a bedtime story. She loved that she and her husband shared all the parenting and household duties.

Dru made it five blocks without getting caught by a red light, but the one up ahead was already on caution. She pressed her foot on the accelerator and raced through the light that changed from yellow to red just as her Mustang zoomed beneath it. If her luck held out, there wouldn't be any police officers on the prowl looking for speeders.

At precisely five after six, she pulled into her designated parking slot, came to a screeching halt, shut off the engine, and got out. Taking a deep breath, she marched toward the back door. She'd been in such a hurry that she hadn't noticed the other car in the back lot or the man standing by the door under the burgundy canopy. She paused a few feet away and looked him over. Customers used the front door, so she didn't think he was a customer. At least, she didn't recognize him. He was of average height and had a stocky build, with a mop of curly black hair. He wore loose-fitting tan slacks and a light blue cotton pullover shirt.

He wasn't a customer and he certainly wasn't a delivery person. So who was he and what did he want?

A tingle of unease vibrated through Dru, nothing major or sinister, just an inkling that something wasn't quite as it should be.

"Hello," she called to him. "Can I help you?"

"Are you Dru Tanner?" he asked, smiling.

He seemed harmless enough. And friendly.

"Yes, I am. And you're?"

When he moved out from underneath the canopy, she noted that he wore a navy backpack.

"I'm new to town. Just moved in a few blocks from here and was told this is the best fitness center in the area."

Dru breathed a sigh of relief. "Yes, it is. Sorry if I seemed a little leery. It's just that customers use the front door."

"Oh. Good to know. I'll be sure to remember that from now on."

As Dru approached him, the key to the back door in her hand, he moved toward her. When he came up alongside her, she noticed that he held both hands, clutched into fists, at his sides.

Odd.

"I guess I'm early, huh?" he asked as his arm brushed against hers.

He was a little too close for comfort, so Dru took a step to the side to put some breathing room between them. Just as she reached the back door, she realized she'd made a deadly mistake taking this man at face value. Before she knew what he intended to do and could manage to stop him, he stuck a needle into her upper arm. She cried out and turned on him, determined to put up a fight. But it was already too late. Whatever drug he'd injected her with was already zinging through her system, making her dizzy and blurring her vision.

"Don't fight it," he told her. "Just relax and go to sleep. I'll catch you when you fall."

She opened her mouth to scream, but no sound came out. In her mind she yelled at the top of her lungs. But only in her mind. In reality, she felt herself swaying. Her knees gave way. And then everything went black.

* * *

Nic and Griff met the Special Agent in Charge of the Charlotte FBI field office, Betty Schonrock, for breakfast and discussed the Scalper case over bacon, eggs, and toast.

SAC Schonrock had made it clear to Griff the moment they met that he was being included only because the killer had chosen Griff, along with Nic, to play his sick, twisted game. But by the time they'd finishing eating and were on second and third cups of coffee, Griff was, at her request, calling the SAC by her first name. In her midfifties with graying brown hair and keen hazel eyes, Betty stood no more than five three and was, to use a polite term, pleasingly plump. And like most women who came into contact with *the* Griffin Powell, she had succumbed to his charm in no time flat.

"I contacted the police department, the sheriff's office, and the highway patrol," Betty had explained. "But there's only so much that can be done. We don't have a name. We don't even have a general area where we can look, and Charlotte's a big town. Do you know how many women in their twenties are into some type of physical fitness as a profession?"

"We realize that it's not much to go on," Griff admitted. "But it's all we have."

"He's playing with you two." Betty glanced from Griff to Nic. "Of course, y'all already know that."

"And he knows we'll keep on taking his calls, listening to his clues, and hoping beyond hope that somehow we can get to his victim before he does."

"You're playing a game you can't win," Betty said. "This guy holds all the trump cards."

"Sooner or later, he'll make a mistake, and when he does, I want to be there to nail his hide to the wall." Nic looked right at Betty. "Someone capable of the horrendous crimes he has committed doesn't deserve to live."

Betty studied Nic closely. Crap! Had she said too much? Said the wrong thing? Had she come off sounding totally obsessed?

"I understand how you feel," Betty told her. "And I agree completely."

Nic sighed with relief.

"Why don't you two follow me to the office and I'll introduce you to some of the other agents?" Betty stood, then reached to pick up the bill.

Griff snatched the bill off the table. "I'll take care of it."

"Thanks." Betty smiled at him. "You've got the address for the office: 400 South Tryon Street."

"You two go on," Griff said. "I'll be right behind y'all."

Nic walked out of the restaurant with Betty, but before they reached Betty's car, the SAC's cell phone rang. She glanced at the caller ID. "I need to get this."

Nic nodded. She tried not listen, since she had no idea if the call was business or personal, but when she heard Betty say, "How old is she? Hmm . . . It could be nothing. Women walk off and leave husbands and kids behind every day. Let's not assume anything at this point."

Nic's heartbeat quickened as she waited for Betty Schonrock to tell her the news she didn't want to hear.

"A woman named Dru Tanner, who manages a physical fitness center, may be missing," Betty said.

"What do you mean, 'may be missing'?"

"It seems when customers starting showing up at the center, they couldn't get inside, so they called her house. Her husband had no idea where she was if she wasn't at work, so he went down to the center and found her car in the parking lot and found her purse and keys lying by the back door."

"I assume the husband called the police."

Betty nodded. "This could be your woman or Dru Tanner may have nothing to do with your case."

"How old is she?"

"Thirty."

Griff came out of the restaurant, scanned the area, and

threw his hand up when his gaze connected with Nic's. "What now?" she asked Betty.

Just as Griff approached, Betty said, "I intend to hold a press conference. I want you there with me. It's time the country knew about this guy." She looked at Griff. "What was it he said he wanted to be called? 'The Hunter'? We'll tell the press that the bureau suspects the Hunter has killed five women and possibly abducted a sixth."

Griff lifted an inquisitive brow. "I take it you've heard something in the past few minutes. He worked fast this time, pretty much overnight."

"There's a woman missing who manages a physical fitness center," Nic told him. "She's thirty."

"Odds are she's his sixth victim," Griff said.

Betty turned to Nic. "We're going to take off the brakes and get things rolling this morning. As far as I'm concerned, you're in charge. And I'll tell Doug Trotter that, and the other SACs whose territories are involved."

"I have only one suggestion concerning the press conference," Griff said.

Nic and Betty looked at him.

"Don't refer to him as 'the Hunter.' He may consider himself a hunter, but we don't want to give him what he wants, do we? So far, we've pretty much been playing by his rules. It's time we buck him again and see what happens."

"What are you getting at?" Nic asked.

"When you announce that the FBI is searching for a serial killer who has murdered five women and possibly abducted a sixth, someone is bound to ask about the victims being scalped. You need to confirm this and once you do, the press will dub him 'the Scalper' and not 'the Hunter.' "

Chapter 12

The small charter plane landed at a private airstrip outside Baton Rouge—with one passenger and four shipping crates. The largest crate was coffin size and the others suitcase size.

Pudge stood and watched while the pilot and the driver of the hired truck load his precious cargo onto the bed of the rental vehicle. When he had placed Dru Tanner in the large crate, he had given her another injection, which should keep her unconscious for a number of hours. But just in case she woke during transport, he had bound her hands and feet and gagged her.

Once the crates were loaded, Pudge settled into the truck cab alongside the driver, a rather brutish-looking fellow, with long, stringy dark hair pulled back into a ponytail. In his peripheral vision, Pudge noted a large eagle tattooed on the man's right arm.

Thankfully the driver wasn't a talker. Pudge despised trying to make idle chit-chat with underlings. The driver, who had introduced himself as Rod, didn't bother asking if Pudge minded listening to the blaring country music the ruffian seemed to enjoy.

They took Interstate 10 southwest, then exited off near Grosse Tête. Pudge gave the driver exact directions, explaining that his home wasn't far, just situated out in the country. They arrived at Belle Fleur a little before two. Once the driver had helped Pudge unload the cargo and place the crates on the veranda, Pudge offered him a beer. He didn't invite Rod into his home. The big oaf didn't seem to mind waiting on the porch.

Pudge retrieved a beer bottle from the refrigerator, took off the cap, and set it on the counter. He pulled out his wallet, removed a hundred-dollar bill, and returned to the veranda.

He handed Rod the beer. "Take it with you." He held out the single bill.

Rod eyed the money.

"Just consider this a bonus for a job well done," Pudge told him.

Rod grabbed the bill and stuffed it into his jeans pocket; then saluted Pudge with his beer bottle, sauntered off the veranda, and headed for the rental truck.

Pudge watched while Rod drove off, waiting until he was completely out of sight before approaching the largest of the four crates. He would dispose of the crates later, break them apart with an ax and put them in the woodshed out back.

Pudge ran his hand over the rough wood. "Are you still resting peacefully, my lovely sleeping beauty?"

Not a sound. Hmm . . . Good.

"I'll be right back and get you out of there," Pudge said. "I have a very special place waiting for you in the basement."

* * *

Griff kept a low profile during the press conference. This was Nic's moment in the spotlight. She had now gotten what she'd been wanting—to head up the bureau's investigation into the series of murders that they both knew had been perpetrated by the second BQ Killer.

SAC Betty Schonrock introduced Nic as the task force leader and turned the microphone over to her. Nic made a brief statement, giving the press the basic facts without revealing too much information. Then she took questions, which came at her fast and furious. The audience consisted of national, state, and local press. Television, newspapers, and some freelancers.

Nic answered the first question quickly, giving a succinct reply, then did the same with the next question and the next.

Yes, there had been five murders in five different states. Yes, they had every reason to believe all five murders had been committed by the same person. Yes, a possible sixth victim had been abducted. Yes, law enforcement in all six states were working together with the FBI.

Then a reporter for one of the national networks asked the question Griff knew someone would eventually ask. "Is it true that all five victims were scalped?"

A hush fell over the crowd.

Nic squared her shoulders. "Yes, all five women were scalped, postmortem."

She answered half a dozen more questions but refused to confirm any other rumors. As soon as she left the podium, Griff moved in alongside her, clasped her elbow, and together he and SAC Schonrock flanked Nic as she exited through the crowd.

Although most of the horde of newspeople gradually dispersed, some of the reporters continued shouting questions at Nic.

"What are you doing with Griffin Powell?" one of the

newspaper reporters hollered. "Rumor has it that you two are engaged."

A loud roar of laughter rose from the onlookers.

"Ignore them," Griff told her.

They made it to the rental car without being followed. Nic shook hands with Betty and thanked her again for her support.

"Grab a bite of lunch and relax," Betty said. "If those autopsy reports come in before you get back to the office, I'll call."

Griff got in on the passenger side while Nic slid behind the wheel. Within minutes, they were back in traffic.

"Do you know where you're going?" Griff asked.

"I haven't the foggiest," Nic admitted.

"Then let's find a fast-food place, hit the drive-thru, and park somewhere so we can talk in private."

Nic nodded.

"The press is going to have a field day with the fact that you and I seem to be a team." She glanced hurriedly at Griff. "You need to go home and stay out of my way from now on."

Griff had figured this would happen. That one sarcastic comment by the newspaper reporter had set her teeth on edge. He'd noted the way she had instantly tensed. Nic wanted not only the press but her superiors to see her as a strictly by-the-book agent. Her recent association with Griff had already compromised her image.

"I'll make you a deal," Griff said.

"Is that a sandwich shop up ahead on the right?" she asked.

Griff checked out the strip mall. "Yeah. Take a right at the next red light." GALWAY COUNTY LIBRARIES

"What sort of deal are you offering?" Nic stopped at the red light.

"Let me go along with you to Betty's office and allow me to take a look at the autopsy reports and I'll go home this evening."

"What sort of deal is that?"

"Once I go home, I won't bother you again . . . until the Scalper calls us."

Nic heaved a deep sigh as she contemplated his offer. "If he stays true to form, he may not contact us again until after he murders Dru Tanner."

"*If* he stays true to form, which he's already proven isn't always the case."

"You think he'll get in touch with us after he sees the press conference on tonight's news, don't you?"

"Assuming it's broadcast wherever he is right now and assuming the fact that you didn't follow his instructions pisses him off, then, yeah, I think he'll call."

"If that's what you think will happen, your deal is worthless."

"There's always a chance he won't call. I could be wrong about him."

Nic took a right, then another right directly into the strip mall parking lot. She eased the rental car into a slot, killed the motor, and turned to Griff.

"You can take a look at the reports, but I want your word that even after he calls us again, you'll back off. I'll keep you updated as long as you stay out of my way. That's my best offer. Take it or leave it."

"I'll take it—with an amendment."

"What?" She glared at him.

"The deal is good only until Dru Tanner is found—alive or dead."

"Then what?"

"Then we negotiate another deal. Agreed?"

"Okay," she replied rather reluctantly. "But I'm agreeing to this because even a few weeks with you out of sight and out of mind is worth the steep asking price."

Griff smiled. "You'll miss me, Nicki."

She groaned. "I seriously doubt it."

*   *   *

Pudge deposited Dru in the basement, restricting her by shackling her with handcuffs and ankle chains. She didn't stir as he adjusted her into a sitting position, her back against the wall, her head slumped forward almost touching her chest. He ran his hand over the side of her face and down her neck.

His gaze rested on her breasts. High, round, and full.

"I'll dream of you tonight. You and I, in the woods together. Those long, trim legs of yours running, running . . ." He skimmed his hand down one leg and up the other.

Leaving only one sixty-watt lightbulb burning, so that she wouldn't wake in total darkness, Pudge left her alone in the basement. When she awoke, he wanted her to see where she was and know that he now controlled her life.

He had a great deal to do to prepare for tomorrow, the first day of the hunt. He would keep her out no more than a couple of hours. Just long enough for her to become familiar with the rules of the game. Each day he would leave her out longer until that final week, he would leave her alone in the woods to fend for herself. She would be forced to forage for food, water, and shelter. And she would have to stay constantly alert, never knowing when he would track her down.

Nic paced back and forth in Betty Schonrock's office. Cursed with nervous energy, she couldn't sit still. The three of them had gone over the autopsy reports on the first four victims. The autopsy results on Amber Kirby weren't ready yet.

The facts were clear, leaving no doubt that all four women had been killed by the same person. Each had been shot in the head with the same caliber rifle. The entry wound was to the back of the head and the larger exit wound in front, leaving each face all but destroyed. Each woman had been scalped either with the same knife or with similar knives.

Betty tapped the papers spread out in the center of her desk. "The autopsies reveal that each woman had been shot more than once—in the arms, knees, ankles, as if he was killing her slowly, one hit at a time."

"He wants them to suffer first," Griff said.

Nic rubbed the back of her neck as she kept moving, wishing she could erase the images flashing through her mind of the victims as they were shot, their battered bodies taking one bullet after another until the final bullet ended it all.

Betty asked, "What do y'all make of the bruises, scratches, and cuts on each woman's body?" Betty asked. "And the fact that their feet were pretty battered, as if they had been doing a lot of barefoot running."

Nic paused and stared at Griff, then said, "I think he's chasing them. He wants to be called 'the Hunter,' so that gives us a major clue. He's hunting these women, possibly for the entire three weeks they're missing. And in the end he kills them."

"If they're allowed to run free for three weeks, why hasn't at least one of them been able to escape?" Betty asked. "And where could he take them so that they wouldn't be anywhere near other people?"

"He either owns or rents land," Griff said. "Somewhere private, secluded, probably out in the country far away from other homes, and it's a place not easily accessible to the public."

"Maybe the reason no one has been able to escape is because there is only one way in and out of the property without crossing a river or a mountain, or simply because the area is so vast." Nic stopped, braced her hips on the edge of Betty's desk, and crossed her legs at the ankles. "He could have hundreds of acres at his disposal."

"Since this is all a game to him, then it's easy for him to think of himself as a big game hunter." Griff's voice had lowered to a husky growl. "He's hunting these women as if they were animals. He's the predator and they're his prey."

Nic sensed some odd vibes coming from Griff and wasn't sure what was wrong. Why had she picked up on something so subtle? A slight change in his voice. A faraway look in his eyes. Tension in his big body. And an underlying anger that he was barely controlling.

She looked at Betty, who seemed completely oblivious. Apparently she hadn't picked up on anything.

"There didn't seem to be much, if any, environmental clues found on the victims," Betty said. "The consensus is that he wipes them down and cleans their nails before transporting them back to the area where he kidnapped them. However, minute particles were removed from under the fingernails and toenails of each victim."

"I want those samples sent to our lab," Nic said. "On the off chance the microscopists can ID the dirt, or pollen, or whatever was under their nails, it could help us figure out the area where he's taking them. We'd know if it's desert or woods or swamps."

"All the women were dehydrated and malnourished," Griff said. "He's withholding food and water. Maybe not in the beginning, but for most of the time. He could use that as a means to control them. If they're good, if they play along, he rewards them. If not . . ."

There it was again, Nic thought. That peculiar feeling about Griff.

"He loves playing God," Griff said. "The whole thing is one giant power trip for him. He's probably impotent under normal circumstances, probably can't have normal sex with a woman. But I'll bet you he gets off tormenting these poor women and he doesn't even have to touch them."

A shiver of unease quivered through Nic. Strange how

Griff was so certain about his facts and stranger still was how she instinctively believed he was right. It was as if he had tapped into some kind of inner knowledge about the Scalper, in a way that only someone intimately acquainted with him would be able to do.

Nic shook off the sense of foreboding as well as her implausible musings about Griff's thoughts. She didn't know what he was thinking, and reading something deep and meaningful into his comments bordered on irrational. She'd definitely been spending far too much time with him. But that was about to change. And the sooner the better. The very last thing she needed—now or ever—was to fall under the spell of the infamous Griff Powell charm.

When Dru came to, she couldn't remember where she was or what had happened. Sleepy. She was so sleepy. Was it the middle of the night? Was she at home in bed? Or was she actually asleep and having some kind of weird dream?

Try to wake up, she told herself.

She reached out, searching for Brian, trying to grab hold of his arm and shake him. *Help me, Brian. I'm having a horrible nightmare and I can't wake up.*

She jerked her hand back, away from the damp, slimy surface she had touched. Her eyelids flew open, but her vision was blurred.

Where am I?

When she tried to cry for help, it took several attempts before she could utter a sound, then she simply squeaked softly.

What's wrong with me?

The musty scent of damp earth and the gloomy semi-darkness suggested that she was possibly either in a cave or somewhere underground.

Don't panic. Stay calm.

Within minutes, her vision gradually cleared and she was able to take a good look at her surroundings.

She was in a basement or some type of old cellar. One lone light prevented her from being in total darkness.

Stand up and walk around, try to figure a way out of here.

She managed to get to her feet but suddenly realized that her ankles were bound with heavy metal manacles.

Oh, God. Oh, God!

Tears filled her eyes as she tried to remember.

When she lifted her hands to brush the tears from her face, she felt the handcuffs. She held her wrists in front of her and screamed.

That crazy man who had been outside the back door of Great Bods had stuck a needle into her arm. He had drugged her.

"Where are you?" she yelled. "Why are you doing this to me?"

The only response was an eerie silence.

Griff took a taxi from the field office in the Wachovia building on South Tryon Street and arrived at the airport shortly before seven. He had made Nic a promise that he fully intended to keep. That didn't mean Powell's wouldn't continue with their own independent investigation, but for the time being he would stay away from Nic and her official fact-finding mission. They could work independently and still share information. Besides, he was better off putting some distance between them. For some unfathomable reason, he'd begun to like Nic.

He had discovered that she wasn't quite as hard-edged as he'd thought. Tough as nails, yes. But he suspected she had a soft side, one she kept well hidden. Maybe her husband's suicide had forced her to put up a defensive wall. If Griff understood anything, he understood self-protection. Maybe something in her childhood had convinced her that she had to fight for the right to be any man's equal. Who knew? He certainly didn't, and if he ever asked her, he felt certain she'd tell him that it was none of his damn business.

He couldn't fault her for keeping her secrets, for being a private person. There were ten years of his life that were a mystery to everyone who knew him. Everyone except Sanders and their friend Yvette.

Those years had changed him irrevocably, making him the man he was today. He seldom allowed himself the indulgence of thinking about what his life might have been like if he'd been able to turn pro after college and continue playing the sport he had loved. He'd probably have remained a cocky, brash young man for quite a few years, loving life and living it to the fullest. But eventually, he'd have matured, probably retired with a hefty bank account and a scrapbook filled with good memories. He figured he'd have been married by now, have a couple of kids, be living the good life. And maybe his mother would still be alive. More than anything, he regretted that he'd never been able to take care of her, to give her all the things she had deserved. He'd wanted to buy her a car, build her a house, hire her a maid.

A flash of memory angered Griff. He had worked diligently putting those ten years behind him, trying to bury the tormenting memories so deep that they could never rise to the surface and torture him again.

He would never forget, of course, but through years of working with Yvette, through meditation, and through sheer willpower, he had managed to control his thoughts. Most of the time.

So, why now, tonight, had *his* face appeared, even momentarily, in Griff's mind?

You know why.

Acknowledging the similarities between the evil from the

past and the evil from the present had allowed old ghosts to resurface.

He had loved playing God, just as the Scalper did. The games *he* had played had been a giant power trip for him. Tormenting others, bending them to his will, and hearing them beg had become his only reasons for living.

Just as Griff boarded the private Powell jet, his cell phone rang. Although he sort of hoped it was Nic, he knew it wasn't.

"Powell here," he said, having a good idea who the caller was.

"You and Nicole aren't team players. It seems you can't follow even the simplest rules."

"Following your rules was getting us nowhere fast," Griff told him.

"Is it my fault that you and Nicole, the Powell Agency, and the FBI can't put all the pieces together quickly enough to save even one woman?"

Griff emitted a derisive chuckle. "Enjoy your game while you can, you sick son of a bitch. We'll find you and when we do, nothing would give me more pleasure than to strip you naked, turn you loose in the jungle, and hunt you down like the rabid animal you are."

Silence. Then in a nauseatingly soft and sweet voice, he said, "How interesting that you and I think so much alike."

Griff didn't wait for him to hang up. He severed the connection and turned off his cell phone, then boarded the plane for home.

Nic checked into the motel at seven fifteen, laid her briefcase on the desk, put on a pot of half-decaf/half-regular coffee, and kicked off her shoes. Tomorrow, she would set the task force into motion. The first thing she needed to do was make sure everyone on her squad was up to speed on the case. Each department needed to share all their information with all the members. Everyone needed to be on the same page from the get-go.

Her head ached, her neck ached, and she needed eight good hours of sleep. A couple of aspirin might help her head and she could get by on six hours' sleep, but what she really needed was for Griff to give her another neck massage.

Damn! Where had that thought come from?

Don't think about Griffin Powell.

He's gone.

You sent him away.

You do not need him within a thousand miles of you.

Knoxville certainly wasn't a thousand miles from Charlotte, but even a few hundred miles would do.

Just as Nic started to pour herself a cup of freshly brewed coffee, her cell phone rang. Crap.

What if it's Griff?

She checked the caller ID.

It wasn't Griff.

"Hello."

"Hello, Nicole. You disappointed me terribly today. I watched your press conference. You didn't follow my directions."

"If you don't give me what I want, I will not give you what you want," she told him.

"Are you already tired of playing my game?"

"Your clues are practically worthless."

"Then I won't give you any more."

"Fine with me."

"Dru is going to play the game," he said. "I'll start teaching her the rules tomorrow. We're going to have so much fun. Don't be jealous. You may not want to play with me, but you will. Just wait and see."

Pure fear jolted through Nic. When she broke free from

that momentary alarm, she started to reply but realized he had hung up.

Her first instinct was to call Griff immediately.

There's no reason to call him. You don't have any information to share.

Throwing common sense out the window, she hit the programmed number. Instead of getting Griff, her call went directly to voice mail.

She tossed the phone across the room and onto one of the two double beds, then she poured herself a cup of coffee, sat down at the desk, and opened her briefcase. She had a lot to do before morning. But one thing she wouldn't be doing was calling Griff again.

Chapter 13

Griff had spent the past two weeks at home, but he had sent agents to all the various locations where the Scalper had abducted the six women. He was staying out of Nic's way and had requested that his agents at the scenes keep low profiles and not lock horns with Nic or anyone from the bureau's field offices in the six states. He had stepped back and would gladly stay in the background. She needed her space and it seemed that he was the one person who had a knack for invading that invisible perimeter surrounding her. He knew all about erecting boundaries and safeguarding them. Compared to him, Nic was an amateur. His whole persona had been created on illusion. Over the years, as he had become more and more comfortable with the public's image of who Griffin Powell was, the real Griff had gone underground into a secure place where nothing and no one could ever touch him.

"Excuse me," Sanders said. "I knocked several times, but you didn't respond."

Griff glanced up from where he sat behind the desk in his private study, his favorite room in the house. "Sorry, I suppose I was deep in thought."

"Barbara Jean suggested that, with the weather being so nice today, we should have lunch on the patio."

Griff glanced out the window. Sunny. Blue sky. A gentle breeze blowing. "Hmm . . . yes. Good idea."

"Yvette arrived almost an hour ago," Sanders said. "I gave her her usual room."

"It will be good to see her. It's been too long."

"Yes, it has."

Griff didn't need to tell Sanders to make sure Yvette had everything she needed. And it went without saying that they would provide her with anything she wanted. She was as dear to them as a beloved sister. She was a sibling reborn with the two of them in a cleansing fire that had destroyed the past and on which they each had built a future.

"Is there anything I can do for you?" Sanders asked.

Griff's gaze connected with his old friend's. "You know why I sent for Yvette?"

"Yes."

"I hate that after all these years, he still has the power to affect me so strongly." Griff rolled his leather chair away from the desk and stood. "You think the past is dead and buried. You want it to be. You need it to be. But something happens, something triggers the memories and there you are—back in hell."

"This killer—the Scalper—is not invincible, no more than York was."

York. The name alone still had power over Griff, a power as dark and dangerous as the man himself had been.

Griff narrowed his gaze to a hard glare. "I thought we agreed to never speak his name."

"Perhaps it is time." Sanders's gaze never wavered.

Griff could not bring himself to verbally agree. He nodded curtly.

"Lunch will be ready shortly." Sanders turned to leave, then paused and added, "Rick Carson arrived this morning around ten and Holt Keinan will be leaving shortly. Do you wish to speak to him before he goes?"

"You gave him his assignment?"

"Yes."

"Then I don't need to speak to him."

"Very well." Sanders closed the door quietly behind him when he left.

Griff rotated Powell agents at Griffin's Rest on a regular basis, keeping one here at all times to oversee the estate security. He had handpicked each agent, and many had been with him for five or more years. A scant handful of agents were more than acquaintances, but none were friends, not in the truest sense of the word. Former agent Lindsay McAllister, now Lindsay Walker, had been and still was a friend.

Under different circumstances, he would be looking forward to seeing Yvette. But the reason she was here was because he had called and asked her to visit. Not simply as a friend but as a fellow survivor. And in a professional capacity as a psychiatrist.

Nic had slept for ten hours straight last night. God, it was good to be home, in her own bed, with her own pillows. Motel/hotel living was okay for a few days, but she'd been on the road for the past two weeks, visiting each of the six states where the Scalper had abducted a victim. Although she didn't want to alienate the SAC or agents at the various field offices by flexing her muscles, she thought they needed to meet her in person, to know that she intended to be a hands-on leader. She had sat in on several of the reinterviews of possible witnesses, none of which garnered them new information. She had personally spoken to family members and visited each of the sites where the killer had hung his victim upside down from a tree limb.

Sitting cross-legged in the middle of the living room floor, various reports, photos, and file folders circling her, Nic held her mug in both hands as she sipped the strong coffee. This was the last cup of an eight-cup pot, actually her sixth cup, since she'd used a fairly large mug.

She had taken the day off—her first in fourteen days—to get some rest. She had even foregone her morning walk, something she seldom skipped, even when she was out of town. But try as she might to relax and put the case out of her mind, she couldn't. All she'd been able to think about was Dru Tanner. Wife, mother, daughter. A woman who was loved and needed.

If they couldn't come up with something that would lead them to Dru, her abductor would kill her in seven days.

I'm so sorry, Dru. So sorry this happened to you. Sorry we haven't rescued you. Sorry about whatever hell he's putting you through.

When Nic's house phone rang, she ignored it. Her mother had called twice this morning already. She knew what Mom wanted. She wanted Charles David to come home for a visit, and she thought Nic could persuade him. It was her own damn fault that she hadn't seen her only son in nearly three years. If in the past she had cared a little more about her son's feelings and a little less about pleasing her overbearing, dominating new husband, she wouldn't be estranged from her son now.

I love you, Mom, but I just can't deal with you and your problems right now.

Nic got up, stepped over the paper ring of data spread out on the floor, and took her cup to the kitchen. While rinsing the pot and filter holder, she scolded herself for wishing that her cell phone would ring instead of her house phone. Griff always called her on her cell phone and the infuriating man hadn't called her since they'd parted company in Charlotte two weeks ago.

Fine with her. She didn't want him to call. Didn't need to hear his voice. Had nothing to say to him.

Liar.

She had gotten used to sharing ideas with him, to bouncing her thoughts off him, using him for a sounding board. As absurd as it sounded, they had actually fallen into a routine of thinking out loud with each other. She had never had that with anyone else, except maybe Charles David when they were kids.

So he hasn't called. That's what you wanted, wasn't it— for him to go away and stay away from you and from this investigation? He'd been true to his word. He hadn't interfered, hadn't put in a surprise appearance, hadn't even telephoned.

Sure, you're not upset that he hasn't called.

Admit it, Nic, you miss the man.

She would not admit something that wasn't true. She did not miss him. If she did miss him, it was the way you'd miss a healed cold sore.

Whatever it took, she had to get Griffin Powell off her mind. And she needed a breather from work. What she should do was shower, get dressed, go the mall, do some window shopping, and call a friend for a dinner date.

A friend? Did she still have any of those? Other than the people she worked with, she hadn't taken the time to cultivate any relationships. Not in years. Not since Greg's death.

Nic filled the pot with fresh water, poured it into the coffee-maker, then put in a new filter and added the ground coffee. After flipping the switch to start the brewing process, she returned to the living room, sat down in the middle of the floor, and picked up the photos of Amber Kirby taken at the scene.

She had spoken to Mrs. Landers only a couple of days ago to ask about her grandaughter Maddie, the six-year-old who had discovered Amber's body.

"She still hasn't said more than a few words and she's having nightmares," Mrs. Landers had told her. "But the child psychologist we're taking her to says that it will just take time for her to recover."

Nic could only imagine the trauma to the child. Imagine being six years old and seeing a woman hanging upside down from her bound ankles in a tree in your grandparents' apple orchard. A dead woman. Covered in dried blood. Part of her face missing and her head scalped.

Nic moaned. God, even an adult would have difficulty recovering from something like that. But Maddie was a child, practically a baby.

Murder always had a ripple effect, as practically every event in life did. Every word, every action, even every thought had consequences.

For at least the millionth time, Nic wondered if something she had said or done had contributed to Greg's mental instability. Had she said the wrong thing that morning? Had her long hours and dedication to her job been factors? Hadn't she loved him enough?

She had loved him a great deal when they first married, and had foreseen a bright, successful future ahead for them. They had been a young, up-and-coming, career-oriented couple with government jobs. Greg had been the type of man she'd been looking for, someone sensitive, kind, and supportive, as well as bright and ambitious. Everything had been so perfect that first year. Almost too perfect. They seldom disagreed, never argued.

When had things begun to change?

She couldn't pinpoint a specific time. No one day stood out in her memory as the day her marriage had started falling apart. At first, she had pretended nothing was wrong, had chalked up the subtle hints of trouble to nothing more than both of them being overworked. By the time she had admitted to herself that their marriage was on the rocks, that they needed help, it had been too late.

Oh, Greg, I'm sorry. I'm so very sorry. If only . . .

No, she wouldn't do this to herself. Not again. Definitely not now. There was nothing she could do for Greg, but she still had seven days to save Dru Tanner.

Gasping for air, Dru doubled over and allowed her aching chest a moment of relief. But only a moment. She didn't dare stop for a second longer than absolutely necessary. If he caught her in less than four hours, he would punish her. Oh, God, she didn't think she could bear it. Not again.

She wasn't sure how long she'd been here, the prisoner of a madman. Probably a couple of weeks, although it seemed more like years. The days were endless, spent alone in the woods. Running and hiding, then running some more. And the nights weren't much better, except that she could rest for a few hours, even sleep for a while. He wouldn't allow her to sleep all night. He set an alarm that went off after four hours.

At dawn every morning, he brought her up from the basement and gave her food and water. Less and less each day. Then he took her deep into the woods and released her.

"I'll be back later," he'd told her those first few mornings. "Don't let me catch you too soon. If you don't play the game so we can have fun, I'll have to punish you."

That first day, she had thought she actually had a chance to escape. Even with handcuffs on, she could run. And that's what she'd done—run like crazy. In every direction, seeking any sign of an escape route. But she'd found only more woods. He had returned later and hunted her down.

"Very good," he'd told her. "You managed to elude me during the hunt for over an hour. Tomorrow, you must do that for two hours."

Each day he had increased the length of time he let her

run free, extending the hunt. He had rewarded her with her choice of food and water or a bath, if she managed not to get caught in the allotted amount of time. But if he caught her too quickly, he punished her.

Don't think about it. Don't. Just keep running.

She heard the roar of his dirt bike.

No, no! He's getting close.

Run, run, run!

Griffin and Yvette took an afternoon stroll along the lakeshore. The warm September breeze caressed Yvette's shoulder-length hair that shimmered a striking blue-black in the sunlight. He thought again, as he so often did, what an incredibly beautiful woman Dr. Yvette Meng was. Small. Slender. Exotic. A delicate porcelain doll.

She had paid an exorbitant price because of her rare beauty. York had chosen only the best. The very best. He had searched the world for a woman as unique as Yvette. But he had misjudged his little china doll, mistaking gentleness for meekness.

Griffin had learned from York's mistake—looks can be deceiving.

"It's already autumn." Griff finally spoke after they'd been walking for nearly ten minutes. "It's beautiful here year-round, but in October just looking out my bedroom window can take my breath away."

Yvette smiled. "Sometimes, Griffin, you can be almost poetic." She paused, reached out, and held her hand over his arm, but didn't touch him. "You have a poet's soul and the heart of a warrior."

He stopped, turned, and smiled at her. "There's an old saying—takes one to know one."

"Ah, so it does." She lifted her hand from where it hovered over his arm and then began walking again. "When I was a child, I loved summer. Now, I appreciate each season for what it has to offer."

"Is there advice in that comment?"

"If one chooses to hear the advice, yes. If not . . ."

"There were two Beauty Queen Killers." Griffin kept walking and did not look at Yvette.

She kept in pace with his slow, easy saunter. "I see."

"Special Agent Baxter and I put the pieces together once we saw the ballistics reports and realized that Cary Maygarden had been hit twice, by two different riflemen. I chose not to pursue the matter because of Lindsay and Judd. Nic tried to get someone in the bureau to dig deeper, but when the killings ended with Maygarden's death, there was no other concrete evidence that a second man had been involved."

"And now there is evidence."

"He called us," Griff said. "He's playing a new game and he decided he wanted us to play with him, to be a part of his game."

"Opponents in the age-old war of good versus evil." Yvette stopped as they neared the curve leading to a path that continued around the lake and veered off toward a dilapidated old boathouse on the estate.

"He's killed five women in this new game of his and has kidnapped a sixth." Griff glanced up at the azure sky, bright and clear, with only wisps of fragmented clouds here and there. "He keeps each woman for three weeks, then he puts a bullet in her head and afterward, he scalps her."

Yvette didn't even flinch, but Griff knew that she was not immune to the horror, simply desensitized by past experience. He doubted that anything would shock her.

She held out her hand to him. "May I?" she asked.

He understood that she was asking for permission to take his hand in hers, to touch him. Only a select few knew Yvette's secret talent, one she considered as much a curse as a blessing. She was an empathic psychic. Before he met her, he had never believed such a thing was possible.

Griff held out his hand to her. He trusted Yvette as he trusted only one other human being—Sanders.

She took his hand in hers and closed her eyes. Neither of them spoke for several minutes. Griff felt only the soft warmth of her hand, but he could tell by the tension in Yvette's face that she was experiencing far more.

She released his hand suddenly and stepped away from him. After taking several deep, cleansing breaths, she opened her eyes and stared directly at him. "You fear he is playing a game that is all too familiar to you."

"He calls himself 'the Hunter,' " Griff said.

"And you refer to him as 'the Scalper.' "

Griff nodded.

"You care about her," Yvette said, her voice a mere whisper.

"Who, Nic? No, you're wrong. I don't have any feelings for her. I just got used to having her around, that's all."

"No, that is not all. She is not what you thought she was. You like her."

"She grows on you."

Yvette's full, pink lips tilted ever so slightly in a fragile smile, then the smile quickly faded. "You have been having nightmares again. York has returned to torment you."

"Yeah, and just when I thought he was gone for good, that I had managed to bury him so deep he could never resurface."

"The only power he has over you is the power you give him."

"Don't you think I know that?" Griff hadn't meant to raise his voice, hadn't meant for his words to sound so harsh. "Sorry. I didn't mean—"

She waved her hand in an it-doesn't-matter gesture. "I wish that I had been able to help you more, but I am too close to you, too involved in what happened to be totally objective as a good therapist should be."

"You've helped me plenty."

"If you could have trusted another psychiatrist, he or she might have been able to help you more than I have."

"No." He would never allow anyone else inside his head, would never share that monstrous part of himself with any other human being.

"Exercise more. Meditate more. Talk to Sanders. Talk to me. And go back to work. Become actively involved in this case again."

"I promised Nic—"

"You will work with her, never again in competition against her."

Griff widened his eyes inquisitively. "She's going to hate like hell to see me show up again."

"I would not be so sure of that."

"Is that some sort of psychic revelation?"

"Actually, it is simply woman's intuition."

Griff chuckled.

"Can you stay a few days?" he asked.

"I will stay as long as you need me."

"We could take one of the boats out tomorrow and cruise downriver. Sanders and Barbara Jean could go with us."

"That sounds lovely. If it is what you would like to do, then we will—"

"What I want is to find the Scalper before he kills another woman." Griff curled his hands into tight fists. "I want him dead so that he can never torture anyone else. I want his rotten soul to burn in hell."

"Along with York's wicked soul." Without asking permission this time, she reached out and took Griff's right hand in hers and slowly, gently unfolded his fist, then did the same with his left hand. "York has no power. You are the one with all the power. Don't give him any."

"Why won't he stay dead?"

"Because you keep bringing him back to life. Only you can make his death permanent."

Damar Sanders stood on the patio alone and looked out at the peaceful lake. He had approved of the choice Griffin had made when he picked this land on which to build his home. Not only was the estate secluded, but the location was serene and peaceful. After so many years of struggle and turbulence, of fighting to survive and reinvent themselves, they had needed a tranquil sanctuary.

He did his best to never think of those years, but a man had only so much control over his thoughts. Even the strongest person could hold the floodwaters at bay for only so long. When the darkness washed over him, he had learned that the only way to come through it and into the light on the other side was to face what he feared most.

Griffin knew that was what he, too, must do. And Yvette would help him.

Some battles had to be fought again and again, the same enemy vanquished repeatedly. And with each victory, the enemy grew weaker. Perhaps someday *he* would become so weak that he could no longer wage war.

Damar had once loved and been loved. By his parents. By his wife. He had lived a good life, had been a proud man, had been greatly blessed.

"Damar . . . Damar . . ." For a brief moment, he thought that the soft feminine voice calling to him belonged to Elora.

"I am here," he replied and turned to warmly greet Barbara Jean Hughes. She was a lovely woman, only a few years younger than his Elora would be now, and with the same vibrant red hair and pensive dark eyes. The physical resemblance between the two women was minor, but the gentleness of Barbara Jean's spirit was almost identical to Elora's.

"I thought we were going to play chess," she said.

"Yes, of course, we are."

She wheeled her chair farther out onto the patio, then halted several feet from him. "I don't mean to pry," she said. "But you and Griffin have been awfully quiet all day, ever since Dr. Meng arrived. Is everything all right?"

He walked over to Barbara Jean, leaned down in front of her wheelchair, and looked into her eyes as he took both of her hands in his. "You mustn't be concerned about Griffin or me. Griffin is worried about this new case, the Scalper murders. And when Griffin worries, I worry."

"And when you and Griffin worry, Yvette Meng shows up."

"Griffin telephoned her."

"She's a beautiful woman," Barbara Jean said. "I know that you . . . you and Griffin both care about her."

"We love Yvette," Damar said. "She is our sister. Do you understand?"

"I understand the concept," she told him. "But unless you choose to explain your past relationship with her—"

"The past is not only my past. I share it with Griffin and Yvette. I cannot share it with you or anyone else unless they, too, are willing for me to speak of it."

She squeezed his hands and smiled, then leaned forward and kissed his cheek. "I don't need to know all there is to know about you. You're a good man. And you're my friend, as is Griffin. I don't like to see either of you unhappy."

"Playing chess with you, my dear Barbara Jean, will make me happy." He stood, moved behind her wheelchair, and grasped the handlebars. Indeed, spending time with her made him exceedingly happy. It did not matter whether they played chess, prepared a meal together, or simply sat quietly and listened to music.

Until Barbara Jean came to Griffin's Rest over a year ago, a woman alone and frightened of the monster who had brutally murdered her sister, Damar had thought he would never care for another woman in the way he had cared for Elora. But day by day, week by week, month by month, as she worked for the Powell Agency and gradually recovered from her ordeal, he had come to know Barbara Jean for the special lady she was. And he had slowly fallen in love with her.

She did not know his true feelings for her.

For now, it was enough that they were friends.

Dru tripped over a dead tree limb that lay across her escape path. Tumbling forward, she held out her arms, trying to break her fall. But her weak limbs gave way to the weight of her battered body and she fell flat on her face.

No, God, please . . .

Get up, damn it, get up. Run. He's close. So close.

But her tired, weak arms and legs refused to cooperate. The earth was cool, the bed of dried leaves soft beneath her. She wanted to rest, to curl up and sleep for hours.

She was so tired.

The deadly roar of the dirt bike alerted her that he was almost upon her, too near for her to escape. But if he caught her, he would punish her. No, no, she couldn't bear another night in the cage or another day without food.

"Game's end," his soft, menacing voice called out to her, as if echoing from a great distance.

She managed to lift herself to her knees.

When she looked up, he stood less than ten feet away, a scowl on his face, his rifle pointing directly at her. She struggled to stand, but didn't have the strength. Dropping back down on her knees, she stared at him, a mixture of sweat and tears clouding her vision.

"It's almost over," he told her. "Just a few more moves in the game and then the conclusion."

"Please, don't . . . don't kill me. I have a child. A little girl who needs me."

"Oh, poor Dru, so pitiful."

Before she realized what he intended to do, he fired the rifle. The bullet hit her in the shoulder. Crying out in pain, she clutched her shoulder as she doubled over. Blood gushed through her grimy fingers.

"Just a few more shots, just a little more suffering, and our game will be concluded."

Game! That's all this had been to him. Her life meant nothing to him. The fact that she had a child, a husband . . . He didn't care. She wasn't a woman to her captor, not even a human being. She was nothing more than his prey.

He shot her in the opposite shoulder. She fell forward onto the ground, the pain unbearable, and yet she had no choice but to bear it.

Two more bullets entered her body in rapid succession as he marched steadily toward her. One shot entered the back of her left calf and the other the side of her right thigh.

When she was on the verge of passing out from the agonizing pain, he reached down, jerked her up by her hair until she was on her knees again. Then as she toppled over, he shot her for the final time.

Pudge leaned his rifle against a nearby tree, then using his foot, he rolled Dru over and inspected his kill. Bending down, he grabbed a handful of her silky, auburn red hair, blood from the wound in the back of her head still sticky and wet matted against her scalp. He ran his fingers through her damp hair. And smiled.

He removed the Razar knife from its leather sheath attached to his belt. The carbon steel blade shimmered like molten silver in the afternoon sunlight. He took his time removing her scalp, savoring every second, memorizing the exhilarating feel of ultimate victory so that he could relive these heady moments over and over again.

Chapter 14

The call came in at nine fifty-three on a cloudy, dreary morning in October. Nic had flown into Charlotte two days before for a conference with Betty Schonrock, the local police chief, county sheriff, and the mayor. Everyone had been holding their breaths, waiting, and hoping that, against all odds, Dru Tanner's body wouldn't show up somewhere in the area approximately three weeks after she had disappeared. Just outside Charlotte, off Interstate 85, near the Catawba River, two retirees on their way for a day of leisurely fishing discovered a body hanging upside down from a tree limb.

The dispatcher who had taken the call, after obtaining vital information from the elderly fisherman, realized the significance of the discovery. Two deputies had arrived on the scene less than ten minutes before the county sheriff and twenty minutes before Nic and Betty managed to make it through the downtown and interstate traffic.

The deputies had effectively secured the scene and although a small group of onlookers had congregated, thanks to the semiisolated location, crowd control wasn't an immediate concern. Nic worked with Sheriff Painter, who acknowledged that Nic was in charge and actually seemed relieved that the FBI would be involved.

"She's one of the Scalper's victims, isn't she? She's that Tanner woman he kidnapped a few weeks ago," The sheriff had shaken his head. "Y'all have to find this guy."

The scene was photographed and videotaped, per Nic's orders. The medical examiner requested a few more photos. He checked the body for stiffness, moving the jaw, neck, and eyelids, as well as the arms.

"She's been dead for a while," he said. "Probably close to twenty-four hours."

They photographed the rope cords and all the lacerations and bruising on the body before taking it down from the tree limb. The rope binding her feet was photographed before being cut in a manner that preserved the knots.

Nic studied the corpse and, from the photographs her family had provided, she recognized the woman, despite the horrid condition her face and body were in now. A butterfly tattoo on the woman's left ankle cinched the ID for Nic.

She tried not to think about Dru Tanner's husband and child. She motioned for the examiner to continue with his work. He loosely covered the woman's head, feet, and hands with bags and closed them off with tape, then bagged the body.

The woman. The corpse. The victim. Nic tried to think of her that way, but she couldn't forget the fact that this was Dru Tanner, wife, mother, and daughter. She was only thirty years old. She should have had another fifty or so years ahead of her.

Doing her best to focus on the job at hand and not on this one victim's personal history, Nic put her emotions aside and did what had to be done. Not that she'd ever been the overly emotional type. She wasn't a cry-me-a-river kind of woman. The last time she'd gone on a crying jag had been about a month after Greg's funeral. One night, as she'd been preparing her dinner, she had broken down and cried for hours.

On the way back to Charlotte, Nic thought about exactly what she would say when she held the next press conference. She needed time, but she couldn't put off speaking to the press for more than a few hours.

"We should set up a press conference for this afternoon," Nic had told Betty. "Three o'clock. But first, we have to speak to Dru's husband."

And I need to contact Griff.

The press probably already had hold of the news that a body had been found, and that in all likelihood, it was Dru Tanner. The sheriff had sent a couple of deputies to ask Brian Tanner to identify the body. Nic wanted to be there when Mr. Tanner arrived to make sure he was protected from reporters.

Griff was on his way to the airstrip that afternoon when Nic called him. He hadn't seen her or spoken to her in three weeks.

"Hello, Nic."

"I suppose you already know."

"Yeah."

"I called the first chance I got."

"Sure."

"I'm holding a press conference in an hour. I wanted to make sure you knew beforehand."

"I'm coming to Charlotte. Today."

"I figured you would."

"I'll try to keep a low profile," he told her.

"I'd appreciate that."

"Have dinner with me tonight."

"Griff, I . . . uh . . . I'm not—"

"We have to talk sooner or later. We both have to eat

tonight. And we know he'll call both of us again. If not today, then tomorrow or the next day."

"Okay. Dinner tonight. Seven thirty. Someplace out of the way."

"Don't want to be seen with me, Special Agent Baxter?"

"I don't want to be harassed by reporters trying to get a scoop."

"We can have dinner in my hotel suite," he said. "That is, if you trust me not to seduce you."

"You could *try*."

"Only if you wanted me to."

"I don't."

"Then I won't."

"Where are you staying?" Nic asked.

"The Westin, downtown on South College Street."

"I'll see you tonight."

"Yeah."

After Nic ended their conversation by simply hanging up, Griff contacted Sanders and gave him instructions concerning dinner tonight in his hotel suite. Knowing she liked steak, he decided to go with shrimp and steak and all the trimmings. He didn't need to go into detail with Sanders. Everything the man did was done to perfection.

Griff suspected that Nic needed a night off more than she realized. She'd probably been skipping meals, eating junk, and existing on a few hours' sleep each night. He had no doubt that she'd been pushing herself as hard as humanly possible and probably thinking that not being able to rescue Dru Tanner was somehow her fault.

The lady definitely needed someone to take care of her.

Griff smiled to himself. If he dared to say something like that to her, she'd take a couple of inches off his hide. Nic needed to think of herself as strong and tough, a woman who didn't need to lean on anyone.

But there are times in life when we all need someone. No

matter how strong, how competent and in control a person was, no one was invincible.

Why he had chosen himself to be Nic's temporary shoulder to lean on, he wasn't sure. He might not be the only man who understood how badly she needed someone, but he'd lay odds that he was the only man brave enough for the job.

Pudge had taken Interstate 77 to Columbia, South Carolina, and checked into a no-name motel southwest of the city, where he planned to spend the night before heading out in the morning for Atlanta. Once there, he would turn in one rented vehicle, take a taxi across town, and then rent another, using different fake ID. There was no way anyone could find him. He was always careful and always covered his tracks.

Late yesterday he and his oversize travel trunk had arrived in Spartanburg, South Carolina, on a chartered jet. Upon his arrival, a rented SUV had been waiting. He had driven straight toward Charlotte and took the route he had mapped out before leaving home. After finding the back road leading into a wooded area near the Catawba River, everything else had been simple. He had chosen the nearest large tree with low branches, then shoved the trunk out the back of the SUV, removed Dru Tanner's bloody body from the trunk, and dragged it across the ground. Leaving her body by the tree, he had gone back to the trunk and taken out the small expandable ladder he'd brought with him and proceeded to hang Dru by her bound feet to a sturdy branch. By the time he had accomplished his task, he'd been sweating profusely and huffing like a freight train. But he'd been smiling.

Mission accomplished.

He had spent the night at a motel outside town, gotten

up at six, showered and put on clean underwear, but had dressed in the same clothes and used the same disguise. He'd eaten breakfast at a fast-food restaurant, but only because he was extremely hungry. Nothing short of being ravenous could have induced him to eat such mediocre food.

If all went as planned, he would drive from Atlanta to Chattanooga and from there to Memphis, where he would take a commercial flight to Baton Rouge.

He would go home.

He needed time before he made his next move, before he upped the ante, so to speak. The next woman he had chosen to play his game would be easy prey because, like all the others, she would not be expecting him.

After stacking the pillows from both double beds against the headboard of one bed, Pudge snuggled into the downy nest, stretched out, and tapped the number he knew by heart into the prepaid cell phone.

She answered on the third ring.

"Hello."

"Hello, Nicole. Did you find the little present I left for you?"

Silence.

"I saw your press conference on TV," he told her. "And, no, I'm not still in Charlotte."

She wasn't responding to anything he said. Apparently, she was upset with him. Ah, poor darling. She was no doubt frustrated because she and Griff hadn't been able to save Dru Tanner.

"I don't like it that the press is referring to me as 'the Scalper.' I told you that in this game, I am 'the Hunter.' I expect you to correct the mistake."

"Tough shit."

"Ah, now, now, Nicole. Such language from a lady."

Silence.

"I'm not going to give you another clue until you do that one little thing for me. If you do something for me, then I'll do something for you. Isn't that fair?"

"You don't know the meaning of the word 'fair,' you son of a bitch."

"There you go, cursing again. Shame on you."

She groaned.

"Once I know that you're playing by the rules—my rules—I'll give you another clue. But not until then."

He hung up, tossed the phone to the foot of the bed, and closed his eyes. He pictured Nicole as she had looked at today's press conference. Neatly dressed in khaki slacks, white shirt, and navy blazer. The afternoon sunlight had hit her sable hair at just the right angle, setting it afire with shimmering highlights. Although she looked tired, as if she'd lost sleep, she had been beautiful. Like an Amazonian goddess. The man who conquered her would have to be a fearless warrior.

A hunter who would make her his prey.

After settling into his suite at the downtown Westin, Griffin removed his suit, shaved for the second time today, and changed into slacks and a casual knit shirt. Just as he set up his laptop computer, his cell phone rang.

Was Nic canceling their dinner plans? Had she gotten cold feet?

Griffin checked the caller ID. It wasn't Nic.

"Hello, Griffin," the now-familiar voice said.

"Well, if it isn't the Scalper."

"You delight in going against my wishes, don't you, Griffin?"

"I *delight* in anything that pisses you off."

"For all your wealth and sophistication, you really have no breeding. You came from trash, didn't you? Weren't both of your grandfathers Tennessee sharecroppers?" When Griff didn't react, the caller continued. "What's that old saying about you can take the boy out of the country, but you can't take the country out of the boy?"

"I prefer the old saying about what goes around, comes around."

"Do you indeed?"

"Why are you calling? Not simply to chat."

"Are you hoping for a new clue?"

"I'm hoping a grizzly bear tears you from limb to limb. Slowly and painfully, and eats you for dinner."

"My goodness, you do have a morbid sense of humor."

"Just say what you have to say and be done with it," Griff told him.

"I've chosen my next victim."

Griff tensed. *God help us.*

"She's very special."

"Aren't they all special?" Griff asked.

"Of course they are, but not the way she is. She will be my prize trophy. I expect the hunt will be exhilarating every day. She won't go down without a hell of a fight."

"I don't have time to listen to this crap," Griff told him. "Either give me the next clue or—"

"Patience, patience. Once Nicole does as she's been told, I'll call both of you again and give you each your clues."

Dead silence. The bastard had hung up.

Griff laid the phone beside his laptop, walked across the room, and retrieved a beer from the minibar.

Out there somewhere was another potential victim, going about her life as usual, without the slightest idea that she had been chosen to play a murderous game with a crazed killer. And time was running out for her.

As Nic knocked on the door of Griff's suite, she wondered what she was doing here. She had agreed to have dinner, in his hotel room, with one of the most notorious playboys in the country. In the past, she wouldn't have been caught dead alone with Griffin Powell. And yet, here she was on his doorstep and actually looking forward to seeing him. Dear God, she *had* lost her mind, or what little mind she had left. That had to be it. Lack of sleep, stress, and brain-numbing frustration had created this lapse in her normally good judgment.

On the verge of talking herself into turning around and running back to the elevator, Nic gasped when Griff opened the door. She stared up at him. Her mouth dropped open. Damn him for looking so good. It wasn't right for a man to be that ruggedly handsome and filthy rich, too.

"Come on in." He stepped aside so that she could enter.

She hesitated for half a minute, then blew out a deep breath and stepped over the threshold, feeling very much like a martyr being tossed into a lion's den. When she noted that the lights were all on, that there was no soft music playing, and that there wasn't a bottle of champagne in sight, she relaxed just a little.

"I've ordered dinner," he told her as he closed the door and joined her in the lounge. "It should arrive within the next five or ten minutes."

She nodded, then surveyed the room. "This is nice."

"Have a seat."

She chose a single chair, just on the off chance that if she'd sat on the couch, he would have sat beside her.

"Care for a beer?" he asked.

"No, thank you."

He sat on the sofa, leisurely crossed his legs, and studied her closely. "Relax, honey. You're safe with me. This is business tonight. Besides, you're not my type."

"Oh, I know this is a business dinner." Why should she care that she wasn't his type? She should be relieved that he didn't find her attractive. So why had his comment bothered her so much? "You're not my type, either." *That's it, Nic, you tell him.*

"Well, now that we have that settled—"

"He called me this afternoon, after the press conference," she blurted out. "He doesn't like it that the press is referring to him as 'the Scalper' instead of 'the Hunter.' "

"Yeah, I know. He phoned me, too."

"I figured he might have." She nervously rubbed her hands together. "He doesn't intend to give us any more clues until I issue a statement to the press in which I refer to him as 'the Hunter.' "

"He's really hung up on terminology. Considering what he does to these women, we could just as easily refer to him as 'the Shooter,' 'the Hangman,' 'the Tormentor,' 'the Abductor,' or half a dozen other terms, but he doesn't see himself as any of those. In his mind, in this game of his, he is 'the Hunter.' That's what it's all about—the hunt. He's playing a psychological game as well as a physical game. God only knows what each day of the hunt involves, what kind of rules he demands that his prey follows."

"Each day of the hunt?" Nic asked. "Did he say something about—"

"He told me that he's chosen his next victim, that she's special, and that he expects the hunt will be exhilarating every day."

"Do you think that means he hunts them every day during the three weeks that they're missing?"

"Probably. But we'd already come to the conclusion, from the autopsy reports, that these women were exposed to some pretty harsh conditions." Griff paused briefly, then cleared his throat. "I think it's a pretty good bet that he's releasing these women in a place he thinks of as some sort of hunting ground, and then he stalks them, hunts them, and . . . All we know for sure is that in the end, he shoots them, again and again. In the legs, the arms, the shoulders and, finally, the head."

Nic pressed her open palms across her cheeks, then slid her fingertips up to her temples and rubbed in a circular motion.

"Headache?" Griff asked.

With her eyes half-closed to barely open slits, she sighed. "It hit me right after the press conference. I took a couple of aspirin and that helped some, but it won't go away."

"If you'd let me, I could—"

The knock on the door interrupted Griff midsentence. Nic breathed a sigh of relief. If he had offered to give her another neck and head massage, she wasn't sure she would have turned him down.

Griff opened the door to allow the waiter to serve their dinner. He wheeled in a large cart filled with a variety of items, then transported everything from the cart to the table.

"Would you like for me to open the wine, sir?" the waiter asked.

Griff nodded.

The waiter opened the bottle, poured a small amount into one of the glasses, and handed the flute to Griff. He sniffed the wine, took a sip, savored it on his tongue, then swallowed. He nodded to the waiter, placed his glass back on the serving cart, and signed the room service bill while the waiter filled both glasses.

As soon as the waiter left, Griff pulled out a chair at the dining table. "Dinner is served."

Nic walked across the lounge to the table and allowed Griff to assist her. He whipped off the silver covers on their plates to reveal steaks, shrimp, baked potatoes, and asparagus smothered in a rich, creamy cheese sauce.

"I hope this is all right," Griff said.

"Oh, God, it's wonderful. I didn't realize how hungry I was until just now."

Grinning, Griff sat down across from her, unfolded his napkin, placed it in his lap, and glanced at Nic as he lifted his knife and fork. "I didn't order salads because I was afraid you'd eat the salad and claim you were full. I know how women are about eating a decent meal."

"Not this woman," Nic told him as she grabbed her knife and fork.

Griff laughed. "I wasn't sure about dessert, so I ordered a variety tray."

An hour later, with their meal eaten, every one of the six desserts taste-tested and two-thirds of the wine gone, Nic sauntered back into the lounge and sat on the sofa. Griff refilled their wineglasses and brought them with him. He handed Nic hers, then sat down beside her, lifted his feet, and rested them on the coffee table.

"Why don't we put off any more business talk until tomorrow?" Griff suggested. "You need to relax tonight and—"

"I thought tonight was strictly business."

"It is. The business of helping Nicole Baxter rejuvenate." He spread his arm out on the sofa back behind her. "You push yourself too hard. Why, honey? What are you trying to prove?"

Nic looked down into the wineglass, deliberately avoiding eye contact with Griff. "You think I'm some angry, militant feminist, don't you?"

"I never said—"

"Well, I'm not." She snapped her head up and glared at him. "You don't know me. You don't have any idea who I am and what I think and how I feel."

"You're right. I don't."

Her gaze locked with his, neither of them able to look away.

"Our relationship was much easier when I didn't like you," Nic told him. "I've judged you just as harshly as you've judged me and as much as I hate to admit it, I've probably been as wrong about you as you have about me."

"Watch out, Special Agent Baxter, you're on the verge of being nice to me."

Nic smiled, then glanced away. "Thank you for dinner."

"You're welcome," he said, then asked, "How's the headache?"

"What headache?" She sighed. "It must have been a hunger headache. Either that or a stress headache. Either way, it's gone now, thanks to the lovely, relaxing meal we just shared." She saluted him with her glass. "And the wine helped."

"You can't drive to your hotel now," he said.

"You aren't suggesting that I spend the night here, are you?"

"Not here with me. This is a one-bedroom suite. But I can arrange a room for you here and—"

"Or I could take a taxi back to my hotel."

"Stay here. We can finish off the bottle of wine, talk a while longer, and get to know each other a little better. Maybe get rid of a few more of our preconceived notions about each other. Then, in the morning, we can have breakfast together and if you'll let me, I'll tag along with you tomorrow."

"Ah, now the real reason you're being so nice comes out. You've been buttering me up."

"You caught me."

She should be angry with him, but she wasn't. She should get up right now and leave. She didn't.

"I'll stay," she told him. "In the hotel, not in your bedroom."

Griff nodded, then got up to make a phone call.

"Where's the restroom?" she asked.

He pointed the direction, then turned his attention to whoever was on the other end of the line.

When she came out of the bathroom, she found him waiting for her back on the sofa. And she noticed that he had topped off their wine.

"You have a room booked for tonight, just down the hall," he told her.

"Thank you."

"Sit." He patted the sofa cushion. "We'll talk."

"I'm fading fast," she admitted. "I'm not sure how much longer I can make it without falling asleep. Maybe I'd better say good night."

"The bellman should be up here with your key shortly and then I'll walk you to your door."

She sat down beside Griff. "I see why so many women find you irresistible."

"Why is that?" He leaned toward her.

"Because you're very charming. And you have a knack for making a woman feel special."

"You are special, Nicki."

They each leaned toward the other until they were face-to-face, only a couple of inches separating them. Was he going to kiss her? Did she want him to?

When the bellman knocked on the door, Nic gasped and jerked back. And when Griff went to get the key from the bellman, she jumped up and met him before he reentered the lounge.

"I should go," she told him.

He cupped her elbow. "I'll walk you to—"

"No! No, thank you. Just give me the key. I'm fine on my own." She held out her hand.

He laid the plastic keycard in her hand, then folded her fingers over it. Her gaze moved from where he cupped his big hand over her fingers up to his face. "Order breakfast for seven, will you? We can talk more then. I'm sure we'll both be more levelheaded after a good night's sleep."

Chapter 15

Nic had stayed in Charlotte for several days after Dru Tanner's body had been discovered, and while she'd continued with the investigation, she had waited for the Scalper to call again.

He hadn't called.

True to his word, Griff had kept a low profile while they were in Charlotte. He'd done his best to avoid the press and although he'd shadowed her every move, he hadn't interfered in any way.

When she'd decided to return to D.C. and Griff had offered the use of his jet, she had refused at first.

But then he'd said, "I thought we were friends now."

"Not friends," she'd corrected him. "Friendly acquaintances."

"How about friendly colleagues?"

"Acquaintances." She would not agree that they were colleagues. She was a federal agent, an authorized law enforcement officer. He was a private detective, one who often used his wealth, power, and notoriety to bend the rules to suit himself.

He'd nodded, but hadn't verbally concurred with her assessment of their relationship. So, they'd left it at that. But she had flown to D.C. on his jet today, and they had once again kept their conversation focused on business.

"He's not going to call again until he gets what he wants, is he?" she'd asked Griff.

"It's been nearly a week and so far, he hasn't contacted either of us with a clue. And as far as we know he hasn't abducted another woman, but we can't be certain about that."

"I should probably issue a press release that refers to him as 'the Hunter,' then wait and see what happens. But it galls me to give in to his demand."

"Yeah, I know. Unfortunately, for now, it looks like we'll have to keep playing by his rules. He needs to think he's more powerful than either of us."

"Or the two of us combined."

Four hours ago, they had landed in D.C. and she'd gone straight to the office and put together a press release. Then she and Griff had driven to her home in Woodbridge.

How long would it take the press release to hit the airwaves? Immediately? Tonight? Tomorrow? When would the Hunter learn that he'd won this round, that Nic had given him what he wanted?

Neither she nor Griff had discussed him staying in the D.C. area overnight, and when he had gone home with her, neither of them had mentioned anything about when he'd leave. She had ordered pizza for supper and they'd laughed when they realized they both preferred thin crust, loaded with a variety of meats and smothered in black olives.

They kicked back in her living room, sitting on the floor as each of them finished off a second beer and eyed the one piece of loaded pizza left on the coffee table.

"We could share it," Griff suggested.

She waved her hands back and forth. "No, no, you eat it. I had three huge pieces and I certainly don't need any more."

"Well, if you insist." Griff lifted the luscious, cheese-smothered piece, brought it to his mouth, grinned at her, and then took a big bite.

Nic studied Griff as he ate. If anyone had told her a few months ago that she and Griff would ever be on friendly terms, she'd have thought them insane. She had spent years disliking the man. Disliking? Change that to practically despising. And there wasn't a doubt in her mind that the feeling had been mutual. They couldn't breathe the same air without wanting to strangle each other.

So what had changed?

She hadn't. And neither had he. They were both the same two people they'd always been.

"What?" he asked as he finished off the last bite of pizza and picked up his bottle of beer.

"Huh?"

"You're looking at me funny," he told her. "Do I have tomato sauce on my face or bits of meat between my teeth?"

"No. I was just thinking how strange this is—the two of us sitting in my living room floor, sharing pizza and beer."

"Friendly colleagues and friendly acquaintances do things like this."

"Yes, I know, but that's what makes this slightly weird—up until a couple of months ago, you and I could barely have a civil conversation."

Griff smiled. "Ten weeks ago everything changed when we received those first phone calls. Odd as it sounds, I suppose we can thank the Scalper—uh, the Hunter—for forcing us to work together and giving us a chance to get to know each other."

"There are things about you that I still don't like," Nic told him with brutal honesty.

He laughed. "Same here."

"And I suppose you know that I've been getting some ribbing from my colleagues at the bureau about our relationship."

"Good-natured ribbing, I hope."

"Yes, but . . ." She could hardly tell Griff that more than one of her coworkers had implied that she had succumbed to the legendary Powell charm.

"But?"

"Nothing." She got up off the floor. "I want something for dessert. I think I have some shortbread cookies in the pantry."

Griff reached up and grabbed her hand. She looked down at him.

"It bothers you that someone might think we're sleeping together, doesn't it? But it shouldn't. We're both single, both consenting adults, and it's really nobody's business."

She yanked her hand from his. "You do know that you have a rather notorious reputation when it comes to women?"

"I've never been one to kiss and tell," Griff said.

"No, but apparently some of the women you've *kissed* have been."

"Nic?"

"Let's drop it, okay? I'm going to get those cookies." She headed toward the kitchen. "Want another beer?"

"No, thanks. I'm fine."

She rushed out of the living room, more to get away from Griff than any urgent need for cookies. Once in the kitchen, she blew out a deep breath and called herself an idiot for bringing up the subject of their relationship. They were friendly acquaintances, but that was it. No romance. No sex.

She opened the pantry, searched for the cookies, saw them, grabbed the box, and turned around—right into Griff's hard chest.

She gasped when she collided with him.

He was way too close, their bodies touching.

"You do know that you can trust me, don't you, Nic?"

She swallowed. She could handle Griffin Powell at arm's length, but up close and personal like this, she wasn't so sure. The drumming roar of her heartbeat thundered through her head and a rush of excitement surged through her body. She felt a tightening sensation between her thighs.

"I'm not your type, remember?" she told him.

"And I'm not your type, am I?"

"No. You're not."

"Then we're in agreement," he said. "I'm not your type and you're not mine. There are things you don't like about me and things I don't like about you. You're not the least bit impressed with my reputation or my money and I'm not impressed by your ball-bashing reputation. Maybe that's why I find you so fascinating."

"You find me fascinating?" She couldn't breathe. If he touched her . . .

"Utterly fascinating. And quite an enigma. You're an aggressive, independent lady and a tough-as-nails federal agent, yet you're completely feminine." He reached up and caressed her cheek, then ran his fingertips down her neck. "And all woman."

She knew that if she didn't stop him, he would kiss her. And if he kissed her, they would make love.

"It'll just be sex," she told him.

"Sure, honey. Whatever you say."

He kissed her. Slowly. Tenderly. Taking his time. Brushing his lips over hers. Nipping at her bottom lip. Outlining her mouth with his tongue before plunging inside.

Stop him now, before it's too late.

But she didn't stop him.

She lifted her arms up and around his neck as she pressed her breasts against his chest. One advantage of being five ten was that even though she couldn't stand eye to eye with a guy who was six four, he didn't tower over her, either. And their bodies aligned oh so right. Almost perfectly.

When he deepened the kiss, he eased his hands down her back and cupped her buttocks. He forced her lower body intimately against his.

He was hard.

She was wet.

They were both ready.

She ended the kiss, gulped in air, and said breathlessly, "We won't pretend this is something it's not."

She grabbed his face between her open palms and kissed him. Ravaged him. He reciprocated, giving back as good as he got.

God, how she wanted this. Needed this.

They went at each other, touching, kissing, licking, and tearing at each other's clothes. She managed to get his shirt over his head, leaving his chest bare. While she worked on his belt, he unbuttoned her blouse, spread it apart, and grabbed her hands. Holding her wrists to either side of her, he lowered his head and placed his mouth over one taut nipple. She shivered when his hot mouth touched her breast.

"Bed." She managed to get out the one word.

He groaned, then allowed her to lead him out of the kitchen. They made it to the living room before he kissed her again. After that, she was lost. He shoved her onto the sofa and hurriedly removed her jeans and panties while she tossed her open blouse and bra on the floor. He helped her loosen his belt and unzip his pants. Within seconds, the remainder of his clothing joined hers on the carpet.

No soft music. No candlelight. No sweet words of love. Just raw passion.

But that's what Nic wanted. What she needed.

It was what it was—sex.

Griff came down over her. She took him into her arms

as he kissed her. She raked her nails down his back, over his spine, and across his firm ass. When he sucked one nipple and then the other, she bucked up, asking him to take her. He lifted her hips to meet his thrust. Nic cried out with sheer pleasure when he lunged into her hard and deep.

In the frenzy of their lovemaking, they toppled off the sofa and onto the floor, but they barely noticed. Nothing mattered except the release they both sought.

Their need was too great, the heat between them too scorching, their bodies far too hungry for satisfaction to make the experience last. Nic came first, every nerve in her body screaming glory hallelujah as her muscles shivered with pleasure.

As if her climax triggered his, Griff growled a deep, throaty groan when he jetted into her. With his big body shaking, he collapsed on top of her, then quickly rolled off her and took her with him, pulling her close.

She lay there, her heartbeat thumping loudly in her ears, her body damp, and her skin sensitive to the touch.

It was just sex, she reminded herself. But it was damn good sex.

Griff ran his hand over her hip. She shuddered. He kissed her shoulder.

"Okay?" he asked.

"Better than okay," she told him truthfully.

"Satisfied?"

She lifted herself up, braced her elbow on the floor, and turned to him. "Very satisfied."

"We didn't use any kind of protection," he said, his voice low and quiet.

"Yeah, I know. We're idiots." She looked him right in the eye. "I don't do stuff like this—unplanned, unprotected sex. I'm not on the pill."

He reached up and skimmed his fingertips across her

cheek and down her throat, stopping at the top curve of her right breast. She sucked in air.

"I keep condoms in my travel kit," he told her.

"Always prepared, huh? I suppose you have to be, considering how many women throw themselves at you."

Nic suddenly felt embarrassed. She wanted to kick her own butt for being so reckless. She'd just had unprotected sex with an infamous womanizer.

She pulled away from Griff and stood up, intending to go to the bathroom. Before she got two feet away from him, he jumped up and grabbed her from behind. He wrapped his arms around her and nuzzled her neck.

"My reputation with the ladies is grossly exaggerated," he whispered in her ear. "I don't screw every woman who throws herself at me. I do have affairs, mostly brief affairs, but I don't bed-hop. While I'm in a relationship, no matter how brief, I don't sleep around."

"And you usually use protection?" She didn't try to jerk away from him; she liked the feel of his arms around her far too much.

"Would you believe me if I told you that I always use protection, that it's been a long, long time since I did something like this?"

She turned in his arms. "I've never done something like this."

"We got carried away with the moment. It happens. I don't want you to feel guilty about it or worry that you might be pregnant."

Nic closed her eyes. Pregnant? Merciful Lord!

Her entire body went stiff.

He grasped her shoulders and shook her gently. "Nic?"

"I don't feel guilty," she told him. "And I doubt that I'm pregnant. But if, God forbid, I am, I'll deal with it."

He ran his hands down her arms, then released her, but he

didn't say anything. Did that mean he was okay with what she'd told him? He probably assumed she meant that if she was pregnant, she'd get an abortion.

"I don't want to play against the odds more than once," she told him. "If you're going to spend the night, you'd better get those condoms out of your travel kit."

Griff reached out, grabbed her, and yanked her naked body against his. He lowered his head, kissed her, and said, "I'm going to spend the whole weekend here with you, if you'll let me."

"If that's the case, then we'd better run into town tomorrow to pick up groceries and a big box of condoms."

"Lady, I like the way you think."

Griff woke slowly, languidly, feeling good. He opened his eyes, intending to see if Nic was awake, but what he saw was that her side of the bed was empty. She was probably in the bathroom or possibly in the kitchen putting on coffee.

He kicked back the covers and stretched. They'd had sex twice during the night, bringing the total to three times. Not bad for a guy who'd soon turn forty. And he had a morning hard-on that he intended to take care of as soon as he could bring Nic back to bed.

"Nic?" he called. "Where are you, honey?"

Silence.

Griff sat up, turned, and put his feet down on the floor. "Nic?"

No response.

Hmm . . . He didn't hear the shower running. Maybe she was in the kitchen and couldn't hear him.

He got up, intending to search for her and for his scattered clothing; then he noticed that someone—no doubt Nic—had gathered up his discarded clothes, folded them neatly and stacked them on the top of the dresser. His shoes, socks stuffed inside, were sitting beside his clothes. He carefully removed his slacks and headed for the bathroom, where he'd left his travel kit last night.

After he showered, shaved, and slipped on his slightly wrinkled slacks, he wondered why Nic hadn't checked on him. All he could figure out was that she must be preparing breakfast. If so, that was another unexpected aspect of her personality. He'd never thought of her as the domestic type.

When he entered the kitchen, he found it empty. He noted the pot on the coffeemaker was almost full and two mugs sat on the counter. No sugar. No cream. They both took their coffee black. There had been a time when he had sweetened his coffee, but as a guy grew older, he had to think about his waistline.

As he poured himself a cup of coffee, he was puzzled by Nic's absence. Then he noticed the note attached to the refrigerator door with a plastic magnet.

He removed the note and read:

Gone for my morning walk. Back soon. Coffee ready. You prepare breakfast. Surprise me. Nic.

Griff chuckled. Surprise her, huh? He had no idea how long she'd been gone or how quickly she would return. At most, a morning walk shouldn't take more than thirty to forty-five minutes, right? He didn't have any time to waste, so he made three hurried phone calls.

Twenty-five minutes later, Jonathan showed up with Griff's garment bag that he'd left on the plane, and no sooner had Griff dressed in jeans, a long-sleeved cotton sweater, and loafers, than the breakfast he had ordered arrived. He had learned over the years that enough money could get a man just about anything he wanted. If he wanted breakfast catered at a moment's notice, all he had to do was offer twice the normal rate, plus a bonus to the delivery person.

He placed the hot dishes in the oven to keep warm, the cold items in the refrigerator, and the variety of jams and jellies on the table. The florist arrived while Griff was setting the kitchen table with Nic's plates and silverware. Since he hadn't found any cloth napkins, he had used the paper ones stored in the pantry. He placed the small bouquet of mixed flowers in the center of the table, then carried the larger bouquet of two dozen peach roses into the bedroom.

He paused, staring at the bed. The comforter lay in a heap on the floor and the blanket hung half-on/half-off at the foot of the bed. He considered making the bed, but decided there wasn't any point, since he intended for them to spend a large part of the day heating up the sheets the way they had last night.

Underneath that tough, controlled façade, Nic Baxter was a wild woman in bed.

Nic rounded the corner near the neighborhood park, three blocks from her house. She hadn't been surprised that she had not seen anyone else out this early on a weekend morning or that only one car had passed by. Most women probably wouldn't have gone for a morning power walk after a vigorous night of lovemaking, but Nic wasn't most women. And the man she had made love with wasn't her husband or boyfriend or even her friend. He was just a friendly acquaintance.

Get real, Nic. Griffin Powell is now your lover.

She should feel like a slut for not only giving in to her baser urges and having sex with a man she had hated up until a few months ago, but because she had done the unforgivable—had unprotected sex. God, how stupid was that!

What must Griff think of her this morning? That she was an easy conquest, just like all the other women he'd known? That she was a sex-starved bitch who'd been insatiable?

When she got back to the house, she'd simply explain that it had been a while for her and she'd needed the release of an all-nighter. The stress of her job had finally gotten to her. He'd understand.

But then what?

He expected to spend the weekend. And she wanted him to stay.

So, why not have an affair with Griff? As long as they kept their relationship private—like he'd said, nobody's business—she didn't see why she couldn't handle a brief affair—the only kind Griff had. In public, they would work together on the Hunter case, equals, if not really colleagues. In private, they would be lovers.

And if I'm pregnant?

She'd cross that bridge if and when she came to it. The odds were in her favor. It was the wrong time of the month. They'd had unprotected sex only once. And besides that, she might not even be able to get pregnant. She and Greg had tried to have a baby that last year of their marriage, but she hadn't gotten pregnant. Thank goodness. She'd been foolish enough to think that a child might have improved their marriage.

Ouch! Nic felt the sting as it pierced her back. Had an insect of some kind stung her through her cotton sweatshirt? Damn, whatever it was, it hurt like hell.

Nic's vision blurred. She felt wobbly, as if she might pass out.

What the hell?

Chapter 16

When Nic didn't return home well over an hour from when Griff had awakened, he began to worry. He knew she hadn't taken her cell phone because he'd found it in her purse. Just how long did she walk? What route did she take? Invading Nic's privacy, he scanned the numbers stored in her cell phone, found Doug Trotter's home number and called him.

"Nic? What the hell are you—?"

"This is Griffin Powell. I'm using Nic's phone." He explained, with as little personal detail as possible, why he was concerned.

"I don't like the sound of this," Doug said. "She takes a thirty-minute power walk most mornings and I know she stays in her neighborhood. Take a look around and call me back in ten minutes."

"I'm not waiting ten minutes," Griff said. "I'm not waiting another second. You get somebody over here pronto. I'll search the neighborhood, but we need to start an all-out search immediately."

"What's got you so upset? You don't think—"

"I'm not thinking anything," Griff lied, "except that Nic could be in trouble."

"I'll contact the Woodbridge police department and get a couple of uniformed officers out there, then I'll call Chris Garmon. He works out of our D.C. office and he lives in Woodbridge."

Griff removed Nic's key chain from her purse, went out into the garage, locked the back door, and got in her car. He drove up and down the streets in her neighborhood searching for her. The more time that passed, the more frantic he became.

Where the hell are you, Nic?

By the time he had gone through the neighborhood twice and returned to Nic's house, two Woodbridge police officers were pulling up in front of her house. They exchanged names and Griff filled them in on what little he knew. The officers asked Griff to wait at the house in case Nic came home, while they covered the same ground Griff already had.

Fifteen minutes later, Special Agent Garmon showed up, asked Griff a few questions, and then called Doug Trotter. When the police officers returned, Garmon took over, but Griff didn't give a damn who was in charge. All that concerned him was that the police hadn't found any sign of Nic.

"Get more people out here," Garmon ordered. "I want the neighborhood canvassed. We need to find out if anyone saw Nic this morning."

"Show me the note again," Garmon told Griff once the officers went back to their patrol car to call for reinforcements.

Griff pulled the note from his pants pocket and handed it to Garmon, who read it aloud. " 'Gone for my morning walk. Back soon. Coffee ready. You prepare breakfast. Surprise me. Nic.' "

"You spent the night here last night?" Garmon asked.

"Yes, I spent the night. I've already told you that I did."

"It just seems odd to me that Nic would let you stay here, considering the fact that you're far from her favorite person."

"Where have you been the past few months?" Griff asked, not bothering to mask the aggravation in his voice. "Nic and I have been working together, unofficially, of course, on the Hunter case. And we've become . . ." He paused, remembering how they'd joked about the exact definition of their relationship. "We've become friendly acquaintances."

"You two didn't get into a fight, did you? You didn't—"

Griff grasped the lapels of Chris Garmon's jacket and shoved him against the wall. "Don't let the words come out of your mouth."

Wild-eyed with genuine fear, Garmon stammered, "You—you do know that—that you're manhandling a—a federal officer."

Griff's jaw tightened. He released the agent's lapels, gave him a warning glare, and stepped back a couple of feet.

Heaving a deep sigh, Garmon straightened his jacket, then cleared his throat. "Nic knows how to take care of herself. Whatever's happened, she'll be okay."

"She went for a morning walk in her safe neighborhood. She didn't take her cell phone and didn't have her gun," Griff said. "Up against your average mugger, she could hold her own, but against the totally unexpected . . ." Griff clenched his teeth.

Goddamn son of a bitch!

Don't think it. Don't dare think it. There has to be another explanation. He wouldn't be stupid enough to target an FBI agent.

Yes, he would. He's just that arrogant.

Griff's stomach muscles knotted painfully.

"You need to get roadblocks set up on every road going

out of Woodridge," Griff said. "And start checking chartered boats and planes and rental cars."

"You don't need to tell me how to do my job." Garmon glowered at Griff but kept his distance.

"Then, by God, get out there and do it!"

An hour later, after Griff had worn the carpet bare with his pacing and had alienated Special Agent Garmon, SAC Doug Trotter showed up, with the Woodbridge chief of police in tow.

Nic's home had become headquarters for the search and rescue mission that was under way. A swarm of local police officers, FBI agents, and state troopers were on the job, doing everything within their power to locate one of their own. And by noon, Griff was half out of his mind with worry.

Nicki, honey, where are you? Are you all right?

Suddenly Griff's cell phone rang. *Let it be her. Dear God, let it be Nic.*

Griff checked the caller ID. No name. And he didn't recognize the number. For half a second, his heart stopped.

He walked out of the living room, down the hall, and into Nic's bedroom, leaving the beehive of activity behind him. "Griffin Powell here."

"Are you missing anything . . . or should I say, anyone?" the male voice asked.

"You tell me." Griff closed his eyes and prayed.

He hadn't prayed in a long, long time. He wasn't sure he still believed in God.

"You didn't see this one coming, did you? You and Nic thought that I was simply waiting for her to give a press release in which she referred to me as 'the Hunter' and then I'd call again to give you the next couple of clues."

"And instead you were buying time and leading us in the wrong direction," Griff said.

Maniacal laughter echoed in Griff's ears.

If he ever got his hands on this sick bastard, he would rip

him apart, tear off his limbs, and shove his severed dick down his throat.

"Aren't you going to ask me how she is?"

Griff didn't respond.

"She's asleep right now. Effects of the tranquilizer gun I used on her."

Son of a bitch! Griff barely controlled his rage. "Let her go and you can name your price."

"Oh, Griff, how sweet. You actually care about our lovely Nicole, don't you? But I'm afraid she is a rare and precious gem and we both know she is priceless."

Don't try to bargain with him. He's not going to release her. No matter what you offer him. He has plans for her that include killing her in twenty-one days. Tell him to go to hell, then hang up.

Before Griff spoke again, the caller said, "For old times' sake, I'll give you a clue today and then another in ten days and a final clue in twenty days. If you can figure them out, you'll know where she is."

Griff held his breath.

"You might want to get pencil and paper and write this down so you won't forget." He laughed again.

"I won't forget."

"Go west, young man, go west, and stay south of the Misssuri River."

Silence.

Message delivered.

Griff tormented.

Conversation ended.

Griff clenched his teeth so tightly that his jaws ached.

He stood alone in the bedroom and accepted the situation for what it was. The Hunter had chosen Nic as his next victim. No doubt he'd been planning her abduction from the very beginning of his evil game. And he'd been right—they hadn't seen this one coming.

Nic, honey, stay strong. Fight him with everything in you. Don't let him win. Stay alive. I'll move heaven and earth if necessary to find you.

Nic came to, groggy and disoriented. Her muscles were sore. Her head ached. She opened her eyes slowly. Her vision was blurred.

What the hell had happened to her?

Think, Nic, think!

She had left Griff asleep in her bed, gotten up, put on her walking gear, made coffee, drunk half a cup, and left the house. She had been on her way home when something had hit her in the back. An insect had stung her and it had hurt like crazy.

Holy shit!

Nic tried to move her arm behind her back so she could check for a bullet wound, but quickly discovered that her wrists were cuffed.

She could rule out being in a hospital.

Was she in jail?

You're not thinking straight, Baxter. Stand up and move around, see if you can get your bearings.

By the time she managed to get to her feet, her vision had cleared enough for her to note that wherever she was, it was dark. All she saw was a single lightbulb dangling from an electrical cord hanging from the ceiling. She took one step, then another, and suddenly realized that her feet were manacled at the ankles.

What the hell was going on?

She scanned the area, right and left, front and back, up and down. She was in some kind of cellar. Dark, damp, dank. And creepy.

At least she wasn't scared of spiders.

Oh, big deal, Nic. You're handcuffed, your feet are mana-

cled in chains, you have no memory of what happened to you, and you're relieved that you aren't afraid of spiders.

Think rationally, will you!

The truth of the matter was she didn't want to accept what she suspected had happened. It would be too frightening to admit that it was possible—even probable—that the Hunter had abducted her.

Oh, God in heaven, please let this be a nightmare. Let me wake up safe in Griff's arms.

The handcuffs were real, as were the chains binding her ankles together. This cold, smelly basement was real, too. This whole thing was a bad dream, all right. She was living a nightmare.

"Where are you?" she screamed as loudly as she could.

No response.

Instinct told her that he might not be able to hear her, but he was nearby and it was only a matter of time before he came to get her, to teach her the rules of his game.

Griff's plane landed at two thirty Monday morning. He hadn't slept or eaten since Saturday night. When he disembarked, Sanders met him, and then instructed Jonathan to put the luggage in the back of the limousine.

"All of Powell's resources are being directed to this assignment," Sanders said. "Per your instructions, every available agent will be working the case."

Griff nodded but said nothing. He was bone weary. And tormented by thoughts of what might be happening to Nic.

Griff slid into the front of the limo and sat beside Sanders, who eased the vehicle out of the parking area and onto the roadway. They drove in silence for quite some time. Griff closed his eyes and tried to sleep, but he kept seeing Nic smiling, Nic laughing, Nic shuddering beneath him as she climaxed.

"He gave me a simple clue," Griff finally said.

"Yes, he did."

"West of Virginia is pretty much the rest of the country. And south of the Big Muddy—the Missouri River—could be any one of the Southern states including Texas."

"If it's possible to find her, we—"

"We have to find her!"

"I understand how much you want to apprehend this man and how concerned you are about Special Agent Baxter," Sanders said.

"No, you don't understand."

"Sir?"

"She might be pregnant," Griff said.

Sanders didn't reply.

"The odds are she's not, but if she is, the baby is mine."

Silence.

"Pregnant or not, she matters to me."

He hadn't admitted to himself just how much he cared about Nic until he realized the Hunter had kidnapped her.

Sanders did not know if Griffin loved Nicole Baxter. It was possible that not even Griffin knew. Just as he himself had done, Griffin had closed himself off from any deep emotions, from loving and being loved. And with good reason.

In the past year, since meeting Barbara Jean, he had begun falling in love. Gradually. Carefully. When the time was right, if the time was right, he would tell her of his feelings.

But loving Barbara Jean did not diminish his love for Elora. She had been the love of his life and her memory would live in his heart as long as he drew breath. Even after such a long time, he could still recall the sound of her laughter, the scent of her perfume, the feel of her flesh beneath his fingertips.

History could not repeat itself. What had happened to

him could not happen to Griffin. They could not allow a madman to destroy Griffin's woman and child as York had destroyed Elora and the baby growing inside her.

Pudge placed his dirty dishes in the dishwasher, a mundane chore that was beneath him. But when one couldn't trust live-in servants, one had to make do.

He was sorely tempted to go into the basement and check on Nicole, to see if she was awake and had realized what had happened to her, to taunt her with hints of what awaited her tomorrow and the next day and the next.

No, mustn't change the rules just for her.

He wanted her to beg, as he'd wanted the others to. He wanted her to suffer, as they had suffered.

But Nicole is special.

Yes, she was, but rules were rules and if he made very many exceptions for her, it wouldn't be fair to the others. They had all played by the rules, as would the ones who'd come after her.

Pudge removed his heavy sweater from the coatrack in the hall, put the sweater on, and walked out onto the veranda. Early November in Louisiana was usually warm in the daytime and chilly at night. But no matter what the weather, he enjoyed sitting in his wicker rocker and looking out over his land. Only a thousand acres now, but in its heyday, Belle Fleur had been three times that large.

If he had lived during those pre–Civil War days, he would have enjoyed being a slave master, would have taken great pleasure in torturing both male and female slaves. And he would have been within his rights to do whatever he wanted. He could have killed openly and no laws would have been violated.

But he didn't let a little thing like murder being illegal stop him from playing his games. After all, he was above the laws that governed other men. His superior intellect and breeding gave him rights that the common person didn't have.

Pudge snuggled into the rocker, closed his eyes, and thought about tomorrow. Nicole would not be meek and compliant. She would struggle and curse and fight.

The very thought of her warrior spirit excited him.

The more powerful the adversary, the sweeter the victory.

Yvette met Griffin in the foyer. Apparently, she'd heard the limousine when Sanders had stopped in front of the house and let Griffin out before he parked in the garage.

"I thought you'd gone home," Griffin said.

"I had, but Sanders called me this morning and I took the first flight out."

"Thanks for coming."

"Where else would I be when you need me?"

She reached over and took his hand in hers.

"Go ahead," he told her. "But whatever you pick up from me won't be pleasant."

She held his hand gently but with her own unique strength. Griff felt a momentary sense of calm. It came and went suddenly. He knew that Yvette was trying to help him, doing what she could to infuse him with hope.

She released his hand. "I had no idea that you cared so deeply for Nicole Baxter."

Griff stared at Yvette, not quite knowing how to respond. "We never really knew each other before, when we were battling all the time."

"And now you do?"

"We were beginning to get acquainted. We even joked around about how there were still things we didn't like about each other."

"You cannot blame yourself for what happened," Yvette

said. "Neither of you could have known what this man had planned."

"Why didn't I wake up before she left the house? I could have gone with her for her morning walk. If I had . . ." Griff ran his hand across his mouth and then cleared his throat.

"You need rest."

"I can't sleep."

"Then let us go to your study. We will sit together and if you want to talk, we will talk. If not, we will be quiet."

He agreed and they walked down the hall to his private den. He removed his jacket, tossed it on one of the chairs flanking the fireplace, and sat down on the green leather sofa. She sat on the opposite end of the sofa.

"I thoughtlessly blurted out something to Sanders," Griff confessed. "He told me that he understood how concerned I was about Nic and how badly I wanted to catch this guy. I told him he didn't understand, that Nic might be pregnant—with my baby. God, how thoughtless was that?"

"He is your friend. He is suffering with you and for you. I am certain that he is thinking what I am and probably what you are—that we cannot bear the thought of another madman destroying another innocent woman and her unborn child."

"I swear to God, I can't believe this is happening." Griff spread his thighs and leaned over. He propped his arms just above his knees as he clenched and unclenched his hands while he stared sightlessly at the floor. "An insane hunter. Unwilling prey. A sick, twisted game that leads to murder."

"Do not allow yourself to return to that other time or that place."

When Griff didn't respond, she said, "Listen to me. Concentrate on the sound of my voice and the words I speak. You must not allow the past to consume you. You must stay focused on the present, on what you can do that might help Nicole."

Griff looked directly at Yvette. "And if nothing can help her?"

"You will think no negative thoughts. For now, there is hope."

"Three weeks. That's all the time she has."

"Miracles have happened in less time."

"That's exactly what it's going to take to save Nic—a miracle."

Nic drifted off to sleep from time to time, then woke abruptly, disoriented and confused. Within seconds, reality slapped her in the face.

The Hunter had kidnapped her.

She hadn't seen him. But she knew he was close.

Why hadn't he come for her? What was he waiting for? Daybreak?

Whatever lay in store for her, whatever happened, she had no intention of giving in or giving up.

She knew that Griff would try to find her, knew that the bureau and every law enforcement agency out there would be doing their damnedest to locate her. But in the end, there was only one person who could help her.

Nicole Baxter, you're going to have to save yourself.

Chapter 17

Nic was wide-awake when he came to get her. He looked nothing like she had expected. No horns and forked tail. No murderous glint in his eye. The man who approached her appeared quite normal, not an evil monster. A little under six feet tall, stocky build, dressed in camouflage pants and matching shirt. An ordinary-looking man with a round, almost pleasant face.

"Good morning, Nicole," that familiar soft voice said.

She stared at him, inspecting him from head to toe. Short brown hair. Light olive complexion. And hazel eyes. She wanted to remember everything about him.

"I'm going to unchain you from the wall and help you up the stairs and into the kitchen," he said. "I have your breakfast ready."

"I need to freshen up before breakfast," she told him, doing her level best to stay calm and in control.

"Being allowed to use the toilet and the shower in the house are privileges you haven't earned. If you need to relieve yourself, you can do it outside."

Nic had already peed in her pants once and was about to bust right now. "Then let me go outside."

"Very well." He removed a key from his pocket, undid the lock that bound her chains to the wall behind her. When she took a tentative step forward, he grabbed her arm.

She jerked away from his touch.

He grabbed her again and glared right at her. "You mustn't do that. If you resist, I will assume you are being disobedient and I'll have to punish you."

Her captor appeared to be just an ordinary man, even meek and mild, but she suspected that he was an egotistical control freak. She needed to remember that he had to believe he was in charge at all times. Nic intended to do whatever was necessary to stay alive and find a way to escape.

"I'm sorry," she said.

He smiled. "You're playing the cooperative prisoner, aren't you, Nicole? Good. In the beginning, it will be easier for both of us. But eventually, you will rebel and when you do, the fun will begin."

He guided her through the basement, up a set of creaky wooden stairs, and into a semidark hallway. From there, he led her into a huge old kitchen that probably hadn't been updated in forty years, except for the refrigerator and stove. The long, narrow windows faced the east, the sunrise still hidden behind the far horizon.

It wasn't quite daybreak yet, which meant, depending on where they were, that it was probably between four thirty and five thirty. When he opened the back door and took her out onto the porch, he tightened his hold on her arm, then helped her down the steps and into the yard.

"You can go over there and do what you need to do," he told her. "But don't think about trying to run off. You won't get far." He glanced down at her shackled ankles.

Nic had a hell of a time getting her sweats and panties

down, but she finally managed. Her skin felt dirty and clammy and she smelled like sweat and pee and fear.

She was not going to allow the fear to dictate her actions. He wanted her scared and humble and obedient. For now. But the real hunt had not begun. When it did, he would want to see the fierce animal in her come out and fight for its life.

Pulling up her panties and sweats was even more difficult than getting them down over her hips, but after several attempts, she made it. She walked back to the house, taking her time and observing everything she could see in the predawn darkness.

He waited for her on the porch. He smiled as he watched her. The cocky bastard. When he grabbed her arm again, she flinched but didn't jerk away. Instead, she allowed him to escort her inside to the kitchen table. After he seated her, he went to the stove, lifted a pot, poured something into a bowl, and then brought the bowl to the table.

"You may have a nice bowl of oats this morning," he said. "But after this, you must earn all your meals. You will be allowed food mornings and evenings. Water must also be earned."

Nic eyed the tan, lumpy oats. No sugar. No cream. No butter.

"You may try to feed yourself or I'll feed you."

She grabbed the spoon he'd placed by her bowl. "I'll do it myself." She looked up at him. "Thank you."

His self-satisfied smile widened. "I knew you would be wonderful. The best of the best."

When he reached out and caressed her back, running his meaty hand across her shoulder blades, every nerve in her body reacted, repulsed by his touch. Her muscles tensed. But she managed not to react, not to withdraw.

If he tries to rape me . . .

No, he won't. That's not his MO. Not one of his victims showed any signs of being raped.

Nic clutched the spoon in her right hand, dug into the cereal, and shoved a heaping spoonful into her mouth. Tasteless gruel. But she was hungry and she had no idea when he might offer her food again. She'd take whatever he offered in order to stay alive and to keep up her strength. She ate hurriedly, downing the entire bowl in only a few minutes.

"Good girl." He patted her on the head. "Now, we're going for your first outing in the woods. We won't stay out long today. Just long enough for you to begin learning the rules. If you please me, I'll allow you your choice of either a bath or another meal tonight."

As desperately as she needed a bath, she would choose food over cleanliness.

"Just tell me what you want me to do."

"I'm going to show you where you will be spending most of your time during the day. I'll explain the rules and I expect you to remember them and follow them. If you break the rules, you'll be punished. If you earn points, you will be rewarded."

"How do I earn points?"

"By surviving the hunt, of course."

She stared at him, knowing he could see the puzzlement in her expression.

"We'll do a little run-through this morning," he told her. "Just a trial run. Then tomorrow morning, I'll take you deeper into the woods and, eventually, I'll remove your ankle chains so that you can run free." He caressed her head, his fingers threading through her shoulder-length hair. "You'll like that, won't you, Nicole? Running free. At least until I catch you."

Sanders opened the den door and peered inside. Yvette lifted her head from the back of the wing chair by the fireplace where she'd been resting, glanced at him, and put her index finger to her lips to indicate she did not want him to disturb Griffin. He lay across the sofa, fully clothed, his feet hanging off one end. From his deep, heavy breathing, Sanders could tell that Griffin was sound asleep.

Yvette rose to her feet, tiptoed across the room, and walked out into the hallway. She closed the door behind her before she spoke to Sanders.

"He finally fell asleep, from sheer exhaustion, about an hour ago," Yvette said.

"I have a pot of tea in the kitchen," Sanders told her. "I thought perhaps we could talk before Griffin awakens and the others begin to stir."

She patted Sanders's arm. "He is going to need us in the days ahead. And if Nicole Baxter is murdered . . . He cares deeply for her. Far more than he realizes."

Neither of them spoke again until they were seated at the kitchen table, each with a cup of hot tea in front of them.

Yvette sipped her tea, then set the cup in the saucer. "What Griffin is going through will not be easy for you or for me. We share his memories. We lived his pain as he lived ours."

"We will share this experience with him, also. And we will see him through, no matter what."

"He was concerned about you. Worried because he had told you that Nicole might be pregnant."

"I pray she is not."

"Yes, I, too, pray she is not. If she is murdered and Griffin discovers that she was carrying his child . . . It cannot—it must not—happen again."

Sanders reached across the table and patted Yvette's hand. "We are as powerless now to stop this great evil as we were to stop the evil that destroyed ones so dear all those years ago."

Yvette gripped Sanders's broad, strong hand. "If Nicole

dies, I do not know if I will be able to bring Griffin out of that dark place where he will go."

"We will try. And, if necessary, we will go there with him."

Yvette tightened her small, slender hand into a fist and eased it out of Sanders's hold. "Griffin will need to stay actively involved in trying to find Nicole. If necessary, invent things for him to do. But be careful that he does not realize he is being manipulated. The less time he has to think, the better. The less time he spends alone, the better. You or I need to be with him as much as he will allow us to be."

"Yes, I agree."

They sat together in peaceful silence and finished their tea, then Yvette stood, came over to Sanders, and kissed his cheek.

A soft gasp alerted them that they were not alone. Sanders glanced in the direction of the sound and saw Barbara Jean in the doorway. Their gazes met briefly, then she looked away.

"I'm so sorry. Excuse me. I didn't realize I would be interrupting." Barbara Jean eased her wheelchair out of the doorway.

"Wait," Yvette called. "Please, come back. I am on my way up to my room to take a shower and change clothes. I am sure Sanders would love to have your company this morning."

Yvette paused as she passed by Barbara Jean, smiled at her, and then went on her way. Sanders stood to face Barbara Jean, who refused to look him in the eye as she wheeled into the kitchen.

When he approached her, she moved away from him, going toward the refrigerator. He caught the handlebars on the back of her small, portable wheelchair and stopped her. Then he walked around in front of her and lowered himself down on his haunches.

"You did not interrupt anything," he told her. "Yvette and I are old friends. I have told you before that she is like a sister to Griffin and to me. She and I were talking about our great concern for Griffin."

Barbara Jean lifted her head and looked shyly at Sanders, then looked back at her folded hands resting in her lap. "He's terribly upset about Special Agent Baxter being abducted, isn't he?"

Sanders clasped Barbara Jean's folded hands. "They have become very close while working together on the Hunter case. Very close."

"Oh. Oh, my."

"So you see, this is extremely personal for him, as it would be for me if anything like this were to happen to you."

Her gaze collided with his, her dark eyes bright and shimmering with a mist of tears. "Damar . . . You've never said anything about—about us."

"And now is not the time to do so," he told her. "Not when Griffin will need me in the weeks ahead. You do understand?"

"Yes, I understand." She squeezed his hand and smiled. "I hope you know that I have feelings for you, too."

He lifted her right hand to his lips, kissed it, and then pressed it against his cheek. Someday, he would tell Barbara Jean about Elora. And about the child he had lost.

Each day for the past three days, he had taken her into the woods and released her. The first day, he had gone over the rules.

"I will tell you only once. You must remember them."

She remembered them. Following each and every one of his rules meant a better chance of survival. He wanted a good hunt, expecting his prey to be cunning, and agile, able to run for her life. Now Nic understood why he chose only women who were physically fit. A slow or weak prey provided no challenge. He needed the woman to be capable of staying alive for at least three weeks, with very little food, very little water, and existing under horrid conditions. Only the strongest could endure the hell he put them through.

The first day she'd stayed out an hour, then he'd taken her back to the house, down into the basement, and chained her to the wall. That night he had brought her upstairs and allowed her to choose her reward for having pleased him during their mock hunt that morning. She had chosen the two slices of bread and cup of water instead of a shower. Yesterday, he had removed the shackles from her ankles and set her free.

"I'll give you a fifteen-minute head start," he'd told her.

Bastard!

She had run as far and as fast as she could, not caring in which direction she went or how much time had elapsed. Finally she had stopped, listened, and waited. But only for a few minutes. Long enough to check out her surroundings and ascertain whether or not he had been following directly behind her. He hadn't been.

By the time he'd caught her, she had been tired and thirsty, and even dirtier than before the chase had begun.

He had come barreling through a clearing on a large, roaring dirt bike. She had done her best to elude him, but he had parked the bike, gotten off, removed the rifle he had slung over his shoulder, and fired at her feet. She'd skidded to a halt.

"The hunt is over for today," he'd called to her. "You did very well, Nicole. You managed not to get caught."

Breathless, she had turned and glared at him.

He had laughed in her face.

"You're wondering why I said that, aren't you? Look at

your handcuffs closely. There is a tracking device in them. You can't escape me entirely."

The son of a bitch hunted her without the assistance of the tracking device for a set amount of time, then when he grew weary of the hunt, he simply activated the device and came after her. But he hadn't taken her back to the house. Instead, he had shackled her feet and chained her to a tree, then left her. Before dark he had come back for her and taken her into the basement again, after giving her bread and water.

When he had released her this morning, he'd told her, "You'll be free all morning. I won't begin hunting you for an hour."

She could tell by the sun overhead that right now it wasn't quite noon. He would find her soon. She had taken full advantage of the hours outside, free to breathe the fresh air, to feel the sun on her face, and to survey her surroundings. She had come to the conclusion that she was somewhere in the southernmost regions of a Southern state. South Mississippi, Georgia, Alabama, or Louisiana. The massive live oak trees she encountered dripped with Spanish moss.

The earth was dark and rich. If she became hungry enough, she would dig for fat worms in that nourishing black soil.

And she had encountered a large swampy area where stagnant green water stood. Today, she hadn't drunk any of the filthy water, only washed her feet, legs, and arms in it. But if she became thirsty enough and couldn't find fresh water, she would drink it.

She had also tried to memorize everything she could about the house. A decaying antebellum mansion with massive columns supporting an upstairs balcony that wrapped around three sides of the old structure.

So far, she had pleased him with each hunt, so she had not incurred his wrath or discovered just how he would punish her if she displeased him. But she knew that it was only a matter of time before he lashed out at her. Instinct told her that he was lulling her into a false sense of calm before all hell broke loose.

The one thing Nic was determined not to do was lose track of time—of the days she was in captivity. Three days down. Nineteen to go.

The chances that the bureau or Griff would find her were practically zero. Her only hope was finding a way to escape.

SAC Doug Trotter had taken over as leader of the task force. He kept in touch with Griff on a daily basis, not to share the bureau's information but to ask Griff if Powell's had come up with any leads. Nic had been missing five days. Five long, agonizing days. Griff slept little, simply taking short naps when he became so exhausted he couldn't stay awake. But even asleep, he could not escape the tormenting images of Nic being hunted, tortured, and finally killed by the Hunter.

Yesterday, he'd been on the verge of making a colossal mistake—he had decided to offer a million-dollar reward for information leading them to Nic. Doug Trotter had advised him not to do it, but it had been Sanders who had finally made him see reason. Every nutcase in the country would crawl out of the woodwork with information for that amount of money.

If not for Sanders and Yvette he would have lost his mind by now. Yvette took long walks with him, speaking to him only when he chose conversation over silence. Sanders worried him continuously with mundane matters that under ordinary circumstances he would have dealt with on his own, not even thinking about asking for Griff's input. And they had played chess every evening.

Even Barbara Jean had been drafted into the grand

scheme to keep Griff so busy that he wouldn't have time to slowly but surely go out of his mind.

Then, this morning Lindsay and Judd had arrived, with little Emily in tow. He'd told them that there had been no need for them to disrupt their lives and come rushing to Griffin's Rest. They had ignored him and set up a makeshift nursery in one of the larger guestrooms upstairs.

"We'll go fishing tomorrow," Judd had said.

"And tonight, you're going to give Emily her bath," Lindsay had told him.

That's where he was headed right now. Upstairs to help Lindsay with Emily's bath.

When they entered the bathroom connected to the guestroom, Griff went down on his knees and carefully placed Emily in the tub where Lindsay had drawn several inches of lukewarm water.

"I've laid out all her special things," Lindsay said. "Body wash, shampoo, favorite bath toy"—she pointed to a big-eyed, green plastic frog—"and I'll lay her hooded bath towel on the bathmat beside you. When you finish, you'll find a clean diaper and her pajamas on the bed."

Bracing Emily's back with the palm of his hand, he looked up at Lindsay. "You aren't going to leave me alone with her, are you?"

"I'll be in the bedroom, if you need me." With that said, she left him to proceed without her assistance.

"Well, it looks like it's just you and me, kid."

By the way she splashed and gurgled and cooed, he could tell Emily enjoyed bath time. He'd probably have to change into a dry shirt once he finished this job. All the while he concentrated on gently washing her mop of blond curls and her fat little arms and legs, Griff couldn't help thinking about what it would be like to have a child of his own. He had convinced himself that he was better off without a wife and children, that no woman could ever love him just for himself, especially if she ever learned anything about his past.

He lifted Emily out of the bathwater, wrapped her in the hooded towel, and breathed in the wondrously sweet scent of clean baby.

Why had he forgotten all about birth control when he'd made love to Nic that first time? It wasn't as if he'd never become carried away with passion before. But the hunger he'd felt for Nic had been different, intense in every way. And she had been just as wild for him.

But because he had not used a condom for the first time since he'd become a responsible adult capable of rational decisions, Nic might be pregnant. And now she was out there somewhere, in the hands of a brutal psychopath, fighting for her life.

"Griff?" Lindsay called his name. "Are you all right?"

He held Emily's little cheek against his as he turned to face her mother. Only then, when he looked at Lindsay through his blurred vision, did he realize he had tears in his eyes.

He swallowed, then cleared his throat. "Nic might be pregnant."

"Oh? How do you—?"

"If she's pregnant, it's mine."

"Oh, Griff, no."

Lindsay rushed to him and wrapped her arms around him and Emily, who whined and wriggled until Lindsay loosened her hold.

Nic huddled in a fetal position, her legs drawn up and her arms lying crisscrossed over her chest. There was no room to maneuver and no way to escape from the tiny cage.

Today, he had finally caught her.

It had been her own fault. She had found a streambed and

hadn't been able to resist the urge to bathe. She had dawdled a little too long when she should have been running, staying one step ahead of him.

Tonight, there had been no bread and water. No reward for pleasing him.

"You disappointed me," he'd told her. "I caught you far too quickly for the hunt to be a satisfying experience. I'm afraid I'll have to punish you."

Her punishment was being shoved into a metal cage large enough for a good-size dog and left in the middle of the woods to spend the night.

She couldn't sleep. Her stomach rumbled with hunger. Her body ached from being forced to remain in one position for so many hours. She was cold. So cold. And nature's nocturnal sounds encouraged her imagination. Every bird coo, every owl hoot, every animal cry, and even the nighttime wind through the trees, announced danger. There were snakes in the woods, right? And a plethora of creepy, crawling insects. And wild animals on the prowl.

But the rational part of her mind told her that the real danger didn't lie out here in the woods tonight. The real danger was the animal who would take her out of this cage in the morning and set her free in the woods once again.

Chapter 18

Ten days. Ten excruciating, torturous, endless days. In the long-ago past, Griffin had spent far more than a week and a half in the bowels of hell and had survived. But this was a new kind of hell, one where it was not his life hanging precariously in the balance, but the life of a woman who mattered to him, a woman he cared for deeply. If not for the support of his friends—Sanders, Yvette, Barbara Jean, Lindsay, and Judd—he wasn't sure how he could have made it this far. They stayed with him, kept him busy, and when any tidbit of information came in via either Powell's or the FBI, they encouraged him to believe in what he was beginning to think was the impossible: that somehow, someway, they would find Nic before it was too late.

When he had changed his mind and gone against their advice not to offer a reward for information, they hadn't argued with him. Sanders had arranged for extra personnel to be hired on a part-time basis at the Powell Agency headquarters to handle all the calls that started coming in immediately. The rational part of his mind told him that offering a million dollar reward was crazy, but time was running out. Desperate times called for desperate measures.

Powell's had followed up on every lead, no matter how flimsy the evidence or how wild a goose chase they were led on. Powell agents spread out around the South, grasping at straws, determined to leave no stone unturned in their search.

Doug Trotter had phoned yesterday, the first time in several days. The bureau was no closer to finding Nic than Powell's was, and Griff had heard the frustration and concern in Trotter's voice.

Lindsay and Judd had driven to the Knoxville airport over an hour ago to pick up Nic's brother and bring him to Griffin's Rest. Griff had invited her mother, too, but Nic's stepfather had told him that their doctor was keeping her sedated and preferred for her not to travel. Griff hadn't liked the colonel's tone and instinctively knew that if he ever met Nic's stepdad, he wouldn't like him. But the moment Charles David had answered Griff's call, he had sensed the depth of his love and concern for her, and he suspected that Nic's brother had picked up on similar emotions in his voice.

Leaving little Emily in Barbara Jean and Yvette's motherly care, Griff put on his lightweight jacket and started to leave the house. Before he made it out the front door, Sanders offered to go with him on his afternoon walk.

"I need to be alone for a while," Griff said. "Just for today."

"Are you sure that's wise?"

"The day he kidnapped Nic and called to give me the first clue, he said he would give me a second clue on day ten." Griff's gaze connected with Sanders's. "It's nearly three o'clock on day ten and he hasn't called."

"And taking a walk alone will make him call?"

"No, but it will keep me from putting my fist through the wall while I wait."

Sanders nodded. "If you're not back when Mr. Bellamy arrives, do you want me to call you?"

"Yes, please do that."

Griff walked outside into the crisp autumn day. The sunshine warmed the earth, but the cool breeze kept the temperatures in the high sixties. Thanksgiving was just around the corner, a time for celebrating with family and friends the bounty of blessings in one's life. He, far more than many, had reasons to give thanks because he had been blessed with so much. But he would give up everything he possessed if it would save Nic.

Nicki.

He smiled as he remembered the way she had reacted the first time he called her that. She had known he had done it simply to piss her off.

But the night they had spent making love, he had called her Nicki.

"My beautiful Nicki. My beautiful, sexy Nicki."

She had laughed, tossed her head back, and crawled on top of him, straddling him as she brought her body over his and her mouth down to whisper on his lips, "So, you think I'm sexy, huh?"

Oh, God, please . . . If you're out there, if you exist, if you actually give a damn about us mere mortals, then do this one thing for me. Protect her.

Griff took the gravel road that led through the woods and wound around past the old boathouse and then circled back to the mansion. He loved these private acres near the lake, enjoyed the solitude and appreciated the beauty. Most of the autumn colors had faded and the trees were partially bare, the landscape painted in shades of gray and brown, with scattered evergreens brightening the drabness.

Damn it, Nic, why didn't you just stay in bed with me that morning? If only you hadn't gone for a morning walk. If only I had been awake and gone with you. If only . . .

Wherever you are, whatever he's putting you through,

stay strong, honey. Stay strong. Don't let him defeat you. You have to know that I'm doing everything I can to find you.

Griff was approaching the boathouse when his cell phone rang. His heart stopped for a millisecond, then he reached into his pocket and removed the phone. Unknown name. And a number he did not recognize.

"Griffin Powell here."

"Did you think I wasn't going to call?"

He wanted to ask, *"How is Nic? Is she all right? Please, don't hurt her. I'll give you anything—everything—if you'll just let her go."* Instead, he said nothing.

The son of a bitch laughed.

"If you ask me nicely, I'll let you speak to Nicole."

"What?"

"You heard me."

Was he kidding? Did he actually intend to let him speak to Nic? If the bastard wanted to hear him beg, he'd beg. Hell, he'd grovel. "Would you please let me speak to Nic . . . to Nicole?"

"Certainly. See how easy that was? All it required was for you to do as I told you to do."

"May I speak to her now?"

"I'll hold the phone for her," the caller said. "She's going to give you your next clue. It's a good one, so listen up."

"Griff?" Her voice was weak. He heard the fear, but also the determination.

"Nic, Nicki, honey. Where—?"

"Spanish moss," she said. "Antebellum house and—"

"You bitch!" the Hunter screamed.

Griff heard a loud slap, then another, and knew Nic had not followed orders, had not given him the clue she'd been instructed to give. The last sound he heard was Nic's gasping grunts.

"Nic!" Griff called. But the line was dead.

Griff tightened his hands into fists, marched several feet

off the road and over to the old boathouse. He pulled back his right hand and rammed his fist into the gray weathered-wood door. Pain shot through his hand and up his arm. But the pain from his bloody knuckles momentarily eased the agonizing pain inside him, pain that was ripping him apart.

Nic licked the blood from her lip and spit on the ground, careful to avoid hitting her captor. She wanted to spit in his eye, but didn't. She knew he would punish her—no food, no water, and another night in the cage. The two hard slaps across her face had hurt, but anything she had to endure would be worth the chance she'd taken when she gave Griff a real clue. What she had told him hadn't been specific, but at least it narrowed down her possible location. If she knew where she was, even what state she was in, she would have called that out to Griff, but she didn't know. The words "Spanish moss" and "antebellum house" wouldn't lead him directly to her, but if they were searching—Powell's and the bureau—and she knew they were, then her words would give them an idea of where to search.

He dragged her across the open field, probably where either cotton or sugarcane had once been grown, all the way to a huge oak tree off to the side, near a rutted dirt path. Two tattered old ropes hung from a massive limb on the tree, no doubt the remnants from where a child's wooden swing had once hung. He shoved her up against the tree.

She gasped for breath.

"Don't move!" He patted the rifle slung over his shoulder.

She stood there, silent and still, waiting for whatever came next.

He removed a knife from his pocket, reached up as high as he could and cut one of the ropes. He knotted the end of the rope twice, then grabbed Nic by the shoulder, whirled her around, and pressed her chest against the tree trunk.

"If you stay put and take your punishment, I won't shoot you."

Shoot her? But today was only day ten, wasn't it? Surely he wouldn't kill her ahead of schedule, would he?

As if he had read her mind, he added, "I won't shoot to kill, only to injure. Maybe shoot off a couple of toes."

She closed her eyes and waited. And prayed. Every instinct within her told her to fight back, not to wait like a cowering whipped dog for her punishment. But if she fought him, he would shoot her. A wound could become infected. And she wouldn't be able to run from him as quickly during the daily hunt if he shot off any of her toes. When the opportunity came for her to escape, she wanted to be ready and able. And escape is what she thought about when the rope snapped across her back, sending a stinging jolt through her soiled, tattered shirt. As he struck blow after blow, she gritted her teeth and endured as long as she could without screaming. By the tenth strike, the rope had cut through her shirt and connected with bare flesh. By the fifteenth strike, tears streamed down her cheeks. By the twentieth strike, she was moaning in agony.

Griff telephoned Doug Trotter and filled him in on his brief conversation with Nic, then he contacted Sanders and ordered him to relay the information to all the Powell agents in the field. Narrow the search to the areas where antebellum houses still existed and where Spanish moss grew.

He tried to erase the sound of those slaps and Nic's wounded grunts from his mind, but they replayed over and over again inside his head. If it took him the rest of his life, he would find the sick son of a bitch and kill him. Slowly. Show him no mercy. Torture him the way he had tortured so many others.

When Griff entered the house through the back door, Yvette met him. Apparently, she had been watching for him.

"Nicole's brother just arrived," she said.

Griff nodded.

"Do you wish to speak to him now or—"

"Yes, of course." When Yvette reached out to place a comforting hand on his shoulder, he withdrew from her touch.

She eyed him questioningly, then visually searched him from head to toe. Her gaze focused on his right hand. "You've injured yourself."

"It's nothing. I'm fine." When he curled his fingers to make a fist, he winced as pain spread through his whole hand.

Disregarding his assurance that he was all right, she grasped his hand. "Do not pull away. I promise I will not trespass into your thoughts."

He opened his hand and relaxed the tension in his arm. She inspected his skinned knuckles, the blood covering them beginning to dry in spots.

"This needs to be cleaned and an antiseptic applied," she told him. "And I believe there are several splinters that need to be removed." She looked directly at him and asked, "What did you do, run your fist through a wooden plank?"

"Through the old boathouse door," he admitted.

She released his hand, then reached up and caressed his cheek.

Words were not necessary. He understood how much Yvette cared that he was suffering the torment of the damned. He had thought neither of them would ever again have to stand by and watch helplessly while the other endured such anguish. He went with her to the bathroom off the kitchen and allowed her to wash and doctor his hand.

Fifteen minutes later, once he'd had a chance to meditate for a short while and center his thoughts on the positive and not the negative, he walked into the living room where Judd and Lindsay were keeping Nic's brother company. The moment Griff entered the room, the young man stood and came toward him. Lindsay and Judd excused themselves. Griff and Charles David met halfway, each with outstretched hands. Charles David was a tall, muscular, exceedingly handsome guy, with dark hair and eyes that reminded Griff of Nic's. The brother and sister bore a strong, almost twinlike resemblance to each other.

They shook hands, then Griff grasped Charles David's arm and gave him a reassuring squeeze. "I spoke to your sister. She's alive."

Tears welled up in the young man's eyes. "How? When? I don't understand."

"Come and sit down." Griff led Charles David over to the sofa and the two sat opposite each other. "Her captor let me hear her voice. He had instructed her to give me the second clue, the one he had promised to deliver on her tenth day of captivity."

Charles David gulped, then cleared his throat. "And she gave you the clue."

"Yes, only not the clue she was supposed to give me. She called out the words 'Spanish moss' and 'antebellum house.' " Griff willed himself to remain calm as he continued. "I heard him scream at her and then the line went dead."

Griff and Charles David shared a hard stare that spoke louder than any words could have. They both knew that Nic had paid a high price to relay her message.

"I contacted Doug Trotter and gave him the information, and my assistant, Sanders, has been in touch with my agents in the field."

"I appreciate everything you're doing to try to find Nicole," Charles David said. "I know that in the past, the two of you have been adversaries. But the last time I spoke to Nic, she told me that since you two had been working together, she'd begun to think she might have to revise her opinion of you, perhaps downgrade you from lethal to merely dangerous."

Griff chuckled. "That's my Nic."

Charles David eyed Griff speculatively. "You care about my sister and she about you. She's more to you than just an acquaintance, more than simply someone you're working with on a case."

"Yes."

"I suspected as much."

When Griff stood, Charles David did, too.

"I'll have Sanders show you to your room. Please, make yourself at home. And if there's anything you need, just let us know."

As if on cue, Sanders appeared in the doorway. Griffin introduced the two men, then excused himself and went directly to his study. He poured himself a drink, downed the aged Scotch in only a few minutes, and then refilled his glass.

He had drugged her last night and when she awoke this morning, her left shoulder blade was sore, as if she had scraped it against the brick wall during the night. Because she had been obedient yesterday and had given him a good hunt, he had brought her back into the house and allowed her to sleep in the basement, but he gave her no food or water.

"I will not completely forgive you for disobeying me," he'd told her.

After days without food, she had grown accustomed to occasionally feeling faint. Thankfully, she had managed to return every day to the stream that trickled through the woods, so at least she had had water.

Slightly groggy when he came for her, she'd tried her best to clear her mind before he released her for today's hunt. If she didn't manage to stay alert and avoid his relentless pursuit, he would punish her by continuing to withhold food and by forcing her back into the cage tonight.

Today was day fourteen.

And from the moment he began their march into the woods at dawn, she sensed that something was different about today. He wouldn't kill her. It wasn't time yet. But he had something planned for her. A surprise?

He always released her in the same spot every day. She wasn't sure if he knew that she was aware of this fact or not. The less he knew about what she was thinking and feeling, the better.

When he removed the leg irons, she stepped up and down several times, walking in place. He grabbed her wrists and unlocked the handcuffs, then pulled them off and tossed them on top of the ankle chains lying on the ground.

She stared at him, silently questioning his action.

"Today, we change the rules and alter our game," he told her.

She nodded.

"You're free, nothing binding you, no tracking device so that I can find you at the end of the hunt and bring you in."

"I don't understand."

"I'm letting you go, Nicole."

She glared at him, knowing there was more, that he would never willingly release her, that this was just part of the game.

He smiled. "You'll be allowed to run free, to find food and water and shelter. I will hunt you today, but if I can't find you, I'll allow you to stay in the woods tonight. Alone. Not in a cage. Not bound by chains. We will repeat the hunt every day until either you escape or on the final day, I kill you."

"Day twenty-one," she said.

"I'll give you only ten minutes' head start today, so you'd better run." He glanced at his wristwatch, then yelled, "Go! Now!"

Nic ran. And ran. And ran.

As soon as she knew she was far enough into the woods where he couldn't see her, she backtracked and circled around from where she had left him, being careful not to let him spot her and figure out her maneuver. When she knew for sure that he was deep into the woods, she crossed the open fields and headed due north, away from the wooded area in which he had released her.

Nic understood that he had not actually set her free, had not given her a real opportunity to escape. This was simply a new aspect of his game and she couldn't allow herself to be duped into having false hope, which was what he wanted.

The most important thing for her to remember was not to panic. Every morning, she had reminded herself of that fact. The urge to run blindly, to flee without giving thought to her actions could result not only in an accident, but could adversely affect her judgment and deplete her energy. Keeping her fear under control was essential to her survival.

Not for one minute did she believe that he did not have a way of keeping tabs on her. Otherwise, this final-week segment of their game made no sense. He had to know that she possessed the skills to stay alive and that given this kind of freedom, she could possibly manage to get away from him.

A niggling sense of knowing something without being aware of exactly what she knew plagued Nic as she thought through a plan of action. She needed food and water and, if at all possible, shelter from the nighttime temperatures, which she guessed were dropping into the forties. But she needed to think, to plot, and to plan as she kept moving. If he hadn't already realized that she had outmaneuvered him, he soon would and he would come after her with a vengeance.

An hour later, winded and thirsty, Nic took a break. She

sat down under a towering tree in a dense area of the woods and scratched her itchy back against the tree trunk. She couldn't stay here for long. She had to keep moving. When she stood, she tried to reach the spot on her back that felt slightly sore and now itchy, but she couldn't get at it by reaching over her shoulder. She twisted her arm behind her back and raked her fingers an inch below the spot. Close, but not close enough. When she brought her arm to her side, she felt something damp on her fingertips. She looked down and saw a red stain. Damn, she was bleeding. Apparently, she had rubbed her back too vigorously against the tree.

Hour after hour, Nic trekked through the woods, across a stream, over marshy swampland, and back into the woods. Only once had she seen anything that vaguely resembled a road. She had crawled over a dilapidated barbed wire fence and onto the dirt path, which obviously had been a road at one time, but was now overgrown with weeds and grass. She followed the path in the opposite direction of her captor's antebellum home, hoping beyond hope that this abandoned lane would lead her to an escape route.

Griff knew that the others were worried about him, about the fact that he slept very little, drank more than he ate, took long walks alone, and for the past several days had begun closing himself off in his study for hours on end. They all meant well, and he appreciated their concern, but there was nothing any of them could do to help him. With each passing day, the chances of their finding Nic grew slimmer. Although he hadn't given up hope entirely—and he wouldn't as long as there was even the slightest chance Nic was still alive—he was enough of a realist to face harsh reality.

There were far too many places where Spanish moss grew and old antebellum homes existed for the FBI and Powell's to find all of them before the twenty-one days came to an end.

It stood to reason that if her captor considered himself a great hunter and Nic was his chosen prey, he would need some type of hunting ground. But that area could be no more than a dozen or so confined acres or it could be hundreds, even thousands of acres. He could own the land or rent it or could even be using land that didn't belong to him.

Griff leaned back in the chair, swirled the last drops of whiskey in his glass, downed the liquor, and got up to pour himself a third drink. When he returned to the chair, he gazed into the fireplace at the glowing flame adding warmth and light to the study. Did Nic have heat tonight? Did she have light? Was she alone in the cold darkness, wondering why he hadn't found her yet?

If we don't get a break soon, it's going to be all up to you, Nic. If any woman I know can find a way to escape, it's you.

Sitting there sipping his drink, gazing into the fire, and allowing the liquor to somewhat dull his senses, Griff barely heard the light rapping on the closed study door.

When he didn't respond, Yvette called his name.

Please, go away and leave me alone.

After calling his name a second time and not receiving a reply, she walked away. Griff heard the *clip-clip* of her heels as she walked down the hall. She would never intrude on his privacy, but she would not leave him to his misery. She would come back later. In an hour or two. And eventually, after several attempts, she would insist that he eat a bite and go to bed. This had become a nightly ritual.

Chapter 19

Pudge stood at the front door and watched the light show in the night sky. Streaks of lightning illuminated the darkness and rolling thunder sounded like the beat of jungle drums. He loved storms and had since he was a child. That was something he and Ruddy had had in common. One of the many things.

Ah, dear cousin, I do miss you. Far more than I ever imagined I would. If only I could phone you and tell you about all the fun I'm having with our lovely Nicole.

When the rain began—thick, heavy droplets splattering against the earth—Pudge opened the door and walked onto the veranda. The late-November wind blew the moisture across the porch, hitting him like soft, fat pinpricks. Nic was out there somewhere, in the woods, alone in the storm, probably wet and miserable. She might get sick. Hypothermia was a real possibility. But tomorrow would be day nineteen and as long as she lived two more days, there was no need for his plans to change. Just the thought of that final hunt, of tracking her down and killing her, one shot at a time, excited him almost beyond enduring.

She had been his most cunning prey, just as he had known she would be. She had played the game from every angle, had been obedient beyond his wildest dreams, and then she had shown him her stubbornness and belligerence. She had obeyed him, had fought him, and on several occasions had outsmarted him. She had given him many days of pleasure. And he would miss her when their game ended. But he would keep her scalp in his secret room in the basement, along with all his other trophies. And when he wanted to relive these heady days of hide-and-seek, he would simply stroke her luscious hair and let his mind drift back to the twenty-one days that Special Agent Nicole Baxter had been his captive.

When the guards threw him into the small prison cell, he fell to his knees. Weak, exhausted, hungry, and thirsty. He couldn't remember the last time he had been given food. Days? Weeks? His mind had begun playing tricks on him, so much so that he couldn't believe any of his own thoughts. He had lost track of how long he'd been here. Six months? Ten? A year? It seemed like an eternity.

He'd had another life, a good life. But that life was gone, taken away from him and replaced with an existence that was neither life nor death, but a vague, unholy purgatory holding him captive.

He heard the key turn in the lock, the heavy footsteps of the two guards as they walked away, and the beating of his own heart. After lifting himself into a sitting position, he scooted across the hard earth floor and braced his back against the stone wall. As his eyes gradually adjusted to the darkness, he looked up at the tiny rectangular window high above his head and saw a twinkling star. If he could reach the window, which he could not, he still wouldn't be able to escape. The opening was barely large enough for him to stick his head through and was crisscrossed with bars. Even though when it rained, the rain blew in through the window, he was grateful for the fresh air that kept the hole in which he lived from suffocating him with its putrid odor: the stench of human sweat, urine, and excrement mingled with the rot of dead rodents.

His stomach growled with ravenous hunger.

"Starving you is simply part of your training," York had told him. "You will learn that rewards are given for obedience."

He understood being in training. He'd been an athlete most of his life, playing football and baseball as a kid and moving on to become the star quarterback for his high school team. Then he had attended UT on a football scholarship. He had been *the* Griff Powell, the young man destined for pro fame and fortune.

Everything within him rebelled against the fate that had brought him here, into the world of a madman who used human beings for his own amusement.

Suddenly he heard her voice calling his name.

"Griff, help me. Please help me."

"Nic? Nic, honey, is that you?"

"You have to find me before it's too late."

"Where are you? Tell me where you are!" He reached into the darkness, sticking his arms through the iron bars. "I can hear you, but I can't see you."

"It's day nineteen," she said, her voice growing faint. "If you don't find me soon, it will be too late."

"No . . . no . . . no . . ." he moaned.

Griff woke in a cold sweat, moisture coating his body. He huffed loudly, releasing the ache in his chest, and tossed back the covers. Sitting straight up in bed, he gave himself a couple of minutes to fully emerge from the past.

Before Nic had been kidnapped, he'd seldom dreamed about his time in captivity, but since she had been missing, the old nightmares had returned, only now, she had become a part of them. His past and Nic's present were merging in his subconscious, reminding him of the similarities between York and the Hunter, between his abduction and Nic's.

Griff got out of bed and walked across the room, flung open the French doors, and stepped out onto the balcony. The cold November air chilled his naked body, sending a rush of adrenaline through his system and clearing his mind.

On the far side of the lake, on the eastern horizon, the first faint tendrils of morning light crept across the dark sky. The dawn of a new day. Day nineteen.

Unable to find a cave or even a rock overhang and unable to build any kind of shelter, Nic had been forced to make do with what was available to protect her from the nighttime cold. Each night she choose a different location and built a new bed of twigs, leaves, and grass, then covered herself with these same materials. But last night a storm had hit, drenching her to the skin. She had huddled beneath the low branches of a protective tree and endured as best she could. With morning light, her clothes wet, her hair damp and plastered to her head, she forced herself into motion.

This was day nineteen. She had a lot to do today. E-Day. Escape Day.

Griffin had known this trapped feeling before, remembered it only too well. He was uncomfortable in his own skin, tormented by his own emotions, and could not control how he felt or what he thought. Although Lindsay and Judd realized that he was on the verge of collapse, only Sanders and Yvette understood the underlying cause.

Sanders had refused to allow him to walk alone, but kept silent as they ventured out into the frosty morning. His old friend realized that the only thing keeping Griff sane was motion. He had walked endless miles around his property the past few days, increasing his time outdoors more and more each day. He paced in his study, in his bedroom, and throughout the house.

Griff had tried to persuade Lindsay and Judd to take Emily and go home, but they wouldn't leave. He knew that they were waiting with him for the twenty-first day, staying nearby so that they would be on hand for the end of Nic's life. Her brother had also stayed. Like the others, Charles David was waiting. To varying degrees they had all accepted the inevitable, although they each gave lip service to hope, the power of positive thinking, and prayer.

After walking what Sanders later told him had been over four miles, Griff began to feel the chill in the air. He glanced at Sanders.

"Why don't you go back to the house?"

"I will walk with you as long as you walk."

"There is nothing you can do for me any more than I can do something for Nic."

"We have at least thirty-six more hours," Sanders reminded him.

They continued walking, the vibration of the bare trees rustling in the frigid breeze the only sound for miles.

"No matter what happens, I will eventually find him and kill him," Griff said.

"Yes, I know."

"He deserves the same fate as York."

"You have returned to Amara. In your nightmares. In your

thoughts. You must leave that place for my sake and Yvette's as well as your own."

"I wish I could rip those memories from my brain." Griff clenched his teeth as unwanted images flashed through his mind. "If only eradicating memories were as simple as amputating a limb."

"If reliving the past could help you save Nicole, then it would be worth the risk, but it cannot help her. It can only cause you great harm."

"Yvette says that York won't stay dead because I keep reviving him."

"Yvette is a very wise woman."

"She's not happy, is she?" Griff asked, the thought hitting like a bolt out of the blue. "She's beautiful and brilliant and wise, but she isn't free of the past any more than you or I."

"She is content with her life, as I am with mine and you were with yours."

"Yvette deserves to be happy. I want that for her."

"Perhaps in time."

"If he kills Nic . . ."

"Your life will go on, and you will survive day by day."

"Have you told Barbara Jean about Elora?" Griff asked.

"No, but I will. When the time is right."

"And will you tell her about York and about the years you spent on Amara?"

"Someday, I will tell her as much as she needs to know to be able to understand the person that I am."

"She has a gentle soul," Griff told him. "How do you think she will react if you tell her what we did?"

"There are secrets that must be kept and not shared."

"Take my advice. Don't wait to tell Barbara Jean how you feel." Griff paused and looked directly at Sanders.

"Reach out and grab whatever happiness you can while you can."

Nic hiked toward the old roadbed. He would be up by now, preparing for his day, and it was only a matter of time before he realized that she was on the move. He would suspect something was wrong and come looking for her. Because she had planned and prepared and had been patient, she now had a chance, slim though it was, to win the grand prize—her life. If she could get a head start and leave false tracks to lead him in the wrong direction, she might be able to stay one step ahead of him, even though she would be on foot and he would be riding his dirt bike.

If he caught up with her, would he kill her now instead of two days from now?

Yes, he would have to. It was the only way he could stop her from running. If she didn't escape today, she was as good as dead anyhow. Unless she killed him first.

Nic used her five senses to guide her, knowing that she must stay constantly alert to everything around her. Every sound. Every sight. Every scent. Even her sense of touch and taste could not be ignored. Despite her debilitating weakness, she had to stay strong.

Going against the urge to run like hell, Nic paced herself, not knowing how far she would have to walk to find any sign of the outside world. She moved smoothly, careful not to catch her bare, callused feet on anything. Quiet a while before she reached the old road, she veered off into the woods in the opposite direction, breaking a couple of small tree limbs and mowing down brush with heavy stomping movements; then she backtracked and headed straight for the road. Her small fake trail might or might not buy her some time, all depending on whether or not he actually followed it.

Repeatedly, Nic had come this way, near the rutted road-bed, so that when she got a chance to return, she would have memorized the route. She had to stay aware of her surroundings, of where she had been and where she was going. Day after day, she had soaked the landscape into her subconscious. From the sun's movement, she could gauge not only the approximate time of day, but the direction. She recalled that in winter months, the sun rises more to the southeast than due east.

Pudge enjoyed the hearty breakfast Allegra had prepared. Smoked ham and thick gravy, with scrambled eggs and fluffy white biscuits. As he drank his third cup of coffee and looked over the morning newspaper that Allegra had brought with her, he fantasized about today's hunt. Nic was proving herself a worthy adversary, a prime animal specimen. He would hate to end their game day after tomorrow.

All the more reason to make the most of today.

Had she spent the night out in the storm, surrounded by lightning, drenched with rain? Of course she had. There were no caves on the property and unless she managed to squeeze into a hollow log somewhere, the best she could have done was find shelter under a tree.

"I'm going out on the dirt bike again this morning," he told Allegra. "When you finish with the cooking and clean up, call Fantine and have her take you home. I won't need you back for a few days. I'll call and let you know when."

Allegra eyed the rifle propped against the corner wall near the back door. "Ain't you done killed every squirrel and rabbit and bird there is to kill around here?"

"Hush up, you old fool. I take my rifle with me for protection. And to get in a little target practice."

After he let his breakfast settle, he would start looking for Nic where he'd left her late yesterday. But there was no hurry. There was no way she could escape from Belle Fleur. Only an expert woodsman would ever find his way back to civilization and Pudge knew that Nic was a city girl, had been her entire life. And all her FBI training at Quantico hadn't prepared her for wilderness survival.

Half an hour later, dressed in his camouflage gear, his rifle slung over his shoulder, Pudge mounted his powerful dirt bike and headed out. He was ready for another exhilarating hunt.

When the sun lay halfway between the eastern horizon and directly overhead, Nic stopped along the stream that followed the same path as the old road. She sat down on the bank and cleaned her bleeding cuts and scratches. The way her back itched, she wondered if during the night an insect had bitten her. Maybe something poisonous.

She stood and hurriedly moved upstream. Finding an ideal spot, she leaned down and cupped her hands into the water. After splashing her face, she lifted a second handful to her lips and drank her fill.

Nic left the stream, made her way across the road and into the woods that edged the old path. She found a thicket and sat down inside it. She needed to rest for a few minutes and renew her strength.

During the days and nights of her captivity, several things had helped keep her sane and focused on survival. First and foremost, she couldn't let that sick son of a bitch kill her and add her scalp to his collection. Of course, she worried about how her mother was handling the situation. Sedated, no doubt. Kept oblivious to reality by her new husband. But what about Charles David? He was so tender-hearted and emotional. He would fall apart if she died, especially if she was murdered.

And what about Griff?

All she had to do was reverse their positions and put him here, struggling to escape from a madman's clutches. She knew how he felt, what he was thinking, and understood that he had spent the past nineteen days as tortured as she had been.

Nic crossed her arms over her belly.

She hadn't had her period.

What if I'm pregnant?

She probably wasn't. Probably hadn't been when he kidnapped her. But if she had been, was it possible that those tiny, microscopic cells that would divide and multiply and grow into a baby could have survived inside her bruised, battered, malnourished body?

She had tried not to think about the possibility that she was carrying Griff's baby. The thought of it was too distracting. She couldn't worry about a pregnancy that more than likely didn't exist, not when her life was at stake.

Get up and get your ass in gear. Don't waste any more time worrying about Griff or your mother or Charles David. Or a nonexistent child.

Hours later, when the sun had reached overhead and was beginning its slow descent westward, Nic heard the roar of his dirt bike. Knowing she couldn't stay hidden indefinitely, that any which way she turned, he could be on her in minutes, she had no choice but to go from defensive mode to offensive. Instead of waiting for him to track her down, she had to attack first.

Nic waited until she heard the bike's motor idling and knew he had stopped, probably to visually inspect the lay of the land. Since it had taken him a while to figure out that she'd been following the old roadbed, he must have followed her fake trail for quite some time; otherwise, he would have caught up with her sooner. She crept slowly to the edge of the wooded area where she'd been hiding, slipped her hand into the pocket of her filthy, ragged sweatpants, and pulled out the short, thick wooden stick that she had shaped into a weapon. She had used a sharp-edged rock to scrape a sharp point on the end of the stick.

Her only hope of overpowering him was a sneak attack.

There was no point in putting off what had to be done. She had one chance to make her move and take him by surprise. The noise of the idling motor worked to her advantage, masking the sound of her footsteps as she approached him from behind. Using her body as a battering ram, she dove into him and knocked him off the bike. She used the force of her weight to hold him down while she positioned the knife-like stick to hit the jugular vein in his neck. Just as she plunged the tip forward, he bucked up and the pointed end sliced across the back of his neck. He yelped in pain and knocked her off him. She clutched the stick between their bodies as he rolled her over.

With his red face contorted in rage, he brought his meaty fist back, intending to hit her. When he lowered his hand, Nic turned the stick so that the sharp edge faced away from her. Just as his knuckles hit the side of her face, she lunged upward, thrusting the makeshift knife into his gut.

He grunted.

She shoved the stick deeper.

He stared at her, his eyes wide with shock and disbelief.

As blood gushed from his wound and he grasped at the end of the stick protruding from his belly, Nic managed to roll him off of her. Struggling to stand, she rose on wobbly legs.

While he stared at the blood gushing out of his stomach, Nic reached down and grabbed for the strap that held the rifle across his shoulder. He clutched the rifle with his bloody hand and held on for dear life. Nic tried to wrestle the rifle from him, but quickly realized she couldn't win this fight. She moved away from him and ran. She glanced over her shoulder and saw that he lay by his bike, unmoving and quiet. She hoped the son of a bitch was dead. She looked ahead of her, up the road toward freedom.

And then, just as she got her second wind and thought she honest to God had a chance of escaping, the rifle shot rang out in the hushed stillness. The bullet ripped into Nic's back, the impact bringing her to her knees.

Chapter 20

Foy and Jewel Calame, on their way home from a week visiting their daughter and grandchildren in Thibodaux, were listening to Reverend Tommy Taylor's daily radio broadcast. At home, they always listened to the young minister's inspiring words every afternoon, right after Foy woke up from his nap. They'd been married forty-six years come February, had raised two sons and a daughter, all of them good, God-fearing Christians. *Thank you, Lord Jesus.* Jewel remembered a time when Foy had been a drinker and a gambler, back in his younger years. But when he'd found Jesus, right after their second son was born, he'd given up all his sinful ways and been a good husband and father ever since. They didn't have much in the way of material things, but they made do on Foy's Social Security check. Their house was paid for and so was this old car. And the kids sent them a little, along with Christmas presents and birthday presents, and just this past Mother's Day, they'd gotten her one of them cute little pink cell phones.

"Lord have mercy, Christy Lou, what am I going to do with a cell phone?" she'd asked their daughter.

"You're going to have it for emergencies when you and Daddy are on the road or if you're in town and want to call home, you can. And I can send you a new picture of Marcy Jewel over this phone every day, Mama."

It had been that last bit that had persuaded her to keep the phone. She had five grandsons, ranging in ages from nine to fifteen, but Christy Lou's baby was their only granddaughter. *Lord forgive me, but I'm plum crazy about that sweet little gal.*

"Look up yonder," Jewel said. "Ain't that the road that'll take us into Orson's Cove? We got some of the best Jambalaya I ever tasted at that little restaurant last time we came through here."

"Are you trying to tell me you ain't going to cook supper when we get home?" Foy chuckled.

"Come on, honey pie, let's splurge a little and eat out. Christy Lou gave me a twenty-dollar bill and said for me to spend it however I wanted. And I want some of that Jambalaya over at the Fishing Shack."

"Then we'll just make a little detour over that way."

When they reached the turnoff, Foy took the two-lane road to Orson's Cove. The pavement had been patched numerous times, just like the road that ran by their house in Centersville. But there were more potholes and at least half a dozen little bridges crossing creeks and a few dried-up streambeds. Foy slowed their ten-year-old Chevy Malibu down to twenty-five miles per hour when he approached the final bridge that led into town. Jewel was surprised that the county hadn't replaced that bridge years ago. It was barely wide enough for two cars, so most folks took turns, letting incoming traffic go first and outgoing go second when crossing the bridge.

"Hold up!" Jewel cried. "There's something in the road up there, right over on the other side of the bridge."

Foy glared through the bug-splattered windshield. "Could

be a big old dog. Or maybe a calf. Looks like it's been run over."

"Well, you be careful and try not to hit it. And if you can't drive around it, you'll just have to get out and push it off to the side of the road."

"If it's dead, I'll move it," Foy said. "But I ain't about to mess with no hurt animal."

Foy eased the car halfway across the bridge, then slammed on the brakes when Jewel hollered, "Stop!"

"What in tarnation's the matter with you, woman?"

"That ain't no animal in the road, Foy. That's a human being. I think it's a woman."

Foy opened the car door and got out. "You're right," he called back to Jewel. "It is a woman. And I think she's dead."

Jewel shoved open the passenger door, got out, and walked across the bridge to where the woman's body lay sprawled face-down on the road. She knelt down and touched the woman's head. When the woman groaned, Jewel jerked her hand away.

"She ain't dead, Foy. But the poor thing is just barely alive." Jewel inspected the woman from head to toe. "Looks like she's been shot."

"No telling what kind of meanness she was into," Foy said.

"Hush up. It ain't our place to judge. Go get me that pink phone out of my purse. We gotta call 911 and get this gal an ambulance out here. It's our Christian duty to do what we can to help her."

Foy did as she'd asked and brought her the phone. She dialed the emergency number, just like Christy Lou had showed her how to do. Then she told the nice young man on the other end of the line where they were and what they had found.

"You'd best get somebody out here right away," Jewel said. "I don't know how much longer she's gonna last."

She handed Foy the phone, then told him to bring her the pillow she kept in the car for their road trips.

"Ain't no telling what kind of germs she's got," Foy said. "Besides that, she's bloody as a stuck hog."

"Get me that pillow, old man. This gal is one of God's creatures and He expects me to look after her and show her a little human kindness."

When Foy returned with the pillow, Jewel eased it under the woman's head. Poor thing. She was a terrible sight. Just terrible.

The battered woman moaned again and then gasped for air. Jewel's eyes widened in surprise.

"I think she's trying to say something," Foy told his wife. "Look how she's working her mouth."

Jewel leaned down real close to the woman's face and asked, "What is it, gal? You trying to tell me something?"

"Grr . . . rrr . . . the sound purred from the woman's parched lips.

"What was that?" Jewel asked.

"Griff," the woman said.

"Griff?" Jewel looked up at Foy. "What's a griff?"

"Never heard of such a thing."

The woman repeated the word one more time, then passed out.

"It's getting cold out here," Jewel said. "Go get my coat and bring me that old blanket out of the trunk so I can cover this gal up. She's shivering something awful."

Foy grumbled all the way back to the car. Let the old fart grumble. Jewel knew she was doing what was right in the eyes of the Lord.

Pudge hoped he had killed the bitch. He knew he had shot her in the back. Maybe she was lying dead somewhere. But whether she was alive or dead, he couldn't stay at Belle Fleur. It would be only a matter of time, after they found Nicole's body, before they started searching the area. They were bound to discover that a distant cousin of Cary Maygarden owned extensive property in the area and they would put two and two together. A search warrant would come next, and they'd pay a visit to the plantation, go through his house, and find his trophy room in the basement.

He had nearly passed out before he'd made it back to the house. All he remembered was pulling his dirt bike up to the back door and hollering for Allegra. Apparently, she'd called her daughter and the two of them had brought him here to the clinic. They'd probably saved his life. He'd have to remember to reward them. But first things first. Right now, he needed to get out of here. He had to go home and make plans as soon as possible to leave the country.

"Please, lie still, Mr. Everhart," Dr. Morrow said, then looked at his nurse. "Call County General and arrange for transportation. Mr. Everhart is going to need surgery as soon as possible."

Morrow was a young kid, new to the local clinic, but he seemed to know what he was doing.

"I can't go to the hospital," Pudge said. "I have some important business that I have to take care of tonight."

"You can't go anywhere tonight," the doctor told him. "I'm sending you over to County General. You lost a great deal of blood and—"

"Just patch me up and release me. Give me some antibiotics and pain pills and Allegra and Fantine will take me home. I'll come back tomorrow, if you think it's necessary, but I am going home this evening."

"Mr. Everhart, I advise you to—"

"Allegra!" Pudge bellowed. "Have Fantine bring the car around. We're going home just as soon as the doctor finishes up in here."

"Mr. Everhart, please. You had a nasty accident. That sharp stick did some major damage. It's lucky you knew not to try to remove it. If you had, you would have bled to death before you managed to get back home. You owe your housekeeper your life. But I've done all I can for you. You need immediate surgery and I'm afraid we're not equipped for it here at the clinic."

Pudge reached up and grabbed the lapel of Dr. Morrow's white coat. "You don't understand. My life depends on—"

The doctor grabbed Pudge's hand. "Your life depends on your having immediate surgery, Mr. Everhart." He motioned to the nurse, who came over and gave Pudge an injection while the doctor held him down.

"I'll sue you. You can't force me to . . ."

Pudge realized the injection had been a sedative. Apparently, a fast-acting one. His last coherent thought was: he hoped Nicole Baxter was dead.

* * *

Nic heard strange sounds. Buzzing. Humming. Quiet thumping. And voices. Soft voices. What was wrong with her? Why couldn't she open her eyes? Why was she so sleepy? Was she dead? Was she in some halfway house between heaven and hell?

"The poor dear," a female voice said. "She's lucky to be alive."

I'm not dead!

She opened her mouth and tried to speak. What was that in her mouth? Yuck. Something was stuck in her throat.

"Mmm . . . mmm . . ." She tried to talk, but only a weird mumble came out.

"She's waking up," another female voice said.

She felt a warm hand on her shoulder. "It's all right, miss. You're in Baton Rouge General in Baton Rouge, Louisiana. You're safe and you're going to be all right."

What was she doing in Baton Rouge? She didn't know anyone in Louisiana. Was she here on official business?

Why am I in the hospital? What happened to me? Why is my mind so screwed up?

She mumbled again. Damn!

Somebody help me.

"Don't try to talk," the softer voice said. "You're on a ventilator. Temporarily."

Nic managed to move her eyelids, lifting them partially open. Her vision was blurry, but she could make out the shape of a full face and short, curly hair.

"Well, hello, there. I'm Geena Kilpatrick. I'm one of the nurses here in ICU."

Hello, Geena. I'm Nicole Baxter. Special Agent Baxter. I'm an FBI agent.

"You're probably feeling pretty groggy," the nurse said. "You're recovering from surgery and we're keeping you medicated for the pain."

Surgery? Why did I have surgery?

"Should I call Sheriff Mitchum?" the other female voice asked.

"Yes, go ahead. He wanted us to let him know the minute she woke up. But tell him that she's not going to be able to talk to him this morning."

Nic lifted her arm and reached for the nurse who stood directly by her bed. Suddenly her vision cleared enough so that she noticed the tubes connected to her arm. When she held out her hand, the plump, sweet-faced nurse clasped Nic's hand gently.

Nic mumbled again and again. Frustrated that she couldn't speak, she squeezed the nurse's hand and looked up at her pleadingly.

"Oh, dear, you want to say something really bad, don't you?"

Nic nodded.

"I'll get you a pad and pen and you can see if you can write down what you're trying to say."

Doing her best to smile, Nic nodded again.

Nurse Geena disappeared.

Nic glanced around while she waited. She was hooked up to various monitoring equipment and she noticed an IV drip. They were probably giving her some high-powered pain-killers and that's why she couldn't think straight, why she couldn't remember.

Just relax and think. What's the very last thing you remember?

Griffin Powell.

They had made love. More than once.

He had spent the night with her. At her home in Wood-bridge.

How had she gotten from Virginia to Louisiana?

She had awakened after their night of fabulous sex. Griff had been asleep, so she'd tiptoed into the bathroom, put on her sweats, made coffee, left him a note, and gone for a morning walk.

"Here we go," Nurse Geena said as she placed an ink pen in Nic's right hand and a small notepad in her left. "You are right-handed, aren't you, sweetie?"

Nic nodded.

Staring at the notepad, she clutched the pen in her hand.

She remembered going for her morning walk. She had been almost back to her house when—Oh, God! Someone had shot her.

But if she'd been shot in Woodbridge, Virginia, what was she doing in a hospital in Baton Rouge, Louisiana?

She needed Griff. He'd know what was going on. Griff would handle everything. He'd take care of this whole mess.

"Want me to raise the head of your bed just a little?" the nurse asked.

"Mm . . . mm . . ." Nic nodded yet again.

She pressed the pen into the notepad and with great effort managed to scribble the letter *G* and then an *R* and finally an *I* before she had to rest.

Nurse Geena glanced at the pad. "Are you trying to tell me your name?"

Why didn't they know her name?

Nic shook her head, then scrawled the letter *F* and showed the word to the nurse.

"Grif?"

Nic nodded.

"Is that part of your name?"

Nic shook her head and wrote four letters, slowly, laboriously, with great difficulty. She tapped the notepad repeatedly.

"Grif Powl? Is he your husband?"

Nic shook her head.

"Is it the name of the person who shot you?"

She shook her head again, growing more and more agitated by the minute.

Someone had shot her. Yes, she remembered. Images flashed through her mind. Chains on her ankles. Handcuffs. Woods. The roar of a dirt bike.

Nic screamed, the terrified sound echoing in her mind, but it came out of her mouth as a muffled, gasping moan.

Nurse Geena called out something to someone as she held Nic's shoulders, trying to keep her still. Nic's struggles ended when the other nurse slid a hypodermic needle into the tube that connected her arm to the IV solution.

Geena had been an Registered Nurse for twenty-five years, the past ten spent as an intensive care nurse. She'd seen some horrible things in her time, but she didn't think anything could compare to what had probably happened to their latest Jane Doe. She'd been shot in the back, though luckily the bullet hadn't hit any vital organs or her spine. That in itself was a miracle. But the large gash in her back, just below her left shoulder blade had been infected. Also, she had been malnourished and on the verge of being dehydrated. From the bruises on her body, the healing welts on her back, and the cuts and scrapes on her legs and feet, the sheriff's department surmised that she'd been tortured.

When she had arrived at Baton Rouge General, she'd been near death. If the old Centerville couple hadn't found her and called for help, she would have died within hours.

As Geena sipped on her cola, she eyed the notepad where their Jane Doe had scribbled a name. Or at least Geena thought it was a name. She had called her daughter and asked her to Google the two words, "Grif Powl." It was possible that it wasn't a person's name.

"I'll run a check, Mom, and call you back," her daughter had told her ten minutes ago.

Isaac Felton, another ICU nurse, came over and sat down beside Geena. "What do you have there?" He glanced at the notepad Geena was absently patting.

"Oh, it's something our Jane Doe wrote down. But she got so upset when we didn't understand what she was trying to tell us that we had to sedate her."

"Mind if I take a look?" Isaac asked.

Smiling, Geena handed him the pad. "We think it's a name. I'm having my daughter Google it to see if she can come up with something."

Isaac read the words aloud. "Grif Powl. Hmm . . ." He repeated the words several times. Then, just as he said, "Griff Powell. Griffin Powell," the telephone rang.

"Is that a name you recognize for some reason?" Geena asked before taking the call.

"Mom, it's me, Megan. I think I may have found out about that name."

Geena held up an index finger as a signal for Isaac to wait a minute. "Yeah, honey, go ahead."

"There's a super-rich private detective named Griffin Powell. He's got offices in Knoxville, Tennessee. And guess what else? He used to be some big hotshot football player for the University of Tennessee, back before I was born."

"Is there a telephone number listed for this guy? An office number?" On the off chance that this Griffin Powell was the person their Jane Doe wanted, Geena decided she'd at least check it out.

"Yeah, there's an office number and an e-mail address."

"Give me the number," Geena said, then looked at Isaac. "Write this down."

He nodded. She repeated the number Megan gave her, then hung up and turned to her coworker.

"I guess Megan told you that Griffin Powell is a football legend," Isaac said. "The guy was Mr. UT football before anybody knew Peyton Manning's name."

"I should probably call the sheriff's office and let them do this, but that poor girl in there needs somebody who cares about her and she needs them now. I'm going to call this guy and describe our Jane Doe and see if he might know her."

Griff hadn't slept in forty-eight hours. Today was day twenty-three. Nic's body hadn't shown up anywhere. The Hunter hadn't called. Nobody knew what the hell was going on.

Sanders didn't know exactly when Griff would break, but it would happen. Today. Tomorrow. Next week. His old friend was on the verge of a nervous breakdown and not even he or Yvette could prevent the inevitable.

Barbara Jean called Sanders's name. He turned from where he stood on the patio, the cold afternoon wind whipping around him, and faced her. She remained inside, just beyond the half-open French door.

"Rick Carson is on the phone. He's calling from the office in Knoxville. He says it's urgent."

Sanders hurried inside and closed the door behind him. "Did Rick say what this was about?"

"He said it was in regard to Nicole Baxter."

Sanders's chest constricted tightly. Was this the call they had been anticipating? The call they had dreaded?

"Did he say anything else? Is she—?"

"He didn't go into detail. He just said for you to call him immediately."

Sanders nodded, then hurried down the hall and toward the state-of-the-art home office. He opened the door and flipped on the switches that activated all the lighting in the huge room, which was divided into three separate work areas. After seating himself behind one of the desks, he picked up the phone and called the Knoxville office. The receptionist put him through to Rick Carson immediately.

"Did they find her body?" Sanders asked the minute Rick answered.

"No," Rick replied.

A whoosh of air left Sanders's lungs as a feeling of intense relief spread through him. "Then this call is not about Nicole Baxter?"

"Yes, it is," Rick said. "Or I think it is. I just spoke to a nurse who works in the ICU at Baton Rouge General. She called wanting to speak to Griff. It seems she's got a patient, a Jane Doe, who had surgery for a gunshot wound and who they believe was tortured and left for dead on a back road somewhere down there. I know this doesn't fit the Hunter's MO, but this woman—she can't speak because she's temporarily hooked up to a ventilator—scribbled Griff's name down on a notepad."

"The nurse who called, did she give you a description of the Jane Doe in her ICU?"

"Sure did."

"And?"

"Late twenties, early thirties. Tall, probably five nine or ten. Dark brown hair. Light brown eyes."

Sanders's heartbeat accelerated. "It could be Nicole."

"Yeah, but it might not be. What are you going to do? How are you going to handle this?"

"I'm going to tell Griffin."

"But what if it turns out not to be Nicole Baxter?"

Sanders knew that what Rick did not understand was the depth of Griffin's despair, that nothing that happened could take him any further down into the hell in which he now resided.

"If it is not Nicole, Griffin will deal with it."

Five minutes later, Sanders knocked on the closed study door.

"Go away," Griffin said, his voice a hoarse growl.

Disregarding Griffin's command, Sanders opened the door and walked into the room. He snapped his head around and glared at Sanders.

Bloodshot eyes. Two-day growth of beard stubble. Rumpled clothes.

A half-empty bottle of Scotch rested on the floor beside the sofa.

Griffin had an obsessive habit of being clean-shaven. A left over quirk from his days in captivity when he had not been allowed to shave. Knowing that Griffin had not touched a razor in days told Sanders more accurately than anything else did that his old friend had allowed himself to sink into the quagmire of hopelessness.

"I thought I told you to go away."

"There is possible news about Nicole," Sanders said.

Griffin sat up straight and looked Sanders in the eye. "They found her body?"

"No, but there is a young woman—badly injured, but alive—in an ICU in Baton Rouge who fits Nicole's general description. It seems this woman, who is unable to talk, managed to write your name on a piece of paper."

Griffin shot up off the sofa. "Call Jonathan and tell him to have the plane ready to go ASAP. Come with me and fill me in on the details while I take a shower, shave, and change clothes."

Chapter 21

Griff had lost faith. He'd given up. He had been waiting for two days for word that Nic's body had been discovered. And then he had received a miracle. Even the chance that this woman in the Baton Rouge hospital might be Nic was more than he had dared hope. On the flight from Knoxville, he had struggled to maintain a balance between hope and reality, between what his heart told him and what his head told him. Under any other circumstances, he would have chosen harsh reality and common sense, but not today, not when Nic might be alive.

Although Sanders and Rick Carson had traveled with him, he had spent the trip in relative silence and appreciated that they had respected his desire for solitude. He needed time to prepare himself for whatever they found when they arrived at the hospital. If Nic was alive, he would move heaven and earth to help her. But if the woman wasn't Nic . . .

God, how he hated the uncertainty.

And he hated being so emotionally charged. For years, he had prided himself on being aloof and unemotional. But then Special Agent Baxter had entered his life five years ago and everything had changed. During the four years that he had been involved in BQK cases, he'd thrived on their verbal sparring matches. No one else got under his skin the way she had.

Now he wondered if all those years of animosity between them had been nothing more than a long prelude to the night they'd made love. Was it any wonder, after five years of foreplay, they had ignited instantly and set each other on fire?

During the past three weeks, he had relived every moment of that night. Every touch, every kiss, every whispered word.

Let Nic be alive. On their drive from the airport to the hospital, Griff's mind repeated the silent plea again and again.

They arrived at Baton Rouge General with a police escort, requested by SAC Doug Trotter, who was now on his way to Louisiana. Before they left Griffin's Rest, Sanders had contacted Nicole's immediate superior and filled him in on the information they had received from the ICU nurse. Rick Carson had flown in with them and Griff suspected that Sanders had requested Rick accompany them so that he could run interference and deal with anything that Griff might ordinarily handle.

Hospital security met them at the entrance and ushered them straight to the elevator and upstairs to the intensive care unit. A sheriff's deputy, who had been assigned to stand guard, met them in the waiting area.

"I'm Griffin Powell." He looked the young deputy square in the eyes.

"Yes, sir. I'm Deputy McNeal."

"I'm here to see the Jane Doe in ICU."

"Yes, sir. The sheriff has given you clearance to go in and see the lady during visiting hours."

"I'm not waiting for visiting hours. I want to see her now."

"I—er—they're awfully strict about this, Mr. Powell. Visiting hours aren't for another hour and—"

"Either you get the head nurse or whoever's in charge out here now or I'm going in, permission or not."

The deputy's brow wrinkled. "Uh, yes, sir. You wait here."

"Griffin." Sanders touched his arm.

Griff breathed in deeply, then released the breath slowly. "I'm okay."

A plump, middle-aged woman with rosy cheeks and curly brown hair approached Griff. "Mr. Powell?"

"Yes, I'm Griffin Powell."

"I'm Geena Kilpatrick. I'm the one who called your office. If you'll come with me, I'll take to you see our Jane Doe. We've kept her sedated all afternoon, but she's coming to and getting agitated again. Maybe when she sees you, she'll settle down."

"Have you asked her what her name is?"

"No," Geena said. "Not again. When we gave her the pad and pen, we thought she would write her name, but she wrote your name instead. At first we couldn't make it out and wasn't sure if it was a name. She left out letters and . . . Well, when we didn't understand what she'd written, she became very upset and tried to get out of bed. We've kept her sedated ever since."

The nurse led him into the ICU and directly to Jane Doe's cubicle. She stepped back and waited for Griff to enter. Before going in, he closed his eyes. *Let it be Nic.*

He walked in, then halted midway to the bed. His gaze traveled over the woman lying there. She moaned as she stirred restlessly. He focused on her face. Pale. Bruised. Eyes closed.

Overwhelming emotion gripped him, constricting his lungs, tightening his throat. Then he released the tension in one huffing breath.

Nic! She was alive.

Thank you, God.

"Is she someone you know, Mr. Powell?" Geena asked.

So overcome with emotion that he couldn't speak, Griff nodded, then moved slowly toward the bed. When he looked down at Nic, it took every ounce of his willpower not to grab her and pull her into his arms. Instead, he dropped to his knees at her bedside, lifted her badly scratched and bruised arm, and brought her hand to his cheek.

"Nic, honey. Nicki, it's Griff."

"Mmm . . ." she whimpered but didn't open her eyes.

The nurse came up behind Griff. "I'll leave you alone with her, Mr. Powell. But first, could you please tell me her name? I need it for our records and I've been instructed to inform the deputy."

Griff nodded, never taking his eyes off Nic. "Her name is Nicole Baxter. Special Agent Nicole Baxter."

"She's an FBI agent?"

"Yes."

"Thank you. I'll leave you now. Stay as long as you'd like. If, when she wakes fully, she's upset, we'll have no choice but to sedate her again."

"I understand." Griff glanced over his shoulder and up at Geena. "What can you tell me about her condition?"

"She's listed as critical. Other than that, I can't say more. You'll have to speak to her doctor. He'll be making rounds in the ICU later."

"All right. Later."

Griff stayed there on his knees, Nic's hand in his, and talked to her. She kept mumbling, kept shifting about as if she were uncomfortable. A couple of times, her eyelashes fluttered.

"You're going to be all right," he told her repeatedly. "I'm here, Nic. It's Griff. Whatever you need, whatever you want . . ."

He didn't know how long he remained on his knees, but

eventually Geena Kilpatrick came back, checked on Nic, and brought in a chair for him.

"Has she opened her eyes?" the nurse asked.

"Not yet."

She patted Griff on the shoulder. "She will. Be patient."

Griff sat in the chair and held Nic's hand. He talked to her for a while longer, then just sat there and waited.

Suddenly, she squeezed his hand so gently that he barely felt it. He looked at her and said her name softly. Her eyelids opened and closed a couple of times, then she opened her eyes completely and stared at him.

She mumbled, unable to speak because of the tube in her throat. Her eyes filled with tears.

Griff squeezed her hand tenderly. "Hey there. It's about time you opened those beautiful brown eyes and looked at me."

Tears streamed down her cheeks.

She tugged on his hand.

He stood, leaned over the bed, and gently wrapped his arms around her. She lifted her hands and weakly grasped the lapels of his jacket. He never wanted to let her go, but he knew she needed to lie still and rest, so he pulled loose, clutched her shoulders, and eased her back into a comfortable position in the bed. She reached for him. He grabbed her hand, brought it to his lips, and kissed it.

She pulled her hand free, then moved her right index finger over her left palm in a scribbling motion.

"You want a pen and paper again?" he asked.

She nodded.

"Are you sure you feel up to it?"

She nodded again and looked at him pleadingly.

He smiled at her. "Whatever you want."

She sighed and squeezed his hand again.

He leaned over and kissed her on the forehead before he left to find the nurse.

"She wants a pen and paper," Griff told Geena Kilpatrick. "I'll get them for you right away."

"Thanks. And would you ask the deputy to tell the two men who came with me that I'm staying until y'all kick me out and for them to get a hotel room and I'll call them if I need them?"

"Yes, of course."

Griff held the notepad for her as she tried to write. Every letter she scribbled took great effort. Woozy, her limbs as weak as wet dishrags and her thoughts slightly jumbled, she struggled to stay focused.

She showed Griff what she'd written.

PLATAION HOUSE

He studied the two words closely. "Plantation house?"

She nodded, then ripped off that sheet of paper and began writing. Once again, she turned the pad so Griff could see what she'd written.

LOTS LAND WODS

"Lots of land. Woods."

She nodded.

"He took you to an old plantation house here in Louisiana. The house was surrounded by woods."

Nic sighed heavily, then tore off that sheet and wrote again.

When she held out the notepad, Griff took it from her, and studied the four words she had written:

LOOK WHER I FOND

And then he said, "You want us to look for him close to where you were found."

"Mm . . . mm . . ." She nodded again and reached for the notepad.

"That's enough for now," he told her. "Rest for a while and later you can tell me more."

She shook her head and waved her hand at him.

"Stubborn as ever, I see." He grabbed her hand, kissed the center of her palm, and said, "Doug Trotter is on his way here. He's got the local field office working on this, as well as the sheriff's department. And Rick Carson came in with Sanders and me. They'll speak to the couple who called 911 when they found you and get all the information about where you were."

She closed her fingers around his hand and shut her eyes.

There was so much she needed to tell Griff, so much information she could give him to help them track down the monster who had held her prisoner for nearly three weeks. But she was tired. So very tired.

Doug Trotter met with Griff at the hospital that evening and they came away from their brief meeting with the knowledge that they shared common goals: Nic's full recovery, and the apprehension and punishment of the madman who had captured her.

"We're tracking down the couple who found Nic," Trotter had said. "I expect to hear something tonight. And we've already spoken to the 911 operator and the paramedics who brought Nic in. We've got all our manpower at work on this one."

"I'd offer Powell's resources if I thought you'd use them."

"Yeah, but you know I can't accept. Not officially. Anyhow, we know where Nic was found, so, if all goes well, it shouldn't take long to figure out just where she was being held."

"When you find out—"

"Someone will give you a call."

Griff understood that Trotter couldn't officially notify Griff, couldn't share info with him. But Nic's boss knew the best way to keep Griff under control was by cooperating with him.

The ICU staff had bent the rules to allow Griff a great deal of time with Nic, so he hadn't protested when he'd been asked to leave and return in the morning. He took a taxi to the hotel, where Sanders had a hot meal waiting for him. After a late dinner, he showered, shaved, and changed clothes.

"I'm going back to the hospital," Griff said.

"You will not be allowed to see her tonight."

"I know, but I need to be there, nearby." *Just in case.*

"You should wait for her brother to arrive," Sanders suggested. "Rick has gone to the airport to meet him."

"Tell Charles David that he'll be able to see Nic first thing in the morning, at nine o'clock. But if wants to stay in the waiting room with me tonight, have Rick drive him to the hospital."

Sanders followed Griff to the door. "I must ask you for a promise."

Griff tensed, then paused and glanced at his friend.

"Promise me that if the FBI finds this man, you will not take the law into your own hands."

Sanders knew him too well. He knew just what Griff was capable of, just how barbarically he could react in certain situations.

"I promise that if the FBI apprehends this man and he is adequately punished by the law, I will do nothing else."

Sanders nodded.

He understood the conditions of Griff's promise and accepted them. He knew, better than most, that there were circumstances under which a man had to do what was necessary, whether his actions were legal or not.

Rosswalt Everhart arranged for a chartered plane to fly him to Mexico where he checked into a private clinic, using fake ID and paying for everything in cash. As soon as he had recovered from surgery, he would move on. But in the meantime, he would use this recuperative period to find and rent a tiny, isolated island somewhere, hopefully not far away. He had always liked the Caribbean.

He had left the hospital in Louisiana the day after his surgery. He'd had no choice. If he had remained in the United States, the odds were that the FBI would have found him. By now, they probably knew his name, his connection to his cousin Ruddy, and were no doubt searching Belle Fleur, both the house and surrounding acres. The thought of strangers tramping through his home, rummaging through his personal belongings, and desecrating the hallowed Everhart grounds enraged Ross. And it was all that bitch Nicole Baxter's fault. She had almost killed him, but only because he had underestimated her. Next time, he would not make that mistake.

Naked, his young, muscular body scarred with insect bites, ugly scratches, and stinging cuts from underbrush, Griffin Powell ran through the jungle. His left forearm dripped blood from where he'd snagged it on a jagged rock when he'd fallen into a deep ravine. Dried blood caked his lacerated feet. The sun beat down on his scorched flesh, burning his already-blistered skin. Adrenaline surged through him. Every survival instinct he possessed urged him on. Keep running. No matter how much he ached, no matter how weary and sleep-deprived he was, he had to keep going. His life depended on it.

A shot rang out, echoing through the dense maze of thick greenery and towering trees. York was closing in on him.

Griff's heartbeat accelerated.

Forcing himself to run faster, he tried to think, tried to figure out where he was and in which direction he should go. Escape was impossible. But temporary asylum was not. He had outwitted York before and he could do it again. That's why he was still alive after weeks of being hunted like a wild animal.

He would not die.

He would not let York destroy him.

He would live. No matter what he had to do.

And someday, he would kill his tormentor.

"Griffin? Mr. Powell? Are you all right?" A man's voice called to Griff, from somewhere outside the foggy memories that haunted his dreams.

Griff awoke with a start and stared into pale brown eyes identical to Nic's. Struggling to emerge from his nightmare, Griff ran his hands over his face and rubbed his eyes.

"What is it? What's wrong?" he asked Nic's brother.

"That was my question for you," Charles David said. "You were mumbling in your sleep and becoming really agitated."

Griff took a deep breath. "I'm okay." He glanced at the wall clock there in the ICU waiting room. "It's nearly six. I must have slept for a couple of hours."

"I think we both drifted off sometime after three," Charles David said. "I woke when I heard you grumbling."

"Sorry."

"No problem." He looked around the waiting room, empty

except for the two of them. "I could use a cup of coffee. How about you?"

"I believe the cafeteria opens at seven," Griff said. "We can go for breakfast and get back in plenty of time to see Nic during the first visitation at nine."

Charles David stood and stretched, then looked down at Griff. "I believe in nonviolence. I'm opposed to hunting for sport. I'm opposed to the war this country is embroiled in. I don't even believe in the death penalty. So, tell me, why is it that I feel as if I could strangle the man who hurt Nic? I honestly think I could kill him with my bare hands."

"A lot of our beliefs change when things get personal," Griff said. "A man can say he'd never kill another human being, but when his life or the life of someone he loves is on the line, how would he react? What would he do? Self-preservation and procreation are the two strongest instincts that we humans possess. And right up there with those two is the instinct to protect what's ours."

"Nic's a lot tougher than I am. She always was." Tears glazed Charles David's eyes. "While she was missing, I kept telling myself that if anyone could survive—" He gulped down tears. "He tortured her, didn't he?"

Griff stood and clamped his hand down on Charles David's shoulder. "He's a monster who derives pleasure from other people's pain—mental, emotional, and physical."

"How will she ever recover from this? How can she forget what he did to her?"

"We don't know what he did," Griff said. "But just like you said, Nic is tough. She's strong and she'll recover, in time." He didn't add, *But she'll never forget.*

Griff had never forgotten those years on Amara. For the most part, he managed to keep those memories buried deep inside him, but since this new series of murders had begun, those old memories had been resurfacing. Awake, he could battle the demons and keep them at bay. But asleep, those demons took control of his subconscious.

Griff squeezed Charles David's shoulder. "Let's see if we can find a coffee machine before breakfast."

"Yeah, let's do that."

Just as they reached the elevator, it opened and SA Josh Freidman emerged.

"Morning," Josh said. "You two heading off somewhere?"

"Coffee," Griff replied. "What about you? What are you doing here?"

Josh glanced at Charles David. "Are you Nic's brother?"

"Yes, why?"

"I'm Special Agent Josh Friedman. I work with your sister. My boss, Doug Trotter, wanted me to fill you in on what's happened." Josh gave Griff a sidelong glance, then refocused on Charles David. "Why don't we go for coffee and I'll fill you in."

The three men entered the elevator.

Griff said, "Start talking."

"A man named Rosswalt Everhart owns a thousand-acre plantation and an old antebellum house about six miles from where Foy and Jewel Calame found Nic," Josh said. "It seems that, in the area where he lives, he's known as an eccentric recluse."

"And?" Griff asked.

"And while we were searching for personal information on this guy, guess what we discovered? Guess who his cousin was?"

Griff tensed, every muscle tight, every nerve taut. "Cary Maygarden."

Chapter 22

LaTasha Davies stood in the open doorway of her eight-year-old daughter's bedroom, which she shared with her six-year-old cousin. It was good to be home, back in Tampa, even if only for two weeks. At least she'd be spending Thanksgiving with her family, something she hadn't been able to do for the past couple of years. She'd been in Afghanistan two years ago and in Iraq last year and would be returning to the war long before Christmas. Being assigned outside the U.S., she'd had no choice but to leave Asheen with her mother.

"That child's growing up without you," LaTasha's mother, Geraldine, had told her. "It ain't good for either of you to be apart so much. Asheen's got to where she's calling your sister 'Mama.'"

"You don't think this is the way I wanted my life to turn out, do you? I'm doing what I have to do to give Asheen a decent life, the kind of chances I never had."

"I did the best I could."

"I know you did, Mama. I'm not blaming you. I blame myself for getting pregnant at fifteen and quitting school and letting Marco back into my life over and over again."

LaTasha had learned all her life lessons the hard way. As a teenager, she'd been pretty and smart and thought she knew more than her mama did about everything including men. Marco Crews had been twenty-five, drove a sports car, and always had money to burn. It wasn't until after she had given birth to his daughter and gone through two abortions that she finally realized the guy was bad news. Turns out, she hadn't been so smart after all. Marco had fathered half a dozen children by three different women, but remained single and on the prowl.

When Asheen was four, she'd been diagnosed with juvenile diabetes. Her daughter's illness had been a wake-up call for LaTasha. She'd quit her two part-time minimum wage jobs, where she'd had no benefits whatsoever, and joined the army. She'd believed that her decision was the best way to provide Asheen with everything she needed. The army could also give LaTasha a chance for a good education. And if she wound up getting her head blown off in Iraq, at least her daughter would be provided for.

"She's a sweet child," her sister Katari said as she came up behind LaTasha. "She reminds me so much of you when you was that age."

"Don't let her forget me entirely," LaTasha said.

Her sister placed her arm around LaTasha's shoulders and gave her a hug. "Mama and me talk about you to her a lot, you know."

"When did she start calling you 'Mama'?"

Katari sighed. "She don't do it all the time, just every once in a while."

"I don't want her calling nobody else 'Mama.' I'm her mama."

"She hears Tyrina calling me 'Mama' and Latarius 'Daddy' all the time," Katari said. "You can't blame her for wanting parents like her little cousin has. But she knows you're her mother. She's not going to forget about you."

LaTasha pulled away from her sister. "I'm going out for a walk. I need to think about what I'm going to do. If Mama hadn't moved in with you and Latarius—"

"Don't go blaming Mama. She's getting old. She's worked hard all her life and her health ain't good. Instead of resenting the bond I've got with Asheen, you ought to be grateful that I'm giving her and Mama a good home."

"I'm grateful." LaTasha swallowed her tears.

Without a backward glance, she rushed down the hall, through the kitchen, and out the back door. *Go for a run,* she told herself. *Work off some of this anger and resentment, then come back and spend the day with your daughter. Make the most of the time you have with her and don't fight with Katari anymore. She's right, you should be grateful to her.*

And she *was* grateful. But that didn't mean she accepted the fact that her child was calling another woman "Mama."

Griff and Charles David had taken turns visiting with Nic at the morning visitation period in ICU from nine to nine thirty. She'd still been slightly groggy from all the drugs, but coherent enough for Griff to tell her about Rosswalt Everhart and his connection to Cary Maygarden. By their one o'clock visit, Dr. Mandel had made his rounds and ordered Nic taken off the ventilator.

Charles David had spoken to Dr. Mandel, and had asked Griff to join them. As the doctor explained Nic's condition, it became apparent that she had suffered a horrendous ordeal. By the time the doctor walked away, Charles David had been crying.

Griff knew Nic's brother loved her and would do anything for her, but he was not strong enough to give Nic what she would need in the upcoming weeks.

Geena Kilpatrick had then explained that Nic's throat would be sore for a couple of days and she'd be a bit hoarse.

The best news was that Nic's condition had been changed from critical to stable.

Griff had taken the opportunity to ask a question that had been plaguing him, but which Geena whould not have been permitted to answer had Charles David not been there as Nic's next of kin.

"I . . . uh . . . need to ask something," Griff had said.

"Yes, Mr. Powell, what is it?"

"Nic . . . Nicole isn't pregnant, is she?"

Charles David's eyes widened, but he said nothing.

"No, Ms. Baxter isn't pregnant," the nurse said, then patted Griff on the arm before she returned to her other duties.

"You go in and see Nic alone," Charles David said. "I know she wants to talk to you. I can wait until this evening to see her, but please tell her that I'm here."

"Thanks," Griff said, thankful Charles David hadn't pursued a conversation about why Griff had thought Nic might be pregnant.

He entered the ICU and hurried straight to Nic's cubicle.

Pausing at the entrance, he looked at her where she lay on her side, the head of her bed tilted slightly upward. God, she was pale, her eyes weak, her body way too thin and badly bruised. He couldn't allow himself to think about what she had been through. He had to find a way to help her look forward, not back.

"Good morning, gorgeous," he said as he walked toward the bed.

She looked at him, a fragile smile curving her lips, but he saw the pain in her eyes.

He wanted to hold her, kiss her, comfort her, but she was still hooked up to an IV and other essential equipment. Stable condition meant she was better, but it didn't mean she was completely out of the woods. She'd been shot in the back, the bullet entering below her shoulder blade and exiting through her side, just beneath her armpit.

"I'm not gorgeous." Nic rasped the words as Griff sat down in the chair at her bedside.

"Oh, yes, you are. You're the most beautiful sight I've ever seen," he told her.

She held out her hand. Griff grasped it and gave it a gentle squeeze.

"Have they caught him?" she asked.

"Everhart wasn't at home, but we didn't expect him to be, if he was still alive, and unfortunately, he is. His housekeeper told Doug Trotter and the parish sheriff that Everhart underwent surgery for a stomach wound at the County General Hospital. But before you ask, no, he wasn't still at the hospital. It seems he has disappeared and nobody knows where is."

"Son of a bitch!"

"Trotter's getting a search warrant so he can go over the house and grounds with a fine-tooth comb."

"Get me a picture of him so I can ID him. Okay?"

"Trotter's going to send us a photo of him as soon as possible."

Nic heaved a deep sigh, and then grunted.

"Are you okay, honey?" Griff asked.

She sucked in air. "I'm sore as hell. My whole body aches."

"They can up your pain meds. I'll call the nurse and—"

"No! I'm tired of not being able to think straight. I want my mind back." She jerked her hand out of his.

"Take it easy, honey. Don't talk. Just rest."

"How can I rest knowing he's out there, alive and free and—"

"Don't do this to yourself," Griff told her. "You've been through hell. You need to give your body time to heal . . . and your mind."

When Nic didn't respond, he noticed that she was looking away from him, her jaw clenched and her hands clutching the sheet that covered her to her waist.

"Charles David said to tell you that he's here, outside in the waiting room. He's giving me the entire thirty minutes to visit with you."

She nodded, but didn't speak and didn't glance his way.

"Nic?"

"Hmm . . . ?"

"When Trotter gets the search warrant, I'm going out there, to Everhart's plantation."

"Belle Fleur," she said as she turned and looked at Griff. "That's what he called his home."

"He told you the name of his plantation, but he never told you his name?"

"He referred to himself as 'the Hunter.' "

Griff noted that she was clutching the sheet tighter and tighter. He reached out and slid his hand caressingly over each of hers, then grasped the fingers of her left hand and forced her to release her tenacious hold on the sheet.

"You're safe," Griff told her. "He can't hurt you, not ever again."

Nic glared at Griff, her gaze riveted to his face. "Find him and stop him."

"We will."

"I tried to kill him." Nic lifted her hands and looked at her open palms. "I made myself a weapon out of a stick." She rubbed her hands together. "When I had the chance, I attacked him. I went for the jugular, but I missed."

Griff watched her as she spoke, understanding that she was reliving every moment as she told him about what had happened.

"He threw me off him and we wrestled on the ground." Nic rubbed her hands together harder and faster. "I turned the sharp stick toward him and shoved it into his gut as far as it would go. I hoped I'd killed him." She coughed. "I wanted him dead." She coughed again and again. "I hated him. He was a—" Nic coughed uncontrollably.

Griff called for the nurse. By the time the woman whose name badge read A. Kennemer came in and took over, Griff was holding a hysterical Nic in his arms, preventing her from flailing about wildly.

Griff held Nic while Ms. Kennemer administered a sedative via the IV tube. Within minutes, Nic was asleep.

"May I sit with her for a while?" Griff asked.

"You have fifteen more minutes, Mr. Powell."

"Thank you."

He watched Nic while she rested. He didn't know if she had ever killed anyone in the line of duty. Whether she had killed anyone or not, the fact that she had not only wanted to kill her abductor but had tried to kill him obviously tormented her. Unlike the madman who had tortured her, she had a conscience.

Griff remembered a time when the thought of killing another human being had been an alien concept to him. But that had been before his years on Amara, before he'd been trained by York to either kill or be killed.

He reached out and caressed Nic's bruised cheek, then eased several matted tendrils of dark hair away from her face and slipped them behind her ear.

It would get worse for her before it got better. A lot worse.

"But I'll be here for you, Nicki. I'm going to help you through this, no matter how long it takes."

Griff and Rick Carson arrived at Belle Fleur around four that afternoon. Sanders had stayed at the hospital with Charles David. A horde of law enforcement officials swarmed the plantation house and grounds, all under the supervision of the bureau's SAC Trotter. Understanding that they had been given permission to be on the scene as observers, and only because Trotter had sense enough to know it was the best way to keep the Powell Agency under control, Griff and Rick stayed out of the way.

Griff figured that at one time the old house had been a showplace, probably not more than thirty or forty years ago. But time and neglect had turned a magnificent mansion into a sadly decaying structure. Why hadn't Rosswalt Everhart spent some of his millions to keep the place up? In the initial report Powell's had done on Everhart during the past couple of hours, they had discovered the man was worth in the neighborhood of eighty million.

Just as Griff and Rick approached the front veranda, Doug Trotter and Josh Friedman emerged from the house. The four men spoke and exchanged handshakes, and then Trotter asked about Nic.

"She was asleep when I left the hospital," Griff said.

"Has she told you anything about Everhart?" Trotter asked. "I've been waiting to question her—"

"Don't," Griff said. "She's not ready."

Trotter eyed him questioningly. "Nobody's going to push her, but the more we know about this guy, the better our odds of catching him."

"I understand. But I'm telling you that other than identifying Everhart from a photo, she's in no shape for an interview. Not yet."

"As for identifying him from a photo—we need Nic to do that for us as soon as possible. Cleo Willoughby, the B&B owner in Arkansas, positively identified Everhart as the guy who rented the Cary Grant room from her the day Kendall Moore's body showed up. She says that she's sure, even though he had a mustache and his hair was a different color."

"Nic and I figured as much when Miss Cleo mentioned her one night guest. I'm glad she was able to ID him."

Trotter nodded. "Friedman, take Mr. Powell to the basement and show him around." He looked right at Griff. "I don't have to tell you not to touch anything, do I?"

"No, you don't." Griff glanced from Trotter to Friedman. "What's in the basement?"

"It's where that sick son of a bitch probably kept Nic and his other victims," Friedman said. "At least part of the time."

"And there's a special room down there," Trotter said. "You do know the only reason you're here is because—"

"The Powell Agency will cooperate with the FBI completely."

Griff and Trotter exchanged quick nods, silently agreeing on the terms.

The interior of the house, filled with priceless antiques, smelled slightly musty, but everything appeared to be relatively clean, the wooden floors waxed and the furniture dusted and polished.

Griff followed SA Friedman down the wide hallway. He paused behind the agent when he opened the door to the basement.

"Watch your step," Friedman said. "These stairs aren't very stable."

Griff stayed a couple of steps behind the agent as they descended into the dark, dank, subterranean level of the mansion. The only illumination came from a single lightbulb hanging on a cord from the ceiling. The moment Griff's feet hit the dirt and brick flooring and the scent of moist soil, human waste, and rotting rodents bombarded his senses, he stopped dead in his tracks. Unbidden thoughts, memories of another time and place, overcame him. But he quickly took control, willing himself to focus on the present.

"Stinks down here," Friedman said.

Griff didn't reply.

"Take a look at the rusted chains that line that wall over there." Freidman shined his flashlight over the row of rusted manacles. "They must have kept slaves down here before the Civil War."

Griff noticed a pair of new chains set into the same wall.

He paused and stared at the metal shackles and knew without a doubt that this was where Everhart had kept his victims bound. Nic had been held prisoner in this basement.

Friedman came up beside him. "Don't think about it. That won't help Nic."

Griff released a harsh breath, barely containing his anger. The rage inside him demanded revenge.

"There's a room down here you'll want to see," Friedman said. "Just remember not to touch anything."

Griff nodded, then followed the agent to the door that had been left standing open at the far side of the basement. On the right-hand side of the midsize room, shelves of glass cases lined the wall, all empty except for seven that sat side by side. A mannequin head stared sightless from each case. For a millisecond, Griff closed his eyes to blot out the scene before him, knowing that the scalp atop each plastic head had been taken, postmortem, from each of Everhart's seven victims.

Nic had been victim number eight.

Suddenly, a vision he'd thought long vanquished appeared inside his head, reminding him of another trophy room as equally gruesome as the one in which he now stood.

"Mr. Powell, are you okay?" Friedman asked.

Griff cleared his throat. "Yeah, I'm okay."

"Have you seen enough?"

"More than enough."

Fifteen minutes later, Griff and Rick met up with Trotter and the local parish sheriff about half a mile from the plantation house. A group of lawmen were standing beneath a canopy of ancient trees, most heavily laden with Spanish moss. The men and women formed a loose circle. Griff stepped forward to get a look at whatever held their attention.

In the middle of the human ring surrounding it, a large metal cage glistened malevolently in the late-afternoon sunlight.

Griff paused, every muscle rigid, as anger boiled inside him. How many hours had Nic spent inside that cage?

He knew what being treated like an animal could do to a person. No matter how strong Nic was, how brave, how competent, she would never be the same again. Her experience as a captive had changed her irrevocably. And not one of these lawmen—male or female—understood that fact. Only someone who had lived through such degradation could ever truly know.

Pudge reclined on the comfortable bed in his private room at the Garabina Clinic. Although medication eased his pain, he had requested that he be given only enough to dull the ache in his belly but not so much that he couldn't function. He needed to stay at least partially alert in order to remain safe and be able to make future plans. He had hired a Mexican realtor to check into all small islands that rented by the month or leased by the year. Once he had fully recovered from his surgery, he intended to resume his normal activities, only somewhere far from Belle Fleur, and out of the reach of the U.S. government.

Other than one suitcase filled with his clothes and another with cash, the only other items that he'd brought with him from home were his laptop computer and a briefcase filled with bearer bonds and the documents concerning his Cayman Island bank accounts.

The doctors had told him he would be here at least a week and if he wanted to stay longer, they would transfer him to the spa area of the clinic where he could remain as long as he wished. Hopefully, by week's end, his realtor would have found him an island hideaway. In the meantime, he could pass the hours quite contentedly by choosing his next victim, the first of many who would share his island paradise.

As he zipped through dozens of choices, so many young, vibrant women in superb physical condition, his mind kept wandering back to one specific woman. Apparently, it was true—you could never forget the one who got away.

Nicole Baxter.

She was alive. Damn her!

Not now, not next week, nor even next month, but someday, he would capture her again. And when he did . . . Just the thought of what he would do to her excited him.

"I'll come for you, Nicole, when you least expect it."

Suddenly, a photo popped up on his laptop screen, catching his attention. Hmm . . . Interesting. The accompanying article was from a Tampa, Florida online magazine:

WAR HERO HOME ON LEAVE.

LaTasha Davies was quite lovely for an army corporal. Long-legged, lean, skin like rich chocolate, and eyes as black as ebony. Pudge studied the photo of the young woman wearing her military uniform, and then he scanned the article. It seemed Ms. Davies had saved the life of two of her comrades and had managed to keep all three of them alive for five days behind enemy lines.

She would make a truly worthy adversary.

Chapter 23

"How's our patient today?" Griff asked the private-duty nurse he had hired as one of three to stay with Nic 24/7. Mrs. Elkins had twenty years of experience and had come with the highest recommendations, as did her counterparts on the evening and night shifts.

"Eager to leave here," Mrs. Elkins said as she motioned for Griff to step back out into the hall.

Outside Nic's room, the nurse glanced at Griff's companion and nodded cordially, then told Griff, "Ms. Baxter is physically ready to leave the hospital tomorrow, but emotionally and mentally, she's unprepared."

"I've tried to tell her doctors that she is not going to respond to the counseling sessions they've provided," Griff said. "No matter how much she may want to open up and talk about what happened to her, she can't."

"Then I don't know what to tell you, Mr. Powell," Nurse Elkins said. "She's been here twelve days and physically, she's made a remarkable recovery. But she needs psychiatric help to deal with the trauma. Unfortunately, she seems to believe she can deal with things on her own."

"That's my Nic. Stubborn as a mule." Griff turned to the lady at his side. "Mrs. Elkins, this is Dr. Yvette Meng. Dr. Meng is a psychiatrist who specializes in posttraumatic stress syndrome. I've brought her here to meet Nic."

Mrs. Elkins surveyed Yvette, from her shiny black hair to her size five and a half bronze leather heels. She held out her hand to Yvette. "It's very nice to meet you, Doctor."

After the ladies shook hands, Mrs. Elkins took her morning break.

Griff grasped Yvette's arm. "Nic will probably fight you every step of the way."

"Yes, I know. I would expect nothing less from Griffin Powell's woman."

"Oh, God, whatever you do, do not say something like that to Nic. She'll go ballistic."

Yvette smiled. "You trust me to care for her. Yes?"

"Yes."

"Your Nicole and I will become acquainted a little more each day and eventually I hope she will trust me as you do."

"She hasn't agreed to come home to Griffin's Rest with me. Not yet."

"When she learns that she has only two choices—either come with us to Griffin's Rest or spend another two weeks in a D.C. hospital under psychiatric care, followed by another month of counseling, then I believe she will make the right decision."

"I just hope she likes you," Griff said. "Hell, I hope you like her."

Griff opened the door and held it for Yvette, who entered Nic's room two steps ahead of him. Nic glanced up from where she sat in a chair near the windows and looked from Griff to Yvette and back to Griff.

"Good morning, honey," Griff said. "How are you today?"

"I'm fine," Nic said. "I've gained back four of the ten pounds I lost, my bruises have faded, my scratches have healed, and my surgical stitches come out tomorrow. I'm ready to go home."

Griff walked over to her, leaned down, and kissed her on the forehead. "There's someone I want you to meet." He motioned to Yvette, who approached cautiously.

Nic eyed her visitor. "Dr. Yvette Meng, I presume."

Griff tensed. "As you know, Yvette's an old friend. Sanders and I have known her for eighteen years."

Nic rose slowly from the chair and held out her hand. "It's nice to finally meet you, Dr. Meng."

"Please, call me Yvette."

Nic shook her head. "If you're going to be my psychiatrist, I think I'd prefer calling you 'Dr. Meng.' "

Griff frowned. "Okay, want to tell me what's going on here? How did you know Yvette had volunteered to—"

"Ah, now, Griff . . ." Nic looked up at him and smiled wryly. "You don't think you're the only one who did some background checking, do you? While you were finding out all you could about me when we worked on the BQK cases, I was doing the same."

"Well, I'll be damned. I should have known," Griff said.

"Yes, you should have." Nic indicated the other chair in the room. "Won't you sit down, Dr. Meng?" Nic looked up at Griff before she sat back down. "Why don't you leave us alone for a while, say, half an hour? Go get a cup of coffee or something."

Griff eyed her suspiciously, wondering just what Nic had in mind. Whatever it was, he wished he could stay and listen to their conversation. If Nic thought she could intimidate Yvette, she had a big surprise coming.

As soon as Griff left them alone and Dr. Meng had sat down across from her, Nic studied the other woman carefully, noting how exquisitely beautiful Griff's old and dear friend was. Just how dear a friend? Was this exotically lovely woman one of Griff's lovers?

"You may ask me anything you wish," Yvette said.

"Anything?"

Yvette nodded.

"Are you and Griff lovers?"

Yvette's lips curved into a pleasant smile. "No, we are not nor have we ever been."

Nic hated herself for asking and hated herself even more for feeling so damn relieved by Yvette's answer.

"You know where Griff was and what happened to him during those missing ten years of his life, don't you?" Nic asked.

"Yes, I know. Sanders and I were with him during those years."

"Were you." The comment was rhetorical, not really a question at all.

"May I ask you something?" Yvette's voice possessed a gentle, almost hypnotic cadence.

Nic nodded.

"Have you spoken to your superior at the FBI this morning?"

"Yes, Doug stopped by earlier."

"Then you know what your options are."

"Oh, yes. It seems everyone is in agreement that I'm in need of psychiatric care. What I say and think doesn't seem to matter. Nobody believes me when I say I'm okay and that once I get back to work tracking down the Hunter, I'll be fine."

"You don't think you need counseling?"

"Counseling—maybe. But I could get that while I'm working, couldn't I? Why can't Doug and Griff and the doctors realize that going after this guy will be the best medicine for what ails me?"

"Of course you realize that that is not an option at present. You will not be allowed to return to work until you've undergone treatment," Yvette said. "Griffin has offered his home to you for the duration of your recovery and he wishes for me to work with you."

"Do you always do as Griffin wishes?" *That's it, Nic, act like a jealous girlfriend.* "Forget I said that."

"It is forgotten," Yvette told her. "Please, consider Griffin's offer. At Griffin's Rest you could recover in peaceful surroundings instead of a clinic. Our daily sessions would be informal. We could mutually agree on the ground rules."

"How long?" Nic asked.

"How long would the daily sessions be?"

"No, how long would this psychoanalysis last? A week? Two weeks? A month?"

"That's difficult to say. It would depend on how you respond to treatment."

"I don't suppose you'd believe me if I told you I'm perfectly all right."

"No one lives through what you did and walks away untouched," Yvette said. "You may believe that you are all right, but—"

"Damn it, why are all you psychiatrists alike?" Nic jumped up out of the chair and stood in front of the windows, looking out, up at the blue sky. She took a deep breath and murmured, "I'm sorry. I think I'm going stir-crazy in here. I want to go home. I want my life back the way it was before . . . before . . ." *Don't you dare cry. Don't give Dr. Meng any proof that you're unstable.*

Although she'd been totally unaware of Yvette Meng getting up and walking toward her, Nic sensed her presence. When she glanced over her shoulder, she saw the woman standing directly behind her.

"I have something in my purse that I would like for you to look at," Yvette said. "Call it a preliminary test, if you would like."

"I haven't agreed to be your patient."

"No, you haven't. And the choice is entirely yours. But

you must know that Griffin needs to be a part of your recovery and if you come to Griffin's Rest—"

"Maybe I don't care what Griffin needs. Maybe making him happy isn't as important to me as it is to you." *You did it again, didn't you? You just can't shake the jealousy thing. Good God, Nic, the woman told you that she and Griff aren't lovers. Besides, even if they were, what difference would it make? You and Griff had one night together. You're not married or engaged or even in love.*

"Sorry," Nic said as she turned to face Yvette. "Okay, show me whatever it is you want me to take a look at."

Yvette pulled her leather shoulder bag around in front of her, opened the purse, and delved inside. She removed a photograph and held it out to Nic.

Nic stared at Yvette's hand for a full minute before she took the photo from her, turned it over, and gazed into the hazel eyes of the madman who had held her captive for three weeks. Rosswalt Everhart looked so normal.

Nausea churned in Nic's stomach. Just the sight of this monster made her sick. Her heartbeat quickened. Her hands trembled. She could hear his voice calling her name. *"Nicole. You've disappointed me. Now, I'll have to punish you."*

She crumpled the photo in her hand, crushing it into a wad. Without saying a word to Yvette Meng, Nic walked across the room and tossed the photo in the wastebasket.

Tilting her chin high, she faced the doctor. "See, I know exactly what to do with trash like that."

"You are trembling," Yvette said. "Your heart is beating very fast. You are sick to your stomach and you are beginning to perspire. And you can hear his voice and see his face in your mind. He will not leave you alone."

"Damn you!" Nic hated herself for being so weak.

"Please, let me help you."

Choking on her determination not to cry, Nic clenched her teeth tightly and glared at Yvette Meng.

* * *

LaTasha's leave would end in two days. If only she didn't have to go so soon. She and Asheen were just beginning to get to know each other again, just beginning to rebuild their mother-daughter relationship. She had allowed Asheen to miss school today so they could have the whole day together, just the two of them. They had spent the morning shopping for Christmas presents, most of them for Asheen. New shoes, a new dress, a pair of jeans, and a tiny gold locket that cost a week's pay.

They sat together in the food court at the mall, shopping bags surrounding their table. LaTasha had discovered that her daughter preferred chicken sandwiches to hamburgers and she hated pickles. But she loved vanilla milk shakes.

"What would you like to do this afternoon?" LaTasha asked. "We could go to the movies or—"

"Could we bake cookies?"

"You want to bake cookies?"

"Christmas cookies. And we could make some of the cookies sugar-free just for me. We can cut them out in the shapes of bells and wreaths and angels and Christmas trees. We could go buy the cookie cutters and all the stuff to make the cookies and we could decorate them and . . . and I could take them to school with me tomorrow and tell everyone that my mama and me made them."

Emotion lodged in LaTasha's throat. She stared at her beautiful child through a fine sheen of tears.

"Mama?"

LaTasha swallowed. "I'd love for us to make cookies."

Asheen clapped her hands together gleefully and smiled as if she'd been given a priceless gift. "Can we buy one of those fancy plastic boxes to put them in? A red and green box with gold glitter?"

"You can pick out any box you want."

Asheen lunged over and hugged LaTasha.

The feel of her child's arms around her and the look of sheer joy on her sweet face gave LaTasha a feeling that no words could ever describe. The feeling existed only in a mother's heart.

"When I come back from this next assignment, I should be able to stay in the U.S. I want you and Grandma to come live with me. I know you'll miss your Aunt Katari and—"

"I'll miss all of them." Asheen hugged her tightly, then lifted her head. "But they can come and visit us, can't they?"

"Of course they can." She caressed her daughter's cheek. "Are you saying that you want us to live together again, the way we did when you were little?"

"Oh, yes, Mama. It's what I want more than anything in this whole wide world."

LaTasha grasped Asheen's hand and gave it a tight squeeze. "I'm glad, because it's what I want more than anything, too."

Tabora Island was three miles wide and four miles long, just a speck in the Caribbean Sea, off the coast of Nicaragua. Pudge had leased the entire island for six months, with an option to extend the lease for an entire year. He would live here as Mr. Palmer Ross, an eccentric millionaire, who valued his privacy above all else. The realtor had arranged for two Honduran women, who did not speak more than a few words in broken English, to come to the island whenever they were needed, to clean the house and prepare meals. They would be staying until tomorrow, making everything ready for Pudge's first guest.

The only transportation on and off the island was by boat. He had purchased a new speedboat, which he could use to travel south to Panama or north to Cancun, where he could catch a commercial jet to anywhere in the world. Tomorrow he would travel to Tampa, using a fake passport, and then the day after, if all went as he had planned, he would bring

LaTasha Davies home with him. Everything had been arranged to transport several crates of newly purchased personal items to his home. From Tampa, he would take a private plane to San Pedro and then a quick boat ride to the island. The empty crates could be tossed overboard in route, saving only the one containing his precious cargo. Her room in the cellar was waiting for her. He had done his best to recreate the atmosphere of the basement at Belle Fleur including a set of shiny new manacles.

Although the house here on the island was not as large and not nearly as magnificent as the mansion at Belle Fleur, it was adequate for his needs. Spacious, roomy, with views of the ocean on two sides, from where it perched on the highest point on the island. Not exactly a hill, more like a grassy knoll.

Pudge walked out onto the front porch, sat in the large rattan rocker, and gazed out over the grounds of his new home. He would never be able to return to Belle Fleur. Nicole had not only tried to kill him, but she had taken his ancestral home away from him. Someday he would make her pay dearly for her sins against him. If she thought her first captivity had been unpleasant, she couldn't begin to imagine what he had planned for her the next time. And there would be a next time.

Griffin Powell wouldn't be there to guard her 24/7 forever. Nicole would never allow it. Pudge smiled. All he had to do was wait for the right moment and use that mile-wide streak of independence in Nicole to bring her down.

Doug Trotter had told her she was making a big mistake. Josh Friedman tried to talk her into coming back to D.C. But in the end, she had gone with her gut instincts. Nic couldn't explain why she had chosen to go home with Griff. For some unfathomable reason, she simply knew it was the right thing to do. The best thing, not only for her, but for Griff. Odd how she felt that he needed her every bit as much as she needed him.

During her stay at Baton Rouge General, Griff had been a daily visitor, always near but never intruding. Not once had he mentioned their last night together in Woodbridge before she'd been kidnapped. Not once had he done more than kiss her forehead or her cheek. He had proven himself to be her friend in more ways than she could count, and maybe that's what she needed most now. Just someone to lean on for a brief period of time. Someone who would make no demands and would give her the time she needed to fully recover from her ordeal.

She had deluded herself into thinking she could simply return to her life as a federal agent, just pick up where she left off, as if she hadn't spent three weeks being tormented by a psychopath.

No one, not even Griff, would understand if she admitted that she wanted to scream and cry and rant and rave and butt her head against a wall. Who could possibly believe that anyone who felt that way wasn't crazy?

Oh, God, maybe she was crazy. Maybe sometime between the morning she'd been captured and the day she'd escaped, she had lost her mind.

One minute she wanted to beg Griff to hold her and never let her go. The next minute she didn't want anyone to touch her. There seemed to be no rhyme or reason to her thinking, no logical reasoning behind her mood swings.

Yes, she knew all her problems—at least most of them—were linked to her imprisonment, to those endless days of degradation and torment. Even though she hadn't mentioned her feelings to Dr. Meng, the very wise lady had explained that whatever she was feeling, whatever wild mood swings and unusual emotional reactions she was experiencing were to be expected.

"Not only are they to be expected, but they're perfectly natural," Yvette had said. "You are not losing your mind, even if sometimes it seems that you are."

Okay, so I'm not losing my mind, Nic told herself. *Even if I think I am.*

So, here she sat on the Powell jet, along with Griff, Dr. Meng, Sanders, and Rick Carson, flying into the wild blue yonder, all the way from Baton Rouge to Knoxville. Charles David had offered to come with them, but she had insisted that he go home to San Francisco, back to his normal life.

"I'll call you at least every other day," she'd promised. "I'm going to be just fine. Griff will see that I have everything I need."

Neither she nor her brother mentioned the fact that although their mother had telephoned Nic several times while she'd been in the hospital, she hadn't come to Baton Rouge to see Nic. Her husband had felt the stress wouldn't be good for her.

Griff sat beside Nic on the plane, but he didn't crowd her and he hadn't tried to make idle conversation. Occasionally, he would take her hand in his or simply look at her and smile. Twice, he had asked if she needed anything.

Poor Griff. He was trying so hard to be her knight in shining armor. She didn't doubt that he genuinely cared about her, but she sensed that more than anything else, he felt sorry for her. God, how she hated that.

Griff felt helpless. More than anything he wanted to do something for Nic to make things easier for her. If only he had the power to erase these past five weeks from her memory. If only they could go back to that morning in Woodbridge and do it all over again. He would awaken in time to stop her from taking her morning walk. He would drag her back into bed and make love to her all day. And somehow he'd figure out that the Hunter intended to kidnap Nic. Then he could protect her.

But he could no more erase her memories of captivity than he could erase his own. He only prayed that Yvette could help Nic the way she had helped him.

Yvette had gone through years of therapy herself, trusting their lives and their secrets to her beloved psychology professor, Dr. Gilbert. She had persuaded Sanders and Griff to seek the old man's wise counsel, but the professor had passed away before they could, and so both Griff and Sanders had turned to Yvette for therapy.

Looking back now, Griff realized that reliving their captivity on Amara and sharing their memories with one another had worked both for their recovery and against it. But in the end, they had each come through their individual trials of fire stronger and wiser. Each of them now dealt with the past in his or her own way. But Griff did not delude himself into thinking that they were completely healed, that the past no longer had any hold over them. Each of them bore the scars of their imprisonment, just as Nic would always bear the scars of hers.

When Jonathan brought the Powell jet in for a landing, Nic reached out and grasped Griff's arm. He laid his hand over hers and squeezed reassuringly.

"I'm only staying at Griffin's Rest for a few weeks," Nic said, but looked down at the floor and not at him. "I'll go through therapy with Dr. Meng, and then I'll go through whatever tests the bureau wants to run on me. After that, I'm going back to work. I intend to track down the Hunter and bring him in."

Griff wondered if Doug Trotter would allow Nic back on the task force or if he would reassign her when she was healthy enough for active duty again. But now was not the time to disagree with her about her future plans.

"You can stay for as long as you like," Griff said. "But

you know you're free to leave whenever you want." He squeezed her hand again. "Selfishly, I'd like for you to stay for a while, at least through Christmas and New Year's."

She stared at him then, a questioning look in her honey-brown eyes. "I hadn't even thought about Christmas. It's only a few weeks away, isn't it? And then New Year's and—" She closed her eyes and bit down on her bottom lip. After taking a deep breath, she looked back at Griff and said softly, "You don't have to feel sorry for me, you know. I'm going to be all right."

"Oh, Nic, honey, is that what you think—that I feel sorry for you?" He turned in his seat, reached out, and with his free hand caressed her cheek. "Nothing could be farther from the truth. I'm angry. I want to kill Everhart. I want to make everything all right for you. I want to take away your pain." He cupped her chin between his thumb and index finger. "I want to keep you safe and never let anything bad happen to you ever again."

She closed her eyes. At first he thought she might be crying, but she wasn't. Perhaps only inside.

With her eyes closed and her hand in his, she said, "I'm going to lean on you for a little while. I'll live at Griffin's Rest and go into counseling with Dr. Meng. But I'm going to get well quickly. And I'm going back to work by the first of the year. I refuse to allow Rosswalt Everhart to destroy my sanity and take away everything that's important to me."

That's my Nic. Tough as nails. Strong. Independent. Determined.

But she had no idea what lay ahead for her. Her dark nights of the soul were yet to come.

Chapter 24

Sanders woke Griff at five thirty on Saturday morning. He came to with a start, his heart racing, his first thoughts of Nic.

"What's wrong? Is Nic—?"

"Nicole is fine. As far as I know she is sleeping," Sanders said. "I apologize for waking you, but Douglas Trotter is on the phone. He says that it is urgent."

Griff tossed back the covers and stood, totally naked. Sanders held up Griff's robe. He slipped into the calf-length silk garment and belted it quickly.

"Line one," Sanders said.

Griff walked over to the desk, picked up the receiver, and tapped line one. "Griffin Powell here."

"I got a phone call less than half an hour ago from some guy claiming to be the Hunter," Trotter said.

"He called you?"

"How the hell he got my cell number . . . Doesn't matter, does it? He called me because, apparently, he had tried to call Nicole and her phone went to voice mail. He's using me as a messenger boy."

"Meaning?"

"He instructed me to contact Nicole and tell her to keep her phone on and with her at all times."

"Goddamn!" Griff motioned to Sanders. "Wake up Yvette. I need to talk to her." Sanders nodded, then exited hurriedly. Griff said to Trotter, "This could mean that he's already set up shop somewhere else and he's preparing to abduct another victim."

"Yeah, unfortunately, I agree."

"I'd give every dime I have to know where that slimy bastard is."

"Make that two of us," Trotter said. "But for now, I need to know if Nic is stable enough to deal with a phone call from this guy."

Hell, no. Nic had left the hospital only yesterday and was as fragile as spun glass. One tap on that thin shell she'd erected around her emotions and she'd shatter into a million pieces.

"Powell, are you still there?" Trotter's gruff voice vibrated with concern.

"I'm here. Just thinking. Nic's not ready to deal with a call from Everhart. But if we don't let her know what's going on and she finds out, it will only make things worse for her."

"And she'll be mad as hell at us."

"Yeah, there is that."

"You seem to be closer to her than anyone right now. As much as I hate to let you make the decision, I'm leaving it up to you."

"I can either steal her cell phone so she never sees his message, or I can tell her what he's up to and advise her to let me handle things, or—"

"There's a third option and we both know it's the one Nic will choose," Trotter said. "Emotionally ready or not, she'll take that son of a bitch's calls. She wanted to nail his hide to the wall before . . . But now—damn it, Powell, do whatever you can to help her, you and that shrink of yours."

"I'll be in touch later this morning." Griff ended the conversation, placed the receiver on the base, and headed for the bathroom.

He had just started shaving when Yvette called out his name through the closed bedroom door.

"Come on in," he told her.

She moved through his bedroom like a floating cloud, as quietly as if her feet never touched the floor. Pausing in the open bathroom door, she looked him over and settled her gaze on his shaving cream–covered face.

He picked up his razor, took a couple of swipes, then rinsed the razor and glanced at Yvette. "Everhart contacted Doug Trotter. He left a message on Nic's cell phone and he wants her to turn her phone on and keep it on. My guess is that he's on the verge of kidnapping another woman and he's ready for Nic and me to play his game with him."

"So soon," Yvette said. "This man is quite driven. Apparently, the single focus of his life is playing this deadly murder game. He is allowing nothing to stop him, not even Nicole's escape, the revelation of his true identity, or the fact he is still recovering from surgery."

Griff continued shaving, and made comments each time he rinsed the razor. "Nic's not ready to deal with this, is she?"

"No, and I'm not sure she ever will be."

"She's not going to give me her cell phone willingly. That phone was one of the first things she asked for while she was in the hospital. I had a hell of a time persuading her to turn the damn thing off and keep it off. If I know her, she'll be turning it on sometime today."

"And when she does, she will see that she has received a message."

"I could steal her phone." Griff turned on the faucets, leaned over the sink, and splashed water over his cleanly shaven face.

"As much as you want to protect Nicole, I advise you not to try to manipulate her or control her. At this point, she trusts you, perhaps more than anyone else in her life. You do not want to do anything to jeopardize that trust."

"So you're saying I should let her talk to the maniac who kidnapped and tortured her?"

"I am saying that the decision must be hers."

"Yeah, yeah. I know." Griff lifted a towel from the nearby rack and dried his face. "Why couldn't she be the type who'd happily let a big, strong man handle everything for her?"

"If she were that type, she would bore you. Nicole is exactly the kind of woman you need."

Griff tossed the towel aside. "I want to protect her."

Yvette's gaze met his, a look of understanding passing between them. When he emerged from the bathroom, she stepped aside.

"And you *will* protect her, as much as she will allow you to."

He nodded. "Be prepared for whatever happens. I'm not sure how she'll react. Probably play tough and in control, at least at first."

"The timing is unfortunate," Yvette said. "She might have been better prepared to handle this in a few weeks. But Rosswalt Everhart is forcing her—forcing us—to adhere to his timetable."

"And play the game by his rules."

The roar of the dirt bike pulsated all around her, as if he were coming after her from all directions. Was he riding around in a circle, surrounding her? If he was, then she was trapped, with nowhere to run. Nic's heart thumped loudly inside her head. Sweat coated her hands, dampened her face, and dripped down between her breasts. Nausea clawed at her belly. She was beyond hungry. She had gone without food for days now.

Suddenly, he appeared from out of nowhere, a heavy rope in his hand. "No, don't!" she pleaded, but he didn't listen. She turned and faced the tree, standing there obediently while he lashed her back repeatedly, the sting of the rope ripping through her clothes and into her flesh. If she did not take her punishment, he would shoot her.

Stay alive. Do whatever you have to do.

Run. Run away from him. Save your life.

He fired the rifle. The bullet hit her in the back. Hot, piercing pain.

The Hunter's laughter echoed all around her. Inside her head, vibrating through her body.

She screamed.

Nic's eyes popped open. She looked straight up at the ceiling. Where was she?

Sitting up, she surveyed her surroundings. She was in a big, comfortable bed, with a down comforter and feather pillows. The colors were soft and feminine, creams and beiges and pale peaches. She wasn't at home, not in her bedroom, not in her bed.

She was at Griffin's Rest.

She was safe.

Nic tossed back the covers and crawled out of bed. The moment her feet hit the floor, she immediately wanted to get back in bed, pull up the covers, and stay there all day. If only she could sleep for the next month and wake up on New Year's Day completely sound in mind and body. Ready to go home. Prepared to return to work.

Stop feeling sorry for yourself. Take a shower, get dressed,

*call Charles David, go downstairs, and put on your happy
face and pretend you're sane.*

First, she needed to find clean underwear. She looked
around the room and decided that her bras and panties were
probably in one of the drawers in the huge Victorian dresser.
Griff had told her that he'd sent a Powell employee to Woodbridge to pack her clothes and bring them to Griffin's Rest.
Last night, when Griff had brought her upstairs to this room,
her pajamas and house shoes had already been laid out for
her.

After a little searching and pillaging, she discovered that
not only were her bras, panties, knee highs, stockings, and
socks in the dresser, but there were new items that she didn't
recognize. Expensive underwear that just happened to be her
size. Griff's doing, no doubt. And when she opened the
walk-in closet, she gasped. She had never owned this many
clothes in her entire life. My God, what had Griff done, ordered her a complete new wardrobe of winter clothes?

After searching through countless brand-new slacks and
sweaters and skirts and jackets and two coats, she finally
found her own clothes, the ones she'd worn last winter and
the winter before that. She chose a pair of comfortable jeans
and her favorite multicolor fleece sweater. While searching
for her old penny loafers, she discovered ten pairs of new
shoes and four pairs of boots.

Griffin Powell, what have you done?

She'd have a talk with him this morning and tell him that
she didn't want his gifts, that she was not some kept woman
who—

Nic stopped abruptly.

*Griff did all this out of kindness and caring. Remember
that fact when you thank him for his generosity. All you have
to do is simply wear your own clothes every day and he'll
take the hint.*

She rummaged around in the closet until she found her old loafers. She hugged them to her chest.

Familiarity. Something that was her own. Security.

Where had she put her purse last night? Hmm . . . On the bottom shelf of the bedside table.

After gathering all her clothing items and laying them out on the foot of the bed, she retrieved her purse, flipped it open, and searched for her cell phone. While she'd been in Baton Rouge General, she'd told Griff she wanted her phone. He'd had someone in the D.C. field office overnight the phone to the hospital, but before he'd given it to her, he had wrangled a deal from her. She had reluctantly agreed not to use the phone except to talk to her mother, her brother and her cousin Claire, and to keep it turned off the rest of the time.

Plopping down on the side edge of the bed, she turned on the phone. It was much too early to call her brother. What with the three-hour time difference between Knoxville and San Francisco, it was practically the middle of the night in California.

Just as she started to lay the phone on the nightstand, she noticed that she had a message. She didn't recognize the number.

Her heart leapt to her throat.

No, it couldn't be.

Her hand shook so badly that she almost dropped the phone.

Get hold of yourself. If the Hunter left you a message, then it may well mean he is preparing to kidnap another woman.

Or he could have called simply to torment me.

Taking a deep breath and garnering all her courage, Nic listened to the message:

"Hello, Nicole. Do you miss me as much as I miss you? If you don't leave your phone on, you can't play

*the game. You don't want to miss your first clue, do
you?"*

God, how she hated the sound of his voice.

Clutching the cell phone in her hand, she slid off the bed,
rushing out of the bedroom and down the hall toward Griff's
suite. She knocked once, then opened the door and barged
into his room.

She stopped dead in her tracks, practically skidding to a
halt when she saw Griff standing in the doorway of the adjoining bathroom, wearing nothing but a loosely belted silk
robe. Yvette Meng, in a flowing pale yellow negligee gown
and robe, stood beside him, her hand on his arm.

"Excuse me," Nic said when Griff and Yvette turned and
looked at her. If only she could disappear. Poof. Be gone.

She started backing up. Griff came toward her. "Wait,
Nic."

"No, I'm sorry I intruded. This can wait until later." She
kept backing slowly toward the door.

Griff caught up with her just as she managed to back all
the way into the hall. He grasped her shoulders gently. "Nic,
honey, you didn't intrude. Whatever is going through that
suspicious mind of yours—"

"Your relationship with Dr. Meng is none of my business.
I just wish you'd told me that you two are still involved. And
I wish she hadn't lied to me." She wiggled her shoulders,
trying to loosen his hold, but he held fast.

"Yvette came to my room because I sent for her. I needed
to talk to her about you."

"Oh, so you want me to believe that talking to her about
me was so urgent that it couldn't wait until after breakfast."
She jerked away from Griff.

"Yvette is my friend. We are not romantically involved.
The only reason she is here at Griffin's Rest is to help you.
And the only reason she is in my bedroom is because Doug

Trotter called me at five thirty to tell me that Rosswalt Ever-hart had contacted him and demanded that you turn on your cell phone and—"

"Oh, my God! I barged in on you because when I turned on my phone just a few minutes ago, I had a message from him."

Griff grunted. "What did he say?"

"He told me leave my phone on if I wanted to play the game and not miss my first clue." Nic glanced past Griff to where Yvette stood just beyond the open doorway. Their gazes met for a split second and Nic knew why the woman was in Griff's room. He had wanted to ask Yvette, as Nic's therapist, how a call from the Hunter would affect Nic and if there was any way he could protect her from Everhart.

"You don't have to take his calls," Griff said.

Nic nodded. "Yes, I do. You know I do." *Don't cry!*

"Nic, honey . . ."

"I'm okay. I'm okay." She slipped her cell phone into the pocket of her pajama bottoms.

"No, you're not." He reached down and took her hand. "Come on back into my room and talk to me or talk to Yvette."

"Not now. Later." She pulled away from Griff. "I need to grab a shower and get dressed. We'll talk after breakfast." She glanced from Griff to Yvette. "Maybe we won't wait until Monday to start my therapy. There's no rule that says we can't start sessions on a Sunday, is there?"

"We will begin whenever you are ready," Yvette said.

Just as Nic turned to go back to her bedroom, a phone rang. All three of them froze instantly.

"It's my cell phone," Griff said.

"Answer it," Nic told him.

He strode hurriedly into his bedroom, picked up his cell phone from the desk, and answered it. Nic hesitated, and then, avoiding eye contact with Yvette, walked straight to Griff, who was speaking in monosyllables. She knew it was the Hunter. Rosswalt Everhart. Cary Maygarden's distant cousin and partner in a murderous killing spree that had lasted five years and had spanned from Texas to Virginia.

Nic waited, holding her breath, Yvette Meng standing nearby, until Griff ended the conversation by slamming his phone down on the desk.

"It was Everhart, wasn't it?" Nic asked.

Griff nodded.

"What did he say?"

Griff glanced past her and looked at Yvette.

"No, don't do that," Nic told him. "This isn't her decision to make. It's mine. Damn it, Griff, tell me what he said."

"He gave me a couple of clues."

"Which were?" Nic's pulse rate increased dramatically.

Before Griff could reply, Nic's phone rang. She tensed instantly, then thrust her hand into her pocket and yanked out her cell phone. She flipped it open.

"Hello, Rosswalt," she said.

"Hello, Nicole."

"I got your message. And the answer is, yes, I miss you. I wish I were with you right now so that I could stab you over and over again with my makeshift knife. How did it feel, Great White Hunter, having your prey attack you and nearly kill you?"

Silence.

"What's the matter, cat got your tongue?" Nic taunted him.

"She won't be as clever as you. She won't be able to escape. Her only hope is for you and Griff to find her before the last day of the hunt."

"Maybe I don't want to play your game anymore. Maybe I don't want to hear your damn worthless clues."

"Very well, if you really don't want to play."

Damn son of a bitch! He knew she wouldn't be able to resist the chance to help another victim.

Silence.

"Say 'please,' " Everhart said.

"No, never again."

Laughter. The memories of that sound sent shivering chills along Nic's nerve endings.

"Hail the conquering heroine."

"What?" Nic asked.

The line went dead.

Nic flipped her phone closed and faced Griff.

"Nic, honey—?"

" 'Hail the conquering heroine,' " Nic said. "I'm not sure if he was giving me a clue or making a statement."

"We'll consider it a clue and add it to the ones he gave me."

"Which were?"

"Why don't you let the Powell Agency and the Bureau work together on these clues and you concentrate on your therapy sessions with Yvette?"

"What were the clues?" Nic demanded.

" 'Boot camp buccaneer.' "

Nic recited the three words silently, then added them to her clue.

"Boot camp buccaneer and hail the conquering heroine," Griff said aloud.

"I'm going to take a shower and get dressed," Nic told him. "Then as soon as we grab some coffee, we'll compare notes. You start thinking now and I'll do the same. Separate boot, camp, and buccaneer, then put them all together, and then try two words together. And we'll do the same with my clue."

When she turned to go, Griff called to her. "Nic?"

"Yeah?" She looked back over her shoulder.

"We'll do this together, on one condition."

"Okay." She eyed him questioningly.

"You start your therapy sessions with Yvette today."

"You've got a deal. When we take a break this afternoon, I'll let Yvette get a sneak peek inside my head."

Chapter 25

Clasping his stomach as he made his way up the stairs from the cellar to the screened back porch, Pudge cursed Nicole Baxter for the millionth time since she had stabbed him in the gut and fled Belle Fleur. Once he stepped out of the dungeon darkness and into the light of the Sunday-evening twilight, he lifted his hand from his belly, inspected his palm, and groaned when he saw the bright red blood. Goddamn it! Carrying an unconscious LaTasha Davies from the speedboat to the house and then down into the cellar had put too much strain on his incision. He would have to clean up, use an antiseptic, and change shirts.

But why was he bleeding? His incision was practically healed, wasn't it? Maybe those damn Mexican doctors at the clinic had screwed up somehow. Maybe infection had set in or maybe the wound had healed from the outside first and was still open beneath the newly formed scar tissue.

He didn't want to leave the island tomorrow to seek medical attention, but if it became necessary, he would do it. He much preferred his original plan—to begin a new hunt with his recently acquired prey.

Getting into and back out of the U.S., using his fake passport, had been even easier than he had anticipated. He'd flown into Tampa on a commercial airliner, but had returned via a private plane. After all, he didn't want any delays in getting his precious cargo home as quickly as possible.

Now, back in the house, he went directly to the small bathroom off the kitchen, stripped out of his shirt, and inspected the healing slash across his abdomen. The pink scar appeared the same as it had yesterday, except for a fine stripe of blood that coated half the surgical line. After removing his ruined shirt, he wiped the blood off his belly and noted that a small tear in the center of the incision was oozing blood and some sort of clear fluid.

This was all her doing. He had suffered terribly because of her. And even now, weeks after her escape, his life was still affected by her vicious attack on him. She might think she was safe, that Griffin Powell could protect her, but the time would come when he would exact his revenge against her.

If only that time was tonight.

If only Nicole Baxter was in the basement, chained to the wall, awaiting his punishment.

For now, he would have to content himself with LaTasha. He knew she would not disappoint him. She would take to the hunt like the trained solider she was and give him many days of pleasure. And in the end, he would reward her for pleasing him by shooting her only once.

Nic waited with Griff in his home office, counting the minutes until they heard back from Doug Trotter. They had spent most of yesterday trying to decode the Hunter's clues. And when Griff had suspected that Nic was growing tired, he had insisted she go to bed.

"Let me just take a break," she'd suggested. "I can talk to Yvette for a little while, then you and I—"

"Talk to Yvette tomorrow. You're asleep on your feet."

"But Griff . . ."

"You had an hour session with Yvette this afternoon. So, either I walk you to your room or I carry you. Take your pick."

Knowing when she couldn't win an argument with Griff, she had allowed him to escort her upstairs. But if she'd thought that would be the end of it, she'd been wrong. He had returned thirty minutes later to find her talking on her cell phone to Josh Friedman.

"Do I have to strip off your clothes, put you into your pajamas, and tuck you into bed?" Griff had asked.

When he checked on her again, he had found her in bed, feigning sleep. She suspected that he knew it would take her hours to fall asleep and that her rest would be interrupted by nightmares.

This morning, she'd had her second one-hour therapy session with Dr. Meng and the honest truth was she felt today's little talk had been as useless as yesterday's. Their discussion had been more like a conversation, each of them contributing information. Nic now knew where Dr. Meng had been born, who her parents had been, and where she had attended medical school. And Nic had shared similar info with the woman she still refused to call Yvette.

By early afternoon, she and Griff had put together a possible description of someone who might be Everhart's latest victim. But they couldn't be sure they were right about anything. And to make matters even worse, they had no idea when the Hunter would strike again.

Boot camp implied military training. A soldier or a sailor? A woman in the armed forces.

Hail the conquering heroine implied that this soldier or sailor had done something heroic, something that might have put her in the spotlight, even if only briefly.

Buccaneer had taken longer to figure out, simply because there were more possibilities. But in the end, Nic and Griff had agreed, as had half a dozen other FBI and Powell Agency minds. More than likely this final clue indicated a location. And with Griff's penchant for sports, his first thought had been Tampa Bay Buccaneers, which translated to Tampa, Florida.

They had surmised that Everhart's next victim was a female soldier from Tampa, Florida, and she had recently been heralded for some type of bravery, probably in the line of duty.

"I wish Doug would call," Nic said as she paced back and forth in an open area of the office.

"He'll call as soon as he has any news." Griff sat on the edge of the large conference table. "In the meantime, why don't we grab a bite of supper—?"

"I'm not hungry."

"You barely touched your food at lunch."

"I'll eat a big breakfast, I promise."

"I'm not trying to be your warden," Griff said. "I don't want you to feel like a prisoner here at Griffin's Rest. Not after . . . Damn, Nic, all I want is to take care of you."

Her fingers itched to touch him, but something inside her held her back. "I know, but I need for you to just let me be me. You can't help me any more than you already have. Some things, I have to do for myself."

Griff nodded. She hated that solemn expression on his face. She knew she was the cause. But if she lied to him and told him she was perfectly all right, he wouldn't believe her and would worry about her even more.

"If Everhart has abducted another woman, you cannot allow yourself to become obsessed with the case," Griff said. "Your first obligation is to yourself. *You* have to be your top priority."

"Logically, I know you're right. If I don't find a way to completely recover emotionally and forget what happened to me, I won't be able to do my job."

Griff looked at her, his gaze oddly sad. She knew he wanted to pull her into his arms and comfort her, and a part of her wanted him to. But if he touched her, she might crumble into pathetic, weepy, hysterical pieces. She couldn't allow that to happen. It would be like pulling the pin on a grenade. Losing herself in Griff's comfort might destroy her.

"Nic, honey, you're expecting too much of yourself if you believe you will ever forget what happened to you. Don't set yourself up for defeat."

"I can tell you've been talking to Dr. Meng about me. You just quoted her, almost verbatim."

"Actually, I haven't talked to Yvette about your session today. And yesterday, all I asked her was whether the first session had gone well and she said that it had. If I sound as if I'm quoting her, it's because Yvette has been my therapist for a long time."

"She's been your therapist?" Nic frowned. "I don't understand. Why would she—?"

The office phone rang. Nic gasped. Griff picked up the receiver and motioned for Nic to grab one of the two extensions.

"Powell, this is Doug Trotter."

"Yeah, Trotter. Nic is on the extension," Griff said. "She's anxious to hear what you've found out."

Trotter cleared his throat. "Nic, are you sure you want to hear this?"

"I'm sure I need to know the truth," she told him.

"Okay, here goes. This morning around seven, Corporal LaTasha Davies went for a walk around her old Tampa neighborhood. Sort of a last good-bye before she reported back to active duty. She was scheduled to report in first thing tomorrow morning and was to be shipped back to Iraq within a week."

Nic held her breath.

"And?" Griff prompted.

"Corporal Davies disappeared. She never returned home to spend the rest of the day with her daughter, mother, and other family members."

"Is it possible that she simply went AWOL?" Griff asked.

"Not likely. Davies has an exemplary record and—"

"He's got her!" Nic said as nausea burned a path up her esophagus.

"We have no evidence that she was abducted," Doug said. "But considering the fact that the clues Everhart gave you match up with Davies's ID and she's now missing, the odds are he has kidnapped her and has taken her to only God knows where."

"If we don't find her, he'll kill her," Nic said, her voice quivering slightly. "But before he kills her, he will put her in chains and he'll starve her and beat her and—" Nic dropped the phone and ran out of the office.

"Nic!" Griff called to her.

She raced to the nearest bathroom, about ten feet down the hall and on the left. She just made it to the commode and managed to flip up the lid before she upchucked. After lifting her head and taking a deep breath, she fought the tears threatening to overtake her. Salty bile rose to her throat. She bent over and threw up again.

She saw Griff in her peripheral vision. He filled the powder room doorway, his shoulders as broad as the opening.

"Nic, honey . . ."

He reached out and placed his hand on her back.

She tensed, then gagged and dropped to her knees on the floor before vomiting again, this time emptying her stomach. While she struggled to calm her agitated nerves, she heard water running.

Griff knelt down beside her and wiped her face with a soft, damp cloth, washing away the perspiration from her brow and the spittle from her mouth. When he slid his arm around her waist and helped her to her feet, she started to protest, to tell him she neither wanted nor needed his help. But for the life of her, she couldn't manage to pull away from him or form the words of protest on her lips. Instead, she leaned on him.

"Better?" he asked.

She nodded.

"Do you want to go upstairs and lie down for a while?"

"No. I'll be all right." She tried to smile, but the effort failed. "What about Doug? Did you hang up on him? You need to call him back and get all the information—"

Griff tapped his index finger on her lips. "Trotter gave us all the relevant information he had. Right now, he's doing what he can."

"We need to—"

He tapped her lips again. "At this point, there is nothing we can do."

Nic heaved a deep sigh. "Everhart is going to put her through a living hell." Nic turned and buried her face against Griff's chest. "Oh, God, Griff, you have no idea what it will be like for her."

He wrapped his arms around her and held her.

That night, long after everyone else had gone to bed, Griff sat alone in his study, the dying embers of a warm fire glimmering in the fireplace. Tonight would be one of those nights when he wouldn't sleep. Before Nic had been kidnapped, he had reached a point in his life where he seldom had nights like this.

He knew that if Nic could cry, the emotional release would help her. But she hadn't cried. Wouldn't cry. Wouldn't let go. She was so all-fired determined to be strong, to hold the anger and frustration inside her. And that self-control damned her to a self-inflicted purgatory.

He understood. They were so much alike, his Nicki and he.

Griff had managed to persuade her to eat some saltine crackers and drink a little ginger ale after her bout of vomiting. When he'd suggested she talk to Yvette again, she had refused.

"Not another session today," she'd said. "Maybe two sessions tomorrow."

Instead of talking about what she was feeling, of working through the reason she had reacted so violently to the news about LaTasha Davies's disappearance, Nic had decided she would help Barbara Jean with plans to decorate Griffin's Rest for the upcoming holidays. Christmas was just around the corner.

Griff knew that Nic was grasping at any excuse not to face the reality of her situation. She wanted to believe that by acting in a normal way, doing normal things, she could prove to herself and everyone who cared about her that she was back to normal.

Griff gazed into the waning flickers of firelight and accepted the threatening memories, ones that could erode years of pride and self-control.

"Oh, God, Griff, you have no idea what it will be like for her." Nic's words haunted him. Why hadn't he told her the truth, that she was wrong? He did know what it would be like for LaTasha to be subjugated by a madman, made to obey his every whim, forced to become a hunted animal in order to survive.

Griff shuddered.

He could feel York's hot breath on his neck.

Griff stood as still as a statue as the man's hands skimmed over his shoulders, down his back, and roughly grasped his taut buttocks.

"You're an incredible male specimen," York said. "Tall, large bones, broad shoulders, muscular, and quite beautiful as only a young man can be."

York sighed as he released his hold on Griff, then he ran his fingertips over the raw welts on Griff's back. Griff winced.

"When you learn to obey my every command, the floggings will stop. It's entirely up to you, Griffin. I don't enjoy having Sanders whip you, but it's your own fault for being so rebellious."

Griff forced his mind back to the present.

More than anything, he wanted to help Nic recover. But at what price to his own sanity?

Chapter 26

If she could elude him for a while longer, give him the kind of hunt he wanted, he might offer her some food tonight. But if he found her too soon . . . *Please, dear Lord, no!* LaTasha tried not to think about the cage. The first time he had locked her inside that terrible cage and left her outside all night long, she had bruised and bloodied her hands and feet trying to break free. After hours of useless struggle, she'd wept like a baby.

She had thought he had broken her that night. And he almost had.

But come morning, she had welcomed the new day. Another chance to escape from the crazy man who had kidnapped her and brought her to this island prison.

Sweating profusely, winded, her legs burning as if they were on fire, LaTasha emerged from the wooded area and ran toward the beach. This was the first time since he had brought her here and begun their daily hunts that she had gone this far away from the spot where he had released her, only a few yards from the house. She wasn't sure how far she had traveled, but it had to be several miles, although she had deliberately gone in circles a couple of times. She had done that to confuse her stalker and buy herself more time.

The sand on the beach shimmered a creamy white, like tiny diamond chips piled high over the ground. Dropping to her knees, she gasped for air. When she brought her head up to drink in the fresh sea air, she saw a dilapidated building, really nothing more than a small shack. The wooden structure was bleached a pale gray and many of the boards were warped.

LaTasha forced herself back on her feet and trudged through the soft sand to the shack. She didn't dare stay here long enough to fully inspect the place. The Hunter could find her at anytime. As she rounded the building, intending to run up the shore as far as she could and then back into the woods farther up the beach, she came to a dead standstill when she encountered the boat.

Turned over, with its underside exposed to the sun, rested a small wooden boat, two oars beside it, braced against the back of the nearby shack.

Thank you, dear Jesus, thank you!

What if the boat had holes in it? What if the wood was rotted? What if—

Don't worry about any of this today. Concentrate on the hunt. Run as far from this place as you can. Don't let him catch you here.

He doesn't know this boat exists. He can't. He has no intention of allowing me to leave this island.

LaTasha knew that she could find her way back here, to this newly discovered means of her escape. But she had to be careful. Be patient. Make plans. Wait for the right moment.

Pudge parked his dirt bike, got off, and removed his canteen from his backpack. Hunting here on this tiny island wasn't as challenging as it had been at Belle Fleur. He had known those thousand acres as he knew the back of his hand. And he supposed, given time, he would learn every inch of Tabora Island. The wooded areas were like jungles—damp, dense, and smelly. Rotting vegetation and small dead animals. The beaches were nice, unspoiled, but a bitch to walk on and it was impossible to maneuver his dirt bike on them except in the places where the sand was packed down, and there weren't many areas like that.

LaTasha had tried his patience those first few days, but once he had punished her sufficiently, she had become his willing prey. She had proved to be quick and agile, a truly magnificent animal.

But she was not as cunning as Nicole. None of them had been.

He supposed he could not expect perfection from all of them, could he? Nicole had been special in a way no one else had been or would be. It wasn't LaTasha's fault that she did not inspire him the way Nicole had. The one time he had whipped LaTasha, the act had not given him any real pleasure until he had pretended he was thrashing Nicole.

He didn't hate LaTasha. He hadn't hated any of them. They were nothing more to him than participants in his game, their only purpose to provide him with pleasure. But he now hated Nicole. Hated her for outsmarting him and escaping. Hated her for trying to kill him. Hated her because she had diminished his enjoyment for hunting other prey.

Pudge upended his canteen and poured the remaining water over his head, then shook his head from side to side and let out a warrior's whoop.

Run for your life, my beautiful ebony antelope. You have only eleven more days before I bring you down with one fatal shot and claim my trophy.

* * *

"Why don't you want to talk about your husband?" Dr. Meng asked.

Nic eyed the lovely doctor, who sat in the white wicker chair directly across from her in the sunroom. Every day for the past week and a half, Nic had spent an hour each day sitting and talking to Griff's precious Yvette. The woman never raised her sweet voice, never became agitated or frustrated or angry. Sometimes, Nic would say something for the sole purpose of getting a negative reaction from the woman. Not once had Nic's tactics achieved the desired results.

It wasn't that she didn't like the good doctor or that she thought she had any reason to be jealous of her relationship with Griff, but damn it, how could you warm up to someone so perfect?

"Nicole?"

"Yeah, I heard you. I was just wondering about your clothes. You've worn a different outfit every day since I met you. You must travel with a shitload of luggage."

Dr. Meng's full, perfect lips lifted in a hint of a smile. "I keep many clothes here at Griffin's Rest. I consider this my second home."

Nic glared at the other woman. "Why am I not surprised," Nic mumbled *sotto voce*.

"You are trying to change the subject, Nicole. Why is that? You have told me about your parents, your brother, and your stepfather, but you have said very little about your husband."

Nic rubbed her hands up and down her thighs, then jumped up and walked to the end of the sunroom facing the woods. Afternoon sunlight cast deep shadows across the ground, dark outlines of the towering trees. The fat evergreens grew abundantly alongside the oaks and maples, their branches now barren in mid-December.

"How is talking about Greg going to help me come to

terms with being abducted and tortured?" Nic did not want
to discuss the details of her marriage with anyone, not even
a trained professional. Not again.

"Nicole, I'm going to ask something of you that requires
a certain level of trust." Dr. Meng rose from her chair and
walked toward Nic.

Nic turned and faced her. "It's not that I don't trust you.
I'm not sure I trust anyone completely."

"Not even Griffin?"

"I'm not sure. Maybe."

"We've tried several different techniques and so far none
of them have seemed to help you, but it is early yet and we
will probably retry some of those techniques again. But I
have a very special procedure that often helps my patients.
Do you trust me enough to allow me to employ this method
with you?"

Nic shrugged. "Sure, why not? We've tried rewriting my
nightmares using imagery where I'm in control of the out-
come, but I'm still having nightmares. No better or worse
than before. So, what's this special procedure you want to try
on me today?"

"May I take your hands in mine?" Dr. Meng asked.

Nic scowled. "You want to hold my hands."

Dr. Meng nodded. "Only for a couple of minutes."

"What's that supposed to do?"

"It will allow me to sense what you are feeling."

"Huh?"

Dr. Meng held out her hands. "Please, Nicole, let me help
you."

Nic hesitated, a strong sense of uncertainty demanding an
explanation. But the look of genuine concern in the doctor's
mesmerizing black eyes persuaded Nic to lift her hands and
place them in Dr. Meng's.

Nic looked down at where Dr. Meng held her hands between them, as gently as if her hands were delicate flowers that would crush easily. A strange sense of calm spread through Nic. Her body relaxed. She shot her gaze up to the other woman's face.

Yvette Meng had closed her eyes and seemed to be in some kind of trance.

"Dr. Meng?"

She didn't reply for a full minute, then she sighed deeply and released Nic's hands.

Nic's feelings of calm and relaxation lingered. "What happened? What was that all about?"

Dr. Meng opened her eyes. "Tell me about how Gregory died and why you blame yourself for his death."

So much for calm and relaxed. Nic tensed, but she felt an overwhelming need to be honest about her feelings where Greg was concerned.

"Greg killed himself. Shot himself." Nic looked away from Dr. Meng, her gaze focusing on a single pine tree standing tall and proud in the middle of so many older and larger trees. "I thought I knew my husband. I believed that whatever problems we were having were the result of our both working so many hours, dedicating ourselves to our jobs. I thought if we had a baby, if I made more time for him, for us . . ."

"It wasn't your fault," Dr. Meng said. "You must stop blaming yourself."

"Greg was in trouble and I didn't know it. I was his wife. I should have instinctively known that he needed help." Nic crisscrossed her arms over her waist, clutching her elbows, hugging her body protectively. "He should have been able to come to me and tell me that he . . . he—Oh, God, even now, after all this time, I still can't admit the truth."

"What was the truth?"

Nic laughed harshly. "My young, handsome, ambitious

husband, a Drug Enforcement Administration agent with a spotless record, became a drug addict."

She had confessed Greg's sin aloud and the world had not come to an end.

"Why didn't I see what was happening? Why did he turn to drugs? Did he think he couldn't come to me for help?"

"You are not responsible for your husband becoming addicted to drugs and you are not responsible for his suicide," Dr. Meng said. "Gregory chose his own path, made his own decisions, just as you and I do. If he did not want to come to you for help, he could have gone to someone else. He could have sought professional help. He didn't. His own weaknesses destroyed him."

"No, please . . . Greg was kind and dear and we were good together, at least in the beginning. He really was the perfect sort of man for me."

"Perfect for you because he was the opposite of your father?"

Nic groaned. "Oh, crap! Do we have to talk about my father again? The man was a macho, chauvinist control freak. We've already established the fact that I became a ball-bashing feminist because of dear old Dad."

"Have you ever considered the fact that the reason you are having such difficulty working through the trauma of your abduction is because you don't want to admit to anyone, not even yourself, that for a brief period of time someone else controlled you completely, just as your father once did?"

"My father did not control me. I wouldn't let him. And I wouldn't let that damn psychopathic freak control me, either. Do you hear me? No one controls me. Not ever!"

"You're wrong," Dr. Meng said, her voice velvety soft. "In such a subtle way that you don't even realize it, your father still influences your thoughts, your actions, and your reactions. And the Hunter creeps into your mind when you are asleep and even sometimes when you are awake and takes control."

"No!" Nic screamed. "No, no, no . . ." She ran from the sunroom, the truth of Dr. Meng's words chasing her like demons from hell.

Chapter 27

Griffin had watched helplessly while Nic withdrew from him more and more each day. It was as if, with her every action, she was telling him that she did not want or need him. And because she was never hostile to him or the other members of the household, was actually pleasant most of the time, he realized that she was playing her own Nic-is-recovering-just-fine game. For the past week, she had been spending the better part of each day helping Barbara Jean and Mark Crosby decorate Griffin's Rest for Christmas. Once or twice, he'd heard her laugh. Talk about sweet music to his ears.

"Nicole is hiding," Yvette said. "She has chosen to pretend that she is well adjusted and capable of living a normal life."

"Yeah, I know. She told me this morning that she's planning on going home to Woodbridge after New Year's and that she expects to return to work as soon as possible."

"Unless she faces what has happened to her and admits the truth to herself, it is only a matter of time before she self-destructs."

"We can't let that happen."

"I cannot help her if she will not let me."

"Damn it, Yvette, there has to be something you can do."

She shook her head. "Until she accepts the fact that she cannot control every aspect of her life and that having been held captive and subjugated against her will does not make her a weak, spineless, easily manipulated woman—a woman like her mother—she won't be able to begin the healing process."

"She's still attending therapy sessions every day, so try a new method of some kind. Talk her into medication or hypnosis or—"

"You are not listening to me, Griffin. I am trying to tell you that before I can help her, you must help her."

Griff's stomach muscles tightened. "What can I do to help her? Tell me and I'll do it."

Yvette held her hand over his. "May I?"

"Yeah, sure."

She took his hand in hers. "You know what she needs from you."

"No."

"You know that she thinks of you as strong, brave, and powerful, a real man's man, similar to her father in some ways and therefore her male counterpart."

"I can't," Griff said.

"I have spoken to Sanders and we agreed that you must do this to help Nicole. We give you our permission."

"You know what you're asking me to do, don't you? You're asking me to bare my soul to a woman that I . . . who means more to me than . . . How can it help her to know that I was stripped of my dignity, that I had my life stolen from me, that I was forced to become a wild animal in order to survive?"

Yvette squeezed his hand tenderly. "I believe that in asking that question, you also answered it."

* * *

Mia O'Dell stuffed three shopping bags into the trunk of her Jaguar, then turned and took two more bags from Logan Carter. She always waited until practically the last minute to do her Christmas shopping. It was so much more fun that way. And Logan was such a dear for staying with her for the entire afternoon at The Summit, the absolutely most divine place to shop in Birmingham. She had spent far more than the amount Daddy mentioned as her limit. But it didn't matter. She had her father wrapped around her little finger. And she had learned long ago that his bark was much worse than his bite. He might shout out orders and get all gruff and huffy, but deep down, he was an old softie. Daddy couldn't say no to his three girls: Mia, her little sister, Meli, and their mom, Joyce.

"I have only a few more gifts to buy." Mia fluttered her dark, thick eyelashes at Logan.

"Ah, Mia, enough's enough." He caressed her butt. "I thought we were going to take advantage of my folks being out of town for the holidays. So far, you've been over at my place only once." When he pinched her, she swatted his hand away. "Hey, honey, a guy's got needs, you know."

She cuddled up to his side and smiled. "Just four more gifts and I promise we'll go straight to your place and I'll give you what you want."

He nuzzled her neck. "I want a blow job just like the one you gave me last time."

Mia sighed. Why did guys like having their dicks sucked? And they all liked it. Every last one of them. She'd found out in high school, when she was sitting home without a date most weekends, that the one way for a not-so-pretty, not-very-popular girl to attract boys was to go down on them. The first time, she'd actually thrown up. The second time, she had merely gagged. But before she'd graduated from high school, she'd perfected her skills and could give head better than the most experienced hooker.

College guys were only older versions of high school boys. And she'd found that even the goody-goody young men who attended Samford University, where she was on the cheerleading squad, appreciated a woman with a talented mouth.

She didn't delude herself into thinking that Logan was in love with her. He liked her, but he dated her for the sex. Unfortunately, she was in love with him.

"Since your folks will still be on that riverboat cruise Christmas Day, why don't you spend the day with my family? You know Mom will be serving a feast. She's had Sophie baking up a storm for days now."

He shrugged. "I guess I could do that. Are you sure your parents won't mind?"

"I'm sure."

Maybe Logan didn't love her now, but that could change, couldn't it? Anything was possible. After all, she had a lot more going for her than just putting out. She had all her daddy's money, too.

Pudge stared at the calendar on his computer. December 24. One twenty AM. Later today most of the people in the world would be celebrating Christmas Eve. He would celebrate, too, in his own special way.

He had become bored with LaTasha. Bored with the same old hunt. That, too, was Nicole Baxter's fault. Despite the fact that she had nearly killed him, or perhaps because she had, he wanted her as he had never wanted another woman. Wanted to make her suffer unbearably before he killed her.

In the meantime, he would take LaTasha on another hunt today before the final one tomorrow. He wondered if she realized tomorrow was Christmas Day or had any idea it would be the last day of her life.

There was one thing about the island that made it superior to Belle Fleur as a hunting ground. He could release his prey, unchained, unmonitored, and know she had no chance of escaping. But that advantage took the edge off the excitement of the hunt. At Belle Fleur, that added risk, that slight danger, had thrilled Pudge.

Yesterday's hunt had been terribly disappointing. He had managed to track LaTasha down far too quickly. It was as if she had given up. Of course, he'd had to punish her. She had spent last night in the cage. Today, she should be more than eager to please him.

But before he donned his hunting gear and revved his dirt bike into action, he had one other little chore to attend to, a preliminary part of his game that he enjoyed. The anticipation of pleasure yet to come.

He laughed at his own play on words.

There was nothing more sexually stimulating than the end of the hunt. Catching his prey, overpowering her, showing her who her master was, aroused him. But he did not pleasure these women. Fucking them would be like screwing an animal, and he was not into bestiality.

A shiver of anticipation rippled through him at the thought of killing LaTasha. At least in dying, she would provide him with some satisfaction.

Pudge opened the file folders he had compiled during the past week. Only by planning the next abduction had he been able to pacify himself and assuage his discontent. He had narrowed the search down to five women. A volleyball player. A ballroom dancer. A cheerleader. A gymnast. And a college team swimmer.

One by one, he studied each woman's picture and the information he had acquired on her. Two blondes. Two brunettes.

One redhead. All of them young. Each of them in prime physical condition.

He paused on the photo of the curvy cheerleader. Large breasts. Long legs. Probably five seven or eight. Chin-length dark brown hair and chocolate-brown eyes. Not pretty, but appealing. And there was something about her that reminded him of Nicole. Perhaps it was that confident glint in her eyes and the self-assured tilt of her chin.

Hello, Mia. How would you like to visit my island paradise? This place is simply . . . to die for.

Sanders had taken Barbara Jean for Christmas Eve services at the Methodist church she attended on a regular basis. And to Griff's surprise, Yvette had gone with them. He realized that was his cue. She was giving him time alone with Nic, the perfect opportunity to tell her something about the ten missing years of his life. After speaking to him only once, Yvette had not broached the subject again, leaving the decision entirely up to him.

But if Yvette believed that the best way—perhaps the only way—to help Nic recover was for him to tell Nic that he had been held captive by a madman and subjected to inhuman treatment, then he had to find the courage to confess at least a part of his deepest, darkest secrets.

"Barbara Jean and I baked three cakes today," Nic said as she curled up in an easy chair near the windows in the living room. "I've never baked a cake in my life. It was fun."

"Didn't you ever bake cookies or cakes with your mother?" Griff asked.

"Nope. She tried to teach me how to cook, but I refused to learn any domestic skills. I was determined not to follow in her footsteps and become a housewife, which to me was equivalent to being a slave."

"My mama was a servant," Griff said. "She cleaned other people's houses. Some people treated her well, but others acted like she was dirt beneath their feet."

"So, it's true that you grew up extremely poor."

"We were as poor as church mice."

"We weren't rich by any means, but we lived in a nice house, we had a nice car, we dressed well. For all intents and purposes, we were your ideal all-American family. Dad owned his own business. Mom stayed home with the kids, one boy and one girl. I took ballet and tap lessons. My brother played Little League. Charles David and I did everything we were told to do until we became teenagers."

"Then you rebelled as most teenagers do."

"It was a little more than that," Nic admitted. "The funny thing is, if Charles David had been the girl and I'd been the boy, everything would have been perfect. My brother was sweet and sensitive and artistic, like our mother. I was rough and rowdy and aggressive, like our father."

"I take it that your father didn't want a sensitive, artistic son."

Nic laughed, the sound hollow and bitter. "I don't know which he hated more, having a sissy for a son or a tomboy for a daughter."

"Why are you telling me all of this now?" Griff asked.

"I suppose it's been on my mind. Dr. Meng keeps making me go over things from my childhood again and again. She's convinced that my choice in a husband and my guilt about Greg's death are connected to my feelings about my parents. And somehow all that mixed-up mess between my parents and my husband is actually connected to the way I'm handling—or, in her opinion, not handling—the recent trauma I experienced."

"And you think she's wrong?"

Nic shrugged. "I want her to be wrong."

"You do realize that Yvette has not shared your confidences with me. All she's told me is that she can't help you because you won't let her. And she thinks—"

"Screw what she thinks!" Nic shot up out of the chair. "Let's forget about all that crap for tonight and tomorrow. It's Christmas. We should be eating and drinking and laughing and celebrating and opening presents." She walked over to the tree and looked down at the mile-high pile of gaily wrapped gifts. "When Sanders drove Barbara Jean and me into Knoxville to shop last week, we bought out the stores. And it's all your fault for giving me your credit card."

When Griff joined her in front of the tree, she turned and faced him. "But I want you to know that I bought your gift with my own money," she said.

"Nic?" He looked right at her, into her beautiful honey-brown eyes.

Tensing her jaw and forcing a smile, she met his gaze head-on. "Yes, Griff?"

"Yvette believes that I can help you."

Nic stared at him, her expression questioning his comment.

"Tell me something," he said. "Describe me."

She emitted a close-mouthed laugh. "Are you serious?"

He nodded.

"Well, you're handsome."

"That goes without saying." He grinned. "What else?"

"You're rich and powerful. You're strong and . . . and brave. And you're the kind of man other men envy, the kind they'd like to be."

"Hmm . . . Do I remind you of anyone?"

Nic's forced smile vanished. She looked away from him.

"Do I remind you of your father?" he asked.

Lifting and dropping her shoulders, she heaved a deep sigh. "A little." She sighed again. "Before I got to know you better, I thought you were just like my dad and I suppose that's one of the reasons I detested you." She glanced over her shoulder at Griff. "I guess you know my opinion of you has changed somewhat. And my feelings for you have pretty much done a complete one-eighty."

"Same here," Griff told her. "You know, don't you, honey, that you and I are an awful lot alike. Yvette told me that I'm your male counterpart and vice versa."

Nic turned around slowly and faced Griff, her eyes wide with wonder and acceptance. "Dr. Meng is right about that."

"We're two halves of a whole."

Nic grinned. "Now, I wouldn't go that far. Saying something like that borders on the romantic and we both know that neither of us are romantics."

"We're realists, aren't we? We see life for what it is and deal with it the best we can."

Nic's smile wavered. "I know what you're trying to say."

"Do you?"

"Yes, I think I do. You think I'm pretending to be all right, when in reality, I'm not. But let me ask you this, Mr. Nic Baxter's Male Counterpart: if what happened to me had happened to you, wouldn't you handle it the same way I am?"

"I did," Griff confessed. "At first, I pretended I was too tough, too strong to need anyone's help. But in the end, I did need help. Sometimes, I still do."

Nic stared at him, studying his face, obviously trying to understand what he had just told her. "You lost me back there with 'I did' and now I'm totally confused."

Nic glanced down at Griff's outstretched hands. After briefly hesitating, she placed her hands in his.

"Let's sit down." Griff led her to the sofa. She went with him willingly, without one word of protest.

When they were seated, he reached out and caressed her cheek. "There was a time when I didn't give a damn what you thought about me."

Her lips quivered in a tentative half-smile. "Ditto."

He ran his hands down her arms, then released her. "What you think of me matters to me now."

"Griff, what are you trying to say?"

"When I was twenty-two, just graduated from UT and was a first-round draft choice for the Dallas Cowboys, something happened that drastically changed my life."

Nic watched him closely.

He forced himself to keep looking directly at her. "I was drugged and kidnapped."

Nic gasped.

"The only other people who know about what happened to me are Sanders and Yvette. I'm trusting you with this information because Yvette believes my telling you about what happened to me will help you."

"Damn it, Griffin Powell, if what you're telling me isn't the absolute truth . . . If you and Dr. Meng have concocted some elaborate tale—"

Griff grabbed Nic by the shoulders. Her eyes widened in alarm.

"If you think that I'd lie to you about something like this, then maybe you don't know me at all."

"I'm sorry, Griff. I—I trust you. I know you won't lie to me."

He released her.

"The man who had me kidnapped was a billionaire who owned his own South Seas island, a place called Amara." Griff did not intend to tell Nic everything. Not tonight. Maybe not ever. But he would give her the basic facts. "He abducted and held captive young men in prime physical condition. He collected them as other men collect stamps or coins or antique cars. He tortured them until they bent to his will. Then he prepared them for the hunt."

"Oh, God, no!" Tears misted Nic's eyes.

"I spent four years on Amara. I became little more than a wild animal, living each day as the captive of a madman. I was forced to kill in order to live. I did unspeakable things in order to stay alive."

When Nic touched his arm, Griff tensed. Their gazes met and locked.

"You don't have to say anything else," Nic told him. "You don't have to tell me everything. Not tonight."

"What matters, is that I survived. I got away from York, just as you escaped from Everhart. And I recovered from my ordeal, just as you can. I'm not a weak, helpless victim. I've spent years being helped by Yvette and Sanders, who were also York's captives. Without them, I wouldn't be the man I am." He grabbed her hand. "How did you describe me—strong, brave, powerful, the kind of guy other men envy?"

Nic swallowed her tears. "Oh, Griff . . . Griff . . ."

He pulled her into his arms and held her fiercely. If only he could absorb her pain and suffer it for her, he would. But where Nic had to go in order to heal her wounded soul, she would have to go alone.

Chapter 28

LaTasha swiped the perspiration out of her eyes and wiped her damp hands on her filthy shirt. Her heart raced as she struggled with the heavy wooden boat. She had to turn it over, place the oars inside it, and drag it to the beach. And she had to accomplish all this as quickly as possible. She knew the Hunter was close. He had almost caught her, probably not more than half an hour ago. She couldn't be sure of the exact time. But she had managed to elude him long enough to get a good head start. Today was the day she'd been waiting for, planning for, ever since she had discovered the old boat.

She had one chance to get away. If she failed . . . No, she wouldn't fail. She had to live, had to find her way home to Asheen.

Grunting as she put all her strength into turning the boat over, LaTasha almost shouted for joy when the boat flipped upright in the sand. Why was the boat so heavy? What kind of lumber had been used in its construction?

The boat isn't all that heavy. It's you. You're so damn

weak because you haven't eaten in days. You have practically no physical stamina.

After sucking in a deep breath and huffing it out slowly, she grasped the end of the boat and tugged. She was surprised when it moved more easily than she had anticipated. Grunting as she strained to drag the boat to the waterline, LaTasha didn't hear the approaching dirt bike. Only when she slid the boat into the ocean and started to climb aboard did she hear the bike's roaring engine.

Oh, dear Jesus, no. Not yet. Please, just a few more minutes.

As she hopped into the boat, sat down, and reached for the oars, the Hunter came into view, barreling out of the wooded area. His dirt bike hit the sand, sending a spray of fine particles flying up around the wheels.

LaTasha grasped the oars and thrust them down into the water.

She ignored the distant rumble of thunder. She didn't have time to worry about the weather.

The Hunter parked his bike, yanked off the strap holding the rifle across his back, and pointed the weapon directly toward her.

"Stop now or I'll shoot you!" he yelled, his eyes wild, his face beet red.

She began rowing, but the boat didn't move, simply sloshed back and forth on the incoming and outgoing waves.

Help me, sweet Jesus. Help me.

The Hunter aimed and fired.

The bullet hit the top edge of the boat, blasting off a strip of wood and turning the fragments into minute projectiles.

LaTasha kept trying to make the oars cooperate. Just as the Hunter shot at her again, she managed to find her rhythm and row the boat away from shore. His second bullet barely missed her head.

The Hunter jumped off his bike and ran toward the ocean, bellowing at the top of his lungs. Cursing. Damning her. Warning her.

He aimed and fired again. The third bullet sailed through the side of the boat, but hit high enough so that it didn't create a leak.

Outraged and screaming louder, he ventured into the water, then aimed and fired again. This time the bullet hit its mark.

LaTasha gasped as fire shot through her body, radiating from the hole in her gut. She was bleeding really bad, but she didn't dare take time to inspect her wound or give in to the unbearable pain. She kept rowing and rowing and rowing. And praying and praying and praying.

She looked back at the island, still no more than a hundred feet away. Her last coherent thought before she passed out was that she had escaped and somehow, someway, she was going to make it home to Asheen.

With her mouth agape, Nic stood in the driveway in front of Griff's home and stared at the big blue truck. Rip Tide Blue, Griff had informed her. A brand-new, shiny Escalade ESV, with all the bells and whistles.

"Merry Christmas, honey," he said as he tossed her the keys.

She looked down at the set of keys in her hand, then up at Griff. "I can't accept this. Do you know how much a truck like this costs? It's a Cadillac, for crying out loud."

Griff laughed. "Would you prefer a Ford or a Chevy?"

"No, that's not what I meant."

Yvette walked up beside Nic and, with humor in her voice, said, "Just say thank you and accept his gift, otherwise none of us will be able to enjoy the rest of our Christmas."

Everyone at Griffin's Rest was aware that if the Hunter remained true to form, he either had already killed LaTasha Davies or he would kill her today. But in the spirit of the season, trying to make the day enjoyable for everyone else, no one had said aloud what they were all thinking. Instead, they had eaten a fabulous dinner, prepared by Sanders and Barbara Jean, had listened to Christmas carols, and had exchanged presents.

Nic grunted. "That cashmere sweater I bought him sure does pale in comparison to what he got for me."

"Think of it this way," Sanders said as he came up on the other side of Nic. "To Griff, the cost of the truck was no more extravagant than the cashmere sweater was to you."

"Come on, honey. Let's take it for a spin." Griff motioned to her.

She zipped up her quilted parka, smiled first at Sanders and then at Yvette—and yes, she was finally calling Dr. Meng by her given name—and hurried out to meet Griff. She smiled at him.

"What did you buy all your other girlfriends for Christmas?"

He chuckled. "I don't have any other girlfriends. Not anymore. I'm thinking seriously about keeping the one I've got. *If* I've got her. Do I, Nic?"

"Do you what?"

"Do I have you?"

"Sure you do. You're stuck with me for at least another week."

She raced around to the driver's side, electronically unlocked the door, and heaved herself up and into the Escalade's plush leather seat. By the time she buckled herself in, Griff was sitting beside her.

"You know I can't keep this truck," she told him.

"Give it a test drive first, before you decide."

She stuck the keys into the ignition, started the engine, and sighed contentedly. God, she loved this truck. But then,

Griff had known she would. No sleek little sports car for her. No trendy SUV.

Of course this vehicle bordered on being sleek and trendy. But it was a truck. A gorgeous, badass truck.

She drove over every paved and unpaved road at Griffin's Rest. Then they got out on the highway and burned a third of a tank of gas before Nic brought them back home and parked in the driveway.

Clutching the steering wheel, she whined, and then cast a sidelong glance at Griff. "You've corrupted me, you know. I'm seriously thinking about keeping this truck."

Griff laughed, the sound a robust rumble inside the truck cab. He reached over, grabbed her, and kissed her. It was their first real kiss since . . .

She returned his kiss tentatively, loving the feel of his lips against hers. Griff ended the kiss and let her go. But he kept smiling.

"Tell me you love the cashmere sweater as much as I love this truck and I might keep my present."

"I love the sweater," he said. "Blue is my favorite color."

"I know. And apparently, since you bought me a blue truck, you know it's my favorite color, too."

"Face facts, honey, we really are just two halves of a whole."

She slapped his arm playfully. "Stop that mushy talk."

Griff laughed again.

"Would it be greedy if I asked for another gift?"

He eyed her suspiciously. "What sort of gift?"

She laid her hand on top of his and looked into his eyes. "I am going home, back to Woodbridge soon, right after New Year's. And do not try to talk me into staying longer."

"I would if I thought I could. But I know better."

"My sessions with Yvette are going well. I'm slowly but surely coming to terms with what happened to me. I'm going to continue therapy with someone in D.C., and, hopefully, Doug will put me back to work soon."

"What does all this have to do with my giving you another present?"

"You and I had one night together," she said. "A rather incredible night. At least I thought it was."

Griff's grin widened. "Oh, yeah, it was definitely an incredible night."

"I think we might have had something good going for us and I'd like to give it another try. Maybe this time, we can even go out on dates and stuff like that."

"Our dating is the other gift you want from me?"

"Yeah, sort of."

"Nicki, honey, don't you know that would be as much a gift for me as for you?"

"I'm thinking maybe we could do something special New Year's Eve."

"It's a date. I'll come up with something really, really special."

Nic squeezed his hand. "Just being with you will make it special."

"Now who's getting mushy?"

They both laughed. And it felt damn good to laugh again, to feel happy again.

Pudge sat on the beach and looked out at the ocean as dark storm clouds swirled in the sky. He could no longer see the small wooden boat that LaTasha had used to escape the island. Why hadn't he inspected every inch of his rental property before he'd brought a visitor here? It had never entered his mind that some previous renter, probably years ago, had left behind that damn little dinghy.

It didn't matter that she had managed to get away. *She's*

dead by now. I shot her. Either in the heart or close to the heart. But if she's not dead, she will be soon enough, definitely by this time tomorrow. There was no way she could survive drifting around out there on the ocean, the hot tropical sun beating down on her. No food. No water. Bleeding to death. Floating aimlessly farther and farther into the Caribbean Sea.

But what if someone finds her? If that happened, no one would have any idea where she'd come from, would they? There was no way they could connect her to Tabora Island. He was safe.

But to make sure, he should take the speedboat and go after her. He stared up at the darkening sky. Loud booms of thunder followed streaks of lightning, the approaching storm coming closer and closer to the island.

Go now, before the storm hits.

Slinging his rifle over his shoulder, he walked back to his bike, got on, and headed for the pier on the other side of the island. But before he'd gone halfway, the storm hit. High winds. A savage downpour. By the time he made it to the house, he was soaking wet.

He couldn't take the boat out in the storm. He'd be risking his life if he did. Smiling to himself, he thought how fortunate for him that this sudden tropical rainstorm no doubt would sink the dinghy quickly and end all his concerns about LaTasha's body ever being found.

There was no reason to let this little setback interfere with his plans to kidnap Mia O'Dell. But not yet. He would wait, listen to the news, and make certain he had no reason to leave Tabora Island. Once he knew for sure that there was no possible way for anyone to locate him, he would fly to Birmingham and bring the bosomy Samford cheerleader back to his island.

* * *

Nic knocked on the closed den door.

"Yeah?" Griff said.

"May I come in?"

"Nic? Sure, honey, come on in."

By the time she opened the door, Griff was only a few feet away, standing there waiting for her. She first noticed there were no lights on in the room and wondered if he'd been sitting in the dark. The second thing she noticed was that he was wearing the blue cashmere sweater she'd given him today.

"Hi," she said.

"Hi."

"I guess you couldn't sleep, huh?"

He shook his head. "Apparently you couldn't, either. Bad dreams?"

"No dreams. I haven't been to bed tonight."

"Come on in. Do you want a drink? Or we can go to the kitchen and fix some cocoa or hot tea or—"

"No thanks."

When she entered the study, Griff reached around her and closed the door. His arm brushed her shoulder.

"I can't stop thinking about LaTasha Davies," Nic said.

Griff placed his hand on the small of her back and guided her toward the leather sofa facing the fireplace. Flames danced from the burning logs, casting warmth and light into the room.

When he reached for the switch on a side table lamp, Nic clasped his hand. "Leave it off. It's cozier this way."

When they sat, Griff laid his arm across the sofa back, directly behind Nic's shoulders. "Do you want to talk about it?" he asked.

"Yes and no. I'd like to stop thinking about her, stop wondering when her body will show up." Nic looked at Griff. "Do you think he'll take her back to Tampa and hang her from a tree?"

"It depends on whether he stays true to form or alters his game plan."

"By now, he's probably already killed her."

"Nic, honey . . ."

She laid her head on his shoulder. "It's all right. I'm dealing with it."

"What can I do to help?"

"You're doing it." She reached for his hand.

He grabbed her hand, brought it to his mouth and pressed his lips into her open palm. "It's been nearly fifteen years since I left Amara and for the most part, I've put that time in my life behind me. But in the past four months, since we've been tracking the Hunter and I've realized the similarities between him and York, my nightmares have returned."

"I haven't questioned you about those years." She squeezed his hand. "After you told me what had happened . . . Well, I knew that if and when you were ready, you'd tell me more."

"Sanders and Yvette were part of those years, not just the four years on Amara, where we were York's captives, but the six years following, when we stole York's billions. That accounts for the ten missing years of my life."

Tilting her head to one side, she gazed at Griff, noting the stern, stock-still expression on his face. "You stole the man's billions? Is that how you—?"

"Stole isn't quite the right word. Let's just say we acquired his billions."

"How? I don't understand."

Griff slipped his arm around her shoulders, then faced her, eye to eye. "We killed York."

Nic took a deep breath. "I assumed you had."

"We stabbed him to death. The three of us. And we watched him bleed to death. Very slowly. We wanted him to suffer."

"Oh, Griff . . ." She caressed his cheek. "I understand. If

I'd had the chance, I would have stabbed Everhart again and again until he was dead."

"These monsters, men like York and Everhart, they turn us into killers. They destroy our humanity and try to remake us in their image."

"That's why we can't let them win. You killed York. You've built a new life—a good life—and you help others, those who have been devastated by cruel, inhuman murderers."

Griff leaned forward, bringing his forehead down on hers. He whispered against her lips. "The brutal savage that York turned me into still exists inside me. And sometimes . . . sometimes that knowledge frightens me."

Nic pressed her mouth against his, wanting to comfort him, and yet wanting far more. They needed each other, on every human level. He understood her the way no one else did. Griff had been right—they were two halves of a whole. So much alike. Male and female counterparts.

When Nic ended the kiss and they came up for air, Griff pulled her into his arms and buried his face against her neck. "You can't know how much I want you."

Sighing deeply, she slipped her arms around his waist and held him close. "I want you, too."

He lifted his head. "I don't want to rush you. I don't want to do anything that will harm you in any way."

"Physically, I'm almost as good as new and perfectly capable of making love. And my body is telling me it needs you."

"What about your mind? And your heart?"

"Oh, Griff, my heart—" Tears misted her eyes. "I refuse to get all mushy and female on you."

"I don't mind, honey. I'd kind of like to see you all mushy and female." He ran his right index finger over her chin, down her throat, and brought it to a standstill at the V-shaped neckline of her blouse.

Everywhere he'd touched her tingled with life. "I'm not going to be the first one to say it."

"Say what?"

"You know—that I care."

He shrugged. "Want me to say it first?"

"Uh-huh."

He cupped her face with his hands. "Nicole Baxter, I'm crazy about you. I don't know how it happened or when it happened." He laughed. "God help me, but I love you."

He loved her? Griffin Powell loved her.

Oh, shit. Shit!

Don't freak out. Isn't this what you wanted to hear? Didn't you want him to say he loves you?

Now what?

Tell him how you feel.

How do I feel?

I love him, too.

So tell him. Now!

"I love you, too, Griff." Tears filled her eyes, trickled from the corners, and dropped onto his hands that were holding her face with passionate tenderness.

Nic had never wanted anything in her entire life the way she wanted Griff. Here and now. With an aching need to love and be loved, a hunger that went beyond the physical.

"Make love to me," she whispered. "Please, Griff. I need you so."

When he gazed into her eyes, she saw her own desperate longing reflected in the cool silvery blue of his eyes.

"You have no idea how difficult it's been for me to keep my hands off you these past few weeks." Pressing his forehead against hers, he closed his eyes and ran his hands down either side of her neck and over her shoulders. "If I take you now, I might hurt you. I might be too rough. After what you've been through—"

She kissed him. No hesitation. No prelude.

He shuddered.

His eyes flew open. "Nic . . . ?"

"You'd never hurt me," she said, her voice husky with desire. "Don't you know that what I want is your passion? I need that. I need to feel totally alive again. With you. Only with you."

Clutching her shoulders firmly, he jerked her to him and bore his mouth down on hers with fierce possession until she whimpered, parting her lips for his invasion. As he plundered the softness of her mouth, he splayed his left hand across her lower back, holding her in place while his right hand reached between them and cupped her breast.

Moaning, on fire to possess him, Nic slipped both hands beneath his cashmere sweater and shoved it higher and higher until she reached the thatch of honey blond hair covering his massive chest. She tugged on the sweater. He lifted his arms and allowed her to remove it. When she lowered her head and flicked her tongue across one nipple and then the other, he groaned savagely. He shoved her away from him and down onto the sofa, then unbuttoned her blouse and unhooked her bra with swift accuracy.

She lay beneath him as he hovered over her, big and hard and overwhelmingly male. His breathing ragged, sweat dotting his brow and upper lip, he gazed down at her naked breasts.

She quivered as he lowered his head. The moment his lips touched her nipple, she cried out with an intense pleasure/pain, her body so sensitive, so hungry for fulfillment. He licked and sucked one nipple while his fingertips tormented the other.

"Now . . . now . . ." she pleaded.

He unzipped her slacks, snaked his hand inside her silk panties and fondled her. She bucked up against his hand as his fingers rubbed her intimately.

"Oh, Griff, please . . . please . . ."

He yanked her slacks and panties down and off. He removed his pants and briefs and tossed them on the floor.

When he cupped her buttocks in his hands and lifted her to meet his first, deep, penetrating lunge, she flung her arms around him and held on for dear life. When he was buried deep inside her, his breathing ragged, his big body trembling, she moved against him. Inviting him. Encouraging him. Begging him.

Gritting his teeth, his muscle strained beyond endurance, he let go completely, relinquishing the tight control over his emotions. He hammered into her, claiming her with primitive need.

Nic clenched her fingers, tightening her hold on him as she met him stroke for stroke, taking from him as he took from her, giving him all that she was as he gave to her. She came first, shivering, shuddering, and crying out as she drowned in pleasure. Moments later, Griff came, surrendering to her completely.

He lifted himself off her, sat up and pulled her onto his lap. She draped her arms around him as he nuzzled her neck.

"I love you," she murmured.

For the first time in her life, she had allowed a man to do more than claim her body. Griff had taken possession of her heart and her very soul.

Chapter 29

Griff watched Nic while she slept.

He had thought this would never happen to him, that he would never truly love someone with a passion that bordered on madness. He wasn't the type. He was a hard-ass womanizer. He'd never had a long-term relationship. Had never wanted one.

But he wanted to keep Nic with him, wanted to bind her to him and never let her out of his sight. Yeah, right. Like she would ever let that happen. He had fallen in love with an independent lady, one who gave as good as she got. If he tried to control her, even slightly, she'd rip into him like a buzz saw. But that mile-wide, self-reliant, liberated streak in Nic was one of the things he loved about her.

He slowly eased the sheet downward until it rested about her hips. Her large, firm breasts rose and fell with each breath she took. An ugly surgical scar peeked out from under her arm. Nic's red badge of courage. A surge of fear gripped him when he thought about how close he had come to losing her.

He could give this woman everything she wanted—

except the one thing she wanted most: Rosswalt Everhart behind bars. Or perhaps six feet under. That's definitely where Griff would prefer to put the psychopath who had tortured Nic.

Sighing languidly, she turned over on her side. Griff watched her closely as she opened her eyes and looked at him. She smiled.

"Good morning," he said.

"It can't be morning already, can it?" She glanced toward the French doors. "It's still dark outside."

"It's raining," he told her. "Actually, it's a rain-sleet mix."

"Hmm . . . a good day to stay in bed." She winked at him.

He rolled over, draped his arm across her waist, and kissed her. "You read my mind."

She reached up and draped her arms around his neck. "Did you pull the sheet off me?"

He laughed. "Sure did. I wanted to get another look at those big, beautiful boobs." He nuzzled her in the center of her upper chest, directly above her breasts, then licked a path downward, going from one nipple to the other. "And I wanted to taste them, and . . ." He slid his hand over her belly, across her mound, and dipped his fingers inside her.

Moaning invitingly, she bucked up, taking his fingers fully inside her. "You're giving me ideas, Mr. Powell." She slipped her hand between their bodies, inched her way across his six-pack lean belly, over his navel, and circled his erect penis.

"God, woman, I love your ideas."

She shoved him off her, rolled him over on his back, and lifted one leg up and across him. Then she hoisted herself into a sitting position and straddled him. After bracing her open palms on either side of his head, and taking the dominant position, she smiled seductively.

"I want you to just lie there and take it like a man," she told him, then kissed his mouth, his chin, and his throat.

He cupped her buttocks with both hands. "I'm yours, honey. Putty in your hands."

With her fingers gripping him firmly, she caressed his penis. "Not exactly putty. More like solid rock."

Griff loved seeing Nic like this. Sexy and flirtatious. Full of life. And love.

She touched and kissed every inch of his chest; then she moved slowly, maddeningly, down over his waist. Her tongue toyed with his navel. In and out. She bypassed the spot he most wanted her to kiss and instead went down one leg and up the other. When she made her way back to his belly, he reached down, forked his fingers through her hair, and urged her to put him out of his misery.

She tossed her head back and laughed. "If I give you what you want, I'll want something in return," she teased.

"Name your price, woman."

"Hmm . . ." She nuzzled the thicket of hair surrounding his straining erection. "I want breakfast in bed. And then I want a bubble bath. You can scrub my back."

"Agreed."

"And—"

"There's more?"

"I want to cuddle in bed and talk about hearts and flowers and moon and June and all that mushy stuff."

Griff chuckled. "You're beginning to sound like a silly, frilly female."

She ran her tongue over his penis, from tip to base and back to tip.

Griff moaned, deep in his throat.

"And you're acting just like a . . . a . . . a man!" she told him, her tone playful.

"Damn right about that."

When she eased his penis inside her mouth, Griff groaned with pleasure. Her lips were soft and moist, her mouth hot. He gently held her head in place while she drove him mad with her flicking tongue and her mouth's milking motions. When he was on the verge of coming, he tried to ease himself away, but she refused to let him go. Not until he climaxed.

Huffing loudly and shuddering with release, his ears rang and the top of his head exploded. His body jerked repeatedly, draining every ounce of pleasure from the moment.

Nic swallowed hard, then slid her tongue over the length of his penis and spread kisses up his belly and over his chest.

He grabbed her, pressed her damp, luscious body down onto his and kissed her. His tongue mated with hers, the taste of his come rich and musky in her mouth.

Griff served Nic breakfast in bed. Afterward, he made slow, sweet love to her, giving her the same pleasure she had given him earlier. Then he drew her bathwater in the claw-foot tub, filled with scented oils and overflowing with foaming bubbles. And he did a lot more than wash her back.

By the time they finally left her bedroom, it was afternoon and they joined the others for lunch. She had skipped her therapy session yesterday because it had been Christmas. But since she would be leaving Griffin's Rest next week, she wanted to take full advantage of Yvette's expertise while they were together.

The sunroom had quickly become their daily meeting place, and as with the other sessions, each took the seat familiar to them.

"I'm going to miss you," Nic admitted aloud.

"And I you." Yvette smiled. Her fragile smiles never quite reached her black eyes, which always seemed sad. No, not sad. Melancholy.

"But I'm sure we'll see quite a bit of each other in the future," Nic said. "I'll be visiting Griffin's Rest fairly often and you will, too."

"I look forward to our becoming good friends, when we are no longer doctor and patient."

"So do I."

"You are very good for Griffin."

Nic sighed contentedly. "And he's very good for me."

"He has been content with the life he made for himself, but never truly happy. Not until now."

Nic's heart did a stupid little *rat-a-tat-tat*. "He's told me some of what happened to him on Amara, but I know there's much more he hasn't told me."

"There are things he may never be able to tell you."

Nic gazed deeply into Yvette's eyes. "He didn't tell me anything about you and Sanders, except that you were both York's captives, just as he was."

Yvette folded her small, delicate hands in her lap. "I was more than York's captive." Her soft voice dripped with anger. "I was Malcolm York's wife."

"Oh."

"He wanted me because I was beautiful and possessed a special talent that he knew he could use against me and against others." Yvette bowed her head. "I was twenty years old and a medical student when he had me kidnapped and taken to Amara. I was what is often referred to as a child prodigy. I was in my final year of medical school when . . ."

Nic wished she could think of something to say, but Yvette's confession had rendered her speechless.

"I hated him," Yvette said. "He was quite mad. And unfortunately, he was also exceedingly wealthy."

"Yvette . . ." Nic leaned toward the other woman, something tender and maternal in her desperately wanting to give comfort.

"I was tormented and tortured and forced to do things

against my will. I became nothing more than an instrument, a tool in the hands of a monster."

Nic slid to the edge of her chair, reached out, and grasped Yvette's tightly clenched hands. The moment Nic touched her, Yvette's eyes widened in surprise and their gazes met in a moment of realization.

Heat suffused Nic's body, as if an electrical current had sent a jolt of mild shock through her nervous system.

"Do not be afraid," Yvette told her. "I did not harm you. You simply picked up on my extremely powerful life force. If I had not allowed my memories to make me so emotional, you would not have felt anything more than a mild warmth."

"That special talent you possess—what is it?" Nic asked.

"I have certain psychic abilities." Yvette spoke so quietly that her voice was barely audible. "Empathic psychic abilities."

Nic pulled her hands free of Yvette's and eased back in her chair, but did not break eye contact. They sat there and stared at each other, neither of them speaking for several minutes.

"You were able to get inside the minds of York's captives, weren't you? You could sense what they were thinking and feeling and—oh, my God, you endured their pain with them, didn't you? And he loved watching you suffer."

Before Yvette could respond, they heard someone clear their throat. They looked toward the open door and saw Sanders standing there.

"Please forgive the intrusion," he said, looking straight at Nicole. "Griffin wishes to see you in his office immediately."

Nic jumped up. "Has he heard something about LaTasha Davies?"

"Yes, I believe so."

"Thank you, Sanders. I'll—" She glanced back at Yvette.

"Go, go. We will talk more later."

Nic rushed out of the sunroom and hurried to the office.

She didn't bother to knock; she simply flung open the door and walked in. She looked around the room, expecting to see Holt Keinan, the Powell agent on duty at Griffin's Rest, with Griff, but Griff was alone.

"Come on in." He sat at the head of the conference table.

When she approached, he stood, took her hands in his, and said, "I just spoke to Doug Trotter. This morning, not long after sunup, a Costa Rican fishing boat came upon a rowboat floating in the sea. There was a woman on board."

Nic held her breath.

"The woman had been shot. She was unconscious and near death."

"Was it LaTasha?"

"Possibly. Probably. Her description fits LaTasha's."

"Is she still alive?"

"As far as Doug knows, she is. He's on his way to Costa Rica right now. He'll send her fingerprints to D.C. If this woman is LaTasha, we'll know right away."

"Oh, God, Griff, if she's alive, she can tell us where he is."

"If," Griff said. "Everhart has to know she escaped, which means unless our government can keep her existence top secret so he won't know that she was found, he won't stay put. If word leaks out that she was not only found but is still alive, he'll run."

"But if he believes she's dead and that no one found her floating around in the ocean, then he'll feel safe and stay right where he is and we can find him."

"The Caribbean Sea is a large body of water," Griff reminded her. "Everhart could be anywhere from Mexico to South America. And there are countless tiny islands, some so small they aren't even charted."

Chapter 30

The FBI and the U.S. Army worked in conjunction to bring Corporal LaTasha Davies out of Costa Rica and back to the United States. All of this was done in a top secret move to keep the woman's identity unknown to everyone, except on a need-to-know basis. She was taken directly to Walter Reed Army Medical Center in D.C., and after five days in intensive care, she remained in a coma, her condition critical.

Doug Trotter phoned Nic with daily updates.

The Hunter had not called either her or Griff with clues about a new victim.

Did Everhart suspect that LaTasha was still alive? Had he stayed put, biding his time, or had he moved on, setting up in a new locale and searching for another woman to participate in his murderous game?

The waiting had been as excruciating for Griff as it had been for Nic. With each passing day, she had grown more and more restless, as had he. But Griff had taken action, doing his best to distract her from her concerns about LaTasha and her fears about the Hunter's next victim. During the day, he'd kept her busy: a trip to see Lindsay and Judd Walker and their daughter, Emily; a visit to a Knoxville firing range so she could practice her marksmanship; long drives on country roads, exploring the northeastern Tennessee countryside; an evening trip to Pigeon Forge and Gatlinburg to see the holiday lights; and a dinner reservation in Maryville, at Foothills Milling, fine dining in the foothills of the Smoky Mountains. And Nic had spent every night in Griff's arms, loving and being loved.

A part of her wished that she could stay here forever. But she had a life back in Woodbridge. A home. A job in D.C. And a maniacal killer to find.

Besides, it wasn't as if she and Griff wouldn't be seeing each other on a regular basis. She'd be coming back to Griffin's Rest as often as possible and when she couldn't come to him, he would come to her. They had agreed that their relationship was long-term. Just how long-term, they didn't discuss. And Nic was grateful for that. She wasn't ready to define their love affair.

Her bags were packed and in the Escalade. Powell agent Shaughnessey Hood would be driving her truck to Woodbridge for her and hopping a commercial jet back to Knoxville.

"I have something special planned for tonight," Griff had told her. "And it involves our taking an airplane ride."

She had asked him for a special date on New Year's Eve. But Griff had made every day and night they had spent together special.

Griff knocked on her bedroom door and called, "Ready to go, honey? It's after eleven and I'd like to be airborne when the clock strikes twelve."

"Be there in a second." She looked at herself in the cheval mirror one more time.

"Don't dress up. Wear something nice but comfortable," Griff had told her.

She had chosen from the array of new clothes that lined

her closet. A pair of dark brown corduroy slacks, brown boots, a red turtleneck sweater, and a camel wool coat. She had taken extra time with her makeup and hair and even agreed to wear a pair of gold and diamond hoop earrings that Griff had hidden in the glove compartment of her truck—as a surprise.

Pudge had spent hours walking along the beach, trying to work through his doubts and uncertainties. LaTasha had floated away in a rowboat nearly a week ago and probably she and the dinghy had been swept into the sea by the storm. There hadn't been one word about the boat being discovered. He had watched every newscast he could find on satellite TV, broadcast from both the U.S. and neighboring countries. He had scoured the Internet, searching for any story that might be linked to his escapee.

She's dead.

If she hadn't been found in this length of time, she never would be. One of his shots had probably put a hole in the dinghy and it had sunk not long after leaving Tabora, taking LaTasha's corpse with it to the bottom of the sea. He had no reason to worry. She was nothing more than fish food now.

He would wait another day or two, and then he would phone Nicole and Griff with their clues. New game. New rules. Only neither of them would know what all of those new rules were, not until it was too late.

Pudge had come to realize that Nicole had ruined his game. She had taken all the fun out of it. That's why he'd failed with LaTasha. She had bored him.

And no doubt Mia would bore him, too. That's why he had devised a new game and would put new rules into play. Mia would not be his prey. She would be his bait.

* * *

Once Nic had settled comfortably on the plush leather sofa in the Powell jet and Griff had given Jonathan orders to take off, she tried again to persuade Griff to divulge their destination.

"Please," she whined unconvincingly. "Tell me where we're going."

He kissed her on the nose. "If I told you, it wouldn't be a surprise."

She crossed her arms over her chest and pretended to pout.

Griff laughed. "You need more practice at those silly girlie tactics. You're absolutely no good at whining or pouting."

"It's because I hate women who do either. But since I seem to be becoming more of a girlie-girl every day that I'm around you, I thought I'd give them a try."

"What makes you think you're turning into a girlie-girl?"

She tapped the dangling earring in her right ear. "Diamond earrings. If these aren't—"

"Made for you," Griff told her. "They're beautiful, just like you."

"Well, it's not just the earrings." She batted her eyelashes at him. "I've turned into a sex-craved femme fatale. And it's all your fault."

Griff laughed, the sound reverberating loudly inside the plane. "Look what you've done to me. You've turned a perfectly satisfied playboy into a simpering, lovesick fool."

She widened her eyes. "Hmm . . . Lovesick, maybe. Simpering, decidedly not. And you, my darling Griff, will never be a fool."

A chime sounded. Nic looked at Griff, who tapped a button on his wristwatch.

"It's midnight," he said.

"Happy New Year, Griff."

"Happy New Year, Nicki."

He pulled her into his arms and kissed her.

When he ended the kiss, he said, "Sanders packed dinner for us. Cold cuts and cheese, freshly baked sourdough bread, and champagne."

"I'm going to have to start dieting," Nic told him. "I'm back up to my normal weight." She laughed. "Actually I'm four pounds over my ideal weight."

"Start dieting tomorrow."

"I believe it's already tomorrow."

"Then make it day after tomorrow."

"Tell me where we're going and I'll put off dieting."

"Blackmail does not work on me."

She ran her hand over his crotch, letting her palm linger over his semierection.

Griff moaned. "You don't play fair, honey."

"Tell me where we're going."

He grabbed her hand. "It'll take us a little over an hour to get to our destination. If you don't want to eat, I can think of another pleasant way to pass the time."

"Hmm . . . Burning calories instead of consuming them. I like your suggestion."

A black limousine awaited them at the airport. Griff whisked her off the plane and into the limo so quickly that she didn't have time to get her bearings. Wherever he was taking her, he intended for it to remain a secret, at least for a while longer. The limo windows were so dark that she couldn't see out to identify streets or buildings.

Sometime later, when the limousine parked and Griffin helped her out, she blinked several times. She knew exactly where they were. Walter Reed Army Medical Center. And Doug Trotter stood there on the sidewalk waiting for them.

The frigid winter wind moaned as it bored through her wool coat, chilling Nic to the bone. But what had she expected? This was January in D.C. The residue of a recent snow hid in dark corners, and pockets of refrozen ice shimmered in the moonlight.

Griff and Doug shook hands. "Thanks for doing this," Griff said.

Doug grunted, then focused on Nic. "It's good to see you. You look great."

"Thanks. I feel good. And I'm doing fine."

"Ready to come back to work?"

"I'm ready whenever you say I'm ready."

"A few more weeks. A few more counseling sessions," Doug told her.

"Sure. You're the boss."

Doug chuckled. "Is this your doing, Powell?"

"What?" Griff asked innocently.

"You've mellowed, Special Agent Baxter. I like it. It's becoming on you."

Nic growled. "Screw you. Sir."

Doug and Griff exchanged a that's-our-Nic look.

"Well, let's go. I'm freezing my butt off out here," Nic told them, then added, "you brought me here so I can see LaTasha Davies, didn't you?"

"Corporal Davies remains in a coma," Doug said. "There's a good chance she'll never come out of it."

"I refuse to believe that," Nic said. "I survived and so will she."

Ten minutes later, Nic stood by LaTasha's beside. Although physically she and the young black woman did not resemble each other, she saw herself when she looked at another of the Hunter's victims who had escaped.

She touched LaTasha's seemingly lifeless hand. "Stay strong, Corporal. You have so much to live for. Think about your little girl. She needs you."

And we need you to wake up and tell us where Rosswalt Everhart is.

* * *

When they left the hospital, Griff took her home to Wood-bridge. Nothing had changed, and yet her home seemed oddly unfamiliar. Strange how that in a month's time, she had, purely on a subconscious level, come to think of Griffin's Rest as home.

"I'm staying a couple of days," Griff had told her. "Just until you settle in."

She hadn't argued. She'd wanted him to stay.

They had slept until past noon on New Year's Day. And when they finally roused out of bed and she trudged sleepily into the kitchen, she found coffee already brewed.

After sipping the delicious hot brew, she sighed. "I'd make breakfast, but there are no groceries in the house."

"Check your refrigerator and pantry," he said.

"Did you . . . ?" She opened the refrigerator and found it fully stocked. "Did you steal my keys, make copies of them, and then send one of your flunkies to Woodbridge to do all this?"

"Yep."

"Thanks."

"You're welcome."

"I'm not much of a cook, but I can whip up scrambled eggs and fry bacon."

"I'll help," Griff said. "I'm a whiz at making toast."

After breakfast, they cleaned up the kitchen and then took a shower together. One thing led to another, and it was after three when they got out of bed again.

Cuddled close, they sat on the sofa, eating popcorn and sipping on Cokes in bottles while they watched an old Clint Eastwood spaghetti western on TV.

Using the remote, Griff clicked off the television. "I can't believe we both like old-western movies."

She snuggled against him. "Hey, it just goes to prove the theory that we really are two halves of a whole." That phrase had now become their own personal joke.

"And as your better half, I think you need for me to stick around a while longer."

"You're not leaving until tomorrow," she reminded him, then punched him in the ribs. "What do you mean, 'my better half'?"

He grunted. "I was thinking I could rearrange my schedule and stay here for a week or so."

"No."

"Why not? If I stay—"

"If you stay, you'll pet and pamper me. You'll watch my every move. You'll smother me."

"If I promise not to—"

She kissed him, then rubbed her nose against his. "I love you, Griff. I love making love with you. I love being with you. But if I'm ever going to be Special Agent Baxter again, if I'm ever going to get my life back, I have to do it on my own."

"Promise me that you won't take walks alone. Not ever."

"I promise that, until we capture Rosswalt Everhart, I will not go on walks alone and I will keep my gun and cell phone with me at all times. I will not take any unnecessary risks."

"I wish all those promises made me feel better," he told her. "But the God's honest truth is that unless I can keep you no more than ten feet away from me, I'm going to worry about you."

"I'll call you every day. Twice a day. Maybe three times on Saturdays and Sundays."

"I'll be here or you'll be at Griffin's Rest on the weekends."

"Most weekends," she agreed.

Hugging her close, he kissed her temple. "Maybe I'll just move to Woodbridge."

"Griff . . ." she whimpered.

"Now, that was an A-1, first-class girlie-girl whine."

"Oh, you!" She crawled all over him, tickling him and kissing him, until they toppled onto the floor.

The second of January came all too soon. Griff had persuaded Nic to let him stay all day and fly home tonight. He didn't want to leave her. Couldn't bear the thought of anything happening to her. If she knew what he'd done, she would skin him alive, but sometimes a man had to go against the wishes of the woman he loved. For her own damn good. He had assigned a Powell agent to watch Nic 24/7. He had chosen Luke Sentell for two reasons: Nic had never met him, and he was a former Delta Force commando.

Where yesterday had been relaxed and fun, today was quiet and serious. She had told him about her husband, Greg, how he'd died, why he'd killed himself.

"I thought Greg was the perfect man for me because he was so different from my father. I just never looked beyond the surface and saw what a weak person he was."

They had shared a few tales from their childhoods and teen years. Despite the abject poverty in which Griff had grown up, his early life had been far happier than Nic's. He had always known how much his mother loved him, how proud she was of him. Nic had never felt unconditionally loved by either parent and had been repeatedly told how deeply she had disappointed her father.

When he opened up more to her about his experience on Amara, she told him about how frightened and alone she had felt being held captive by the Hunter, how she had feared each day might be her last. But she had never given up.

"We had to kill all of them," Griff told her. "After we executed York, we had to take out his guards. They were hired henchmen who would do anything for money."

"How many were there?"

"Ten."

Silence.

Nic sat quietly, her gaze cast downward, her breathing slow and even. And then she looked at him. Compassion and understanding in her eyes.

"You feel that their blood is on your hands," Nic said. "Even though they were paid mercenaries who did York's bidding, you wish you hadn't had to kill them."

"They were human beings."

"But it was kill or be killed. You had no other choice."

"We thought we had no other choice at the time. Looking back, I wonder."

"What good does it do to look back? Learn from it, then let it go. Isn't that Yvette's advice?"

"Yvette is very wise."

"Very. Beautiful and wise and psychic and rich."

"Rich?" Griff questioned.

"If she was York's widow and he was a billionaire—"

"*I* have York's billions, not Yvette."

"Why? How?"

"We spent six years claiming Yvette's inheritance, going through both legal and illegal channels. Some of York's investments were in legitimate corporations. Others were connected to organized crime and even to countries with ties to terrorist organizations.

"Yvette's father had been a diplomat and her mother's family had connections throughout Europe. She used those connections to open doors for us. And Sanders had been a Gurkha solider, as his half-English/half-Nepalese father had been. The Gurkhas are the most fearsome warriors in the world, their skills unmatched by others anywhere on earth. He taught me how to fight to win, to fight dirty when necessary. The knowledge and skill he imparted to me kept me alive on Amara and sustained me for our battles with lawyers and judges as well as when we made deals with numerous devils on Yvette's behalf.

"Yvette stayed with us for the first year after we left Amara, but she returned to medical school, did her internship and residency in London, while Sanders and I obtained her inheritance for her. In the end, almost everything that had belonged to York was Yvette's."

"Then what happened?" Nic asked. "Did y'all split the money three ways or—"

"Neither Sanders nor Yvette wanted York's blood money."

"But you did."

"Yes, I did. At the time, I felt that I had earned it. That we'd all earned it. Yvette signed everything over to me. I set up accounts with unlimited funds for both her and Sanders. Neither of them has ever touched a dime of that money.

"When I finally came home after ten years, back to the U.S., back to Tennessee, Sanders chose to come with me. It was his decision to pose as my servant, but we both soon realized that we were more comfortable with him acting as my right-hand man. I spent a great deal of money at first, buying everything I thought I'd ever wanted. But after less than a year, I realized I wanted—no, I needed, to do something more with all my money."

"And that's when you founded Powell Private Security and Investigation Agency," Nic said, "and decided to do what you could to help people who had been harmed by others, to try to put a stop to criminals destroying lives and—"

He grasped her shoulders. "No matter what I do, how much I give to charity, how many criminals I help put behind bars, it doesn't change who I am and what I did."

"You're not perfect," Nic said. "No one is. Yes, your past sets you apart from most people. The horrible things that happened to you on Amara helped mold you into the man you are today. But don't you understand that you could have become as evil as York and you didn't? You didn't because, deep down inside, you're a good man. You want justice and fairness. There's nothing wrong with that."

"I never thought . . ." He grasped her hands. "God, no wonder I love you so much. What other woman could look past the ruthless, selfish bastard I've been and see what's good in me?"

Nic pulled on his hands, dragging his arms around her.

Her cell phone rang. She jumped.

"I'll let it go to voice mail," she said.

They sat there, holding each other.

Griff's cell phone rang.

"Damn," he muttered.

"Get it. I've got a bad feeling."

Griff reached over on the coffee table and picked up his phone. "Powell here."

"Hello, Griffin."

"Hello, Rosswalt."

Laughter.

"Make that 'Mr. Everhart.' I allow only my friends to call me by my given name."

"And we're not friends, are we, you Goddamn sick son of a bitch?"

"Temper, temper. Play nice or I won't give you any clues."

"I didn't realize you had started a new game," Griff said. "No one has found LaTasha Davies's body hanging upside down from a tree."

"Circumstances change. Rules have to be altered. I disposed of LaTasha in a new way. I don't think her body will ever be found."

"But you killed her and scalped her and now you're ready for a new hunt, with a new prey."

"Yes, something like that. And I do so want you and

Nicole to play with me. Maybe this time you'll figure out the clues before it's too late to save the poor girl I've chosen."

"I'm listening."

"One clue for you. And one for Nic."

"Have you already called Nic?" Griff asked, certain that the call Nic had let go to voice mail had been Everhart.

"I left her a message."

Odd that he'd left a message. He had done that only once before. He had always wanted to hear Nic's voice. "You gave her a clue in the message?"

"I'm sure she'll contact you to let you know. You two are still partners, aren't you?"

"What Nic and I are or are not is none of your damn business. Just give me my clue."

"Very well." There was a lingering pause before Everhart said, "Vulcan." Then he hung up.

Nic tugged on Griff's sleeve. "What?"

"He left your clue in a voice mail."

"He did?" Nic laughed nervously. "Apparently, he doesn't love the sound of my voice as much as he used to. So, what are your clues?"

"Clue. Singular. Only one for each of us."

"Hmm . . . What's yours?"

"Vulcan."

"Damn." She got up. "My cell phone's in the bedroom. I'll get it and be right back."

While Griff waited, he repeated the one-word clue several times and a couple of possibilities came to mind. Vulcan, the Roman god of fire and metalworking. Was the woman a firefighter? Or maybe the word referred to the Vulcans of *Star Trek* fame. Could the Hunter's next victim be a young astronaut in training? Probably not.

When Nic returned to the living room, her cell phone clutched in her hand, she had an odd look on her face.

"What's wrong?"

"Nothing. It's just that hearing his voice again . . . I didn't realize it would unnerve me so much."

"He can't hurt you. You're safe. I'll keep you safe, no matter what I have to do."

Nic smiled. A forced smile for his benefit.

"He gave me a two-word clue," Nic said. " 'Six bits.' "

"Six bits? Six bits, as in money?"

Nic nodded. "How much is that—seventy-five cents?"

"What could money have to do with his next victim?"

"Bank teller? But that hardly implies physical fitness."

"I need to stay here," Griff said. "At least overnight. I'll contact Sanders and you get in touch with Trotter. The more minds we have working on this, the better."

"If we haven't figured it out by morning, it'll be too late. He's going to kidnap her tomorrow."

Chapter 31

Birmingham cheerleader Mia O'Dell disappeared on January third. The fact that Griff and Nic had figured out Everhart's clues the night before had been of little help. Birmingham was Alabama's largest city, filled with high school and college cheerleaders. A statue of Vulcan high atop Red Mountain was a Birmingham landmark. And one of the oldest and most popular cheerleader yells was, "Two bits, four bits, six bits, a dollar, all for our school stand up and holler!"

During the past week, Nic had begun counseling sessions with a bureau psychiatrist, had stopped by the field office every day, and had spoken to Griff on the phone morning and evening. It had taken her four days to figure out she was being tailed. The fact that it had taken her that long to suspect someone was following her proved to her that she wasn't quite ready to return to work, even if she had been trying to convince Doug to reinstate her as soon as possible.

She was going nuts not being able to work, especially now that the Hunter had abducted another victim. At least Doug had agreed to let her sit in on the task force meetings. That way she could at least stay up-to-date and be ready to dive back in as soon as the bureau's headshrinker deemed her fit for duty.

Photos of both Rosswalt Everhart and Mia O'Dell had been sent to every country bordering the Caribbean Sea, from Mexico to Venezuela, from Jamaica to Trinidad. Even though all the law enforcement agencies had been issued copies of the photographs, the Powell agency had hired locals to distribute the photos in every city and town.

Nic hung her coat on the back of a kitchen chair, got a beer out of the refrigerator, and headed for the living room. Once slumped comfortably on the sofa, the beer bottle open and the first swig downed, she kicked off her shoes and reached for the portable phone on the coffee table.

She hit the programmed number for Griff's cell phone. He answered on the first ring. Nic smiled. She liked the fact that she had him trained so well.

Oh, God, he'd be pissed as hell if he knew she'd even thought such a thing.

"Hi, honey. How was your day?" he asked.

Nic loved his voice, that gravelly baritone. Tough-guy deep. And sexy as hell.

"Same old, same old," she told him.

"Hmm . . ."

"I stopped by the hospital today to see LaTasha."

"No change?"

"Nope. I hate that we can't tell her family she's alive."

"Once we catch Everhart—"

"Will we ever catch him?"

"You know we will. It's only a matter of time."

Nic huffed. "But will it be in time to save Mia O'Dell? God, Griff, she's only nineteen."

"We're getting dozens of calls every day from all across the Caribbean. So far, none of the leads have panned out, but somebody's going to call with some info we can use to track down Everhart."

Nic took another sip of beer and set the bottle on a coaster on the coffee table. "I want you to do something for me."

"Name it."

"Call off the dogs."

"What?"

"Don't act innocent with me," Nic said. "It's taken me longer than it should have to realize you've got somebody tailing me. Call him off."

"I don't know what you're talking about."

Nic growled. "Damn it, Griff."

"Okay, okay. But he's there for your protection. And for my peace of mind."

"What about my peace of mind? I do not want one of your agents—"

"He won't interfere. He'll be completely discreet."

"No. Call him off, now."

"And if I don't?"

"Then I won't come to Griffin's Rest and I don't want you to come to Woodbridge."

"You don't mean that."

"Try me and see."

"Damn it, Nic, I—"

"Call him off. Tonight."

"Okay, but you have to promise me that you'll be careful."

"I'll be careful."

"And you'll come home to Griffin's Rest this weekend?" Griff asked.

"Maybe."

"Either you come to me or I'll fly there tomorrow evening."

"Miss me?" she asked, feeling triumphant, knowing she had won this battle with Griff.

"I miss you something awful, honey."

"Same here. And I miss everyone else, too. How are Sanders and Barbara Jean and Yvette?"

"Everyone's fine," he replied. "Yvette left this afternoon.

She's going to spend some time in London with old friends while she's attending a conference over there."

"Hmm . . . Griff, what are you wearing?"

"My blue cashmere sweater. Why?"

"Anything else?"

He laughed. "What if I said no, nothing else?"

"I'd say I've never had phone sex, but I'd be willing to give it a try."

Griff grunted. "Bad girl."

Nic breathed heavily, then deepened her voice to a husky tone, and told him exactly what she was going to do to him the next time they were together.

Pudge had brought Mia to Tabora on Saturday and for five days she had tried to amuse him. She had begged and pleaded and even offered him oral sex. The pathetic little slut disgusted him. She didn't have an ounce of grit in her. Spineless little twit. He had thought perhaps she would provide a temporary diversion. She hadn't. That's why she had spent every night in the cage. She had screamed and cried so loudly the first night that he had been forced to move the cage farther from the house. But if all went as planned, he'd be rid of her very soon. One way or another.

Taking the phone outside with him, he sat in the big rattan rocker on the porch, closed his eyes, and visualized the woman he wanted here with him. The woman he would punish for tormenting him day and night. No matter what he did, how hard he tried, he could not erase Nicole Baxter from his mind. The bitch had gotten inside his head and was driving him crazy. The only way to get her out of his head was to bring her here to Tabora and kill her.

He dialed the familiar cell number and waited.

"Hello." He had once loved hearing her voice. Now he hated it, as he hated her.

"Do you want to save Mia O'Dell's life?" he asked.

Silence.

He rephrased his question. "What would you do to save Mia's life?"

"I'd do almost anything," Nicole said.

"Would you exchange your life for hers?"

Another long silence, then Nicole replied, "Are we bargaining for her life?"

"I want you, Nicole. If you'll come to me, I'll release Mia. Alive."

"How do I know you'll let her go?"

"How do I know you won't try to double-cross me?" he asked.

"I don't suppose my word would be good enough."

He laughed. No way in hell would he trust her. Not ever again.

"I'll tell you when and where to meet us," Pudge said. "If I even suspect you didn't come alone, I'll kill Mia immediately. And I'll kill you, too, and as many other people as possible."

"Give me the details. I'll meet you. I'll exchange my life for Mia's."

Ah, sweet victory!

Not yet. You can't celebrate until Nicole is here on Tabora with you. Not until you slice the flesh from her bones and hear her scream in agony.

Doug Trotter met Nic at the field office at ten thirty that night, along with other D.C. and Virginia members of the task force. She laid out Rosswalt Everhart's proposition, explaining every detail.

"You can't think for one minute that I'll allow you to go through with this." With his features contorted in sheer aggravation, Doug got right up in Nic's face. "There will be no exchange. Do you hear me, Special Agent Baxter?"

"Yes, sir, but—"

"Hell, Nic, you're on medical leave."

"Please, Doug, just listen to me."

"No!"

"We can make this work. Everhart wants me. He's risking everything for the chance to have me under his control again. Since I escaped, he's probably fantasized about recapturing me. Don't you see? We can use this to our advantage."

"You're as crazy as he is if you think—"

"You'll know where I am at all times. You can track me. I'll wear a pair of those athletic shoes that contain a tracking device and you can follow me to wherever he takes me."

"Damn, Nic, those shoes are experimental at best. There's no guarantee—"

"I have to do this. It's my chance to stop this monster, to prevent him from killing anyone else."

"But at what cost?"

"I'm willing to take the risk if it means bringing Everhart down and saving God only knows how many future victims."

She could see that Doug was considering the proposition, that he was weighing the options. "The shoes were designed mostly to keep track of people with Alzheimer's and other mental illnesses, right? Hell, Nic, we don't know how long it would take to get hold of a pair—"

"The manufacturer would overnight us a pair if the bureau put in an immediate request. Or you could make some phone calls and see if maybe somebody in D.C. can come up with a pair for us."

"I don't like this."

"You don't have to like it. Just let me do it."

"Does Griffin Powell know—?"

"No! And I do not want him told anything," Nic said.

"When is Everhart getting back in touch with you about the exact details?" Doug asked.

"In the morning."

"If you meet him, I'm not sending you in alone. Got that?"

"But he said—"

"We'll stay far enough away where he won't suspect anything. But once he sets Mia O'Dell free and takes you, once you're on the move, we'll come for you immediately, before he can escape."

"Agreed."

"We're making a bargain with the Devil. You know that, don't you?"

"A bargain that is going to send him straight to hell, where he belongs."

Luke Sentell had reported in to Griff at midnight that evening, informing him that Nic had left her house and driven into D.C. Griff had promised Nic to call off the Powell agent guarding her back. He had lied to her. No way was he going to leave her out there unprotected.

"She went directly to the field office. Got there around ten thirty," Luke told him. "She's still here."

"Something's up," Griff said.

"So, what do you want me to do?"

"Stay put. Keep her under surveillance, but try your best to make sure she's not aware of your presence."

"Yes, sir."

"Call me the minute she leaves the field office. Let me know who else leaves before she does."

Griff paced the floor in his study.

Something was going on. Something that involved the bureau. And if Nic was in on it, that could mean only one thing: they had a lead on Rosswalt Everhart.

So, why hadn't Nic called him?

Because whatever is going on, she doesn't want you to know.

And what did that tell him? It told him Nic was going to do something dangerous. Something stupid. Unless he got there in time to stop her.

He picked up the phone and called Jonathan. "Sorry to wake you, but I want the jet fueled and ready to go immediately. I need to be in D.C. as soon as possible."

Griff tried calling Nic on her cell phone. He left her half a dozen messages before he boarded the Powell jet at two that Saturday morning. He had also tried contacting Doug Trotter and Josh Friedman. He'd gotten voice mail. He'd left them messages, pretty much warning them if they let Nic do anything stupid, they would have to answer to him. Actually, he had threatened both federal agents with castration and painful deaths if anything happened to Nic.

At four AM he arrived outside the D.C. field office, met up with Luke Sentell, and was informed that there had been a great deal of coming and going, but he had not seen Nic leave the office.

Griff phoned Trotter again, this time informing him that he was waiting outside his office. Within five minutes, Trotter returned his call.

"Don't do anything stupid," Trotter said.

"I want to talk to Nic."

"Nic's on an assignment."

"What the hell do you mean she's on an assignment? She's still on medical leave."

"Look, Powell, this is an FBI matter. Go home. Stay out of this. Nic will get in touch with you when she comes back."

"Back from where? Is she not there with you?"

"I told you, she's on an assignment."

"I want to talk to Nic. Now."

"She's not here."

"Then where is she?"

"I'm not at liberty to say."

Griff cursed a blue streak.

He gripped his cell phone with crushing strength, then turned to Luke. "You're sure she hasn't left the office?"

"As sure as I can be."

"Stay here and keep an eye out for her. I've got some government bigwigs to wake up."

Griff intended to call in every favor anybody in D.C. owed him. One way or another, he was going to find out what the hell was going on.

Chapter 32

Nic had never been so scared in her whole life. False bravado had brought her this far, all the way from D.C. to some little seacoast town in Costa Rica. Doug had whisked her out of the field office this morning, along with several other agents, and they had boarded a private plane. Only someone with top security clearance could find out just where the agents had been sent. A few diplomatic strings had been pulled to get clearance for this operation on foreign soil. And as luck would have it, a pair of athletic shoes containing a GPS tracking device embedded in the heel had been delivered only moments before they left D.C. Cutting-edge technology had created a GPS real-time tracking and location device small enough to fit inside a shoe.

Nic tried to stay focused on the task at hand and not think about what might go wrong. But she knew only too well that if Rosswalt Everhart had his way, he would torture her to death.

That wasn't going to happen. Her fellow agents had her back.

At precisely one fifteen, just as Everhart had promised, Nic's cell phone rang.

Her hand trembled as she flipped open the phone and said, "I'm in Sabino, at the airport."

"Alone?"

"Yes, alone." The other agents had remained on the plane, waiting for further instructions.

"Take a taxi and go to the Garcia Fish Market. Wait there for my next call."

Before she had a chance to reply, he hung up. She ducked into the ladies' restroom and called Doug. Once she'd told him where Everhart had instructed her to go, she caught a taxi that took her across town to the fish market. She knew that the other agents weren't far behind, but they would keep their distance and stay far enough away to be undetected.

She waited outside the fish market, doing her best to remain calm, as locals coming in and out of the open-air building gave her quizzical stares. A couple of the younger men even whistled at her.

As the minutes ticked by, she began to worry that Everhart had realized she hadn't come to Sabino alone. But how could he possibly know?

Educated guess. He might be crazy, but he wasn't stupid.

He had to want her desperately to risk his life for one more chance to kill her.

Nic's phone rang.

Her hands shook so much that she dropped the phone on the ground. Damn, damn, damn! She picked it up, and not bothering to brush the dirt off, she flipped it open and said, "I'm here at the fish market. Now what?"

"What are you wearing?" he asked.

"Uh, I'm wearing jeans, a T-shirt, athletic shoes, and a ball cap."

"That's it?"

"Yes."

"No weapon."

"No weapon," she said.

"Take off the ball cap and toss it in the garbage. Do it now."

She threw away the cap. "That's done."

"Roll your T-shirt up in the back and front and tie it in a knot at your waist."

"Okay." She stuck the phone in her jeans pocket and rolled up her T-shirt.

"That's done. Now what?"

"Roll your jeans up as far as they'll go."

"Done," she told him once she'd managed to turn up her jeans to midcalf. "What next?"

"Find someone there at the fish market and give them your cell phone."

"What?"

"After I tell you where to meet me, I want you to leave your phone on and give it to someone at the market."

"All right."

"Once I give you your instructions, give the phone away. I'll take it from there. If I don't hear a man's voice speaking Spanish, the deal is off."

Nic understood that Everhart was making sure of two things: One, she couldn't call anyone to tell them her final destination. And two, she wouldn't have a cell phone with her when she met with him.

"I'll do as you say," Nic told him.

"Good. That way Mia will stay alive." He paused for a moment. "Walk down the block and take a right, then walk two blocks and you'll see a sign that says Sabino Marina. Look for a silver and red speedboat. Mia and I will be waiting on board for you."

Griff was less than two hours behind Trotter and his group of agents that had accompanied Nic to Costa Rica. When he had received word—through an informant privy to top secret info—Griff and Luke Sentell had been waiting at the D.C. airport, ready to leave as soon as he could tell Jonathan where to take them.

Sabino, Costa Rica. A sleepy, little coastal town not yet overrun with tourists.

They were an hour away from landing. With each passing minute, Griff sank deeper and deeper into hell. If he got his hands on Doug Trotter, he would strangle the SOB. What was he thinking letting Nic risk her life this way? He had to know that he couldn't control the situation, that there were no guarantees that Everhart wouldn't simply shoot Nic on sight.

Nic approached the marina cautiously. There didn't seem to be anyone around and from the best she could tell, there was only one boat near the pier. A shiny red and silver speedboat. At the far end of the wharf.

Her pulse quickened. Her throat tightened. Her heart pounded.

You can do this. Backup is only a few minutes away. Walk down the pier and show yourself. Let Everhart see you.

Before she took the first step onto the pier, flashbacks of Belle Fleur bombarded her. The dank basement. The chains. The roar of his dirt bike. The cage.

Stop! she screamed at herself. *Don't do this.*

Not only did Mia O'Dell's life depend on Nic being brave, but also the lives of all the Hunter's future victims.

Squaring her shoulders and praying for courage, Nic took the first step. And then the second. *I'm going to be okay. I can and I will do this.*

When she was within twenty feet of the speedboat, she saw Everhart come up on deck, a rifle in one hand and his other hand clutching the arm of a dark-haired young woman.

Mia. Even from this distance Nic could see the terror on the girl's bruised face.

"Stop right there," Everhart called.

Nic stopped dead still.

"Come on board," he told her. "But keep your hands where I can see them."

"Let Mia go."

"I will. As you're coming aboard, I'll allow her to leave."

Just do it. Do it now, before you lose your courage.

Her heartbeat drummed so loudly in her ears that she barely understood him when he shouted, "If I see one sign of another agent, one hint of a lawman, I'll kill both of you."

Nic nodded, then started walking toward the boat, her steps picking up speed as she reached the end of the pier.

Everhart released his hold on Mia and gave her a shove toward the edge of the boat. She looked at Nic as the two passed each other while Mia climbed out and Nic climbed in. Once Mia's feet hit the pier, Nic cried out, "Run, Mia. Run!"

Everhart grabbed Nic, shoved her onto the deck, and pointed his rifle at her.

"You're mine now. All mine."

The Powell jet had landed in Limon, since the runway in Sabino didn't accommodate jets. Griff had then chartered a small plane to take them from Limon to Sabino. When he and Luke arrived in Sabino, Josh Friedman met him at the airport.

"Where's Trotter?" Griff asked.

Josh swallowed hard. "Tracking Nic."

"Tracking her where?"

"Not sure. She's on a speedboat."

"Then the GPS system in her shoe is working?"

Josh nodded. "So far. Hey, how'd you know—?"

Griff growled. "How many men does Trotter have with him?"

"Enough."

"Enough to do what?"

"Rescue Nic."

"And why did you stay behind?"

"Somebody higher up the food chain than Doug called him," Josh said. "His orders were to allow you to come in behind the rescue team."

"Then what the hell are we doing standing around here wasting time?"

Everhart had taken Nic with him to the cockpit, shoved her down onto the U-shaped seating area, and handcuffed her to small round table in front of the seats. He had then taken the helm and guided the speedboat out of the marina and into the sea.

She forced herself not to glance at her shoes, but she couldn't stop thinking about them, praying that the tracking device was working. If Doug Trotter couldn't track her movements, he'd have no way to find her.

Nic wasn't sure how long they were at sea, but it hadn't seemed long, maybe thirty minutes, before land came into view just up ahead. A small island.

Everhart docked the boat, unlocked Nic's cuffs, pointed the rifle at her, and ordered her to stand up. He made her disembark first and then he followed.

"Hold up," he called to her. "Turn around."

Was this it? Was he going to shoot her here and now?

She turned slowly and faced him. Once again she noted how completely ordinary Rosswalt Everhart looked.

"Take off everything. All your clothes and your socks and shoes."

"What?"

"Strip off everything." He waved the rifle muzzle at her. "Do as I say and you may live to put up a fight. If not, I can shoot you. In the foot. In the arm. Kill you little by little. Right now."

Nausea churned inside her. She untied her T-shirt and pulled it over her head, then threw it down on the beach.

He stood there watching her, a look of terrifying lust in his eyes.

She bent over and reluctantly took off her shoes and socks. She stuffed the socks into the shoes and threw them as far inland as she could. Less chance of the tide reaching them and washing them out to sea.

"Hurry up," he told her.

After removing her jeans, she stood there in her bra and panties. She lifted her arms over her head. "You can see I don't have a weapon and I'm not wired."

"Take off the rest."

She closed her eyes and begged for strength. Then she unhooked her bra, tossed it aside, and slid her panties over her hips, down her legs and off.

"You are a beautiful woman, Nicole."

She shivered.

"But when I finish with you, you won't be so beautiful."

He should have known she would double-cross him. How they had found him, he didn't know. Lucky for him, he'd listened to his instincts and kept watch; otherwise he wouldn't have seen the boats heading for Tabora.

They had found Nicole far too soon. He hadn't had a chance to enjoy himself with her. He'd had such delicious plans for her. He'd even sharpened all the knives in her honor. They could have had so much fun together. Him slicing off a finger here, a toe there. A nipple. A nose.

He sighed. But it wasn't meant to be.

He had risked everything to bring her here, knowing all along that she would find a way to outsmart him. That's one of the things he had so admired about Special Agent Baxter. She was a woman with brains.

But he did not intend to go down without a fight.

It would take a while before they arrived at the house. He still had time to play one final game with Nic.

Trotter and his team of agents spread out over the island, searching for any sign of Nic and Everhart. SA Lance Tillman found Nic's shoes, the ones with the tracking device. Then SA Charlie Durham picked up her clothing.

"Goddamn son of a bitch made her strip!" Doug cursed. "We've got to find her. Go, go!"

The island plantation house was set on a grassy knoll. So far it was the only structure, other than a dilapidated fishing shack, that they'd found on Tabora. On Doug's orders, his men surrounded the house.

A single rifle shot rang out.

Someone inside the house was firing on them.

While Doug and a couple of other agents returned fire, three agents moved in from the back, with orders to enter the house and apprehend the suspect. They all knew, without anyone saying it aloud, that Everhart wouldn't hesitate to kill Nic. If she was still alive.

Pudge knew he was not going to die. There was always a way to escape. The FBI agents were closing in on him. It was only a matter of time . . .

He supposed that on some subconscious level, he had known Nicole wouldn't surrender herself to him, wouldn't exchange her life for Mia's. But his desire for her, his need to have her under his power again had overruled his common sense. He had risked everything for the chance to punish Nicole.

And at least in that, he had won the game. She would not leave this island alive.

She had two hours to live. Two hours to wait for death and perhaps in those last moments, to long for death.

Pudge clutched his rifle to his chest as he maneuvered through the house, careful to stay away from the windows. If he could get to the cellar, he could make his way to the outside through the exterior cellar door, and once outside, he would make a run for his speedboat.

If these stupid federal agents thought they were going to capture him, then they were fools. They weren't dealing with some run-of-the-mill criminal mind, but with a genius.

Doug and his agents separated, two of them making their way around to the back of the house, while Doug and the others guarded the front and sides of the sprawling plantation cottage.

"Give it up, Everhart," Doug called out to him. "We have you surrounded."

No reply. Just the eerie quiet of the wind blowing softly, the surf rolling in and out, and Doug's own heavy breathing.

"Send Nic out first," Doug ordered. "Then once she's safe, come outside on the porch, your hands on top of your head."

God in heaven, let Nic be alive. If Everhart had killed her, Doug would never be able to live with himself. If he came out of this alive. If Griffin Powell didn't kill him for allowing Nic to risk her life.

"Time's running out," Doug shouted. "Nobody has to die here today. It's up to you."

Everhart's answer was succinct and deadly. Repetitive

shots, one barely missing Doug's foot and another hitting SA Murray in the chest, burrowing into his bullet-proof vest and knocking the agent to the ground.

Pudge had them right where he wanted them. Scared and begging him to surrender. They wanted Nic. Wanted her alive. As long as they believed she was with him, they wouldn't storm the house. For the time being, he was safe. And little by little, he was making his way to the cellar door.

Nobody has to die here today. Pudge chuckled to himself as he replayed the agent's words inside his mind.

Oh, but you're so wrong. Even if I don't manage to kill any of you, someone will die today. Nic will die. And there is no way you can save her.

He patted his shirt pocket and laughed.

His laughter filled the room.

When he was gone, safely on his speedboat and out in the Caribbean Sea, on his way to freedom, they would find the note. He would leave it behind for them, in the cellar. And none of them, not even Griffin Powell who was sure to arrive at any time, would be able to figure out the clues to Nicole's whereabouts. Not until it was too late.

His laughter tapered off and he smiled thinking about Griffin's reaction when they finally discovered Nicole's body.

Nicole's corpse.

Pudge crept through the dining room, dropping on his haunches when necessary to keep from being seen through the windows.

Something was wrong!

Although he hadn't actually heard the back door open, he had sensed it, had felt the air rushing into the house, felt the presence of unwanted guests.

He had not expected them to enter the house, not when

they believed he held Nic hostage. Did her life mean that lit- tle to them? If so, he had badly misjudged his enemy.

He had to hurry. Had to make it to the cellar.

In his peripheral vision, he caught a glimpse of a shadow in the doorway. Pudge pressed himself against the wall, lifted his rifle, aimed and fired. Immediately, the agent re- turned fire. Pudge dropped to the floor, taking refuge behind the couch.

Bullets ripped into the soft leather of the Chesterfield sofa as repeated gunfire erupted all around him.

Lance Tillman motioned to his fellow agent, Charlie Durham, indicating for him to go in the opposite direction and come up behind Everhart through the dining room. Charlie nodded, then slipped away while Lance covered the door leading from the living room into the front foyer.

Charlie took his time, his movements stealthy, the ability acquired from years of training. He eased into the dining room, edging closer and closer to the door that led into the living room where Rosswalt Everhart was now trapped.

If the Hunter had Nic with him, using her as a shield, Charlie knew he'd get one shot. One chance to take Everhart out before he killed Nic.

He managed to make it to the door before Everhart spot- ted him and opened fire. Charlie dropped and rolled, diving through the doorway and taking refuge behind a heavy wooden desk near the windows.

As he returned fire, Charlie's mind registered one single thought: Everhart didn't have Nic with him.

How could this be happening? It wasn't possible that these morons had outwitted him, that they had trapped him between the two of them.

Pudge's mind swirled with thoughts, creating hopeless escape scenario after scenario.

He couldn't die like this. But he would never surrender, never turn himself over to the FBI. He would kill himself before he let them take him alive.

His one consolation was that he could savor the last kill in his game. Nicole would die today. He could have killed her quickly, shot her in the head the way he had the others. But a swift death was far too good for her. His obsession with her had, in the end, cost him everything, including his life. He had wanted time with her, time to torture her, to kill her little by little and watch her suffering. But there hadn't been time for that.

Pudge's hands trembled, his finger on the trigger damp with perspiration.

He didn't want to die.

He wanted to escape. Wanted to live. Wanted to . . .

There had to be a way. His life couldn't end like this.

Think. Just stay calm and think. You'll be able to figure out a solution.

He had to kill both agents in order to escape through the cellar.

How simple. The perfect solution. He smiled.

All he had to do was kill the agents.

Feeling confident and invincible, he rose up from behind the sofa, his rifle aimed, ready to do his bidding. He would take out the man in the foyer first, then he would kill the one in the dining room.

He moved forward, heading straight for the foyer and as he neared the doorway, he began firing.

Suddenly, return fire startled him. But it was the unexpected sneak attack from the rear that pierced his back with two bullets. He turned and opened fire on the shooter, whose next shot ripped into Pudge's gut.

He slumped to the floor, his rifle heavy in his hands.

That wasn't supposed to happen. He was smarter than his opponents. He should have been able to kill them both before they shot him.

He covered his bleeding belly with his hand and stared down at the wound.

When the two agents moved in on him and one of them knocked the rifle from his loose grip, Pudge looked up at them, moving his gaze from one to the other, and laughed.

"Where's Nic?" the younger agent asked.

Pudge smiled, knowing they would never find her in time to save her.

The sounds of repeated gunfire inside the house told Doug that his agents were exchanging fire with Everhart. Even though it was his duty to bring suspects in alive if at all possible, he really hoped that in this case the suspect didn't live to go to trial.

A few minutes later, SA Durham came out on the porch and hollered, "We've got Everhart."

When Doug entered the house, the other agents behind him, they found Tillman standing over a man lying on the living room floor in a pool of blood. His eyes were open. Blood and saliva trickled from his mouth. The bastard was still alive, but probably not for long.

"Where's Nic?" Doug asked.

"She's not in the house," Tillman replied.

"I want every room searched again," Doug ordered. "And if there's a basement, I want it gone over thoroughly, every Goddamn inch."

Doug walked over to Everhart, bent down on one knee, and grasped him by the throat. The Hunter gurgled, choking on his own blood.

"Where's Nic?"

Everhart grinned, then patted his chest pocket.

The son of a bitch died that way. With a grin on his face and his eyes wide open.

The water surrounded Nic. Under her, around her, over her. Everhart had submerged her. Buried her alive in a watery grave. She blinked beneath the scuba mask covering her face.

Why had he strapped the oxygen to her back before lowering her into the water?

Because he didn't want to kill her quickly.

He wanted her to die little by little from sheer terror, knowing that her oxygen supply would eventually run out and she would drown.

"They're coming for us," he'd told her. "But they won't find you. Maybe not ever. But certainly not before it's too late. You have two hours to live, Nicole, and then I'll see you in hell."

Nic's feet touched the bottom of the well. He had tied her ankles with rope, but the knot had been loose so she'd been able to work her feet free. Looking up, she could see daylight at the top. She spread her arms out and up until her hands touched the edges of the well's rock wall.

She clawed at the wall, trying to find something to grasp. Nothing. Then she lifted her leg and tried to find a foothold. There wasn't one.

She was trapped. With no way out.

Griff came ashore on Tabora Island, along with Luke Sentell and Josh Friedman, thirty-five minutes after Doug Trotter's agents had stormed the plantation house. When the three of them arrived at the house, they found Doug sitting on the porch, his shoulders slumped, his head bowed.

"Where is she?" Griff shouted.

Trotter lifted his head, then motioned for Griff to come to him.

Griff took the porch steps two at a time. When he approached Trotter, the SAC held up his hand. Griff noticed a small sheet of paper clasped between his forefinger and thumb.

"What's that?" Griff asked.

"The only clues we have to help us find Nic. Everhart left this in his shirt pocket."

Griff reached down, grabbed Trotter by the lapels of his jacket, and jerked him to his feet. They stood there and stared at each other.

"Are you telling me she's not here?"

"She's here on the island somewhere," Trotter said. "But Everhart hid her before we got here."

"What do you mean, he 'hid her'?"

"Take a look at the note."

Griff released Trotter. "Where's Everhart?"

"Dead. In a shootout with my men."

Griff snatched the note out of Trotter's hand.

There, in a barely legible scrawl, were the clues that could save Nic's life.

Water, water everywhere. Two hours until she dies.

Beneath the words, a line of oval shapes repeated over and over again. Were they part of the clue?

Griff crushed the paper in his fist.

"I've got every man out searching the island," Trotter said. "We'll find her."

Don't look at your watch again. There's no point. The last time she had checked the lighted digital face of her waterproof watch, not more than five minutes ago, she'd had an hour of oxygen left.

One hour to live.

After Greg killed himself, Nic had wondered what his last thoughts had been. What did a person think right before dying? If a person knew in advance that they had only two hours to live, how would they spend those final two hours?

How would she?

Griff's face appeared in her thoughts. Strong, ruggedly handsome. Ice-blue eyes. Hair so blond it was almost white. He was smiling at her, holding out his arms, asking her to come to him.

She went into his embrace, loving the feel of him holding her.

She felt his warm breath on her ear, felt his lips against her neck.

Don't ever let me go, Griff.

While Trotter and his agents scoured the island, keeping in touch with Griff and Luke by cell phone, Griff studied Everhart's cryptic clue.

What the hell did "water, water everywhere" mean?

The obvious was the fact the island was surrounded by the sea. And if he took the quote at face value, how did the rest of it go? "Water, water, everywhere, but not a drop to drink."

Could Nic be somewhere near the water and yet unable to drink any of it because it was saltwater?

Griff tromped across the porch, then back again, repeating the trek as he kept thinking.

There was no time to put dozens of bureau minds at work trying to decode the clues. And there was no point in calling Sanders. There was no time for that, either.

Two hours until she dies. Two hours from when? From when she and Everhart first arrived on the island? If so, it might already be too late. Or from the time Trotter and his agents stormed the island? That had been—how long? Well over an hour ago.

Tick, tick, tick.

Time was running out.

Griff sat down on the porch steps, pulled the crumpled note from his pocket, smoothed it out, and looked at it again.

Everhart's clues usually involved time and place. And a clue about the woman herself. But since they all knew Nic was the woman, then only time and place were involved.

Time: two hours.

Place: Water, water everywhere.

"She's in the water." Griff shot to his feet.

"What?" Luke asked.

"Nic. He put her in water."

"You're sure?"

"No, I'm not sure of anything, but it's the only thing that makes sense. He submerged her in water. It's all around here. 'Water, water everywhere.' "

Griff walked into the yard and gazed past the dunes and the sandy beach, off into the distance. "He'd have to find a way to keep her alive underwater for two hours."

"Scuba gear," Luke said.

"Yeah, scuba gear!" Griff shouted. "He put her underwater, with enough oxygen for two hours." He stopped, balled his hands into fists, and moaned. "We've already wasted too much time. We'll never find her—no, damn it, I won't give up."

"I'll call Trotter and tell him to get his men into the ocean, just offshore. Everhart could have tied her hands and feet and dumped her just offshore in some shallow water."

"If he did that, she'll soon float out to sea."

Luke gripped Griff's shoulder. "We'll find her before that happens."

"Yeah, we'll find her."

*　*　*

Nic could not stop herself from looking at her watch. Ten minutes. Ten minutes of oxygen left. And then . . .

She would never go home again, back to her house in Woodbridge. She'd never go back to Griffin's Rest. Never wake up in Griffin's arms again.

Oh, Griff . . . Griff . . .

Don't mourn for me too long. Don't build a fortress around yourself and withdraw from life.

If I could wish one thing for you, it would be that you'll find happiness again.

You deserve to be loved. You should get married and have children and live to be a very old man.

And from time to time, remember me. Remember how much I loved you.

"We've searched everywhere we possibly can. We've gone into the ocean and found nothing." Josh Friedman, wearing only his wet pants, came up to Griff. "Doug has called in backup. We'll have divers out here in an hour. And they're sending in search and rescue crews and—"

"Nic doesn't have an hour," Griff said.

"Yeah, I know. I know." Josh swallowed. "I'm sorry. I—" He turned around and walked away.

The murderous rage inside Griff threatened to overtake him. He hadn't felt such uncontrollable anger since he had left Amara. And he had not known this type of pain, not ever, not even in the four years York had held him captive.

If he lost Nic, he lost everything.

Nothing mattered. Only Nic.

He slid his hand into his pants pocket and pulled out Everhart's note. As he took one final look at the only hope they had of finding Nic before it was too late, tears pooled in his eyes. When he closed his eyes, several teardrops fell on his hand. He sucked in a deep breath. He blinked several times, then, when his vision cleared, he reread the clues. And that's when he noticed that one of his teardrops had landed in the center of one of the oval shapes at the bottom of the note.

"Water, water everywhere."

Water inside the oval. Inside the circle. The odd marks beneath the clues were circles.

Water everywhere inside a circle. Inside a ring. Inside a round bowl.

Inside a well.

"I know where she is!" Griff shouted.

Luke and Josh came running toward Griff.

"She's in a well. Look for a well," Griff said. "It should be fairly close to the house, if this is the original house."

"What makes you think she's in a well?" Josh asked.

"No time for explanations," Griff told him. "Call Trotter. Tell him to bring his men in and start looking near the house for a well."

"There's no need to do that," Josh said. "While we were searching for Nic, I saw what I think is an old well about a hundred yards behind the house."

"Show me," Griff said. "Now!"

Two minutes. She wouldn't look at her watch again.

She didn't want to die.

She wanted to live.

She wanted to make love with Griff again.

She wanted to have babies, wanted to grow old and become a grandmother, wanted to . . .

Was there really life after death? Was there a heaven and hell?

She wanted to believe that this one brief life wasn't all there was.

Maybe there really was a heaven.

Or maybe reincarnation wasn't just a pipe dream.

If she could come back again and have another life, would she?

What if she and Griff came back in a future life, one where they could spend a hundred years together?

Don't fight it. Just accept it. Death is simply the next stage of life.

Nic felt herself floating slowly away, drifting into unconsciousness.

Oh, Griff, there you are. I knew you'd come for me. Hold me close. Don't let me go. She lifted her arms and wrapped them around his neck. I love you so very much.

It felt so good to be safe in Griff's arms.

Griff held on to Nic tightly as he tugged on the lines leading to the top of the well, indicating to the others that he was ready for the agents to bring them topside. If the well had been any smaller, neither he nor any of the other men there would have been able to go down inside and bring Nic up. Luckily, the well gradually widened from the top to the bottom. When they reached the narrower area near the top, Griff lifted Nic up and over his head. Eager rescue hands reached down and pulled her out, then brought him up and out of the well.

When he stood on firm ground again, he saw Nic lying on her side, her naked body draped with someone's jacket. The scuba gear had been removed and lay on the ground beside her. A circle of bureau agents stood watching while Luke gave Nic mouth-to-mouth. She gasped for air, then coughed.

Luke looked up at Griff and smiled.

Griff dropped to his knees and pulled Nic into his arms.

"Am I dreaming?" she asked groggily.

"No, you're not dreaming, honey."

"Did I die and go to heaven?"

"No, you're alive. Heaven's going to have to wait another fifty or sixty years."

Epilogue

Nic sat between Griff's spread legs in the middle of his huge king size bed, the back of her head resting on his naked chest. His big, strong arms circled her body, just below her breasts.

She had come to Griffin's Rest for a long weekend. Griff had sent the Powell jet to D.C. last night to bring her home to him.

"I want us to spend Valentine's Day together," he'd told her.

"That means I'll have to miss work Thursday and Friday."

"I've already cleared your time off with Doug," Griff had said.

She had fussed at him for going over her head to her boss, for making decisions for her, for trying to run her life. But in the end, she had forgiven him, as she knew she always would. After all, she loved Griff just as he was. She wouldn't change anything about him.

She was so happy right now that she could hardly believe that it had been barely five weeks since she'd come within sixty seconds of dying.

During his nine-month murder game, the Hunter had abducted ten women. He had killed seven. Only three had escaped with their lives. Nicole felt a strong bond with LaTasha Davies, who had come out of her coma and was recovering at home with her family. And with Mia O'Dell, who had the support of a loving family, and a boyfriend who was going with her to her counseling sessions.

"I have a proposition for you," Griff said as he nuzzled her neck.

"What kind of proposition?"

"I'd like for you to come and work with me at Powell Private Security and Investigation Agency."

She laughed. "You're kidding. Why would I give up my job at the bureau, where I'm now in line for a promotion, to come work for you as a Powell agent?"

"Your working *for* me is not quite what I had in mind. I believe I said I'd like for you to work *with* me."

She tilted her head, looked up at him, and eyed him questioningly. "Isn't that just a matter of semantics?"

"No, not really." He cupped her breasts in his hands.

"Then you're going to have to explain your offer in more detail." She grasped his hands and moved them back to her waist.

"What I had in mind was a partnership. A full partnership. And, if you insist, I might even consider changing the name of the agency to Powell and Baxter Private Security and Investigation."

"I'm totally confused, Mr. Powell. Why would you make me a partner and hand over half the agency to me?"

"Well," Griff said, "let's call it a wedding present."

"Wedding present?" She turned halfway around and stared at him. "Unless I'm mistaken, a wedding implies marriage, right?"

"Right."

She crawled out from the warm cocoon between his legs

and sat beside him. "A marriage is usually preceded by an engagement."

"Uh-huh."

"And before there can be an engagement, someone has to ask someone else to marry them."

"That's correct."

"Well?"

"I had planned to wait and do this tonight," Griff told her.

"Then you sort of jumped the gun, didn't you?"

"Your ring is in my safe downstairs."

She leaned over, got right up in his face, and said, "You must be pretty sure of yourself if you bought me a ring."

"Just hopeful."

She smiled. "I might marry you. That is, when you ask me."

"That's good to know." He pulled her over and onto his lap. "What about the other proposal? Any possibility you might accept that one, too?"

"Hmm . . . I'm not sure. But if I do, there won't be any need to change the name of our agency."

"Our agency?"

"Yes, our agency. After all, once we're married, I'll be Nicole Powell, won't I?"

"You want to take my name?"

She wrapped her arm around his neck and kissed him. "Just call me an old-fashioned girlie-girl, but I can't wait to become Mrs. Griffin Powell."

Griff chuckled. "Whew, that's a big load off my mind. I was afraid you might expect me to become Mr. Nicole Baxter."

They both burst into laughter.

Then Griff rolled her over onto the bed and took her breath away with a kiss that sealed their bargains.

Please read on for an exciting sneak peek of
Beverly Barton's
next thriller,
COLD HEARTED,
coming soon.

Prologue

Perhaps the best thing he could do for himself and everyone he loved was to commit suicide.

Dan Price stared at the Glock pistol lying atop his desk. He had bought the 9mm automatic for his wife, but she had refused the gift, politely reminding him of her aversion to guns. But at his insistence, she had gone with him to the practice range and learned to use the weapon, only to please him. But to his knowledge, she had never carried the pistol, never kept it in her room or in her car.

If his sweet Jordan had any idea that he was contemplating taking his own life, she would do her best to convince him that no matter what the future held, she would stand by him. It was her basic integrity and loyalty that had first attracted him to the woman who had become his greatest political asset.

Dan lifted the half-full glass of Kentucky bourbon to his lips and finished off the remainder. The liquor burned a path down his esophagus and hit his belly like fire. He coughed a couple of times, then wiped his mouth, picked up the bottle and poured himself another drink.

If he was going to do this—and he fully intended to end

his life tonight—he knew he couldn't do it stone cold sober. He wasn't that courageous. Before he could put the hammer-forged barrel into his mouth and pull the trigger, he needed to be more than a little drunk.

He sipped on the bourbon as he leaned back in the swivel desk chair and let his gaze travel over the room. His private study, as it has been his father's and grandfather's before him. An impressive room inside a two-hundred-year-old antebellum mansion, part of an estate that had been in his family since before the War Between the States. Generations of Price men had severed their country, first in wartime and then in local, state, and national politics. In Georgia, the name Price was synonymous with public service.

If he killed himself, how would that affect his family's good name? No Price man had ever taken the easy way out of a bad situation.

But could he continue, knowing what the future held for him? Could he condemn Jordan to such a life? And what about Devon? And his brother, Ryan? They would never desert him, and that would mean great sacrifices for each of them.

You don't have to do this tonight. You have time.

But how much time? Six months? A year?

Dan finished off his second drink and poured himself a third.

The grandfather clock in the hallway struck twice. Two in the morning.

He unlocked the file cabinet in the bottom drawer of the desk, rummaged through the folders until he found the file he wanted. A copy of his will. His lawyer kept another copy and a third was inside his safe at the house in Alexandria. The contents of his will were not secret to anyone. Everything he possessed would be equally divided among Jordan, Devon and Ryan. Jordan had protested, telling him that she didn't expect such an enormous legacy, but he had quieted her protests with a tender caress.

"I owe you more than I will ever be able to repay," he'd told her.

Dan finished off his third drink.

Minutes ticked by as he contemplated the Glock on his desk. Grandfather Price's antique desk. Family lore claimed the desk had belonged to Jefferson Davis, a contemporary of his ancestor, General John Ryan Price.

Dan poured another glass of bourbon, picked up the bottle and the glass and walked over to the leather Chesterfield sofa. He sat down, placed the bottle on the floor, and considered his options. Death was preferable to the fate that awaited him.

Dan's eyelids flickered open and shut. In the twilight zone of being half-awake/half-asleep, he didn't immediately realize where he was or what had awakened him so abruptly. Woozy from sleep and overdosing on bourbon, Dan recalled that he had contemplated suicide to solve his problems, but in the end, drunk and oddly enough thinking more clearly than he had when he'd been sober, he had realized killing himself would have been the coward's way out.

Dan swatted at something cold against his cheek. His fingertips raked across the metal object. He opened his eyes fully, stared up at the woman leaning over him, and smiled. She did not return his smile. His gaze zipped from her familiar face to his own hand holding the 9mm, its barrel pressed firmly against his head. And it was only when he tried to ease the gun away from his head that he realized her hand covered his, her index finger squeezed tightly over his against the trigger.

"What the—!"

Before he could react, she forced his finger down against the trigger, firing the gut at point-blank range directly into his brain.

Dan's last thought was that someone he'd trusted completely had just killed him.

THE DYING GAME

Beverly Barton

If looks could kill . . .

It's the ultimate game.
To win, you have to kill.
To lose, you have to die.
If he's chosen you to play, then it's Game Over . . .

A brutal serial killer is on the loose. Each victim is a former beauty queen, a single rose placed next to their mutilated bodies.

The scenes of unimaginable carnage have become familiar to Detective Lindsay McAllister. For the last 5 years, dozens of beautiful women have been slain and lives have been shattered, including Judd Walker whose wife was one of the first victims. But when the killer strikes again Lindsey knows she needs Judd's help. The murderer is getting bolder, faster, and more ruthless. The game has escalated, the rules have changed, the body count is rising . . . and no one is safe.

PRAISE FOR BEVERLY BARTON:

'Shocking and terrifying, it will chill you to the bone.'
Tess Gerritsen, author of *The Bone Garden*.

ISBN: 978-1-84756-020-9

Out now.

CLOSE ENOUGH TO KILL

Beverly Barton

He woos. He stalks. He kills . . .

Welcome to Adams County, Alabama, population 10,374 – and falling . . .

Adams County, Alabama is the kind of town where everyone knows each other's business, the kind of place where doors stay unlocked. Until a psychopath comes calling.

Dubbed 'The Secret Admirer', he woos his victims with phone calls, love letters and gifts, before stalking, kidnapping and then brutally murdering them.

A terrifying game is underway. Sheriff Bernie Granger – in her first big case and following in her father's footsteps – is desperate to stop this depraved serial killer before he slaughters another young woman. But is she getting closer to catching him – or being drawn even deeper into his deadly web?

Guaranteed to make your nerves jangle as much as Tess Gerritsen and Karin Slaughter.

ISBN: 978-1-84756-000-1

Out now.

LOST SOULS

Neil White

A ritual murder. Abducted children mysteriously returned. Why?

A woman is found butchered on a Lancashire housing estate, her tongue and eyes brutally gouged out. Ritual murder or crime of passion?

Children are abducted and then returned to their families days later, unharmed but with no knowledge of where they have been – or who took them.

DC Laura McGanity, having relocated from London to the old mill town of Blackley, quickly learns that life up North is far from peaceful. She needs to solve these mystifying cases – but keep the local police on side.

Her reporter boyfriend Jack Garrett – the reason for McGanity's relocation – is back in his hometown and finds himself entangled in the two mysterious cases. His investigations reveal murky connections and sordid secrets.

But when Jack meets a man who 'paints' the future – prophecies of horrific events which he then puts onto canvas – it's becoming terrifyingly clear that many people, including his own family, are in grave danger . . .

ISBN: 978-1-84756-018-6

Out now.

THE TROPHY TAKER

Lee Weeks

A serial killer is on the loose. His target? Lone Western women lured to Hong Kong by the promise of easy money. As **The Butcher's** killing spree escalates, bags of mutilated body parts are found all over the island – and more girls are disappearing.

Taking on his first major homicide case, **Detective Johnny Mann** is determined to stop The Butcher's brutal reign. Haunted by the memory of his father's death by the Triads, he's the only man who can track down a killer who's paralysing the city with fear.

Georgina Johnson has left her tragic past in England to start afresh in Hong Kong. But soon her life is in peril as she is sucked into the sinister world of the city's hostess clubs.

Venturing into dark and dangerous places, Mann unearths chilling evidence about the killings. And then another body is found, one which brings the murders closer to home . . .

Bolt the doors, turn on the lights and pray for mercy – you'll be up all night with this disturbingly addictive debut from a writer being hailed as the female James Patterson.

ISBN: 978-1-84756-078-0

Out now.

BLOOD LINES

Grace Monroe

Blood is thicker than water – and far more deadly . . .

A woman is lured to a remote spot in the Scottish Highlands and strangled almost to the point of death. As she begs for mercy, her tormentor begins to carve her face, before burying her alive.

In Edinburgh, unorthodox young lawyer Brodie McLennan becomes tangled up in the case. When it emerges that Brodie was the last person to see the victim and crucial evidence is found at her flat, she must fight to clear her name – and save her own skin.

Meanwhile in an asylum in Inverness, a deranged patient writes the name Brodie over and over in her own blood . . .

As another mutilated body is discovered bearing the same ritualistic markings, Brodie is running scared from unknown forces, eager to see blood on her hands . . .

Prepared to be shocked in this dark and gripping thriller, for fans of Ian Rankin and Mo Hayder . . .

ISBN: 978-1-84756-041-4

Out now.

THE MOZART CONSPIRACY

Scott Mariani

**An ancient murder . . . A clandestine society . . .
A conspiracy that will end in death . . .**

Ben Hope is running for his life.

Enlisted by the beautiful Leigh Llewellyn – the beautiful
opera star and Ben's first love – to investigate her brother's
mysterious death, former SAS operative Ben finds himself
caught up in a centuries-old puzzle.

Officially Oliver died in a tragic accident whilst investigating
Mozart's death, but the facts don't add up. His research
reveals that Mozart, a notable freemason, may have been
killed by a shadowy splinter group of the cult. The only
clues lie in an ancient letter, believed to have been written by
the composer himself.

When Leigh and Ben receive video evidence of a ritual
sacrifice being performed, they realise that the sect still
exists – and will stop at nothing to keep its secrets.

From the dreaming spires of Oxford to Venice's labyrinthine
canals, the majestic architecture of Vienna and Slovenia's
snowy mountains, Ben and Leigh must forget the past
and race across Europe to uncover the truth behind
THE MOZART CONSPIRACY . . .

An electrifying and utterly gripping must read for fans of
Dan Brown, Sam Bourne and Ludlum's *Bourne* series.

ISBN: 978-1-84756-080-3

Out now.